FOREVER A JETT GIRL
BOOK THREE IN THE BOURBON SERIES

MEGHAN QUINN

MEGHAN QUINN

Copyright © 2015 Meghan Quinn

bookmark: Copyright
Published by Hot-Lanta Publishing
Copyright 2015
Cover by Meghan Quinn

All rights reserved.

ISBN: 1514863529
ISBN-13: 978-1514863527

1
"BLACK WIDOW"

Goldie

"Why, hello, Kitten. You've just made my night."

Oh, my God, what the hell was I doing?

Standing in front of me was Rex Titan with a look that screamed he was going to rip my panties off, not bothering to take my pants off first, and eat me up. Maybe a few months ago I would have welcomed the carnal munching, but right about now, with a heavy heart and a sad image of Jett in my mind, I wanted to run away.

This was a mistake.

How was I going to go through with this? How was I going to keep Rex's dick out of my orifices? Because, right about now, I was pretty sure he would fuck my ear if I pushed back my hair. No doubt about it, he was going to want to bone-a-roni, but I couldn't let that happen. If I let Rex touch me in any kind of way, even a good ear fucking, that would be the end of any chance I had with Jett.

I had to come up with a plan and fast, something I should have thought of before I showed up at his front door with a bag in my hand.

Clearing my throat, I looked up at Rex through my lashes—playing the ever-pathetic victim—and said, "Hi, Rex. Can I...come in?"

Good stutter, I congratulated myself, knowing I was about to step up my acting game.

Act weak, act fragile, act like you've been torn into shreds, I coached myself. Give him your best Oscar worthy performance! Pretend his dick is a camera and work the fuck out of it.

"I would want nothing more than to have you in my home, Kitten. Please, come in."

I wanted to smack the smug look he was sporting off his face, but refrained from physically assaulting him.

"Thank you," I said meekly, as I stepped inside his home and took in the surroundings.

Thanks to Carlos, my dearest bartender from Kitten's Castle, he was able to locate Rex's home for me and give me the address so I could follow through with my plan, my not very well constructed plan. I've never been to Rex's house, and from the looks of it, I was kind of glad. Um, can you say borderline hoarder?

While looking around, I knew he was rich, but I didn't know he was close to Jett Colby Rich. Instead of the modern feel you get when you walk into the Lafayette Club, Rex's style was more old money with rich red and brown tones, old leather and oak furniture with a massive amount of collectibles gracing his walls, making it almost impossible to see the paint. It was nice-ish, but it was straight-up stuffy.

"Can I take your bag?" Rex asked, as he came up behind me and pressed his chest to my back.

Yup, home boy was going to have to be put in his place sooner rather than later, because there was no way in hell I would be dropping trou for him.

"Sure, there's not much, just my suitcase."

"That's fine," he replied, while taking my suitcase and setting it down next to the grand staircase that curved up to a second floor. "Are you hungry?"

"Oh, I couldn't eat," I said, grabbing my stomach. "I'm not feeling so well."

"Are you sick, Kitten?"

Was I sick? I could be sick. I knew how to cough on demand, but being sick would lead to probably seeing a doctor, and then he would say there was nothing wrong with me, and then Rex would see that I was a liar, so taking the whole sick route to avoid Rex's penis wasn't going to work. At least, that's what I expected.

"No," I answered. "It's been a bad night for me."

Surprisingly, my voice choked up at mentioning my night, adding to the distress I was trying to portray.

In reality, I really was stressed and heartbroken. I hated, hated, taking off my necklace. I felt unprotected, empty, and lifeless without it on. I felt disconnected from Jett, like a little piece of me died when I handed him back the necklace. His face was still running rampant through my mind, but I tried to squash it. I was here for a reason. I was here to take back the life I wanted to lead with Jett, and I wasn't going to leave until I accomplished my mission.

"Come, sit down and talk to me," Rex suggested.

I didn't like how nice he was being, almost too nice. He wasn't usually this attentive, this accommodating, but then again, all my experiences with him were a little more animalistic than talkity-talk time. Most of the time, we would forgo conversation when we met up and the only talking Rex ever really did was to tell me to bend over and take him all the way in. I mean, that's good conversation, polite sexual conversation, you know, never talking with your mouth full of dick and all, but not the type of conversation that was necessarily trying to make a connection…well, no, it was making a connection that was for damn sure, but not the type of conversation that helped you get to know the other person.

I followed Rex past a living area and into a giant family space. Why humans needed two "living rooms" would be something I never understood. What did someone do with two living rooms? How did one decide which one to hang out in on a given day? Did they ever feel bad that they didn't spend enough time with one of the living rooms? Did the living rooms fight over their master?

What stupid thoughts, I chastised myself, as I sat next to Rex on his couch. I needed to clear my head; it was show time.

"What happened, Kitten? Why am I so lucky to have you sitting next to me?"

Here goes nothing…

"I feel so stupid, Rex."

"Why?"

"You know Jett Colby, right?" Have to make it seem like I

know nothing."

"Yes, we have a history."

"Oh, that's right. You're a part of his club."

"I was, but I've recently reneged on my membership. I found that ever since a certain little honey-haired girl was no longer performing, my need for my membership was useless."

"Oh, so you know I'm no longer a Jett Girl?"

"I gathered that from the fact that you are here with me, and since I didn't see you there the other night."

"Were you looking for me?"

"I was, Kitten."

"Why?" I asked, slightly curious.

"We will get to that. Please, continue with your story."

"Okay," I felt my shield flair up, wanting to protect myself. I didn't like the ease in his voice, like he'd been expecting me all along. I didn't feel like I had the upper hand at the moment. "This is so embarrassing," I shook my head and buried my head in my hands.

"Don't be embarrassed, Kitten. You can talk to me."

Bah! More like I could talk to his dick.

Brushing my hair out of my face, I looked up at Rex and said, "I fell for him, Rex. Even though he told me not to, even though I signed a contract with specific guidelines, I still fell for him. I had hope when he started taking me to events with him, ushering me around on his arm like he was proud of me, but he was just using me."

"Using you?" Rex asked, as he maintained a respectable distance from me, but still showed concern. What was this mother fucker up to?

I nodded to confirm his question as I squeaked out a tear.

"He doesn't care about me. He said he was using me to distract someone off of Lot 17. I have no clue what that is or who he's talking about, but once I accomplished whatever goal he had, he let me go. Kicked me out."

I watched Rex's jaw work back and forth as he mulled over what I told him. Was he angry? He seemed angry, which wasn't the Rex I knew. The Rex I knew didn't really care about me as a person; he just cared about my body.

"That's why you're here?"

With shame, I hung my head and nodded. "I'm sorry, Rex. I

had nowhere else to go. When I left Kitten's Castle, I lost touch with everyone. The only person I could rely on is you. If you want me to leave, I can. I would understand."

"No, please don't," he said with sincerity. "I can't tell you how long I've wanted you to come here. I think about it every day, how I wish I had come to you sooner, before you were sucked into the grasp of Jett Colby. He's a terrible man, who uses women and throws them away when he's done. I'm so sorry you had to go through that."

Finally making a move, he pulled me into his chest and wrapped his arms around me. Good thing too, because I was pretty sure my eyes were spitting fire. Jett was by far the most amazing man I had ever met and he had a giant heart. He didn't use people, he helped them, he helped them have a do-over in life, and I just despised the fact that Rex was talking so poorly about him, but to save my plan, I let the insults roll off of me.

"Thank you," I replied once I gathered myself. "I don't know what to do. I'm at this crossroads in my life. When I was at the Lafayette Club, I had hope, I could see a future for myself, but now, I feel like I've gone back to square one but with no direction. I'm so confused, so lost."

Rex tilted my chin up with his finger and forced me to look him in the eyes. He was a handsome man, no doubt about that. The deep brown of his eyes almost looked sinister to me now, and the strong features of his jaw showed that he wouldn't be messed with. He was a powerful man, and I'd only realized it recently. I was taking a huge chance by fucking with him. I just hoped it didn't blow up in my face.

"No need to feel confused, Kitten. Do you want to know the reason I went by the Lafayette Club the other day?"

"Yes," I said breathlessly.

Seriously, award winning performance.

Grabbing my hand, Rex stood me up and led me out of his living room.

"Where are we going?" I asked nervously.

"Just come with me, Kitten. You'll see."

The house was dark, and as Rex led me through an unlit hallway, he flipped on the light, revealing pictures of old civil war paintings and memorabilia.

Bleh, boring!

Swords and old guns were mounted on the walls in glass cases, as well as documents that seemed pretty old, like they were once a piece of parchment on a scroll. I was tempted to break the glass, grab the paper and shout "Hear ye, Hear ye," while holding it in front of me, but refrained from making an ass of myself.

I never knew Rex was a history buff kind of guy, but by the looks of his decorations, I was pretty sure he would spring a boner if George Washington walked through the door right about now.

Just when I was gearing up to see the Declaration of Independence pop out of a corner and bitch slap me with its old time writing, Rex led me into a private den and turned on the light. The room matched the rest of the house with its colonial style decorating, but instead of ancient swords and guns gracing the walls, they were lined with rows and rows of books.

It was like I was in the movie, *Beauty and the Beast* when the Beast shows Belle his library. If I was a reader, I would be impressed, but who has time to read, am I right?

I tore my eyes off of the books and saw what Rex brought me into this room to see. In the middle of the floor was a dark colored console table, and on it was a constructed model of a building sporting multiple rooms. This had to be Rex and Jett's dad's plans for Lot 17, no doubt about it.

"What is this?" I asked, while taking it all in.

The building was a modern looking skyscraper that twisted in the middle like someone took the building and tried to wring water out of it. The small rooms off to the side of the model were what I could only assume were different floors of the building. In one room was an almost exact replica of the Toulouse Room, where Jett Girls put on presentations, but instead of using the purple theme Jett was known for, Rex and Leo kept everything black and gold. Yeah, it was slightly bad ass. Another one of the models on the table was full of some of the equipment I saw in Diego's club with the restraints, but where his materials looked fun to play with, Rex's looked almost sinister, like a torture room.

Yikes, my lady flaps cringed from thoughts of what would possibly happen in those rooms.

Interrupting my thoughts, Rex said, "This, Kitten, is Masquerade. It's a club I've been putting together with my friend Leo."

His "friend" Leo...pfft. I kept my breath steady as I listened to Rex, making sure to show no tells that I knew anything.

"Wow, is it a hotel too?" I asked, observing the height of the building.

"You're very observant. It is a hotel, but the top floors are where all the fun happens. The club will be very much like the Lafayette Club, but will differ in the fact that the girls are naked and the men are allowed to touch and take any girl of their choice back to one of the playrooms."

Holy shit. Rex and Jett's dad were running a modern day brothel. Scandal!

Even though I was surprised, I shouldn't be, because I knew Rex through illegal sexcapades; it shouldn't shock me that he turned his hobby into a lucrative business.

"Are you allowed to do that?" I asked, feeling a little uneasy about the fact that this was what Rex wanted to show me, what he wanted to talk to me about. How could this possibly involve me?

"We're allowed to do anything we want, Goldie. We know people in the city."

Nodding, I touched the model of the building and asked, "What does this have to do with me?"

Taking my hand, Rex made me sit down with him on a couch in his office. With his deep brown eyes staring directly into mine, he said, "After observing you with Jett and hearing Leo report back to me about Jett's interactions with you, I knew it would only take some time until he, once again, messed up something good in his life. He did the same thing with his ex-fiancé Natasha."

I wanted to say, "Nuh-uh, you stole her," but I kept my mouth shut and let him continue.

"We need a lead girl, Goldie. I need someone with experience to teach the girls we're hiring how to please a man, how to dance for the city's elite, who will be frequenting our club. You're the only girl who can do that for me. You're the only one who has experience and who I can trust."

He wanted me to train the girls? Bad move, because I would train them to get their asses the hell out of that club.

Rex and Leo were running a brothel, and as I pondered that for a second, it hit me. This was what Diego was telling me when he said Rex and Leo were up to something illegal. This is what Jett was trying to find evidence for. This was how I was going to bring down Rex and Leo; I just had to figure out what the parameters were. Jackpot!

Rex continued, "You will be compensated well for your guidance…"

"Will I have to be one of the girls?"

"What do you mean?" Rex asked, as he tilted his head to the side.

"Will I have to be naked with the other girls? Will I have to go into the playrooms with the men who choose to be with me?"

"Is that going to be a problem?"

Uh, yeah, it was going to be a major fucking problem. I was made for one man and one man alone; there was no way in hell I would spread my legs or take my clothes off for anyone else.

"It will be," I answered honestly, trying to gauge Rex's reaction, hoping this wasn't going to be a short attempt at revenge.

He sat back and studied me as his hand stroked his chin. Why did it take me so long to figure out that the man sitting in front of me was just an awful, awful man? He was manipulative and he emotionally fucked with people. I could see it plain as day in his eyes. He didn't care about my well-being; he cared about himself and that was it.

While looking me up and down, Rex asked, "Why are you really here, Goldie?"

Oh, shit.

If I answered wrong, were there going to be dogs popping out of a secret doorway to tear me to pieces? Rip my lady bits apart for a possible loin harvesting company Rex might be secretly working with? I wouldn't put it past him to have such a connection…the man was straight up frea-kay!

Taking a deep breath, I looked Rex straight in the eyes and said, "I've been used my whole life, and I am just realizing now that I can't live my life like that anymore. I need a new start, a fresh one, and you're the only one I know that will be able to help me."

Twisting his lips, he thought about my answer before saying, "No, you won't be one of the girls. You'll be a manager of sorts, but you will have to wear more revealing clothes."

"I have no problem with that," I responded, feeling a weight of relief fly off my chest.

"You will receive a decent salary and will be required to work more than forty hours a week at first, until we get everything started up. We are currently training in a location that will work for us, but if we are awarded Lot 17, we will be building a whole new club. You will live here with me, in my bed, and if I'm housing you, I will be requiring something in return."

And there it was, the one thing I wanted to avoid. I would give Rex credit for having a good set of balls and coming right out with it. If I was living under his roof, I would be paying him with sexual favors, aka, suck my dick, bitch. Yup, not something I was okay with.

Knowing my next words were either going to make or break this secret operation I'd put myself on, I chose wisely what came out of my mouth.

With a sad smile, I nodded and said, "I can understand that."

"Then, why do you look so sad? We were great together, Goldie."

"We were," I answered. "But..." I took a deep breath and placed my head in my hands. "I'm sorry." I waved my hand in front of me. "I don't mean to get so emotional. It's just...I was really hoping for a fresh start. Ever since I lost my parents to Hurricane Katrina, I've been selling my soul to stay afloat. I let men use my body in Kitten's Castle, I let you use my body to help pay my rent, and I let Jett use me as well. I don't want to be that girl anymore. I don't want to be the girl who sells her body for money or possessions anymore. I'm at a breaking point in my life, Rex, where I've been passed down from man to man to a point where I don't think I can do it anymore. I need a break. I need some time to think. I need some time to find myself and figure out what I want."

"Do you still want Jett?" Rex asked, looking a little angry. I didn't blame his anger; I'd denied his cock.

"No, I don't want anything to do with that pitiful man. You were right, he doesn't care about anyone but himself."

"Then, do you see me in your future?"

I glanced down at my hands and then looked up at him through my eyelashes, preparing for the biggest lie of my life.

"I can definitely see a future with you, Rex. I want to have a future with you, that's why I came here, but before I see that future, I would like to build a friendship first."

A small smile spread across Rex's face as he nodded his head and said, "I think I can wait then."

Bless all the crying vaginas in the world. I just bought myself a few sex free weeks with Rex, but I didn't foresee him waiting terribly long. He was going to want something from me; I was on borrowed time, meaning I had to act quickly.

"Thank you," I replied, while gripping his hand and squeezing it.

"You know, Goldie. You deserve to be treated well, to be given everything you've ever wanted, and in due time, I will be the man who gives you that."

"I wouldn't want it any other way."

"Good enough," he replied while standing. "Come, I will show you to your room so you can get settled. Tomorrow, we will go to the club so I can get you acquainted with some of the girls and your new surroundings. I have great hopes for this new relationship we'll be starting."

Such a fancy fart.

We walked back out to the main hallway, where Rex grabbed my suitcase and led me up to the second floor. To the left, I could see the master bedroom, it was hard to miss with the French doors and immaculate four post bed that stretched the length of one of the walls. Luckily, Rex guided me to the right side of the second floor and into a more modest room. It had beige walls, an oak sleigh bed, and red comforter, shock alert…wasn't expecting that color scheme.

"This will be your room."

"It's lovely," I lied, as I made eye contact with a picture of Thomas Jefferson that hung over my bed. I knew he was dead, but I was pretty damn sure he was reincarnated to live in the picture that hung above the bed I would be sleeping in, because the former president was staring at my breasts, pervert.

"Are you hungry?" Rex asked, as he set my suitcase on a padded bench that sat at the foot of the bed.

"No, just tired. It's been a long night."

"I'm sure," Rex said, while he looked at his watch. "I'll let you get to sleep. The door to the right is your closet and the door to the left is your private bathroom. I will be up around eight for breakfast, and then we can head on over to the club. Does that sound alright with you?"

"Yes, perfectly fine."

Rex took a step forward to, what I could only assume was going to be a kiss, but mid-step, he backed off and gave me a small wave. "Good night, Kitten."

"Good night," I replied, as he walked out of my room and shut the door softly.

The minute he was gone, I exhaled a long breath that I felt like I'd been holding in ever since I walked into Rex's house. I flung my body on the bed and was surprised when I found the mattress was as hard as a rock.

"Jesus, Rex. Invest in some mattresses not made in the 1920's," I mumbled, as I tried to soften the sturdy rock that lay beneath me by trying to channel my inner pussy cat and knead the fuck out of it. But there was no use, I was slumming it with Thomas and all of his other historic friends.

Overall, I thought I'd done a good job infiltrating the enemy's lair. Actually, it wasn't that hard at all. All I had to do now was do a little video work with my phone, interview some of the girls, and then send the video off to the police. Simple. No one was going to stand for a brothel in this town!

Feeling happy about my success, I opened my suitcase and started to unpack my things. I only brought limited items because I really wanted to make it look like I had nothing, even though I had everything back at the Lafayette Club, and when I say everything, I mean Jett.

The itch to call him, to hear his voice ran through my body, but I knew that would be a bad idea. For all I knew, Rex would be able to see who I was calling by posting cameras in my room.

Cameras.

My eyes shot to Thomas Jefferson above the bed and his beady little eyes. With determination, I jumped on the bed and lifted the picture off of the wall while saying, "Ah ha!"

To my dismay, there wasn't a secret peep hole or a camera, it was just a plain old wall and Thomas Jefferson just had creepy eyes.

Still not comfortable, I spent the next half hour scouring my room, bathroom, and closet for any kind of small camera or listening device, but came up short. There was nothing. Did Rex really trust me that much?

I was just about to lay down in bed after I had taken a quick shower and brushed my teeth, when I heard the faint sound of Rex's voice rising to an angry level. Wanting to know who he was talking to, now that I was a secret agent, well, in my mind I was a secret agent…I quietly cracked opened my door and tiptoed to the banister of the stairwell, where I perked up my ears to hear what Rex was saying.

"Yes, she's upstairs. No, she's not wearing a collar. I know. No, I didn't take her phone, why should I? She said she's no longer with him, that she wants nothing to do with him. Because I can trust her. She's desperate Leo; she'll do anything to not have to live on the streets again." He paused for a second and then said, "No, she will not be a girl, not just yet. I gave her a manager position at first..." He paused again, but then raised his voice, malice lacing it, frankly scaring me. "Because, I can't just force her to be the main attraction of the club at first. I have to gain her trust, give her everything she needs, and then break her down, take away her entire life in exchange for what we want. It's all about manipulating your subject. I know what I'm doing; we'll get what we want. We'll be sure to prove to Jett never to fuck with us."

Heavy footsteps rang across the hardwood floors, making me jump out of my listening position and scamper back to my room. Carefully, I clicked the door shut and then sat on my bed.

So, I wasn't as clever as I thought I was. Rex didn't want me; he wanted to use me to get back at Jett, but why? Were they still convinced Jett and I were an item?

No, they couldn't be. There was something I was missing.

With a new understanding of what I had gotten myself into, I turned out the lights of my latest bedroom and thought about what tomorrow was going to bring and how long it was going to be until I was able to see Jett and hear his voice once again.

There was a reason I was doing all of this; there was a reason why I was in Rex's house, depriving myself of the man who had stolen my heart. I was doing this for Jett; I was doing this for us so that we could live the life we wanted to live, not under someone else's rules.

With a flip of the bird to Thomas, the creepy perv, I shut my eyes and went to sleep.

2
"BANG BANG"

Rex

The phone rang in my ear and I impatiently waited for Leo to pick up. Kitten showing up at my door was exactly what we wanted. We knew only time would tell when Goldie would come running from Jett. We pushed him to his limit and made him drive her away. Who was he trying to kid? We had seen his passion for my Kitten ever since Leo called Jett out on his new girl. It was written all over him. I wasn't sure if he loved her, but he had deep feelings for Kitten...that was unmistakable.

"Yes," Leo grunted into the phone.

"She's with me."

There was a pause on the phone before Leo spoke. "Goldie?"

"Yes, she came over tonight, asking for a place to stay, a place far away from Jett."

"She's in your house?" he asked with a little bit of disbelief. We were hoping she would find her way to me when she was ready, but we weren't sure it would actually happen, especially since she left the Lafayette Club a while ago.

"Yes, she's upstairs."

"Is she still attached to Jett? You know we can't have any

complications."

"No, she's not wearing a collar."

"She's not? That's interesting. He must have really done a number on her. That bastard of a son of mine never knew a good thing when it smacked him in the head. He's willing to give up Goldie for Lot 17. Never thought I would see the day."

"I know."

"Did you take away all of her communication?"

"No, I didn't take her phone, why should I?"

Leo blew out a frustrated breath, and I could envision him running his hand through his hair. Like father like son. "Because, what if she's playing you? What if she's lying? We can't be too cautious right now, Rex."

"She said she's no longer with him, that she wants nothing to do with him," I responded with confidence. I saw it in her eyes; she was done with Jett Colby.

"And you believed that? Why?" Leo asked, growing irritated with me.

The moment I went into business with Leo, I knew it wasn't going to be easy. He was just as stubborn as his son, but when it came to trusting someone else, Leo had zero trust. He was constantly checking on me, making sure I was making the right moves. It had started to get annoying...the fact that he thought he could make all the decisions in our partnership. I was not one to be micro-managed, especially since what we had was a partnership, something he often forgot.

"Because I can trust her," I spat back. "She's desperate, Leo, she'll do anything to not have to live on the streets again."

"Desperate enough to be one of the girls?"

"No, she will not be a girl, not just yet. I gave her a manager position at first..."

"Why the fuck would you do that? You know the plan. She is to be one of the girls, not some damn manager."

Rage boiled inside of me from Leo chastising my decisions, once again. I knew what the hell I was doing. I didn't need him riding me about it. Even though he thought he knew everything, he really didn't. The one thing he didn't know was Goldie. She was headstrong, stubborn, and could be flaky. I wasn't about to act on our plan the first second she walked through my door. No, I had to ease her in, show her that I can give her everything, and then when she's settled, when she thinks she couldn't have it any better, I would take it all away from her.

Taking a deep breath, I answered, "Because, I can't just force her to be the main attraction of the club at first. I have to gain her trust, give her everything she needs and then break her down, take away her entire life in exchange for what we want. It's all about manipulating your subject."

This was true, it was how I had done it with the other three girls who'd signed on to the club. I promised them a life they couldn't possibly dream of, lavished them with everything they could want, learned their innermost secrets...secrets that were not to be spoken of, and then when they were content, I turned their secrets against them. I forcefully threatened to expose their misdoings, had them sign a contract, and then took all of their privileges away. It was the only way I could get them to do what they would be offering to the men of my club. It was either fuck or get fucked for them.

"You better be right. We have plans for her, Rex. She is the key to bringing Jett to his knees, and you and I both want that."

"I know; we'll get what we want. We'll be sure to prove to Jett never to fuck with us," I replied, while walking down the hall.

"Very well. Don't fuck this up, Rex. Goldie is in your hands. Be sure to show her who's in charge of this city...who owns this city."

"I will."

We both hung up the phone and I walked up the stairs to my bedroom. Things were finally starting to fall into place. Lot 17 was so close to being in our grasp; we had the winning pawn to the game we were playing with Jett, and I could see the total destruction of the man in the near future. It wouldn't be too long until we had Goldie under our command, only to annihilate Jett.

3
"GONE"

Jett

I've suffered losses in my life, losses that have shaped me into be the man I am today, that have taught me valuable lessons, and that have inspired me to be a better person. But I've never experienced such a loss as I did the moment Goldie took off her collar.

From the window of her bedroom, I watched as a cab pulled up outside the back of Diego's club and took my Little One away, leaving me a broken and bitter man.

Her words kept resonating through my head, "Have faith in the power I have."

From the very beginning, when I asked her to stay with Diego and trust what I was doing for the both of us, I asked her to have faith, faith in me and faith in us, but now with the tables reversed, with her doing the protecting, my faith was non-existent and the main reason was because the one hold I had over her, the one object that gave me security in our commitment to each other was now lying neatly in a box in my hands.

My heart was rapidly beating in my chest, hammering against my ribcage, begging to be taken back by Goldie, to sit in her perfect little hands.

Not able to stand from the blinding pain that was ricocheting through my body, I sat on her bed and dropped the box I was holding to the ground so I could grip my head. Like a madman, I pulled on my hair, trying to figure out what Goldie was up to, why she found it necessary to leave me, to do this all on her own.

A small knock sounded at the door, disrupting my thoughts. I didn't have the energy to look up, so I just mumbled for whoever it was to come in.

The creak of the door echoed through the empty room and the heavy footsteps of Diego entered. I've known Diego for a while now, and I've been quite fond of him, but today, after he brought Goldie to the party, a dark part of me wanted to take him out, destroy him…because by some off-chance if he hadn't taken Goldie to the ball, maybe, just maybe, she would be in my arms right now.

"What do you want?" I said in a gruff tone, trying to hide the pain in my voice.

"Listen, Jett, I just wanted to make sure you were okay."

I tilted my head up ever so slightly so I was just barely looking at the man. He was strong and confident, arrogant at times, just like me, but where I excelled in hiding my emotions, Diego did not. Visibly, he was shaken from seeing Goldie leave; I could see it in his stature.

"Diego, I'm going to make this very easy on you. You're going to tell me exactly what Goldie said to you before the party, and then you're going to get the fuck out of my sight. Got it?"

The menacing tone in my voice was clearly heard by Diego, as he took a deep breath and then rested his body against the doorframe and ran his hand over his face.

"Fine. Goldie came up to me while I was eating a sandwich and asked me about Lot 17. She wanted to know everything and I told her. I told her about your dad, about what Lot 17 entailed and what you wanted to do with it. I told her what I knew."

"Why?" I asked while standing up, growing angrier by the second. "Why would you tell her when you knew I specifically wanted to keep her out of it and as far away as possible?"

"Besides the fact that she practically ripped my nipple off? She deserved to know. You were stringing her along, keeping her in the dark, she was bound to do something. If I didn't tell her, she would have gone off to find her own answers, and who knows what would have happened then."

With precision, I picked up the box with Goldie's collar in it that I'd dropped, and walked over to Diego, where I stood an inch away from him. Taking in a deep breath, I sized him up and said, "Meddling in my relationship, trying to fix a problem that wasn't yours to fix will not go unnoticed, Diego."

"Is that a threat?" Diego asked, feeling more confident now.

"It damn well is. Don't meddle in my life, because it's going to come back and burn you."

"Funny thing is, Jett, you're the one who brought her here; you're the one who needed a safe haven for her, and I provided that. Just because you wanted to keep her in the dark doesn't mean I had to. She deserved to know."

"That wasn't your decision to make," I said, raising my voice.

"Someone had to tell her, and your arrogant ass wasn't going to, so I did."

"You're dead to me," I huffed out, as I pushed past him, knocking his shoulder on the way.

"Blaming me for your problems isn't going to help. You know I'm not the reason this happened. Try pointing the finger at yourself. Relationships are about being open and honest. You failed in that aspect when it came to Goldie, and you're the reason why she left," Diego pointed out, as I stopped halfway down the hallway.

"Relationship advice coming from someone who has been unsuccessful at keeping his own submissive longer than a few months...think I'll pass."

With that, I walked down the stairs of Diego's club and out to the idling car that was waiting for me. My driver opened my door for me and drove me back to the Lafayette Club.

Diego's words ran through my mind as I watched the lights of Bourbon street filter through the side streets of the French Quarter. Scandal and debauchery were conducted every night on Bourbon, yet, were wiped away in the morning; if only life was that simple. If only I was able to sweep away my problems like the sanitation crew of Bourbon Street did.

Life was never that easy, though. Life was never easy for me, from the day I was born, I had drawn a bad hand. I was privileged; I had everything I ever wanted. Money wasn't ever an issue, stature was a given, popularity and fame were something I exuded every day without even trying. I was given a posh life, but that was to the outside eye.

Internally, I struggled every day. My father tried to shape and mold me into the man he was; he kept me away from my mother, destroyed her life right in front of me, and mentally abused me every damn day of my life, telling me I would never live up to his expectations.

The one thing I craved, the one thing I yearned for from the cold-hearted bastard was love, a simple gesture, an unconditional feeling that a father should have for his son, but I was never granted such a concession. Instead, I was mentally assaulted by my father, forced to grow up faster than any kid should, and turned into an emotionless man who sought love in the wrong places.

The only time in my life I ever felt happy, ever felt that unconditional feeling that I've craved ever since I was a little boy was when Goldie was in my arms, smiling up at me and busting my balls every chance she got. She was the one true delight to grace my life, and as usually happened in the abhorrent life I lead, she was taken from me.

She was taken away from me not because of Diego, not because of my miscommunication, no, she was taken away from me because of my father, because he saw I was happy and wanted nothing more than to ruin that happiness.

One way or another, I was going to make sure my dad paid. I was going to make sure he got what he deserved. He was a vile, heinous human being, who didn't deserve to live the life he was leading. He needed to be brought down.

The minute the car arrived at the Lafayette Club, I didn't wait for my driver to hold the door open. Instead, I bolted out of the car and headed to the back of the club, to Kace's room. Not even bothering to knock, since Kace didn't show me the same decency, I barged through his door, but regretted it the minute I heard a girl scream.

In Kace's bed, was a very naked Kace and a similarly naked Pepper.

"What the fuck?" I roared as I spotted their guilty faces.

Pepper covered up with a sheet, which was asinine, given the fact that I've seen her naked too many times to count, and tried to push her hair out of her face. While Pepper covered up, the very cocky and pompous Kace turned away from Pepper and sat on the edge of his bed, not caring one bit about his nudity.

"Do you care to explain yourself?" I asked, ready to plow my fist through Kace's face. Too much had happened in one night, and Kace was about to see all my frustration lashed out on him.

"Not really. Care to fucking knock?" he asked, while folding his hands in his lap, dick still erect.

"How long has this been going on? Is she the only one? Or have you been fucking all of them behind my back?"

"Why do you even care?"

"Because they're Jett Girls; they belong to me. They are contracted for my pleasure, not yours."

The words coming out of my mouth were vulgar, they were flagrant, and they were not me. I didn't think of the girls that way; I considered them more as friends than anything, especially since Goldie entered my life.

The rage boiling up in my body was too much and there was only one cure, but unfortunately, that cure was taken away from me today.

Shaking my head, I turned around and started heading out of Kace's room while I called over my shoulder, "Start finding a replacement Jett Girl."

"What?!" Pepper yelled, as she stumbled out of bed and pulled on my shoulder. "You're seriously kicking me out of the club? You can't be serious. What am I supposed to do? Just not get any while you and Goldie fuck like rabbits upstairs? How is that fair?"

Slowly, I turned around and faced Pepper. With a steely voice, I looked her in the eyes and said, "Did you or did you not sign a contract?"

Taking a second to answer, she finally nodded her head as anguish laced through her eyes. "You can't do this to me, Jett. I need the club; I'm not ready to leave. Please, Jett."

I ran my hand over my face and then looked her in the eyes. "The replacement isn't for you, Pepper."

Kace approached Pepper and me, wearing shorts now, and asked, "Who's the replacement for, Babs?"

"No," I said, while turning around to head up to my third floor. "The replacement is for Goldie; she's done."

Not wanting to talk anymore, I left without answering their

questions. I was too tired, too drained to deal with anything.

Pepper and Kace? How long had that been going on? I really couldn't be mad, and if I was honest, I wasn't mad. I actually couldn't care less. If they wanted to have sex, then by all means, let them have sex. I was at a point in my life where the Bourbon Room was meant for one Jett Girl and one Jett Girl alone.

The minute I got to my office, I poured myself a generous glass of bourbon and sat in my chair, facing the window, so I could look out at the streets of the Garden District. The streets were clear and the pale light of the moon shone down on the trees that covered the sidewalks like a canopy. I used to take pleasure in the view from my office, feeling like I could see all the sinners and saints from my desk chair, but now, the world was just black and white to me; the color that once filled it was gone.

The stairs up to the third floor creaked, and I knew it was Kace; I didn't have to turn around to confirm my suspicion. I was surprised it took him so long to actually come up to check on me.

"Dude, what's going on?" he said, as he sat in the chair in front of my desk.

Not turning around, I answered, "She left me; she gave me back my collar."

"Why?" Kace asked, sounding just as distraught as me.

"Didn't quite get a clear answer about that," I said, as I turned around and rested my hands on my desk. "She said it was about time someone protected me, and that she would be back, but…" I shook my head as I gathered myself. "She took it off, Kace. She took off her necklace. What the hell am I supposed to think? That was the one thing I could rely on, the one piece of security I had when it came to keeping Goldie as mine. Now what?"

"She said she would be back?"

"Apparently, but I have no clue if it's the truth, if she was just stringing me along. Fuck," I swore, as I took a huge gulp of my bourbon. "Kace, I can't function. I don't know where the fuck she is, what she's doing, or who she's with. What does she think she's doing? Going to ride into who knows where and start karate chopping people?"

"I wouldn't put it past her," Kace joked. "I'm sure she has a plan."

I gave Kace a pointed look. "This is Goldie we're talking about."

"True," Kace said. "She's a wild card, though, no one knows what she'll do, let alone what will come out of her mouth. You have to have faith in her, Jett."

And there it was. That's what this all came down to, faith.

But to me, without being able to have any control over the situation, I had a pretty hard time having faith. Ever since I could remember, I've always had control in every aspect of my life, even when I was living under my father's roof, I had control, but with Goldie, I lacked that control. She really was a wild card, and taming her was an enjoyable challenge for me, but right now, I fucking wished she just would have let me take care of things.

I felt helpless.

Needing to change the subject, I sat back in my chair and asked, "How long have you and Pepper been fucking?"

The eloquence my dad tried to instill in me at a young age quickly vanished the minute my world was flipped upside down. Now, I really didn't give a fuck what came out of my mouth. I had no filter.

Shifting in his chair, Kace answered, "Not that long. This was only the second time we've been together. First time was a drunken mistake, second time was a horny one."

"Not getting any lately?" I asked, while finishing off my glass.

"Been kind of difficult lately, given all the bullshit happening around here. Haven't really had much time to go pussy perusing."

"So, might as well dip your pen in the company ink."

"Hell, you do it," Kace replied with a smirk. "Why can't the right hand man get a little action?"

"Have you ever touched Goldie?"

I knew the answer, I didn't even have to ask it, but the jealous fool I was let the question flow out of my mouth.

"No," Kace answered, while looking me square in the eyes. "We both know she wouldn't do anything with me."

"But you would welcome it?"

Why I felt the need to torture myself, I had no clue.

"Yes, no doubt about it," Kace answered honestly. "Every damn day of my life I wish Goldie had never signed the contract, because the minute she left this club, I would have jumped on the opportunity to make her mine. She's, by far, the most uniquely beautiful woman I've ever met."

I ground my teeth while I listened to Kace. I only had myself to blame for the answer to the question, but I was in a masochistic kind of mood and apparently was trying to sink myself into a deeper hole of depression.

"If you can't handle the truth, then don't ask," Kace said, noticing my discomfort.

He was right, I shouldn't have asked, but I couldn't help it. I hated that he liked her, possibly had stronger feelings for her, feelings that only I should have for my Little One.

"I hate that you have feelings for her," I replied, voicing my thoughts. "It drives me insane that I see the same look in your eyes that I have for her."

Kace shrugged and sat forward in his chair.

"We might have the same feelings, but the difference between you and me is that she only has eyes for you. From the very beginning, she's always been made for you."

She might have been made for me, but I didn't deserve her. It was God's cruel joke, to grant me such a beautiful and vivacious woman, but take her away the minute I open up, the minute I fall for her.

I was about to answer Kace back when my phone chimed with a text message. Desperate to hear from Goldie, I pulled out my phone and read the message. Unfortunately, it wasn't from Goldie, it was from Rex Titan.

Rex Titan: Funny little visitor I had tonight, looking for a place to stay, a place as far away from your controlling dictatorship as possible. I will be sure to keep her nice and warm in my bed for you.

Pure rage rapidly flowed through my body as I read the text message from Rex a few times over and over again. Not just rage, but embarrassment...embarrassment for, once again, not being able to hold on to a woman, for once again losing another woman to Rex. I should have known.

Kace was badgering to know who the text was from, but shame washed over me, so instead of letting him know what was going on, I put on a strong façade, looked Kace in the eyes, and said, "Find a replacement for Goldie. We'll need one with Babs doing a new night course for her business and Goldie no longer being a Jett Girl."

"Jett..."

"Do your job and find a fucking replacement," I gritted out, not wanting to hear Kace's lecture.

"Fine," Kace conceded, while getting out of his chair. "Same contract?"

Did I want the same contract? Did I want to revert back to my old ways of calling up a girl every night?

Turning around in my chair to look out the window again, I lightly said, "Same contract."

4
"I NEED A DOLLAR"

Goldie

"These dishes were actually imported from Europe. The queen used them in one of her cottages. I was able to win them on auction; they are worth well over one hundred thousand dollars," Rex educated me about his stupid ass plates.

All I heard was that they were a giant waste of money. The dishes were wretched. Some creepy square gold and red pattern ran along the edge that was supposed to symbolize family or some bullshit like that, I wasn't quite sure because I zoned out halfway through the historic details of the dishes.

Who knew such a strong alpha male could be such a dork, with his collection of teacups, swords, and paintings. The more I saw of his house, the more I realized the man was a hoarder of old crap. Rugs from the White House that smelled like musty old man balls graced the floors, chairs from president's houses that had permanent sweat stains on them, and books that didn't even have pictures graced his house. Where were the sex swings, the crops, the lubes, and edible undies? Non-existent, unless you considered the pantaloons from a late Martha May type lady that were hanging in the hallway to be edible.

Fucking pantaloons.

"They're just lovely," I lied, as I envisioned breaking every last one of them.

There were so many collectibles in his house that I started devising a plan in my head last night to slowly steal items from his collection, so when I left, nothing in his house would be complete. It would be the ultimate burn. First thing to go, one of his damn teacups, and then one of the little silver spoons he collected. Why would someone need a mini spoon that they didn't even eat with?

"Are you ready to go?" Rex asked, as he checked his watch.

"Yes, just let me grab my phone."

"No phones," Rex said. "Any kind of electronics that are taken in the club will be confiscated. We take our privacy very seriously. Every employee will be searched before entering."

Well, fuck. Talk about uptight. There went my idea of getting proof of the whole operation.

"Not a problem," I said causally. "Let's go."

Shit.

Rex eyed the table we were just eating at and said, "Are you going to clean your plate?"

I looked over at the paper plate Rex had given me with a dried out croissant on it. The man clearly didn't trust me with his precious plates, which was evident by what I had to eat off of. Not that it bothered me...eating off of a paper plate; hell, I had once eaten off of an old sock. I've seen worse.

"Oh, sorry. Great thing about paper plates is you can just throw them out, unlike those king plates you have."

"Queen. They are plates from the queen," Rex corrected me.

"Oh, yeah, that old bird. Did you know she carries a purse around with her everywhere she goes? Like, hello, you're the queen, what do you need a purse for? If you see something you like, you just bust out your queen card and it's yours. What do you think she keeps in there? Lipstick, obviously, she's not a beast, but do you think she has things like hand sanitizer? Gum maybe. Oh, wait, no. Do you know what she has? She totally has butterscotch candies. Classic Queenie and her butter..."

"Enough," Rex said, growing angry. Hello, moody pants.

"Sorry," I said weakly. "I ramble sometimes."

"I suggest you don't," Rex said, as he walked out of the kitchen.

Touchy!

Wanting to break his dishes right then and there, I refrained, and followed after Rex to his garage, where he held the passenger side door open for me to one of his cars. At least his temper didn't make him lose his chivalry.

Once Rex was inside the car himself, he strapped his seat belt on and started the car. Before he pulled out of the garage, he turned to me with a gentle look on his face and said, "I'm sorry about losing my temper back there, Kitten. I'm a little sensitive right now. We were supposed to hear about a property we are bidding on today, but because there were so many bids put on the table, the city will be evaluating every proposal and conducting interviews."

He had to be talking about Lot 17, which meant Jett was most likely punching every wall he comes across from that news. I knew he was hoping to hear about the property soon, but of course, in true city fashion, the decision was pushed further back.

"I'm sorry to hear that. But an interview seems like it might be a good opportunity to talk about your plans. It looks like your business venture would bring a lot of jobs to the city."

Everything directed toward Rex that came out of my mouth was a lie, but I felt it was necessary to boost the man's ego every chance I got. The more I showed him I was Team Rex, the better.

He nodded and pulled out of the garage. "That's a very valid point, Kitten."

"Are you going to tell them about the club?" I asked, curious what their plans were.

"No, that won't be a part of the proposal. The city officials who are interested in the club know about our plans, but that is more of an idea that stays behind closed doors."

"I can understand that," I answered, while Rex drove through the streets of New Orleans. "Where is your club now? I didn't know there were so many gentleman's clubs in New Orleans. How does one choose?"

"We own a building off of Canal Street that is covering as an apartment building, but really is the club inside. You'll see."

"So, then why move the club if you already have the space?"

"We would like to have more playrooms in the club; right now we only have four. We would also like to have a bigger floor show and hotel rooms for those who would like to take one of the girls for the night. Plus, we would like to have space to house the girls. Right now, they are going in and out of the building, and it's starting to look suspicious."

So, the man really didn't have any original ideas whatsoever. Everything he was saying was an exact replica of the Lafayette Club, but just skankier.

Jett had rules and limitations for a reason...that was because the Lafayette Club was all about the girls and bettering their lives, while taking advantage of the rich and filthy. Masquerade wasn't for the benefit of the employees. No, it was for the benefit of the owners, at least that's what I could surmise from what Rex had already told me.

With each passing moment I spend with Rex, I'm starting to see how much of a self-centered man he actually is. I'm just glad I met Jett before Rex made his offer for me to be with him, because at the state in my life I was in back then, I would have said yes to him, and who knows where I would be right now? Especially after the conversation I overheard last night.

They wanted to make me the main attraction? What the hell did that mean? Was it like Diego's club, where the girls performed stunts and had sex with someone on stage? That wouldn't fly for me.

We rode in silence for the rest of the ride, only speaking occasionally about the weather. To say the man was a bore was an understatement. Why did I use to like this guy so much?

Rex pulled up in front of an old looking building made of brick that actually looked kind of creepy. There was one door in the front, and it was black with no windows. Yeah, I could see how scantily clad women walking in and out of this door would look suspicious. Jesus, I was even smart enough to know that you had to change the façade of the building to make it look less skeezy.

"See why we want a new building?" Rex stated, as he got out of his car and buttoned up his suit jacket. He walked around to my side, as he handed the keys to a valet, who had popped out of nowhere. Rex opened my door and held out his hand for me. Reluctantly, I took it in mine and let him lead me inside.

"How do the members get inside the building? Do they walk through this door? It doesn't look very nice."

"No, there's a back entrance they use. We wouldn't ask the members to walk through the front. We try to keep things as discreet as possible."

"So, why don't you have the girls walk in the back as well?"

"Because, they are employees; they're not allowed to intermingle with the members unless granted permission. The building really is too small for the operation we're trying to run."

"I can see that," I replied, as I walked through the front door with Rex. The hallway to the front was dingy with torn black walls and filthy floors; it really surprised me how disgusting the place was, especially since Rex and Leo were running it. Not that I had met Leo, but if he was anything like Jett, he would require things to look immaculate at all times. Right now, their club, Masquerade, looked more like a crack whore's den rather than a club for the elite of New Orleans.

"As you can see, the front entrance needs a little work, but we're trying to avoid making any more improvements, since we're trying to grant the club a new location. The interior is much more presentable, I promise."

At the end of the hallway, we came to a dark door that looked like it was almost metal. To the side was a scanning mechanism that threw my whole life off. Were we entering some kind of secret underground storage space for the FBI where they kept the aliens and Elvis Presley?

With precision, Rex entered a code into the keypad, which lifted the door of the scanner thing and he bent forward to have his eyes scanned.

He could not be serious. For a club? Get real, buddy.

"We have the most advanced security system money can buy. We don't let just anyone in here."

"I can see that," I said, as I waited for the door to pop open.

"We'll get your information keyed into the system later today."

"Good morning, Mr. Titan. Do you have a guest with you?" A robot lady said over a loudspeaker in the hallway. Earth to Rex, there's something called volume control.

Talk about peeing my pants.

"Who the fuck was that?" I asked, as I slowly crouched, looking around for a machete woman to pop out of the corner and start whacking away.

"That's the system. It records everyone who enters and leaves and who they brought with them. The system can tell if you have a visitor or not. We keep a log of who is coming and going at all times."

Paranoid much?

"Saki, I have one guest with me, Goldie, our newest member."

Saki? Sounds awfully close to Suri. Did Rex rip everything off? Fucking weirdo.

"Very well, sir."

The door clicked open, and with curiosity, I walked closely behind Rex, peeking over his shoulder and taking in Masquerade.

Surprisingly, there was no greeting space in the club. Instead, it opened up to a room that looked very much like the Toulouse Room, but instead of purple gracing the walls, they were covered in black and trimmed in gold. The gold paint was miraculous. It shined against the black and glittered in the light. I had never seen anything like it. There was a main stage in the middle of the room, with leather chairs circling around it, and above the stage were gold chains hanging from the ceiling, making the center of the room look almost sinister. I wondered what the hell they planned on doing with all of those chains…only time would tell.

Continually absorbing everything around me, I noticed around the room were little doors that must have led to the playrooms Rex talked about. I was most interested in seeing one of those rooms, to see if they were like the rooms Diego had set up, or if they were darker, less sexy.

A long bar rested against the back wall, holding only top notch liquor; I wouldn't expect anything less. Bar stools also sat in front of the black marbled bar, offering a heightened view of the main stage.

The feel of the room was dark, perverse, and almost dangerous.

"Welcome to Masquerade, Kitten. What do you think?" Rex said, while opening his arms and showing off his pride and joy.

"The gold is divine," I answered honestly, as I ran my hand up one of the moldings.

"Gold is the equivalent to power in New Orleans."

Thanks to Jett, I already knew that.

"How does the club work?" I asked, eyeing the stage.

"Come with me," he led me to one of the chairs and pressed a button on the armrest.

A door to the right opened and two women immediately walked out into the room, completely naked. Hello nipples! They kept their heads hung low and walked hand in hand up to the stage. They were both brunettes, roughly the same size in every aspect. They were bare of all hair and had boob jobs for sure, because there was no way their boobs were that perky naturally.

I watched as they ascended the stairs of the stage and started grabbing the chains from the ceiling. The chains clanged together as they moved them and adjusted their heights.

"Every girl submits to the males in the club, they are not to look us in the eyes and they are to always stay silent."

"Interesting," I replied, not really knowing what to say to such a thing. Honestly, I would rather eat his dick than alter who I was to be one of Rex's fem-bots. "What are they doing?"

"They're preparing the main attraction."

AKA, what I would be doing once Rex got his way.

With morbid curiosity, I sat at the edge of my seat and watched as one of the brunettes stood in the middle of the stage and allowed the other brunette to attach chains to her wrists and ankles. Once she was secure, the brunette who wasn't chained stepped away and went back to where she came from.

So the girl just stood there naked, strapped to chains? That didn't seem like that big of a deal.

Before I could ask another question, Rex stood up and took off his jacket. He rolled up his sleeves and stepped up on stage. Things were about to get awkward.

He looked the girl in the eyes and said, "Do I have permission to touch you?"

At least he had the decency to ask. I would have thought, after the way it seemed like he treated these girls, he wouldn't even care to ask if he could stick his finger in their cooche.

This girl nodded, and in fascination, I watched as Rex ran his hands up and down the girl's body, making her writhe under his touch. Her nipples were erect and her eyes were shut. So, it was like Diego's club; she practically orgasmed on stage. Was that so bad?

Rex bent down and opened a panel that was on the floor. He dug around for a second and then grabbed a flogger. He ran it through his fingers right before he struck the girl on the back of the thighs. The pain coming off of her face was almost unbearable to watch.

"What the hell are you doing?" I asked, as I stood and got up on stage to stop Rex.

"Goldie, please step down. Only one member is allowed on stage at a time."

"One member? You mean more than one person comes up here?"

"Yes, the members take turns coming up on stage and practice dominating our girls. We have demonstrators come in to show the technique of flogging a woman, and when they're ready, they are allowed to come up here and do what they want to the woman."

"And how does she feel about that?" I asked, as I lifted the girl's chin so she would look me in the eyes.

"She's paid, right sweetheart?"

"Yes, sir," she said weakly.

I wanted to scream at the girl and tell her how messed up this was. Everything about this club went against every moral in my body. I was okay with stripping and giving lap dances, I wasn't a damn moral compass, but having no say in what happened to you by multiple men? Oh, fuck no.

Then it dawned on me, this was what Rex wanted me to be, the main attraction, the girl all the men flogged, touched, and fucked.

Holy shit! Jett would have a coronary if he found out what Rex was planning.

Sweat started to trickle down my back as I tried to figure out how the hell I was going to get out of the predicament I put myself in.

"Do you have a problem with this, Goldie?" Rex asked, eyeing me with that devilish glare.

Yes, I had a problem with it, Jesus, but Lord knows I couldn't say that. I kept reminding myself I was doing this for Jett; I was doing this for us. I had a purpose for being here, and it clearly wasn't going to be easy, but I was bound and determined to make sure that not only did I get to live my life with Jett, but now that these girls were involved, I was going to find them justice, just like Jett would.

Lifting my chin, I looked Rex square in the eyes and shook my head. "Not a problem at all. Where are the other girls? I would like to meet them and have a run-through of what is expected of them, what kind of training you would like me to conduct, and form some sort of a schedule. Is the club running now?"

A grin spread across Rex's face from my "eagerness" to start my roll.

"Only a few members are testing things out right now. Since we have you on staff now, we can start really training the girls and getting them ready. We are looking to officially open in two weeks, to see how things might run so we can prepare for our new space."

"How many do you have on staff?"

"Three girls, four including you, and one bartender, Blane."

"Blane?"

"Yes, he is also in charge of the demonstrations."

Interesting, I thought. I didn't like Rex grouping me in with the other girls, that terrified me and I promised myself that by opening day, I would be taking down Rex's operation, because I didn't want to come close to that stage.

The clunk of a bag hitting the bar sounded, and both Rex and I turned around to find a very muscular man with tattoos running up his forearms standing behind the counter. His hair was blond and cut stylishly, while his blue eyes stood out against his tanned skin. From what I could tell, he must be Blane because he had Dom written all over him.

"Speak of the devil," Rex said. "Blane, please come over here and meet Goldie."

Blane looked up at me and gave me a wicked grin, as if I was fresh meat. Instantly, I put up my guard. I didn't trust this guy one bit. He reeked of trouble.

With a swagger that was unfortunately sexy, he walked over to us, while eyeing me up and down, sizing me up. Once in front of me, he stuck his hand out and offered his name.

"Blane, nice to meet you, Goldie."

I gripped his hand in mine and was frightened to feel such a tight grasp when he shook.

"Nice to meet you," I lied, as I pulled my hand away. "How do you know Rex?"

"Rex and I go way back, isn't that right, buddy?" Blane said, while clapping Rex on the back.

"It is."

The way Rex smiled had me wondering what the hell their

history was. Whatever it was, it wasn't good. Right about now, I wanted to run back to Jett and bury my head in his shoulder. Things were getting a little too intense for me, and I was for sure in over my head.

"Why don't we let Blane show us what he does up on stage?"

Rex led me off the stage and back into my chair. He kept his hand on my thigh while we watched Blane prepare for his "show." I wanted to flick Rex's hand off of me, but reminded myself to keep the illusion, to make it look like I was here for Rex, not for Jett.

The way Blane spoke softly into the girl's ear reassured me that what I had seen Rex do wasn't close to what Blane was going to do, and I was right. Instead of pain, I saw pleasure cross the girl's features. Blane wasn't cruel or hard on her. No, he was gentle, yet commanding, he sort of reminded me of Jett.

Lord help me…

5
"UNFAITHFUL"

Jett

"I didn't expect to find you in here, boss man," Babs said, as she walked into the gym wearing her Jett Girl gym attire. "Working off some pent up frustration?"

I huffed at her, wiped my face with my towel, and turned up the speed on the treadmill I was working on. I usually worked out with Kace, but he was out recruiting this morning, so I was on my own, which I was enjoying until Babs walked in, breaking my concentration.

"Not talking today? Alright, then I'll talk," Babs continued. "She loves you, you know that? Maybe if you showed one ounce of love for her, she would have stayed."

"It's not like that," I gruffed out, as I continued to run on the treadmill, increasing my speed to a sprinting pace.

"But, isn't it? You've always been a prideful man, an emotionless man, and then Goldie comes along and turns your world upside down, shows you what it's like to have someone truly care for you, truly want you not for your body or your money, but for your mind and your kind heart. But what do you do? You go and fuck it up."

"Enough," I said, while slamming my hand on the treadmill and stopping the conveyor belt. "I suggest before you start slamming your boss, you get the facts right first, Barbara," I seethed, using Babs' God-given name.

Flustered from my tone of voice, Babs started backtracking. "What do you mean? Is there something I don't know?"

"Yes, as a matter of fact, you don't know everything that is going on in this club like you think you do."

I walked over to the little fridge in the gym and pulled out a water for myself. Without chancing Babs a glance, I opened the cap and started draining the liquid. The workout that I was hoping would give me a little escape from the torment running through my head did nothing but irritate me more.

"What's going on?" Babs asked, with her hands on her hips, gaining confidence in her defiance once again.

Babs was my first ever Jett Girl. I found her one day, offering up her services, saying she could blow me for only ten dollars, and it would be the best blow job I ever received. At that moment, I knew she needed help; she needed someone to take care of her, so I took her in. It took me a while to tame her, to dominate her, since she was dead set on pleasing me constantly for the "fancy digs" I was putting her up in, but I told her she didn't have to pay me back, but just to work hard on her Jett Girl skills and education.

Now that she was months away from graduating and launching her makeup line, she had gone back to her old self, not throwing herself at me, but defying me every chance she got. She was just as mouthy as Goldie, but where Goldie spoke randomly about things that popped up in her head, Babs was more forthcoming with putting me in place. Ever since Goldie arrived at the Lafayette Club, Babs had made it her mission to butt into my business and make sure I wasn't screwing up my chance with Goldie.

"This doesn't concern you, Babs. So drop it."

I tried to walk past her, but she placed her hand on my chest and said, "Oh, no you don't. Everything about this club concerns me, Jett. I helped make this club the way it is today. You, Kace, and I built this club together, so when one of my girls goes missing, I get to know why."

The unsaid mother hen of the group spoke; she was right. Without her and Kace, I would never have been able to start the Lafayette Club and make it the success it was today, a success for the women involved.

Running my hands over my face, I said, "Goldie left me. She returned her collar. There, you happy?"

"No," she answered honestly. "Why did she do it?"

This was the part I didn't like talking about. What did I say? She left me for another man? Once again, I'd failed? I would rather just tell people she left me because I was a bastard, because the thought of telling people she was out doing who knew what, trying to protect me, drove me insane, it made me feel inferior.

She was trying to protect me, me! Fuck, I did the protecting; I was the one who took care of the ones in my life. I wasn't the one who had to be protected. It gutted me knowing I wasn't able to do my job, and my Little One was forced to go out into the world on her own to take matters into her own hands.

It gutted me that her "protecting" led her to Rex.

Fury started to run through my veins once again, as I thought about Rex's text. Last night I had tried to figure out why Goldie would run to Rex, what could she possibly do with him? Yes, she knew about Lot 17 and my dad, but how the hell could she make things better by being with him? All she was doing was ripping us apart.

"Well…" Babs encouraged me to continue.

"Jesus, you're frustrating."

"I'm persistent, so don't test me," she replied.

Rolling my eyes, I grabbed one of the workout balls and sat on it as Babs did the same.

"To make a long story short. My dad is after Lot 17 and found out I was putting in for the same property. He knew I had something over him, so he took it upon himself to break up me and Goldie by threatening her life. Goldie got sick of the distance between us, and not being able to live our lives together, so she gave me back my collar and said she was going to protect me. She said to have faith, but honestly, Babs, I have absolutely zero faith in the matter." I took a deep breath and said, "She went back to Rex Titan."

"What? Are you sure?" Babs asked, growing concerned.

"I have no clue. What I do know is Rex sent me a text last

night saying she was with him. I tried contacting her friend Lyla, her old roommate, to see if Goldie possibly asked for her room back, but Lyla hadn't heard from Goldie in a while. No one has, which leads me to believe that she truly is with Rex."

"She hasn't contacted you?"

"No, and her phone is turned off. I couldn't even track it if I wanted to."

"Ah, yes, stalker Jett wouldn't let me down by missing out on that key factor."

"I'm not a stalker," I defended. "Just efficient in my tracking capabilities."

"Clearly, not efficient enough. Do you want me and the girls to get involved?"

"No," I said rather harshly. "I don't want any of you involved. I want you to stay out of this. Kace is out recruiting a new girl as we speak. I will need you and the other three to welcome her with open arms."

"Where are you going to put her?" Babs asked, slightly confused. "The only room that's open is Goldie's."

"Yes, and it's currently being cleaned out."

"Jett, you can't be serious."

"I am," I said, while getting up and heading toward the door. "She returned her collar, Babs. It's over."

"It is not," Babs said, while pushing my shoulder, throwing me off a bit. "She's trying to make it better. She's not leaving you, Jett."

"With Rex? How is that better? How is her running off with another man making it better? No, we're done," I answered, while I headed for my office.

My phone rang, and without checking the caller ID, I answered.

"Jett Colby."

"I found your new girl," Kace spoke into the phone.

"Perfect, bring her in. Her room is being set up right now."

"Jett, do you really want to do this?"

"Yes, now don't question me," I said, right before hanging up the phone.

Truthfully, the last thing I wanted to do was bring in a new Jett Girl. I was happy with the group we had. I was pleased with the dynamic of the girls, and bringing in someone new was always a risk, because most of the time, personalities clashed. Given the fact that I was bringing in a new girl because one of their own left, it wouldn't be easy on the new girl. I actually felt bad for her, because she had huge shoes to fill.

The house was much quieter, much more subdued, like all the girls were in mourning. Kace was always a moody bastard, but now that Goldie was gone, he almost seemed like a piece of him had left. I could tell he was mad at me…mad at me for inviting a new Jett Girl to come on board, but what choice did I really have?

In the off-chance that maybe, just maybe, Goldie actually didn't leave me to be with Rex, then I needed to carry on, show my dad that, in fact, I didn't mind that Goldie was gone, even though my heart was ripping out of my chest with each passing moment she wasn't in my arms.

The third floor didn't have its appeal anymore and, if anything, I wanted to change out my room for Goldie's. I wanted to stay in her room, where it was bright and cheery. I wanted to sift through her closest, smell her, feel her…

"Jett," a male voice rang from my office.

Quickly looking up, I saw George, my lawyer, standing in the doorway of my office. Who the hell let him in?

"George, how did you get up here?"

Clearing his throat, he looked at the ground and said, "One of the girls let me in and led me upstairs."

"Was she wearing a mask?" I asked, starting to grow angry once again.

"Yes," George said quickly. "I have no clue who it was."

Patting my face with my towel, I nodded, and led us both into my office. Since it was still morning and I just got done working out, I left my bourbon alone and offered George a water bottle instead, which he declined.

It was very rare that I allowed anyone to see me in anything but a suit and tie, especially when it came to my business, but George was an exception; I've known him my whole life.

Sitting down in my chair, I looked over my desk and asked, "To what do I owe the pleasure of seeing you today?"

"Lot 17," George said, while pulling out a folder from his briefcase.

"Did we get it?" I asked, leaning forward to look at the file.

"No." My eyes shot up to his, while devastation enveloped

me. "No one got it just yet," George finished. "Since there has been great interest in the lot, they are going to interview some of the candidates. Luckily, we are one of them."

"What do you mean, luckily?" I fumed. "We should have been granted the property in the first place. What more do they want?"

"They want to know your plans for the property; they want a presentation with visuals. They want you to show them that your plans will benefit the city."

"Who else is in the running?" I asked, as I sat back in my chair, trying not to take my anger out on George. He was just the messenger.

"There are only three interviews being conducted. You, of course, Zane Black, a real estate developer in New York City, and Rex Titan and your dad."

My teeth ground together as I puffed out a frustrated breath. Of course my dad and Rex were in the running. Why wouldn't they be? They'd bribed practically everyone in the city.

"Do you know who has the upper hand? Who the city is looking more strongly at?"

"Not at this time, but I can do some digging for you."

"Yes, I need to know what my chances are, what kind of ideas I need to throw together."

"Stick with your original proposal, Jett. Don't change it now; it would look like you're nervous, that you're original proposal wasn't good enough. If it wasn't good enough, it never would have been considered."

Even though I didn't want to admit it, because I was a stubborn man, George was right.
If I changed things now, it would look bad for my character. If I changed my plans, it would be showing weakness, and that was one thing I never did; I never showed my weakness.

Besides Goldie, but that was an emotion I couldn't control. Goldie swept me up with her sassy mouth and crippled me, she was the one and only thing that could bring me to my knees, that could tear me open for the world to see.

"You're right," I concurred with George. "When are the interviews?"

"Two weeks. You have some time to pull together some graphics and put together a presentation, which needs to be short and concise, because you only have twenty minutes altogether for your presentation and questions at the end."

"Not a problem," I said with confidence. This wouldn't be my first interview for a property. I wasn't nervous about the presentation; I was worried about what my dad had up his sleeve. The man would do anything to win Lot 17, even sinking to the level of locking me in my own damn house so I didn't make it to my interview. The man would stop at nothing.

"I will draw up the official plans once again for you to hand out at the interview. Do you want me to get in touch with Jeremy, your assistant, so he can start on the graphics?"

"No, I can handle that," I answered. "I will be in touch with Jeremy. Thank you for coming over here to tell me, George. I appreciate it."

"Anytime," George said, as he handed me the folder he'd pulled out of his briefcase earlier. "Please call if you need anything; if not, I will be in touch if I hear anything else, and when I hear about the time of your interview."

"Thank you."

I dismissed George and opened up my computer to look through my emails, hoping maybe there would be some kind of contact from Goldie. I would take just about anything from her right now, for her to confirm that, in fact, she still thought about me...that she wasn't with Rex.

When I searched through my emails, scanning for one email address only, I didn't find anything from her. So, I sat back in my chair and ran my hand through my hair, trying to tamp down my frustration. There was business I needed to tend to, plans for different properties around the city that needed to be discussed, but all I could think about was the little honey-haired girl who took over my heart.

What was she doing? Was she lounging in the arms of Rex Titan right now? Was he really keeping her warm? The mere thought of that happening had me wanting to pull out every last strand of my hair.

"Hey," came Kace's voice and a knock to my door.

Looking up, I saw him standing sturdily with someone behind him. Did he really bring up the new Jett Girl with him?

"What are you doing?" I asked, assessing my appearance and disheveled heart. I was by no means prepared to meet a new Jett Girl, especially when it wasn't on my terms.

"Thought you might want to meet the new Jett Girl," Kace said with a smirk.

"Now is not the time," I warned.

"Oh, please, stop being a priss," a strong, yet feminine voice came from behind Kace.

One of my eyebrows rose at the nerve of the new girl who was about to join my club.

"Excuse me?"

Stepping aside, Kace allowed the new Jett Girl to come forward, and I nearly toppled over.

The beautiful mocha skin of Lyla, Goldie's old roommate came forward, wearing the Jett Girl gear, minus the mask. She walked toward me with purpose, and from behind her back, she dropped her Jett Girl file on my desk with purpose.

With a smirk on her face, Lyla pointed at the folder and said, "Papers are signed, but I've made a few revisions."

"What gave you the right to do...?"

Lyla held up her hand and interrupted me. "I'm going to stop you right there, buster. You can take your controlling and dominant ways and shove them up your ass. Frankly, I don't need this job; I'm more than capable of pulling in enough money to make things work for me at the bar. Give me some water and a white T-shirt, and I'll make the room rain with boners and cash. But you need me for a couple of reasons. One, you need another Jett Girl, since Goldie is now gone. I know how important it is to meet the members' needs, believe me. Two, I'm here to make sure you don't do anything stupid because your poor little feelings have been hurt. And three, you need someone to help you find Goldie. I'm the closest thing you'll get when it comes to that girl. Keep my identity hidden, and during the day, I'll make it my duty to find out where Goldie is."

"I don't care where she is," I replied arrogantly.

"Yup, calling bullshit on that right away. Nice try, though," she smiled at me. "So, here's what's going to happen, I'm going to room with Babs because the room that you were going to give me is Goldie's, and you're not going to change that. You can take your Bourbon Room and shove it up your ass. Don't even ask any of the girls to come up to it, because collectively as a whole, we choose not to submit to you. That room is meant for you and Goldie. I will learn how to present myself and be a fill-in, but the moment Goldie comes back, I'm out. I'm here mainly to make sure you don't do something completely stupid, like ruin the best thing that's ever happened to you."

She folded her arms across her chest and smirked at me, as if she knew everything. Her cockiness reminded me of myself, and I hated it. But what I hated more was the lack of control I had; there was zero. I felt like I didn't have a say in anything, and that was what was going to drive me to do something that I shouldn't be doing.

"Before you get all huffy, why don't you let me figure out Goldie, and you focus on your business," she added, clearly seeing how uncomfortable I was.

"Why should I trust you?" I finally asked, after her demands were over.

"Because I know what's best for Goldie, and that would be you. I've known her for a very long time now, and nothing has brought her such great joy as when she's with you. You think she lights up a room on her own, try watching her when you're near. She is so bright, so enthusiastic, so completely Goldie that it's intoxicating to see. You two are meant for each other, and I'll be damned if I see it any other way."

I mulled over her statement. There was one thing she was missing; Goldie wasn't the only one who changed…I was not the same person when I was around Goldie. I wasn't a controlling bastard, I was completely different, I was happy, enthralled, completely, without a doubt…in love.

Fuck.

Shaking my head, I turned around and looked out my window. Love? Did it really come to that?

Visions of Goldie ran through my head. The first time she was asked to come up to the Bourbon Room and how nervous she was, the first time we went out on a date and how beautiful she looked in her yellow dress. The first time I gave her a Jett Girl set, the look of joy on her face. The moment I gave her my collar…fuck.

My throat closed up on me as I thought about the loss I was suffering…how I would do anything to have her standing in front of me with my arms wrapped around her waist and my chin resting on her head.

"I'm not going to look for anyone else," Kace said, backing

Lyla up. "It's Lyla or no one."

The two pains in my ass must have communicated beforehand, because they were a united front on Goldie's behalf.

In a surprising moment of complete and utter weakness, I turned my seat so I could rest my elbows on my desk and run my hands over my face. I didn't do emotion in front of people, but I was so fucking exhausted, I couldn't help it.

"She's not with me anymore," I stated weakly. "I received a message from Rex; she's with him."

The room fell silent at my confession. I wasn't sure what Lyla was thinking, but I could feel Kace's eyes boring a hole through me. He knew about my past history with Rex and how losing my Little One to him could bring down my stone façade in a matter of seconds, which it proved to do.

"How do you know?" Kace asked, sounding more confused than anything.

"Rex texted me that she was with him. Since he's not the most trustworthy man, I checked around, and no one else has heard from her. That's the only place she could be."

"Shit," Kace muttered.

"Rex, as in the guy she used to bone for money? No way, he was hot, but she wouldn't go back to him. Although, he did offer her a life with him a little while back..." Lyla thought out loud.

"What?" I asked, fury starting to pour through me, washing out the debilitating pain of feeling weak and useless.

Startled, Lyla said, "When she first started here, Rex wanted to take her back, once he found out she was becoming a Jett Girl. He offered her a place to stay, so she didn't have to stay with you. At the time, Rex didn't know she was desperate for help."

Vaguely, I remembered Goldie talking to Rex before I gave her a set. Was she taking him up on his offer now? After so long? That didn't make sense.

"Fucking hell," Kace said, as he ran his hand over his face.

"What?" Both Lyla and I asked at the same time.

He was silent for a second, and I was about to yell at him to spit it the fuck out, but he continued, "I bet you anything she's trying to take down Rex's club. Diego told me he told her what he knew about it. She said she wanted to protect you; without a doubt, that's what she's doing."

Fucking hell was right.

6
"SECRETS"

Goldie

The last crack of the flog Blane used echoed against the walls as the girl he was pleasuring screamed in rapture from the orgasm that ripped through her.

What the hell did I just watch?

Whatever it was, I felt a little wrong for watching it, but watching the girl orgasm was fucking hot, like if I had a cock, I would be stroking it right now.

From the corner of my eye, I looked at Rex to see that he was smiling brightly and purely satisfied with Blane's performance with the fem-bot; I mean, how could he not be pleased? My armpits were sweating and my legs wanted to spread just from watching that.

"Well done," Rex said, as he stood. "Please release her so she can meet me in the back. I hope you don't mind, Kitten, since we are building a friendship now."

I scrunched my face, as I tried to comprehend what he was telling me.

"Don't mind what?"

Rex pointedly looked down at his crotch and that's when I

noticed his arousal.

"You can take care of it if you want; I would prefer it, actually."

Gah! Gross. I usually like a good old fashioned boner against the pants, but after the way Rex was practically panting during the whole demonstration and the creepy look on his face now, yeah, I couldn't be more turned off. Lady boner shriveled up…good job, Rex.

"Uh, yeah, sure," I replied, really not knowing what to say.

"Really?" Rex asked, "You would rather go to the back with me?"

"What? No!" I shouted, and then realized I needed to bring it down a couple of decibels. "I mean, no," I replied more calmly. "I misunderstood; I don't mind if you, uh…let her take care of that," I pointed at his boner.

Taking a deep breath, he leaned down and pressed his head against my ear. "Don't worry, Kitten, she will only be pleasuring me; I'm holding out myself to be with you…emotionally."

Oh, well fucking lucky me. Jesus. When did Rex become such a creep?

"Got to get it somewhere," I smiled and shrugged my shoulders, wondering what the hell was coming out of my mouth.

"You're not mad?" Rex asked, looking a little worried.

"You do what you have to do, Rex. Get at it!" I said, while pumping my fist in celebration.

I'm fucking certifiable today.

Taking a good look at me, he ran his hand across my face, making a coarse thrill run through my body from his touch. His mouth connected with my ear and he said, "Believe me, I will be thinking of you the whole time. I can't wait to get my hands on your pussy. I've been dreaming about it for months. Explore the club; I'll be back, Kitten. Until then, think of me."

Bah! Yeah, that won't be happening.

"Okay," I said meekly, trying to make him feel bad.

He should feel bad. What kind of sick creep went off with another woman to relieve himself when he was trying to be with me? If I needed an indication that he had ulterior motives, then this was it. He didn't want me. He was just using me to get back at Jett in the worst possible way, and the longer I stayed here, the sooner the day would come when I was the one naked on stage, getting flogged up by Blane the muscle man.

"Be good," he winked and walked away with the girl who'd been shackled to the stage.

In awe, I watched as she followed after Rex with her head down, in a completely submissive state. To say the club was a bit frea-kay was an understatement. Um, how about downright wrong? Men came to Masquerade to watch "demonstrations" on how to dominate a woman, and then they took them to the back rooms to have their ways with them, or they held one-on-one instructional sessions with Blane on stage. Yeah, that's just fucking weird. Who comes up with something like that?

I thought about the Lafayette Club and how it was more of a high class strip club; no one was ever naked, and the only thing that ever touched the Jett Girls was a man's lap…that was about it.

Diego's club was slightly different. I wasn't quite as immersed in his club, but from my understanding, it was a sex club for couples or singles looking for coupling. There were acts that were performed center stage, but they were works of art, well thought-out erotic dances, not some sex shackling. No one was cuffed, no one was forced to have sex; unlike Masquerade where the women walked around like slaves. Where did they even find the women to participate? Even at my lowest, I don't think I would have stooped this low.

"Are you just going to let your boyfriend go off with that girl?" an Australian accent asked from the stage.

A little shocked, I looked over at Blane, who was wiping some sweat off of his forehead and looking down at me with a judgmental eye. How dare he judge me? He was the one practically beating a woman a few minutes ago.

"Fuck off," I said, while turning around and taking in the club, trying to figure out how the hell I was going to bust Rex without bringing in my phone to record everything.

"Cheeky, eh? Don't be mad at me when you're being a doormat."

"Excuse me?" I said, while turning back toward him and practically spitting fire out of my eyes. "Not that it's any of your business, but I'm not with Rex; I actually despise the man and wish that he would burn in hell along with his partner Leo. I am, by far, the farthest thing from a doormat; I don't take shit from anyone, and I especially don't take shit from a highlighted haired man with clothes that are entirely too small for his body," I stated, while looking Blane up and down. "And your accent is stupid."

Good one.

I turned back around, and that was when the realization of what I said crossed my mind. Holy shit. Blane was Rex's friend, they went way back, he was going to tell Rex everything I just said and who knew what would happen from there?

Quickly, I turned around to wipe up my mouth diarrhea, but was faced with a smirking Blane, who started to walk toward me with determination, like he owned the room. Little did he know, I had my fair share of experience with alpha males, and I knew how to put them in their place...easily.

"Listen, I didn't mean..."

"Don't talk," Blane said, as he grabbed my wrist and started walking me toward a door that was off of the bar.

"Where the hell do you think you're taking me, you beast?" I scathed, as I tried to claw my way out of his grasp, but was unsuccessful in getting away from the burly man holding on to me.

"Just stop, will you?" he said, as his accent grew stronger with his irritation.

Scratch that...his accent wasn't stupid...it was press-my-pussy-button sexy.

We pushed past a mini-kitchen and into an even smaller room that only had a desk and a chair in it. The room reminded me of a manager's office you would find in a restaurant, stark and depressing.

With his foot, he closed the door to the room and turned on a small desk light before turning toward me and leaning on the desk.

I looked around, and then eyed him suspiciously. "So, what now? You gut me and sell my organs on the black market? Well, too bad for you, I'm missing my appendix, so good luck selling everything as a whole package. Suck it." I crossed my arms over my chest as he studied me with crystal blue eyes. So what, the man was hot, wouldn't be the first time I came across a hot, domineering man.

"You're a piece of work, you know that?"

"I do, actually," I replied smartly.

Nodding, he smirked again and said, "So you don't like my dearest friend Rex?"

Sweat instantly pricked at my temples, as I tried to figure out what to say. The man seemed too relaxed to be having this conversation with me. I felt like, if he was truly mad, he would have grabbed me by the hair and dragged me across the floor until we reached Rex, where he would toss me at Rex's feet and yell "traitor" at the top of his lungs while shaming me for everyone to see.

Maybe that was a little farfetched, but he seemed too calm and collected right now.

"He's cool," I shrugged. It was the best I had. I mean, the man was fucking another girl in the other room. Oh, wait, pardon me, he was letting her "pleasure him," completely different, apparently.

Laughing, Blane shook his head and said, "You're so full of crap, but that's okay. I'm not a fan either."

"Wait, what?" I asked, a little shocked to see how easily Blane spoke of his distaste for Rex.

"What? Do you think hating Rex only belongs to you? Well, you're wrong, the guy is a prick."

I eyed him, looking for a tell that he was lying. "Is this one of those moments where you trick me into telling you how much I don't like him only for you to record and divulge my secrets to the man in question later?"

"No," he laughed. "You already let me know about your feelings for the man without me tricking you."

"So, you are trying to trick me, then," I poked his chest, only to find that I probably sprained my finger from how strong his muscles were. I should have known better. Men in New Orleans, in the circle of Jett and Rex, equaled, hot, dominant, muscular, and downright irritating.

"No, I'm actually not. I'm trying to find someone to finally be on my side," he said, more seriously.

Oooh, he wanted to be in cahoots. Things just got interesting!

I leaned forward and said, "You really hate him?"

"Do I hate a man who is blackmailing me to be in his club, forcing me to do things to girls that I, by no means, want to do? Yeah, you could say that."

"He's blackmailing you?"

"We're not getting into that now," Blane said with authority, snapping me into my place.

God, I hated myself, I reacted so well to a dominant man; it was annoying.

"Fine, what do you want then?"

"The same thing you want."

"And what do you think that is?" I asked with my hands on my hips.

"Freedom, you want to bring them down and live your life, just like me."

Well, slap me on the hammy hams, he nailed it.

"I'm going to try to forget why you know that about me…"

"I don't know you at all," he cut me off. "But I see the same look in your eyes that's in mine. You're repressed, you can't live the life you want because he's casting a black cloud over you, holding you back. Am I right?"

"Yes," I nodded, a little sadly. What I would give to be wrapped up in Jett's arms right now…It was the one and only thing I wanted, but stupid Rex and Leo were ass cocks and couldn't let the poor guy live his damn life.

"Good. I've been waiting for someone like you to come around. I have some ideas, but we have to act quickly."

"Why?" I asked, starting to grow anxious.

"The interviews for Lot 17 are coming up, and from what I've heard, Rex and Leo are in the running to take it. If that happens, we'll be trapped here forever, because the new club will be improved…it'll be bigger, more exclusive, and more erotic. I want out of this, and I know you do too. I've heard what Rex has planned for you, and believe me, you don't want to be a part of it."

"Gang bang," I mumbled.

"Something like that," he mumbled back, making my eyes pop out of their sockets. "The only way to keep them from getting the property is by exposing them and their business."

"Duh, that's why I'm here," I pointed out, so he knew he wasn't the only one with the genius plan.

"The only problem is, there is no way we can with the security Rex has on this place. We need to devise a plan, and I think I have one, but you might have to get your hands dirty."

"How dirty?" I asked, with a quirk to my eyebrow.

"Not too dirty, but you won't have the luxury of just sitting around, teaching the girls. We have about two weeks to watch Rex's pattern and take advantage of it. We need to get him in a routine when he walks in here…"

A slam of a door cut Blane off from speaking as he looked toward the door.

"You have to go. You can't let Rex see you with me. He'll know something is up."

"Okay," I said, while opening the door.

"I plan on seeing you every day. Don't approach me; I will approach you when the time is right. Until then, do what Rex says, don't let him think any differently."

I nodded, and without a glance back, I exited the small room.

With renewed confidence, I walked down the service hallway to the main room, feeling like a secret spy. I wanted to crawl against the walls and do hand motions to Blane to tell him the room was clear. Where were my spy glasses? My magnifying glass? We were going to bust this joint wide open!

"Goldie, where were you?" Rex boomed as he came toward me.

My inner excitement was squashed instantly by the fury pouring off of him.

Taking a deep breath, I looked around, and then grabbed my crotch instinctively and started dancing around.

"Can you believe I almost went to the bathroom in the sink over there? Where's the damn pisser?"

The worry lines that were etching Rex's face relaxed as he watched me pretend to struggle with my over-filled bladder.

"To the right," he pointed. "Second door."

"Thanks," I said with a pained voice. I ran toward the bathroom and locked myself in it. I looked in the mirror and took a deep breath. My heart was racing from almost being caught with Blane in the little closet office. Rex would have had a man-fit if he saw us exit at the same time. As if he had the right…he was just with another woman. I was still trying to get over the audacity he had of going through with such a thing. What a squid.

After I went to the bathroom, I washed my hands and opened the door, where I was greeted by Rex. He was leaning against the wall, waiting for me. He was definitely paranoid.

"All set?" he asked, eyeing me.

"Yup, are you? Did you have a nice time?" I asked with a sweet voice, trying to show that what he did wasn't the weirdest thing in the world.

Taking a deep breath, he leveled with me and said, "It was just fine."

"Just fine? Do I need to teach her some moves?" I asked, swiveling my hips.

"No, you just need to fuck me," Rex said, while grabbing my waist and pulling me flush against his body. "I won't be able to wait long for you, Goldie. Especially with you sleeping such a short distance away from me. You belong to me, simple as that."

So, the man was a creep, but I still got a little excited when he talked to me in his dominant voice. There was something about his dark, stubble-caressed jaw and the deep gaze in his eyes that turned my insides into a little flutter. I was a lady with an overactive vagina that drooled when an alpha walked in the room; I couldn't help it.

Clearing my throat, I gently nodded and pushed away. "Am I going to meet the girls? When do I start? I'm still a little unclear on what you're looking for from me."

"Fair enough," he nodded and grabbed my hand. "I will introduce you to the girls."

Rex dragged me through the back of the club and into a small room that was closed off by only a curtained door. The back of the club was a disaster. There were exposed pipes and beams and garbage scattered everywhere amid the construction; it appeared to be in a constant state of disrepair. It surprised me how unprofessional it was, but then again, the members never came to the back, and it wasn't like the health code inspectors were invited for a tour. I guess I just expected more from Rex. From the way he presented himself, I would have thought he had the same standards as Jett, but boy was I wrong about that.

The two men were complete opposites. Jett was modern and dignified, a real man. Rex was a crusty old hoarding historian with a pack-rat problem. Lesson learned, never judge a book by its cover, because where Rex is more open and welcoming, he really was a terrible man. Jett was closed off and rude when you first met him, but he's a true gentleman at heart.

Rex cleared his throat to gather the attention of the room. I peeked around Rex's shoulder and saw three women, stark naked and sitting in chairs like robots. They weren't talking, they weren't moving, just staring at the wall and sitting in a row, waiting to be commanded to do something.

Holy hell, was I living in some kind of sex slave paradox?

"Ladies," Rex greeted them, but they didn't lift their heads.

"This is Goldie; she will be your manager and teacher when it comes to the acts you will be performing out on stage. She comes with great experience, and I encourage you to listen to her." Rex turned to me and grabbed my hand to bring to his lips. "I have to go work on some paperwork. Please start working on some choreography for a still-life show. I would prefer to see them slowly touch each other in different positions."

Gross! Fucking pervert.

Smiling and nodding, I allowed him to kiss my hand, even though I wanted to punch him square in the teeth.

"When will they need to know the choreography by?"

"We need them to know it by this weekend, and they need to know it without you leading them, because you will be attending a gala with me Saturday night."

"Oh, really?" I asked, feeling a little apprehensive of who might be at this gala.

"Yes, your dress will be picked out for you. We'll go over the details later. Be useful, Goldie, and whatever you do, stay away from Blane; I saw the way he looked at you, and I didn't like it."

Swallowing hard, I smiled brightly and said, "Not a problem. He's got that whole jock thing going on anyway, too bulky, you know?" I asked, while flexing my muscles. "Like, where's your neck, dude? Bench much?" I elbowed Rex, but he just looked at his arm where I touched him and then took off.

Pull the fucking stick out, dick wad.

Despite what I said, Blane wasn't too bulky at all; he was just perfect and he had a neck, boy did he have a neck. The perfect neck to lick...

Fuck, I was horny. A couple of days away from Jett and already I was envisioning my tongue running up some other guy's neck. Shaking the thoughts out of my head, I turned to the girls and eyed them all. Their heads were down and their hands were in their laps, all posed the same way.

They either went through some crazy sex slave shock therapy or they were desperate for cash. I would say it was the latter. I didn't blame them; I knew exactly how they felt.

Clearing my throat, I stood in front of them with my arms crossed, channeling my inner Kace and screamed at the top of my lungs, making all of them jump about a foot out of their chairs and look at me as if I was some crazy banshee on the loose.

"That's better," I said, while I started to pace the room, looking at all of them. If I only had a whip and a whistle, I would be ready to teach these girls a lesson in submitting to a man. Defiance was the true key to submission. Without defiance, what was the point of having a dominant man? They wouldn't be challenged, and you would just be a doormat. Plus, a good spank to the old backdoor melon was a pleasant way to spend a night.

"Listen up you swaying kumquats, when I'm in the room, you look me in the eye, you puff your chest out with pride, and you own the fact that you are naked with two other women in a room that is less than satisfactory for our fine asses. Yes, that's right, you ladies are fine, you're beautiful, you're more than just a smooth piece of skin with a beating heart. You're women, damn it, you have the power to take down any man you want to, and do you know why?" I pointed at them and then gripped my tits and crotch. "Because we hold the ticket to that pestering one-eyed pant snake that is trying to eat up our gentle lady folds any chance it gets. We get to tell it when it can enter and when we can clench around the swiveling little worm and suffocate him until he squirts his man seed." I clenched my fist and held it in the air as I spoke. "We hold the cards, ladies. Now, let's stand up, smack our tits together, and show those men who's in charge."

I held true to my fist pump and waited for the cheer from the women below from my incredibly inspirational speech, but was greeted with silence instead of a loud victory call.

Tough Crowd.

I lowered my arm and looked at them to see they were all staring at me as if my vagina just fell off. Glancing at the ground, I made sure that wasn't the case, and then clapped my hands together to lift the silence in the room.

"Up and at 'em, ladies. Let's go, stand up, yup that's it. Get on those feet."

Timidly, they stood up and looked at each other, wondering if they were going to get in trouble. What the hell had happened to them all?

Wanting to make them feel more comfortable, I said, "I'm Goldie, like Rex said. The only reason I know him is because he used to pay me for sex. I used to live on Bourbon Street, where I worked at Kitten's Castle as a half nude waitress until I was recruited to be a Jett Girl." All their heads popped up and their eyes lit with interest.

"You were a Jett Girl?" one of the girls asked meekly.

"I was, and it was amazing. I learned a lot from that experience, and I'm going to teach you guys the same thing, but first, we need to drop the submissive act and learn about each other."

"We can't," the girl who'd gained enough courage to open her mouth answered for everyone. "If Rex saw us speaking, he would fire us, and we can't be fired; we can't afford it," she trailed off.

My heart turned in my chest. They were in the same position I was a few months ago, but to my luck, Jett Colby offered me a contract, not Rex Titan.

"Well, when you're around me, you can talk, because hell if I'm going to teach a lap dance to a bunch of muted mannequins. If Rex has a problem with that, he can talk to me. So, tell me your names."

There were three girls, two with brown hair and one with the same color hair as me; they were distinctly different from one another, though. One of the girls had short brown hair that fell to her chin. Another girl had long honey-colored hair same length as mine and she was blessed with bright green eyes, and the girl who had enough courage to speak to me was the other one with brown hair. She was very exotic looking, quite gorgeous.

Looking around, the girl who spoke looked me in the eyes and said, "I'm Evangeline, but everyone calls me Eva. This is Bizzy," Eva said, pointing to the girl with the short hair, "And this is Mercy," she finished, pointing to the girl with the bright green eyes.

"Well, have Mercy," I said, channeling my inner John Stamos, and while waving my hands in the air, garnering not even one smile from any of them. "Okay," I cleared my throat, "You guys are kind of boring, but we'll fix that. Mercy, Bizzy, nice to meet you. Eva, thank you for having the courage to speak. I promise I'm not here to report you three. I'm here to help, okay?"

They nodded their heads, still acting a little stand off-ish. This was going to be so much harder than I thought. Where were Babs and Francy with the shot glasses when you needed them?

7
"MY SUNDOWN"

Jett

"Why are we sitting around the stage? Shouldn't we be practicing?" Pepper asked Kace.

"Jett has to talk to us, so quit your bitching and hold still until he gets here," Kace replied abruptly.

They all sat in silence, listening to Kace's direction, while I watched them from the doorway.

Ever since Goldie's departure and Lyla's arrival, there had been a lot of questions running around, and it was time I settled them before things got too out of hand and rumors started to float around the club.

I straightened my tie and walked into the room, noticing all the girls in their uniforms. Lyla fit in perfectly with the other girls, wearing her shirt well. She was quite beautiful, gorgeous actually, but even though she was very pleasing to the eye, I felt nothing for her. I felt nothing for anyone except Goldie.

My soul ached for her. My body pleaded with me, begged me to go over to Rex's house and take her away, but my brain stopped my body from acting on its needs.

My Little One was in danger; I could sense it. She was with an evil man, someone who would take what he wanted and would have no qualms about who he hurt in the process. Rex Titan was just like my father, maybe even worse, because he enjoyed gloating about his victories.

Needing to put on a strong façade, I pushed the thoughts of Goldie's circumstances out of my mind and addressed the girls. I cleared my throat as a cue for them to direct their attention toward me. Kace was sitting on the stage with a somber expression on his face, while the girls looked slightly confused. I could tell he was hurting just as much as I was. Even though I hated the fact he had feelings for Goldie, I understood how he was feeling, because my heart was going through the same battle.

"Thank you for taking time out of your schedule to meet with me," I said to all the girls.

"You know you don't have to be so formal with us, right?" Babs asked with her legs swung over one of the arms of the chairs she was sitting in.

I ignored her and continued. "As you all know, Goldie has left the Lafayette Club, and we replaced her with Lyla…"

"Stop," Francy said, while standing up, shocking me a bit. "Can you seriously just talk to us, Jett? I can tell you're hurting; I can see it in your eyes, even though you're trying your hardest to hide it from us. We know how much Goldie meant to you…we saw how she made you feel, how she lit up your room when she walked in. You love her, Jett."

I pulled on my cufflinks and studied the floor as I listened to Francy. I love her, yes, that was an accurate statement, a feeling I never thought I would succumb to, but somehow Goldie made me feel, she made me fall for her; I had no choice in the matter.

Once again, ignoring Francy, I looked back up and continued. "Lyla will be staying with us in the meantime, making sure the members stay happy until we can find a permanent replacement. Lyla has made it quite clear she is just helping us out temporarily."

As I spoke of Lyla, I watched as Kace scanned Lyla up and down. He might be hurting about Goldie, but he sure as hell wasn't having a hard time making himself feel better. There was heat in his gaze when he eyed Lyla.

"What about Goldie? Aren't you going to bring her back?" Pepper asked, looking a little angry.

"Goldie has made her choice," I swallowed hard.

"Bullshit," Pepper spat at me. "You're such a coward, you know that, Jett? You're just going to let her walk out of your life? What the hell is wrong with you? I thought you were the kind of man who took what he wanted and didn't let anyone get in his way. Never did I think I would see the day when you would just roll over and play dead. Frankly, it's disgusting."

"What do you want me to do?" I cracked, as my voice roared. "She thinks she can save the world by going back to Rex. I can't do anything about that."

"Yes, you can," Babs cut in. "You can walk up to Rex's place and take back what's yours."

"It's not that simple," I said, as I ran my hand over my face. "If I'm not careful, they'll harm her. I can't have that, even though she left me, I can't fathom the thought of her getting hurt."

The room fell silent as there was a knock on the door. Jeremy, my assistant, popped his head in and said, "May I come in, sir?" I nodded my head and he entered, holding his iPad close to his chest.

He sidled up next to me and practically whispered, "I have some news you might be interested in."

Looking at him with a raised eyebrow, I asked, "What kind of news?"

"I heard from one of my friends that Rex Titan is going to be at the gala this weekend. He plans on talking up some of the city council members about Lot 17 before the interviews start the following week." He paused for a second and then spoke softer. "He RSVP'd for two."

Instantly, my stomach fell to the floor at the thought of Goldie showing up to the gala latched on to Rex's arm. Would she really attend an event with Rex, knowing there was a slim possibility I would be there? If she had any concern for me, she wouldn't. She knew it would tear me apart.

"Is the other RSVP for my father?"

Shaking his head, Jeremy said, "No, he declined his individual invitation."

Fuck.

"I'm sorry, sir," Jeremy spoke. "Would you like me to cancel your invite?"

Seeing Goldie with Rex at the gala would be devastating, it would completely crush me, but on the other hand, getting a chance to see Goldie was an urge I couldn't squash.

"No," I responded. "I will still attend, and would you please invite Keylee to go with me? Apologize for my late notice, but I will need her there for appearance purposes."

Jeremy nodded and took off. I turned back to the girls to find them all glaring at me.

"You're kidding me, right?" Francy asked. "You're going to take Keylee to that event. Are you trying to hurt Goldie?"

"No, I'm trying to make it seem like I'm not about to lose my fucking mind since she left me. I have to make it seem like I don't care about her."

"Why?" Pepper huffed out.

"Because my dad will harm her if I don't. Until I have some kind of leverage over him, some kind of evidence that the man is the actual low life he is, then I have no choice but to act like Goldie means nothing to me, or else, he will harm her. He would do anything to hurt me, to crush me, and right now, he knows Goldie means something to me. He knows," I broke off while rubbing my forehead.

"What can we do?" Babs asked. "How can we make this better?"

"You can't. Leave it to me and Kace. You keep conducting business as usual and make sure Lyla knows the routines. We can't show that there has been a ripple in the club, because if it gets back to Rex and my father, they will take full advantage of it."

"How long is this going to go on for?" Babs asked.

"I'm not sure."

It was the truth. I really had no clue how long this tug-of-war would go on. I was tired, though. I wanted it to all be over, and honestly, I was moments away from pulling the plug on Lot 17. It's caused more hurt than good. I could build a park for the kids somewhere else; I would donate millions to update their facilities if I needed to, but the one thing that kept me from pulling the plug on the project was the fact that if I did, my father would see that as a sign of weakness and he would know that he had me by the balls, that Goldie was the key to what he wanted and I couldn't have that. I couldn't put her in that position, no matter how bad she hurt me.

Speaking with a gentle tone, I looked at the girls and said, "I appreciate your concern. I will try to make this better, somehow."

"If she came back, you would take her, right?" Francy asked while Tootse sat in her lap, completely silent.

Would I take Goldie back? My heart would, my soul would reach out and grab her faster than I could tell her no, but if she slept with Rex, if she shared a bed with the man, I didn't know if I could ever recover from that. I knew my heart wouldn't be able to survive it, knowing the one person who was made for me, who was brought to me by my mom was with someone else; the thought was unforgettable, no matter her intentions.

I shrugged my shoulders and just said, "Depends. I do ask you all to stay out of it, though. I'm at a loss as to what to do at this point, and I don't need you trying to make things better and making them worse instead. Please, just take care of the club for me."

They all nodded their heads in understanding.

With a heavy heart, I turned and walked out of the Toulouse Room, just as my phone rang.

"Jett Colby," I answered.

"Jett, it's George. I have some news."

"What is it?" I asked, growing anxious.

"I was able to find out about the interviews and who the front-runner is. Unfortunately, right now, Rex and Leo have the advantage. They've made some promises to some elites in the city that are outweighing your plans for the lot, as well as Zane Black's plans."

"You can't be serious?" I asked, while stopping in the hallway to pace and run my hand through my hair. "Fuck, what can I do?"

"Not sure. Unless there is something you can find out about Rex and Leo, we are pretty out of luck."

"What about the mayor wanting to run a clean bidding process? What happened to all of that?"

"He's not the one who will be making the decision; it's a panel. He only has so much pull in the matter. Rex and Leo have infiltrated the right people."

Grinding my teeth together, I thought about what my next step was going to be. Goldie was out trying to gather information about Rex, at least that's what we assumed she was doing, that was what I was trying convince myself of, but I couldn't rely on whatever scheme she had in her head. I needed to take control of the situation; I needed to figure this out on my own.

"Thank you for the information, George. I will be in touch."

"What are you going to do?" George asked, with a bit of skepticism in his voice.

"That is none of your concern at the moment."

"Jett, please don't do something stupid."

"George, how little you know me. Have a good day."

I hung up, but didn't put my phone away; I had one more call I had to make.

"Mr. Colby, do you need me to meet you?" Jeremy asked into the phone once he picked up.

"Jeremy, I need you to do something for me."

"Anything, Mr. Colby."

I loved how loyal the man was.

"Gather all the information you can on a Zane Black from New York City and schedule a meeting with him. Sometime soon, please, within the next couple of days. I will fly to him."

"Can I ask what this is for?"

"I need to make some special arrangements," was all I said, and then hung up for Jeremy to be left to his task.

Feeling a little more in control, I walked back up to my office to take care of some of my business. I still had an empire to run. I still had to be the Jett Colby everyone expected me to be, even though I could feel how broken I was inside.

8
"THE GIRL"

Rex

 Kitten flowed through the club with ease. It was thrilling to see her fall right into step with our plans. At first, she seemed to have a little resistance with how we ran things around the club, but she warmed up quickly and had the girls moving flawlessly to a seductive song that would entice our members most definitely.

 The way the club was set up was, the members would come in for a show at a designated time. They would have to reserve chairs beforehand with a deposit, and once they arrived, they were showered with food and drinks. Once they were comfortable, the girls would come out to do a dance or whatever kind of act Goldie prepared for them. Then the men would vote as to who they would want the main attraction to be for that night for Blane to do a demonstration on. The voting process would only be until I was able to permanently make Goldie the main demonstration, a goal both Leo and I had set in our sights to tip Jett over the edge. From the look of Goldie's dedication, we were going to have her on stage quicker than we expected.

 After the demonstration, if a member paid extra, they would have a chance to have a one-on-one with Blane and Goldie, but if not, the men would be able to take one of the girls back to a playroom. Right now, we only have three girls, but Leo and I are confident in being able to recruit more, especially after we secure Lot 17. We will be able to expand our operation.

Masquerade was a play off of the Lafayette Club, but much better. Where the girls were covered at the Lafayette Club, the girls here had to be naked at all times. Lap dances were as close as you could get to the girls at the Lafayette Club, and you weren't even allowed to touch them, but at Masquerade, touching was allowed, and fucking was encouraged. The girls were there for a reason; they were there to be used.

I watched as Goldie had the girls bending in all different directions, while mingling their bodies together. I was getting a hard on just from watching them, and I wasn't one to sit and watch with a hard on. When I was excited, I had someone take care of it for me.

I adjusted the crotch of my pants so I was slightly more comfortable. "Mercy, come with me," I called out, as I started walking to one of the back rooms.

Mercy was, by far, the most beautiful specimen I had ever seen, even more beautiful than Goldie, which was rare. They were quite similar, though, in their build and hair. But where Goldie was smart mouthed and challenging, Mercy was the perfect submissive. She was also my accomplice. She kept an eye on Goldie for me, to make sure she wasn't up to anything crazy.

So far, Mercy was only able to report back about Goldie's first initial speech to the girls, where she told them to drop the submissive act. Luckily, I trained my girls well and they didn't falter much. Eva, I had to keep my eye on, because according to Mercy, she was more outspoken than she should be.

I could hear Mercy's padded footsteps behind me, trailing like the good girl she was.

My conversation with Goldie when she first showed up at my door constantly rang through my head. She wanted to be a part of my future; she saw herself as being with me in the long run. That night, I felt a little nostalgic over what we used to have, the suspense of it all, but after I met Mercy, I knew there was no turning back. Right now, Goldie was a means to an end for me, the end of Jett Colby, and if I had to lie to her, to let her believe I was waiting for her, then so be it.

Leading Mercy into one of the playrooms, I watched as she walked past me into the black out room. Everything in the room was black, from floor to ceiling. You could choose the lighting you wanted reflecting off of the walls, so for today, I chose yellow, because Mercy looked gorgeous under the color.

Clicking the door shut, I turned to see Mercy, kneeling before me in a submissive pose, just waiting for my command, just the way I've instructed her in the past. From the look of her kneeling before me, I felt myself grow harder, it was that easy when it came to Mercy.

"Mercy, you have such a way of pleasing me."

She didn't speak. She just continued to look down at the ground like a good submissive. Kneeling before her, I lifted her chin so she was forced to look me in the eyes. Her green eyes found mine and, once again, I got lost in them. With just one look, she was able to make me surrender every wall I put up around my heart.

"You're so gorgeous," I whispered softly, taking a nip on her lips, an action I couldn't keep myself from engaging in. "Stand, I want to talk to you."

She did as was told and waited for me to direct her. I took a seat in one of the black sofa chairs in the room and patted my knee. Silently she walked over to me and straddled my lap, making her breasts even with my eyes. My mouth watered as I examined her plentiful chest. She was natural, everything about her was natural, from her hair color to her body. I couldn't get enough of her.

"Tell me, Mercy, have you missed me?"

The green in her eyes sparkled as her head nodded with contentment.

Mercy was the exception of all the girls. Initially, I trapped her into working with the club the same way Leo and I forced the other girls, but after a few interactions with Mercy, I realized she was different. I realized she appreciated the dominance, she thrived on it, and that was what made us so compatible.

"Have you heard anything new today? Did everything seem to be in order?"

She nodded her head with a small smile to her lips.

"I want to hear that beautiful voice of yours. Tell me, how was your practice with Goldie?"

I stroked her sides as she spoke softly to me.

"She's nice, Rex. She tells us how beautiful we are every day, and is confident in our abilities."

"Do you not get the same thing from me?" I asked, a little concerned.

"No, I do, but I don't think the other girls do."

I nodded in understanding. "Don't worry, baby girl. Once we have more members, they will feel the same way you do. Now, enough talking, I need to feel myself inside of you."

Bowing her head, she returned to her submissive self and waited for me to direct her.

"Pull off my tie and wrap it around your eyes; I only want you feeling tonight."

Carefully, her small hands ran up my chest and started undoing my tie. I watched as her body flexed over mine, her nipples puckered, only arousing me even more. Once my tie was undone, I watched as she wrapped the tie around her eyes and tied it off against the back of her head. Her breasts fell heavy against her chest when her arms returned to her side, enticing my tongue to reach out and flick them.

"Lean back," I commanded.

Her body angled back, with her hands propped against my thighs, giving me a great view of her breasts. I ran my hands up her sides to just under her breasts, watching her chest heave up and down from my touch. Mercy was very receptive to my caresses, and I marveled every time I had her under me how she reacted to each press of my finger.

With my thumbs taking the lead, I ran them over her nipples...just barely caressing them. I tortured her with precision until I could tell she couldn't take it anymore, and that's when I pinched them. I pinched them until her mouth flew open from pleasurable pain.

"You're allowed to voice your pleasure tonight," I told her.

Instantly a groan came out of her and her hips moved against my hardened erection. Looking down, I could see how wet she already was, another aspect of Mercy I absolutely adored. She was always so ready for me.

"Tell me, Mercy. What do you want from me?"

"Your cock," she responded without hesitation. "I want your cock, Rex."

"Stand up."

She stood straight in front of me and I kicked her legs apart, giving me better access to her pussy.

I told Goldie I was the only one being pleasured in the room, but that was a lie. There was no way I could not pleasure Mercy, not by the way she reacted to me so easily. I needed every aspect of her, and I wouldn't let her think any other way.

My hands ran up her inner thighs until they barely caressed her heated core, where she was wet, just waiting for me to plunge into her. Deftly, my fingers started to rub her clit, causing her head to fall back and her legs to buckle slightly.

"How does that feel, baby girl?"

"So good," she moaned. "Please, I need more."

I pulled my hand away and spoke sternly, "Mercy, what do we not do in here?"

"Tell you what to do," she said meekly.

"That's correct; don't make me remind you again."

With a nod, she stood straight again. Instead of going back to rub her out, I undid my belt and pants and pulled them down, feeing my erection pop free. It was so easy to be hard around Mercy; it didn't take much. Just watching her up on stage was intoxicating. Knowing members wanted to do her, would soon be taking pleasure from her like I did, was an even bigger turn on.

I liked knowing I could pass around what was so precious to me. Some dominants didn't share, didn't dare pass around their submissive, but that wasn't me. I got off on the fact that Mercy could be fucking another man, but in the back of my mind, I knew she was thinking of me the whole time. Call me fucked up, but I couldn't help what I liked.

I rolled a condom on and said, "Come, sit on top of me, Mercy; take me inside of you."

Mercy turned her body away from me and backed up until her calves hit my shins. Carefully, she sat down, gauging where I was. She grabbed ahold of my erection with her hand, and then guided me inside of her.

Every inch of her was perfection. Even with a layer of protection around us, she still felt amazing. It would never get better than Mercy, never.

Once she was seated on me, I pressed my hand into her hair and grabbed a chunk of it, while pushing her forward. I grabbed my phone from my side pocket and angled the camera so you could see her hair and our connection. Holding my hand steady, I took a picture of the erotic scene to save for later.

After I took care of business, I focused on just me and Mercy. I yanked on her hair and pulled her close to my body so her back was rubbing against my chest and I could speak into her ear.

"I want you to ride me, Mercy. Ride the fuck out of me."

Without a tell of emotion, her hips hypnotically moved against my crotch, taking me in and out of her, squeezing me with each plunge. Her chest rose and fell with the intensity of our connection. Easily, I could feel my orgasm start to peak, I could feel my balls tighten from the pressure she was putting on my cock. The feeling of numbness started to cloud my legs as my body started to float with the sensation of pure ecstasy.

From the bottom of her throat, Mercy groaned and clenched around me as her orgasm took her into a frenzy, working my cock up and down until I grunted into her ear and released everything in me.

"Fuck," I groaned closely to her ear, letting her know how much she pleased me, how much she was able to take me over the edge.

Her hips slowed until there was no more orgasm for her to ride out. Her back fell against me and I released the grip I had on her hair, letting her relax against me.

I kissed the side of her neck and then allowed her to stand. Like a good little submissive, she grabbed my cock and removed my condom, and then cleaned me up.

She was perfect. Everything about her was just so damn perfect. Once she was done, she knelt in front of me and waited to be excused.

"Mercy, once again, you've pleased me. Look up at me."

Her eyes peeked up from under her heavy eyelashes, seductively pulling me into her gaze once again.

"Mercy, are you jealous of Goldie, that she is living with me? Be honest."

She took a second to think about it, and then shook her head no, causing a little ricochet of pain to run through my chest. I wanted her to be jealous, to be the only one to have the privilege of being with me.

Her eyes matched mine as she spoke. "I'm not jealous of

someone who is no competition to me. I see the way you look at me, compared to the way you look at her. I know the difference. Do you want me to be jealous?"

She ripped me open. Did I want her to be jealous? Yes, I would prefer her to want me the same way I owned her, but the confidence coming off of her was, by far, more enticing than the notion of her being jealous of Goldie.

No, I adored the fact that she knew she wasn't competition, that she had me wrapped around her pretty little finger.

Pleased, I stood up, put my pants back on, and then grabbed her hand to make her stand as well. My lips found hers for one last kiss, and then I shooed her away. She needed to get back to the other girls before Goldie started becoming suspicious. I was surprised Goldie even let me be with Mercy, but then again, she was desperate, desperate to prove herself and to build a "relationship."

I laughed to myself at the thought of that. The only thing she would be developing with me would be a permanent spot on my center stage. Every elite in New Orleans would know who Goldie was, what she looked like naked, and how it felt to be buried deep inside of her.

Jett had fucked with the wrong men.

9
"FRIEND LIKE YOU"

Goldie

Two days working with Eva, Bizzy, and Mercy and they were still just as closed off as when I started with them. There would only be one reason why they weren't opening up and it had to do with Rex. He had to be holding something over their heads, something more than just being fired from working at the club. Blane was the same way, he was reserved, kept to himself over at the bar and would occasionally work with one the girls on a demonstration, something I would never get used to watching.

For some reason, seeing another dominant work a submissive hit too close to home for me. When I was watching Diego, it was different; he wasn't entirely dominating the woman he was with when they were practicing, he was more like dancing with her…in a sexual way, but still, watching Blane with the girls was different. It was like having an out of body experience, watching myself and Jett together, especially when it was Mercy and Blane working together.

After a long day of showing the girls how to pose properly, asses out, breasts up, and figuring out when they should rotate in tandem with the music, I was pooped and ready to sink into my rock hard mattress, thank you, Rex.

Once again, the man went off with Mercy today. The whole concept was so strange to me and it made me think he really was playing me. He was using me as a tool against Jett, the only thing he didn't realize was, I was using him as well.

After a quick shower, I settled into my bed, turned on my phone, and took a look at it. Every day when I got back from working at Masquerade, I begged for there to be a message on my phone from Jett. I know I left him without a clear answer as to what I was doing, but I just hoped he was able to push past his thoughts, the thoughts that I knew were clouding his mind.

To my disappointment, once again, there were no messages left for me on my phone, nothing. Not even from the girls.

I had never felt so lonely in my life. Even after my parents passed, I at least still had Lyla; right now, I had no one.

It was my doing; I did this to myself, but I thought maybe, just maybe, the relationships I built with the other girls were genuine, but after not hearing from them, it seemed like I was wrong.

Setting my alarm, I put my phone back down and rested my head on my pillow and waved good night to Thomas Jefferson...the man was growing on me.

Rex had already turned in hours ago; he was by no means a night owl. I spent some time in the "library," flipping through some of the books that were dustier than a mummy's vagina. None of them had pictures, all of them had words I couldn't understand, and not one single book talked about sex. What was that about? A touch to the wrist was a scandal. Boo! Give me flying tits and probing dicks.

After I got tired of searching for a book that at least wrote about a man's giant sword, I took a shower and went to bed. Sleeping in Rex's house was not comfortable. I didn't belong here. He didn't make me feel welcome; he made me feel like a prisoner. Shock alert, the man liked to suppress women, should have seen that coming.

Lately, it's been hard for me to fall asleep. There were too many thoughts running through my head. Thoughts like, how the hell was I going to expose Rex and Leo before the interviews for Lot 17 when I had no time away from Rex? When I wasn't in his house, being trapped in the confines of his crusty historian walls, he had me working with the girls. I hadn't had a chance to talk to

Blane, and I hadn't had a chance to explore the club to devise a plan. It was almost as if he knew I was up to something.

I blanched at the thought. He couldn't know, could he? No, he was too caught up in Mercy's pussy to even be concerned about what I was doing.

Even though my mind was wandering, my eyes started to drift shut, just as a clunking sound came from my window. I turned just in time to see it opening, causing me to stifle a screech.

Before I could pull out one of the ancient machetes Rex had lying around, Kace fell through my window, making a bump on the ground.

"Jesus," I said, as I scrambled to the end of my bed to look at him. "What the hell are you doing? You did not just climb up the house and through my window."

Lifting himself up, he brushed off his pants and then stood. "I did."

"What if my window was locked?"

"Why wasn't it locked?" he asked gruffly, while crossing his arms over his chest…classic Kace move.

"Why are you here?" I countered.

"Why did you leave?"

Gah! Infuriating man.

"God, you're frustrating," I complained, while keeping my voice down. "And how did you find me?"

"Rex texted Jett."

I could feel my face turn white and the blood drain from it in a matter of seconds. Rex texted Jett? Of course he did. Why wouldn't he? He was a prideful man, and when he felt like he won, he wasn't a gentleman about it. No, he liked to rub it in.

"You can't be serious. How is Jett?"

"How do you think he is?" Kace asked, as he sat on my bed next to me.

My body heated instantly from having him around, from having someone familiar and safe talking to me. I didn't feel like I had to have my guard up.

"Shit," I muttered. "I told him I would be back, that he needed to have faith."

"Yes, but he's a man who needs control at all times, and by leaving, you took that away from him. I've never seen him like this. He's confused; he's unprepared. He's going back and forth constantly about how he feels. You've completely uprooted him."

I buried my head in my hands and felt tears rush to my eyes as my throat clogged. With a gentle touch, very unlike Kace, he pulled me into his chest and held me as I cried. From the kind gesture and the comfort of his arms, I felt myself fall over that edge, the edge I was hanging on to by a thread. All the stress and mental abuse I put myself through came tumbling down.

The sweet caress of Kace's hand ran up and down my back as he held on to me while I soaked his shirt with tears and, unfortunately, snot. I was a guaranteed ugly crier, happened every time.

"Come back with me," Kace said into my ear. "Come back to the club."

"I can't. If I go back, I can't live the life I want to live."

"What life is that?" he asked, while lifting my chin to look him in the eyes.

Lust poured out of him, the same kind of lust I'd seen from him on multiple previous occasions. Not that he opened up to me…he wasn't very good at hiding his feelings when it came to the unmistakable tension between us.

"Kace…" I said softly.

He exhaled harshly and pressed his forehead against mine.

"Why did you have to sign the contract, Goldie? Why did you have to pick him?"

Tears rained harder down my cheeks as I stared into Kace's soulful eyes. He always had a strong veneer to hide behind, he never really showed his true feelings, ever, so to see him breaking in front of me, cracking, had my heart falling to pieces.

"I fell for him the moment I heard his voice in Kitten's Castle. There was nothing I could do, Kace. I'm sorry. He saved me, he gave me hope, and he gave me a new beginning and stole my heart at the same time."

I felt Kace nod against me in understanding.

"Do you think I would have had a chance with you if we met elsewhere?"

The vulnerability in his voice cut through me. Why was he asking all these questions?

"I don't even want to think about that," I admitted honestly. "Why are you asking? Where is all this coming from?"

Pulling away, Kace ran his hands through his hair and actually looked distressed. It was rather shocking. I never thought I would see Kace crawling through one of my windows one day, let alone showing me one ounce of emotion.

"I need closure, Lo. I just need to drop this and move on, so I needed to know how you truly felt." He paused for a second and shook his head. "You know, for a little bit, I thought that maybe I had a chance from the way you looked at me, but the moment you saw Jett, actually met him, I knew it was all over, but I still hung on."

"I'm sorry," I all but whispered.

"Don't be. Your heart wants what it wants. It's not the first time I've lost something in my life."

"I want you to be happy, Kace. Maybe you will find what I have with Jett with someone else. Maybe Pepper?"

Kace laughed softly and shook his head. "That would never happen. We're just good at fucking, which Jett caught us at, by the way."

"Seriously?" I asked, while pushing Kace's shoulder.

"Yeah," he replied, while pulling on the back of his neck and looking over at me. "It was right after you left; he wasn't happy."

The smirk on Kace's face mended the pieces of my heart that had fallen apart. Was this what it felt like to be Kace's friend? To have a normal conversation with the man without it escalating? I liked it; I liked it a lot.

"Look at us joking and being friends," I teased.

"Never friends," he smirked at me.

"Always friends." I pinched his side, making him grab my hand and give my pinchers the death grip.

"Do that again, and Rex will be barging in here from the noise that comes out of your mouth when I start tickling the shit out of you."

A tickling war with Kace? Yeah, I wouldn't pass up that opportunity. My heart belonged to Jett, but I had a vagina, and she knew what a little touching spree would be like with Kace.

"So, how's the club? Does anyone miss me?"

"They do," he reassured me. "We're not allowed to contact you, actually, but it's not very often I pay attention to the rules."

"Hence, you boning Pepper."

"Watch it," he warned, but with a smirk, making it hard for me to take him seriously. "Lyla is a Jett Girl."

"What?" I asked, as I felt my eyes pop out of their sockets. "Lyla, my roommate? My friend Lyla?"

"Yeah, she's filling in for you right now, keeping the members happy, and swears she can help bring you back."

"She's high," I joked. "I bet she is one hot piece of ass up on the stage. She would put me to shame if I was next to her."

"She's pretty damn gorgeous," Kace admitted, as he looked away from me.

Oh, my God!

"You like her! Oh, my God, Kace, you like her! You like Lyla!"

"Squeal one more time…pretty sure the neighbors didn't hear you."

"Eeep! I'm sorry, but you and Lyla. Oh, my God, you would make the most gorgeous babies. Jesus, I'm kind of getting a lady boner over the thought of you two together."

"Cool it," Kace said, getting tense on me once again. "I just said she was gorgeous."

"No, you said pretty damn gorgeous and then had this look in your eyes, like you wished she was pumping up and down on your shaft right now."

"This is why we're not friends."

"Have you talked to her?"

"Of course I've talked to her; I'm not a mute."

"Oh, really? Because I'm pretty sure you don't ever talk when I'm around."

"That's because I want to see what kind of insane shit comes out of your mouth. You never cease to amaze me."

"I aim to please," I smiled. "Seriously, though. Are you going to ask her out?"

He shrugged. "Who knows? Maybe. She has a mouth kind of like yours. You should have seen her when she walked into Jett's office and told him how things were going to be if she was a Jett Girl. Jett didn't even have a chance to get a word in. I kind of wanted to fuck her right after that."

I sat there with my mouth open, hanging to the floor. I was shocked, not just because Kace was telling me about his feelings for Lyla, but because he was able to speak more than a few sentences. Maybe the man did need closure, because right now, I felt lighter, happier to just be talking with Kace, not fighting, not trying to dodge the sexual tension between us.

"This makes me so happy," I giggled with joy, making Kace roll his eyes.

"Jesus, this is why I don't tell you things, because you do this girly shit."

"I'm sorry, should I pretend I have a dick and jerk off to the information?"

"Is that what you think guys do? Jerk off when they tell each other shit?"

"How else would you celebrate? Dick high fives?"

"Normally, we don't just whip our dicks out when we're around each other. Pretty much keep those wrapped up."

"That's boring. Guys have that whole vision of girls hitting each other with pillows in their underwear at slumber parties. Well, in my mind, when you're all together, you hang out with your wangs out and just jostle them around when talking. You know, like, 'Hey, man, great game today,' jostle, jostle," I said, while pretending to jostle my own pretend dick.

Kace gave me a questioning look and then shook his head. "There is something so beyond wrong with you."

"So, I take that as a no?"

"No," he said, while blowing out a loud breath. "So, has he been treating you well?" Kace asked, while taking in the surroundings of Rex's room.

"Sure. He hasn't really done anything bad to me. He's kind of moody, and even though he says he wants me, he wants us to be together, I know he's lying, because when he's at his club, he goes and fucks some girl in the back."

"And you're mad about that?"

"Well, I mean, I don't want to sleep with Rex, obviously, but it does something to a girl's ego when a guy goes off with another woman when she's supposed to be having a fake relationship with him. You know? I mean, how rude."

"Don't you have bigger things to worry about than who Rex is having sex with? Maybe like what the hell you're doing here in the first place? What are you trying to accomplish?"

Sitting back on the bed and resting against the headboard, I said, "Diego told me about some illegal business Rex and Leo might be conducting, and I knew if I could get some evidence, figure out what they were doing, I would be able to bury them and live my life with Jett. I'm sick of hiding. I'm sick of not having a relationship with the man I want to spend the rest of my life with."

Kace cringed for a second and then asked, "Are they doing illegal stuff?"

"Oh, my God, yes. So, it's like a sex club, but worse. The girls are crazy fem-bots that walk around with their heads down, waiting to be plucked away by one of the members to be fucked in the back room. I haven't really seen what goes on back there, but I know the girls are getting paid for sex. It's consensual, believe me, I've asked them, but it's paid for. I just don't know how to pin him for it."

"Can you record it?"

"That would be the easiest solution, but I'm not allowed to bring in any kind of phone or electronic device. I'm surprised I'm allowed to wear clothes in there. You should see it, Kace. The girls are naked all the time. I know who has a mole where and what cup size each of the girls are. I mean, who wants to be naked all the time, in front of people, and with other girls? The shit going on over there is so fucked up. And, get this, the bartender, his name is Blane, and apparently..."

"Blane Wilson?" Kace asked, cutting me off.

"Uh, I don't know his last name. He has blond hair, and he's a beefcake."

"Blane Wilson," Kace said, shaking his head.

"Do you know him?"

"Yes, he went to school with us. He hung out with the wrong people at school and ended up getting into drug trafficking."

"Holy shit, seriously?"

"Yes, he's not from here though. He grew up in Australia and moved here to be with his uncle when he was young. Technically, he shouldn't be in the states, but if he goes back to Australia, there are men there waiting to kill him."

"Noooo," I said dramatically, as I leaned forward.

"Yes, the dude is a good guy, but made some bad choices in his life."

"That explains what Rex has hanging over his head. Pretty much, Rex is blackmailing him to work at the club and dominate the women in front of all of the members. Rex calls them demonstrations; it's so fucking weird."

"Sounds like it. How do you plan on exposing Rex and Leo?"

"I don't know yet, but I'll figure something out. I heard that they were in the lead for Lot 17; they're the top contender right now. Without this information to expose them, I'm afraid they might win the space, then what happens? Would I ever be able to live my life with Jett the way I want?"

"I don't know," Kace shook his head. "I wish I had a more solid answer for you, but Leo, especially, is a dangerous man, and he will do whatever it takes to make things happen for him. He won't stop until he gets what he wants or he's exposed, and I know damn sure, he's never fully satisfied."

"That's what I was afraid of," I admitted. "Blane wants to work together to get the information we need. We just have to figure out how to do it first. We have a week still, right?"

"Pretty much, a little over a week. Interviews are next Friday."

I nodded and then said, "I have an event I have to go to with Rex. Please tell me Jett is not going to be there."

"Not sure," Kace said, while looking away from me, making me believe he was lying.

"Kace..." I warned.

"He might be there, Goldie. Whatever you do, avoid him. I know you, you're going to want to coddle him, but you have to be cold, you have to stay away. If you don't, you're going to tip Rex off, and then everything will go downhill from there."

"That makes sense," I swallowed, trying not to panic from the thought of seeing Jett on Saturday. I wanted nothing more than to see the man, to touch him, or just even be close enough to smell his masculine scent, but I knew I had to keep my distance. I had to act like I despised the man, when in fact, I loved him.

10
"HARD WORK"

Jett

"Mr. Black is available now," Aubrey, Zane Black's assistant said, as she escorted me back to his office.

She was your typical secretary, blonde, busty, and sexy. I applauded Zane for having good taste; I wouldn't have expected anything less from the man. Even though she was quite beautiful, there was something about her that told me her hair didn't match her mind. She seemed intelligent and loyal; I liked that about her. And what I liked best about her was she didn't seem to eat me alive with her eyes. It was refreshing.

We walked up to a grand door and I allowed Aubrey to open the door for me, escorting me into Zane's office.

"Mr. Black, Mr. Colby is here to see you."

Zane Black, a real estate mogul in New York City, stood up from his desk while buttoning his jacket and walked toward me. The man had quite a story, working from rags to riches, making a name for himself without help from anyone. He was a man to be admired.

Sticking out his hand, he introduced himself, "Mr. Colby, what a pleasure."

I took his hand and said, "You can call me Jett."

"Then, please, call me Z. No one really calls me Zane, and Mr. Black seems too formal for both of us. Can I get you anything to drink?"

"I'm quite fine right now, thank you."

Quietly, Aubrey closed the door on us and Zane led me to the sitting area in his office, a move I found to be quite humble. Any other power hungry man would have had me sit across from him at his desk, but not Zane, he welcomed me into his office and offered me an even playing field. I liked the man already.

"Thank you for seeing me on such short notice, Z."

Zane crossed his foot over his knee and relaxed in his chair, making me feel more comfortable with the ease in his posture he was displaying.

"I have to admit, when I heard you wanted to meet, I was intrigued as to what you wanted to talk about, since we're both bidding for the same piece of property. Does this have anything to do with that?"

"It does," I said, shifting in my seat and adjusting my jacket.

There was a limit of information I wanted to divulge when it came to talking to Zane. I didn't want him to know about Goldie, because that would show weakness, and I didn't want him to know about my feud with my father, because that would show jealousy. I wanted him to know the basics, but I wanted him to work with me.

"How important is Lot 17 to you?"

A small grin spread across Zane's face as he thought about what I asked him. I could see this wasn't going to be as easy as I thought it was when I first walked in. He was easygoing, but he was still a business man.

"It would allow me to expand my racing business. I have some thoughts about racing down in New Orleans, and Lot 17 would help with that."

Zane Black owns Black Top Racing, an underground racing company in New York City. Black Top Racing wasn't how he made all his money; it was a hobby he developed once he made his billions. The whole concept of Zane's racing was actually intriguing, and I considered standing in on one of his races one day because of the uniqueness of his speedway. Thanks to Jeremy, I knew all about his underground secrets.

"What would you say if I told you I had access to the

Riverfront Expressway Tunnel and could get you the rights to the underground road?"

Visibly, Zane perked up at my mention of the unfinished underground expressway in the heart of New Orleans. It was a tunnel the city started to build to ease traffic in 1960, but it was never completed, and instead of opening it up, it was closed off to the public. The Expressway was an attribute I knew Zane would be interested in obtaining, since he kept his speedway private.

"You've peaked my interest. What do you need from me?"

Smiling inwardly, I folded my hands together and said, "There are three bids up for interview next week, you, me and Rex Titan. Lot 17 means a great deal to me. I have plans to make a park for the local Boys and Girls Club, an organization that's very dear to me. Right now, Rex Titan has the upper hand, due to his illegal plans, which have caught the eyes of some city officials."

"What do you mean illegal?"

"Currently, he has a gentleman's club, which a good portion of the city's elite attend…"

"Don't you have a club like that?" Zane asked.

"I do, but mine differs from theirs in a vast way. In my club, the women hold the cards. They are never touched, never naked, and earn all the money from the members. It's a classy form of debauchery where they use choreography and handmade outfits to entice the members. Rex's club is, unfortunately, more of a brothel, where club members pay to have sex with the girls. Although, I don't have proof of the inner workings of the club."

"And you want to bring them down, but need information on the inside, and can't do that yourself," Zane cut to the chase.

"No, I can't."

"And that's where you want me to come in, am I right?"

"Yes," I said, without hesitation.

"I'm not really down with paying for sex and getting caught."

I knew this was going to be an issue, so that was why I'd already talked to one of my friends who was a detective in New Orleans. Ordinarily, I would have let the police handle such a call, but Rex knew everyone in town; he wouldn't just let anyone in his club. There had to be a reason as to why Rex would allow someone on the outside to come into his club.

"I can understand that. That's why I talked to a detective friend about giving you immunity for going into the club and gaining evidence to take down their business."

Zane rubbed his chin and asked, "And what would I receive in return?"

Smart man, always wanting to know what was in it for him.

"If you back out of the bidding process for Lot 17 and assist me with infiltrating Rex's club, I will guarantee you the Riverfront Expressway Tunnel."

"How do I know you can guarantee me the tunnel?" Zane asked, looking skeptical, but hopeful.

From my jacket pocket, I pulled out a piece of paper and handed it to Zane. He glanced up at me in question and then unfolded the paper carefully. He studied the paper for a few moments and then looked up at me with a little bit of shock on his face.

"This is the deed to the expressway. How do you have this?"

"I'm an influential man in New Orleans; it's my city, Z."

"If you're so influential, how come you're having such a hard time acquiring Lot 17?" he asked, sitting back in his chair.

Cocky bastard, I liked him.

"Public bidding process. I can't do anything about that besides work behind the scenes to make things happen. What do you say? Do you want your second speedway?"

I watched as Zane quirked his lips to the side and thought about the proposal I was offering him. I knew I had him; there was no way he would give up the rights to the Expressway Tunnel…it meant too much to him. I had something he wanted, and he was going to have to work with me to get it.

"I believe I can help you, but I need to know what it entails first. How much of my time will be spent down there? What exactly is the plan of getting into his club?"

Grinning, I adjusted my seat again and leaned forward to lay it out for him.

"Like I stated before, Rex won't let you in the club unless he trusts you, and a sure-fire way to get him to trust you is to devise a plan to take me down."

Nodding, Zane rubbed his chin and said, "I take it you two have a history."

"You're correct, but I won't bore you with such petty back stories."

"Thank you," he smirked.

"First course of action is for you to call Rex and set up a time to meet up with him. He will be intrigued to hear what you have to say, since you're in the bidding process."

"That will be easy."

Zane and I talked for the next hour, devising a plan to find a way into Rex's club without getting caught. I explained to him the no phone policy, so we would have my detective friend outfit Zane with a hidden camera to record the inner workings of the club.

The time spent with Zane was rather enjoyable. The man had the same attitude toward business as I did, and he was grounded. He wasn't like every other business man I had to work with. I could foresee a friendship developing between us.

Once we finished, Zane stood and walked me to his door.
"Thank you for seeing me today," I said politely, as I buttoned up my suit jacket and adjusted my tie.

"I appreciate the offer," Zane said with a smirk. "I can't tell you how thrilled I am to get my hands on the Expressway. Never thought my racing would be taken outside of New York City, but this is an opportunity I just can't possibly refuse."

"That reminds me," I said, while holding my hand out. "I will take that deed for now," I smirked.

"Damn, thought you would forget," Zane laughed, as he handed it over to me.

"Let me know how your conversation with Rex goes. I'll be interested to see how he takes your offer. When you come down, be sure to visit when all is said and done. I would love to show you around town."

"You can count on it," Zane answered with a smile. "Just after everything is completed."

"Naturally. I'll be in touch. Thank you, Zane, I can't tell you how grateful I am for your help."

"No, thank you, you made me a better offer than what I was shooting for."

With those parting words, I took off to catch my plane back to New Orleans.

Everything seemed to be coming together. Zane was going to contact Rex and fly out to New Orleans as soon as possible, and I had my detective on hold. Hopefully, sooner rather than later, I would be able to finally take my dad and Rex down, and if it wasn't too late, hopefully claim Goldie once again.

11
"SHE KNOWS"

Goldie

"I have a meeting, Goldie, an important one, so please clean up your dishes and go up to your room," Rex demanded, as he wiped his mouth with a cloth napkin and then took his plate to the kitchen.

I missed Kace already. It was torture being with Rex, and then trying to go to the club to teach the girls, who remained cold and stone-like toward me. I had hope when Blane tried to approach me, but all he asked was for me to give the girls a break...that was it. I wondered if he really was trying to be in cahoots with me, because I didn't even get the smallest of nods from him.

Rex had been an uptight ass-hat ever since he took a call earlier today. It was like someone strung his balls up and occasionally pulled on them, just to piss him off.

His maid cooked us a delicious platter of lasagna, and did the man even thank her? No. He just ate the food on his plate without even talking to me. I had more of a conversation in my head with George Washington on the wall than I did with Rex.

"Hurry along," Rex said, while he looked at me, waiting for me to move.

"Do you mind if I finish?" I said in a snappy tone, getting pretty annoyed with his pestering.

"I would tell you to finish upstairs, but I don't allow food on the second floor. Please, just finish; I need you out of here."

"It seems like you're trying to hide me," I stated with my mouth full of lasagna.

"I can't imagine why," he rolled his eyes and ran his hand through his hair.

"I thought I meant something to you, Rex. I'm sorry, but with the way you've been treating me, it seems like you don't even want me here."

Where the hell did that come from? And why the hell did I even care?

Looking frustrated, Rex got in my face and said, "You're the one who wants to build a friendship first. If you were my girlfriend, you would be treated a little differently, maybe with a little bit more respect."

Ahh, so the man wanted access to the Goldie garden. Not going to happen.

"Well, it would be nice if we could be friends first, seems like it would build a solid foundation. How am I supposed to know if I want to move forward with you if you're going to continue to treat me like this?"

Irritation laced Rex's features, but I could see him ease up a bit.

"I'm sorry, Goldie. I'm just stressed, and having you in the next room is killing me. I will do better at being a gentleman. I apologize."

He sounded almost like he meant it.

Deciding to throw him a bone, I got up from the table, shoved the rest of my lasagna in my mouth, and rinsed my plate off in the kitchen sink. I was about to turn to him and give him a conciliatory hug when his doorbell rang. The look in Rex's eyes made me think I should probably get the hell out of his sight, or else I would be dragged up the stairs by my hair. Scary.

"Uh, I'll just head up to my room."

"Take the back stairs," he said curtly, ushering me away.

Flipping him off behind his back, I walked to the back stairs and pretended to climb them with great force. I was too curious just to let him get away with tucking me away. I needed to know what this meeting was all about, especially if it possibly had something to do with Masquerade. I was a "manager" of sorts; I needed to know what I was working with.

I heard Rex greet whoever was at the door in the hallway in the fakest tone I've ever heard from him. A very strong male voice greeted Rex back, making me wonder who the hell he was meeting with.

Carefully, I padded across the kitchen floor and perched my ear against the door to get a better listen.

"Glad to see you had a safe flight," Rex said. "I was surprised you contacted me, Zane. I wasn't expecting to hear from the competition."

"Call me, Z," the man said back. "Shall we go somewhere to sit and talk?"

"Yes, follow me back to my office."

The sound of their footsteps retreated across the hardwood floors back to Rex's office. Once I heard the door click shut, I pushed past the kitchen swinging door and looked around before falling to the ground and army crawling across the floor.

As I glided along the hardwood, I made a mental note to commend Rex's maid, Sally, on her formidable waxing capabilities, because what I thought might be a difficult task, going unnoticed while crawling on the floor, was actually quite easy.

I pulled up next to Rex's office door, under a console table that rested in the hallway, just in case I had to do some quick camouflaging, and pushed my ear next to the crack of the doorway.

"Drink?" Rex asked.

"I'm good, thank you, though."

The clanking of a decanter sounded off in the room as I heard footsteps retreat away from me.

"So, to what do I owe the pleasure of you coming to see me? I was surprised, yet intrigued, to receive your phone call."

"As you know, I've put in a bid for Lot 17, and from the looks of it, my scheduled interview is more of a courtesy than anything. I don't have a chance up against you and Jett Colby."

Realization hit me as I thought about who Rex was talking about. He must be Zane Black, especially if he was the other one bidding on the property. If he knew he wasn't going to have a chance with winning Lot 17, then why was he talking to Rex?

"Is that confirmed?" Rex asked.

"It is, unfortunately."

"So, why are you here?"

"I want in on your club."

Silence fell across the room, and I could just see Rex trying to understand what Zane really wanted.

"Why would I allow you into the club?"

"We both want something the other has. I know there are some city officials on your side, because of what you've offered them when it comes to your club. I have the other few votes to sway in any direction I want, from the connections I've made since I've been down here. I can guarantee you Lot 17 if you allow me to be a member in your club."

"And why would you want that?" Rex asked, with skepticism lacing his voice.

The sound of leather being shifted on rang through the room before Zane began talking again.

"Two reasons, when I come down here, I have a lot of city elites to entertain, and I would like to entertain them properly, if you know what I mean. Secondly, Jett Colby needs to be shown that he can't have everything."

My stomach dropped at the mention of Jett's name. How did this guy know Jett? I'd never heard of Zane Black until the Lot 17 bidding came up.

"Do you have something against Jett Colby?" Rex asked.

"I do. Jett Colby stole property from me in New York City. Stealing property isn't something I take softly. I've built an empire with my real estate aspirations, and when someone fucks with me, I hold a grudge. Jett Colby fucked with one of my properties, costing me millions of dollars, and I will be damned if he gets away with it."

Was that true? The way Zane's voice rose with anger made it seem like what he was saying was, in fact, the truth, but Jett wouldn't do that, would he? He always prided himself on being an honest and fair businessman. He wouldn't screw someone over for property...his father would, but Jett wouldn't. At least, that's what I convinced myself.

"The man seems to get away with everything," Rex scathed. "How do you plan on taking Jett Colby down? He has a golden reputation in this town."

"Ah, he does in this town, but he doesn't in New York City. I have a few sources who are ready to come forward at the interviews to shed a rather unflattering light on the man. With my persuasion of some of my connections and the evidence I have of Jett being less than honorable in his real-estate dealings, Lot 17 is guaranteed for you, but like I said, I want in. I want to be a silent partner in your club."

Zane had evidence of Jett doing something wrong in New York City? What the hell was he doing that was so bad, and the better question was, when the hell did he do it? Because, if he was with me at the time, the man was going to be castrated, that was for damn sure.

"Are you demanding a say in what happens at the club?"

"Not necessarily. I just want to be able to entertain when I'm down here, show my friends a good time." Zane paused for a second, and then said, "Listen, Rex, you don't have to hide from me. I know from a good source that what you're doing isn't quite legal, and that's what I like about it. It's the forbidden. I want to be able to offer that. Everything about my racing business is forbidden, so why not have access to a club that is as well?"

"These witnesses will come forward to testify against Jett?"

I leaned forward a little more to hear how Zane was going to answer, when someone above me cleared their throat.

Stifling a scream, I covered my mouth and looked up to see Sally, the maid, standing over me with her arms crossed and tapping her toe. Quickly, I shimmied out from under the table and stood up.

"Shhh," I said while covering my lips with my finger and pulling Sally to the side, out of earshot. "Sally, please don't say anything to Rex. I was, umm, just trying to find out what he, uh, wanted as a birthday present."

God, that was a lame excuse, but I really had nothing else up my sleeve.

She gave me a pointed look that said, "I'm going to blow up your spot."

"Please, don't say anything," I begged. "It's important he doesn't know I was listening. Did I mention how nicely you waxed the floors, by the way, and how amazing your lasagna was? Top notch, Sally. You totally nailed that lasagna."

A light smirk played across her lips as she nodded and moved past me, allowing me to blow out the pent up breath I was holding in. Note to self, Sally likes to be complimented.

Not wanting to get caught again, I went back to the kitchen and walked up the back staircase to my room. Thomas Jefferson greeted me by staring at my breasts once again, while I flopped myself on the ancient bed.

I couldn't be any more confused than I was right now. Did Jett really screw over that Zane guy? Zane seemed so passionate. Granted, I hadn't see his face, but if he was anything like all the other guys in my life, he probably didn't show much emotion.

My gut twisted at the thought of Zane and Rex ganging up on Jett to acquire Lot 17. Where was this Lot 17 anyway? It seemed like it wasn't even that great of a property. Was there even a bar nearby? Maybe a Target? What's the point of buying property if you can't get drunk and then drunkenly wander over Target to purchase over a hundred dollars' worth of unnecessary crap?

I was in way over my head. I still had yet to find a way to gather information on Rex's club, thanks to the no phone policy. None of the girls seemed like they were in a position to testify, and neither was Blane. It was weird; they all seemed like they were having less than a stellar time working at the club, yet they clammed up when I tried to get any information out of them.

Besides the one conversation I had with Blane, it seemed like everyone had some strange loyalty to Rex. I tried approaching Blane a couple of times, but he just shook his head no at me, and on top of that, whenever Rex was around, Blane was a giant ass.

I was lost; I was drowning, actually. I needed Jett. I needed to hear his voice, to feel his touch, but I knew if I reached out to him, if I tried contacting him, he would force me to come back, or at least that's what I hoped. Maybe he wouldn't. Maybe he'd moved on.

Last I heard, Rex sent Jett a text about me being with Rex, and I just hoped and prayed Jett kept faith in my feelings for him. I hoped that he hadn't given up on me yet.

I was lost in my thoughts when my phone started ringing. Praying it was Jett, I fumbled around until I was able to grab it and check the caller ID.

Diego.

My heart sank as I answered.

"Hey," I said softly.

"That's not the kind of greeting I was hoping for," Diego said on the other end.

"Sorry, I thought maybe you would be Jett."

"Are you expecting a call from him?" Diego asked, using a curious voice.

"No, not really. I mean, it would be nice to hear from him, but I guess we didn't have a scheduled call or anything."

"Goldie, you left him. Did you really expect him to call you?"

"I didn't leave him," I snapped. "I told him I would be back. I'm trying to work some things out; I'm trying to make things better for us."

Diego was silent for a second before he responded, "And how are you doing with that?"

"Not very well," I admitted. "I'm not doing well at all, Diego. I thought this was going to be easy, that I was just going to waltz into Rex's life and grab what I needed so I could ride off into the sunset with Jett, but right now, I feel like there is no way I will be able to ever solve this."

"What are you trying to do exactly?"

"I want to bring Rex and Leo down. I want to release myself from the shackles they have me strapped down in. With them still around, they're going to keep dragging me and Jett through their negative lives. They're going to continue bringing us down, and I don't want to live like that anymore. I don't want to be in hiding; I don't want to have to watch my back or hide behind the closed doors of the Lafayette Club. I want Jett to claim me, for everyone to see. I want him to take me on dates, for him to be proud to have me on his arm."

"You know he is proud to have you on his arm already, Goldie."

"I like to think so, but now I don't know. I think he's moved on."

"What gives you that impression?"

I sighed and flipped onto my stomach so I could prop my legs up and talk on the phone like I was a teenager in some fifties sitcom.

"I don't know, I mean, I haven't even…"

"Who are you talking to?" Rex asked, as he barged through my door without even knocking.

"Rex," I said in shock, dropping my phone.

Rex eyed it on the ground and quickly picked it up before I could grab it off the ground. He held the phone up to his ear with a look in his eyes that said he was about to explode in seconds. I've never seen the man so mad before in my life.

"Who is this?" he spat into the phone. "Why are you talking to Goldie?" Rex asked after a brief pause. Turning toward me, Rex eyed me suspiciously and said, "Don't call her again," and then he hung up and pocketed my phone. "Why did you answer your phone?"

The way Rex was breathing heavily and searching me like he was crazed, set my warning bells off. Maybe the meeting didn't end well.

"I'm not sure," I responded, starting to fear what he was going to do.

"Don't talk to anyone. I don't trust you," he eyed me up and down.

"Wh-why?" I asked, stuttering from the way he was closing in on me.

"Because, until you fully give yourself over to me, I won't trust you. I will always think you're still interested in Jett. You don't even come near me...you barely look at me," Rex stated.

Oh, shit. I, apparently, wasn't doing a good enough job in fooling the man. But how was I supposed to show him I wanted to "be with him" if I didn't want to have sex with him, let alone touch him? Rex was a very physical man, and the way you proved your loyalty to him was by showing him how physical you could be. Right now, my physical level was at zero and slowly declining into the negatives with each passing day I was near him.

"I want to, Rex. I want to be with you," I pleaded, as he pushed me back on the bed and surrounded me with his strong body. Sweat started to trickle down my back from the strength he was forcing on me and the proximity of his body. "I just can't," I gulped. "I don't want to be used anymore."

"Do you think I like to be used?" he asked with venom in his voice.

"No," I shook my head.

"Because, right about now, it seems like you're the one who is using me."

Where was this coming from? Why was he all of a sudden

attacking me? What the hell went wrong in the last twenty minutes that set him on fire?

"Then, I'll leave. I don't want you to feel like I'm using you. I'll go somewhere else, but I would still like to see you," I bluffed.

His face softened for a second, right before he pulled away and ran his hand through his hair while pacing the length of my room.

"Don't leave," he gritted out. "But don't fuck with me, Goldie. I swear, if I find out you're fucking with me, I will destroy you. Do you hear me?"

Swallowing hard, I nodded my head and let him walk out of my room with my phone, taking my last connection to the real world.

He slammed my door shut, leaving me completely perplexed as to what had just happened.

Fucking weirdo and his mood swings.

Sinking into my stiff-as-a-board bed, I bid Thomas Jefferson a good night and tried to get some shut eye. I still had a lot of work to do at the club, especially since I had no way of proving what Rex and Leo were doing.

I shut my eyes, but was disturbed when Rex flew through my door again. His shadow was booming through my room with the hallway light backing him.

He spoke firmly and said, "Saturday night, I have some business to attend at the club before the gala. I will meet you at the house. My driver will bring me back here to pick you up before the event."

"You don't want me to go to the club with you? It's the girl's first…"

"No, I don't want you there. Just make sure you're ready for the gala. Be sure to look pristine; I'm counting on showing you off to everyone." With that, he slammed my door shut.

When he said he wanted to show me off to everyone, I knew he was bullshitting me, because there was only one person he wanted to show me off to…and that was Jett.

12
"UPSIDE"

Rex

The sweet taste of my cigar drifted out of my mouth as I puffed the thick smoke into the air. My temper got the best of me after I got off the phone with Leo the other night, the controlling fuck.

After Zane Black presented me with his business merger, I couldn't be happier about the prospect of securing Lot 17 and tarnishing Jett Colby at the same time. It was a win-win for me. Granted, I had to relinquish some of the rights to my club, but Zane was a good business man; I trusted him to bring in more members than I could imagine, especially since most of the men he raced with were from foreign countries.

Overall, it was a smart business move, but unfortunately, I was the only one who believed so. After I saw Zane to the door, I called Leo to tell him the news, but he was less than thrilled. He said he didn't trust the man, and wouldn't put it past Jett to set up the whole deal.

The man was paranoid. Jett wasn't smart enough to set up

such a deal, and what would he get out of it in the first place? There was no point.

I wound up arguing on the phone with Leo until I hung up on him. When I walked upstairs, I heard Goldie talking, and that's when I lost it. After hearing Leo talk about Goldie being an insider for Jett and this whole Zane thing, I saw red. I started connecting the dots, and that's when I went ape shit on her.

When I grabbed her phone, I was expecting to hear Jett's voice, see his name on the screen, but instead, it was Diego, a harmless piece of trash on Bourbon Street that happened to put on a suit and tie occasionally. The man was trying to be competition with our club, but fell short, with his less than elegant reputation. It didn't surprise me Goldie would talk to him; they came from the same gutter.

Even though she wasn't talking to Jett, I still took her phone, because frankly, I really didn't trust her. I had my own agenda, but sometimes, there was a look in her eyes that led me to believe she had her own agenda as well, and that's what scared me.

What could she possibly do, though? She wasn't smart, she wasn't intelligent at all, actually. She was a pair of tits with a good body. Yeah, she said funny things on occasion, but she was crude, crass, and classless. She belonged up on stage, for all the men to play with her, because that was all she was, a plaything. She would never amount to anything; she wasn't someone you really took to an event or introduced to your mother. No, she was the girl you fucked in a shady motel to get your fix, and then left for something more sophisticated.

The sooner she figured that out, the better.

Irritation about tonight filled me as I thought about the time constraint I was in. I was in the club, waiting for Zane Black to show up, but had a gala to attend with Goldie. The main point of me attending the gala was to confirm a couple of votes for myself for Lot 17, but what I was looking forward to the most was seeing the look on Jett Colby's face when I showed up with Goldie on my arm. Just the thought of it had my anxiety hanging back.

Everything seemed to be falling into place. Lately, I'd been a little harsh on Goldie, but in the end, I could see her needing me more and more. After we secure Lot 17, I'll be making my move with her. I don't want to play around anymore. I want her to be the one up on stage, the one the members dominate. It would be the final nail in Jett Colby's coffin.

Checking my watch, I thought about how Zane was a couple minutes late. He didn't seem like the type of businessman to be late, especially when we had a scheduled time set up to meet.

The girls were ready for their first performance. Blane was going to be demonstrating on Bizzy tonight, leaving Mercy alone. I found that I didn't want her to be the first to go; I wanted her to be a show-off item, a woman men wanted to come back to see. Bizzy would be a good starter, but Mercy was the girl the men would crave, no doubt about it.

From the corner of my eye, I saw Zane come to the front door on the security camera. Straightening my tie, I approached the front of the club. All the other members who were attending tonight were mingling in the main room, getting their drinks and talking about the festivities. I had Zane enter from the front, because I wasn't quite confident yet in giving him full access to the club. I wanted to read his initial reaction when he we toured the facility. Plus, I needed to confiscate his phone, just in case.

From the security camera, I could see he wasn't shifting in place; he didn't seem nervous, he looked confident and excited. I was a man who read people's body language and looking at Zane, he seemed like he wasn't the least bit concerned about showing up tonight, a sign that he was here at my club for the right reasons, to have a damn good time.

Opening the door, I greeted Zane with a warm handshake.

"Z, so glad you could make it."

"Thank you." I shook his hand while he looked around the entryway. "I'm glad you sent a driver, because I'm not sure I would have been able to find this place."

"We keep it low key on purpose. Once we induct you as a member, we will give you access to the back entrance, which is more private and easier to find."

"Can't wait," he said with a crooked smile.

He stepped forward, but I stopped him with my hand. "Before we walk in, I need you to put your phone in one of the safe deposit boxes that you can access once you leave. We don't allow any recording electronics in the club; I'm sure you can understand."

Without a blink of his eye, he nodded, grabbed his phone from the inner pocket of his jacket, and handed it over. I showed him where the boxes were and how he could access it once he left. The girls did the same thing with their personal items.

"Alright, let's get started," I smirked, as I led Zane back into the club.

Light mood music was playing over the club speakers, setting a more provocative tone for the members. Yellow lights bounced off of the base of the walls, casting a small glow around the room, giving it an almost sinister look. Everything about the club, I loved. It was dark, it was dangerous, it gave men like me, men who had to be on their best behavior in the public eye, a chance to let go, to have some fun without being judged.

The members nodded at Zane and myself as we walked in, acknowledging our presence. When entering the club, you might see someone you know or work with, but the business side of our lives was never discussed. That part of our lives was never brought up because the club was a safe place for us, a place to step outside the professional lives we lived and indulge. No one talked about the club and what happened outside of it.

"This is the main room," I told Zane, who was looking around in appreciation.

"I could see bringing my guys here, easily. Are you going to stick with the same theme when you win Lot 17?"

When I win, I was really liking this guy.

"Blane is in charge of the bar and also the demonstrations."

"Demonstrations?" Zane asked, while we walked over to the bar.

"Yes, we pick one girl a night, who Blane dominates in front of the men, shows them how to properly dominate her. The members love it; it allows them a chance to fulfill a fantasy they might not get back at home."

"Ahh, so some of these men are married." Zane nodded his head as he looked around, worrying me slightly.

"We have a non-disclosure contract each member has to sign. Whatever they happen to see in the club is not to be mentioned outside of these walls. It's a general understanding."

"Naturally," Zane replied. He nodded at Blane and said, "Two fingers of Jameson, please."

Blane acknowledged Zane's order and started filling it. He was a good bartender, kept to himself, did the job correctly, and then entertained after. Blane was one of the best decisions Leo and I had made for our club. The members looked up to him and the girls obeyed him. It was perfect.

The day Leo approached me about hiring Blane, I was apprehensive at first. I went to school with him and he was much larger than me, when it came to his muscular frame, but sometimes brains beat brawn, and when it came to Blane, he made the wrong moves in his life. Leo and I were able to capitalize on his wrong decisions, just like with the girls in the club.

When we were searching for employees, we made them take lie detector tests, to find out their darkest secrets, what skeletons they were hiding in their closets, and like the master manipulators we were, we used those secrets against them. Did I feel like I was cheating them? Yes, but then again, that was business. Only the strong survived.

Taking a sip from his drink, Zane surveyed the room once again, fidgeted with his watch, and then said, "Tell me about the back rooms. Those are what I believe my friends will enjoy the most."

"Yes, I believe that's what every member enjoys the most," I said, as I started walking to the back hallway. "Once we acquire Lot 17, there will be more rooms, but right now, we have four playrooms where members can pick one of the girls to come back here with. Mind you, it's a handsome fee to have sex with one of the Masquerade girls, but well worth it. They have signed contracts to allow the members to do whatever they want to the girls, within reason of course."

"Of course," Zane tipped his cup toward me. "How did you get the girls to participate in the club? Do you plan on hiring more? Three doesn't seem to be enough."

"We have plans for more to come in. It's hard to find willing girls. They have to be desperate, they have to need the money, and they have to have something we can hold against them."

"Like what?" Zane asked, starting to ask too many questions for my liking.

Brushing him off, I said, "We can get into that later. It's something we don't need to discuss right now. Come with me; I'll show you the back rooms where members aren't allowed."

For the next half hour, I gave Zane a tour of the club,

explaining the inner workings, and how we were able to get away with having such a club in the city. Thanks to my connections, we flew under the radar. Zane grew more and more interested with each passing moment, leading me to believe we were going to have a deal by the end of the night, a deal that would clinch everything I'd been striving for.

I took a look at my watch and realized the gala started an hour ago and the girls were going to be coming out soon. So, I took Zane back to the main room and introduced him to a couple of the men that would be sticking around.

"Unfortunately, I have another event I have to attend, or else I would stay longer."

"Oh, please don't let me hold you back," Zane said with a grin. "I'm sure I'll be plenty entertained."

From what I had seen Goldie put together over the last week, I knew he would be very much entertained.

"Shall I call you in the morning to arrange contracts?" I asked, while holding my breath.

The light music in the main room cut and the lights dimmed, pointing to the opening where the girls first showed themselves. Mercy's honey colored hair arrived first, as she strutted out onto the stage. She was a show stopper, no doubt about it.

Looking back up at me after seeing Mercy, Zane nodded his head and placed one of his business cards in my hand. "We'll be in touch."

I shook the man's hand with a new-found excitement brewing inside of me.

Taking one last look at the club, I acknowledged my accomplishment, and went back to my town car, in which I would be taken back to my house to pick up Goldie. I was quite excited to see how the dress I picked out for her fit, and I was even more excited to see the look on Jett Colby's face when I walked into the gala with her on my arm.

This was just the beginning of the end for the man. You should always tread carefully when dealing with such powerful men, because you never knew who they might know and what they might do to stay on top. Unfortunately for Jett, his time was coming to an end.

13
"NO ONE'S GONNA LOVE YOU"

Jett

"I can't get over how beautiful it is in here," Keylee cooed as she held onto my arm a little too tight for my liking.

To say I was annoyed with the little tart hanging all over me was an understatement. Goldie was right in not liking the girl; she very much had an end goal of becoming a Jett Girl, and she didn't hide it one bit.

Once again, she was wearing a purple dress, this one a little sluttier than others I've seen her wear. This one was decorated with a full slit up to her hip and her breasts spilling out the top. Men around the event gawked and women judged. I wondered if she hurt me more than helped me when going to these events. She gave the illusion that there was something between us, since she accompanied me, but by the way she dressed, it made it look like I enjoyed such a woman, when there really was only one woman who caught my eye, and she wasn't even in attendance like I thought she would be.

A little piece of me was annoyed about the fact that she wasn't here. I wanted to see her, my soul needed to see her, to just catch a glimpse of her beautiful face, her smart mouth, and perfect body. I craved her like a drug, and no matter what I did, I couldn't tamp down the feelings.

I didn't just need to see her because it would settle the craving I was fighting, but because I needed to see how she reacted around Rex; I needed to see if my heart was still being held tightly in her hands, or if she really had let me go. Did I still matter to her? Was she really still thinking about me?

Many sleepless nights had greeted me from such thoughts. It killed me not knowing where we stood, whether she was meant to be in my life.

My phone buzzed in my pocket, pulling me out of my thoughts. Ignoring Keylee's blabbering, I pulled it out of my jacket pocket and looked at the message from Zane.

Zane Black: Got everything. Will see you in the morning for delivery. You're home free, man.

The faintest of smiles crossed my lips at Zane's news. I wanted to celebrate; I wanted to run to Rex's house and steal Goldie for myself, but I knew I couldn't react until I had the evidence in my hand. I couldn't divulge any secrets until I knew for certain that what Zane gathered was enough to take down my father and Rex.

"What a pleasure to see you here," came a voice from behind me.

Speak of the devil.

Turning slowly and dragging the ever annoying Keylee with me, I came face to face with my father.

"Dad," I nodded. "You remember Miss Keylee Zinc, don't you?"

He wasn't supposed to be here tonight; he wasn't on the list of attendees, but leave it to my father to change his mind and make an appearance.

"How could I forget such a gorgeous face?" he said, while taking her hand and kissing it, all the while staring at her breasts. He most likely did so to make me mad, but he could stare all he wanted. I could care less. "Why is such a beautiful woman as you hanging out with a boy when you could be wrapped up with a real man?"

Keylee giggled and pushed him away gently, while I gritted my teeth. The man never passed up an opportunity to put me down.

"Mr. Colby, your flattery doesn't escape me. If only I ran into you first," she winked at me. It took every muscle in my body not to roll my eyes at her. Little did she know, I would gladly hand her over.

"It's never too late to upgrade, my dear."

Giggling some more, she covered her mouth and shook her head. "You're terrible."

My father bit down on his lower lip and took her in one last time before pulling his gaze back to my annoyed one. I wasn't annoyed that my father was blatantly flirting with my date, no, I was annoyed that I was related to such an embarrassing human.

"Tell me, Jett, are you worried about the interviews next week?"

"Not in the slightest," I replied with confidence.

"Word on the street is your bid isn't the one being considered."

Not wanting to talk about Lot 17 in front of Keylee, I said, "It's improper to talk about business at a social event with a female present. It would be rude."

Anger crossed my father's face as I threw his words back at him, the same words he would say to me all the time when growing up.

Straightening his tie and clearing his throat, he glanced at Keylee and said, "I do apologize, Miss Zinc, for being so improper; will you forgive me?"

"Of course," she replied, looking a little uncomfortable from the tension rising between my father and me.

"I just don't know if that apology will do; let me make it up to you. Will you do me the honor of joining me on the dance floor?"

Keylee looked up at me, and I just nodded, letting her know it was fine.

With a bright smile, she took my father's arm and he led her out to the dance floor, but not without turning around to look at me. The look on his face was one of victory, but what he didn't know was, he already lost.

Scanning the room, I watched members of the elite of New Orleans milling about, introducing themselves to one another, mingling and forming new partnerships. Women held onto their men's arms and the men held small tumblers in their hands, gradually sipping on the contents.

Being part of such a society was always boggling to me. New Orleans was full of old money and traditions. These galas weren't really for charity. Yes, the money was to benefit a cause for that week, but mainly they were for the powerful to conduct business out from behind their desks. To make deals in public without anyone knowing. It was shady, it was political, and I hated that I lived in such a world. I wanted to do good, I wanted to offer opportunities to those less fortunate, but in order for me to do so, I had to be a part of such a community.

A sharp laugh came from the dance floor, where my dad was twirling Keylee around. Her head was thrown back and, clearly, she was having a good time with him, something I would never give to her. Maybe they were made for each other.

Glancing at the door, my heart stopped beating in my chest the moment I saw Rex Titan walk through the door with my Little One attached to his arm.

The noise and clatter in the ballroom stopped registering in my mind as Goldie walked in. The air was knocked out of my lungs from the mere sight of her. She was in a teal silk dress that belted loosely at her hips, with a slit on both sides. The dress was held up by two thick straps that covered her breasts, but the neckline was non-existent as the front and the back both fell to the waist of the dress. Her hair was pulled back tightly in a ponytail, and she was wearing dark makeup around her eyes, making her look more exotic than normal. Long earrings dripped from her ears, as well as a very small chain that wrapped around her neck and connected to the waist of her dress. She was beyond exquisite. Every bone in my body wanted to run up to her and claim her, but I stood in place instead, as Rex's hand guided Goldie by her lower back into the room.

I needed to pull away, to show that I wasn't affected by her presence, but I couldn't stop staring at her. It seemed like months since I had seen her, when it had only been a week.

The crowd of the room parted as Rex walked forward, making an obvious beeline for me. As if the room fell silent, all eyes were on us as Rex made the final steps. I glanced at Goldie, whose head was down, avoiding all eye contact with me. Why was she not looking at me? Was she ashamed of what she did? Did she not want to look at me? Did she find me repulsive?

"Jett Colby, I had no clue you were going to be here," Rex said with a smarmy smile, as he pulled Goldie in closer to him. "I believe you know Goldie."

With a deep breath, I nodded and looked down at her. Her gaze lifted ever so slowly and her bright blue eyes peeked up, stabbing me directly in the heart. Her face flushed when she noticed the small smile that played on my lips in greeting.

"Good to see you."

"You too," she all but whispered.

"Doesn't my Kitten just look absolutely breathtaking tonight?" Rex asked, while squeezing her side. I watched as Goldie picked her head up and smiled at him.

Rage boiled from the tip of my toes to the top of my head from the lighthearted look she just gave Rex. That smile, that gleam in her eyes, they didn't belong to anyone but me. Rex didn't deserve to be looked at by her like that. That look was reserved for one person and one person alone, me.

Calming my raging heart, I thought about the consequences of me lashing out, of letting Rex get to me. So, instead, I swallowed the aching feeling running through my body and allowed my pride to take a hit.

"Quite lovely," I replied, just as Keylee and my father stepped up next to me. Keylee snuggled into my side once she saw who Rex was with. She clung onto my arm and practically humped my leg to stake her claim.

"Leo, what an honor to see you," Rex said, while sticking out his hand to shake it.

"Rex, pleasure. What a beautiful date. Goldie, you get more gorgeous every time I see you, maybe because this time around you're attached to a real man."

The dig didn't fail to annoy me.

Without saying a word, Goldie just nodded and smiled. I had never seen my Little One act so suppressed, so quiet, so reserved. I didn't like it. She was normally a bright spot in the room, but right now she was quiet, almost like she was threatened not to speak. The realization startled me. Why was she doing this?

I shook my head at the thought; only a day or so more and then I would be able to claim her again, to open my arms back up to her, that's if she wanted me.

My pride took over my thoughts as I wondered if she really did want me. I didn't want to go after her if she wasn't into me anymore, if she really wanted Rex.

I needed to get her alone.

"Come, dance with me," Keylee whined into my ear, while pulling on my arm.

From Keylee's voice, Goldie's head snapped up to see the offending woman. Once realization hit her, she looked back up at me with daggers sprouting from her eyes. I knew she didn't like Keylee, and it was a little thrilling knowing Keylee still had the same effect on her, no matter if we were together or not.

"Not right now," I dismissed her. "Please, excuse us, we have some other people to say hello to. Rex, Dad...Goldie," I nodded, while escorting Keylee away from them. There was only so much I could take, and by the way Goldie was looking at me, I was about to crack. I needed to remove myself from a volatile situation.

"I was having fun with them, why were you so rude?" Keylee complained, while I walked her into the depths of the crowd.

"I think you're failing to realize your role here," I whispered, deathly close to her ear. "You're supposed to smile and shake hands. Your opinion is not warranted."

That shut her up. Did I feel bad for treating her so poorly? No, not at all. She had a privileged life and needed to hear the word "no" on occasion. She couldn't always get what she wanted, and even though she wanted nothing more than to be accepted into the Lafayette Club, that was one wish she wouldn't be granted.

"Keylee!"

Three screeching women came up to us with their hands raised in the air, holding champagne, and looking completely inebriated.

Forgetting all sense of decorum, Keylee screeched with them and ran into their arms.

"I didn't know you bitches were going to be here," Keylee exclaimed.

"Last minute change of plans; come have some shots with us," a blonde exclaimed, while swaying back and forth. Maybe shots weren't the best idea for her, but it would garner some alone time for me.

"I would love to, but..."

I cut Keylee off before she could finish. "Go on, have fun," I winked at her for good measure.

"Really?" she asked.

"Yes, it looks like you girls need to catch up."

"Oh, my God, he's so swoon worthy," a red head said, while eye fucking me.

"Thank you," she giggled, while placing a kiss on my cheek and walking off with her friends.

Feeling lighter without Keylee hanging on me, I surveyed Goldie's movements from the back of the room. I watched as she was introduced to Rex's comrades. She smiled gracefully, listened intently to their stories, and laughed while everyone else laughed. She fit in, the only problem was, she was with the wrong man.

I saw my father look around the room and then whisper into Rex's ear. Rex nodded his head and turned to Goldie. He said something to her, and then pointed to where the bathrooms were located. She looked confused, but then pulled away when Rex's gaze turned stern. She stepped away, fumbled with her purse, and then walked away. Rex shook his head and then pulled my father out of sight, behind some pillars.

It was time to make my move.

14
"TAKE ME TO CHURCH"

Goldie

I couldn't breathe; my heart started beating at an alarming rate against my chest the minute I locked eyes with Jett Colby.

Like always, he looked impeccable in a sharp, fitted, black tux with black bow tie. His hair was long at the top and shaved on the sides, making him look almost sinister, but incredibly sexy at the same time. I could see how the fitted shirt under his jacket pulled against his well-defined chest, making me want to forget everything that happened between us and throw myself at him.

But what made my heart drop wasn't the mere sight of the man I handed my heart over to, no, it was the kiwi that attached herself to him.

My heart sank from the thought of Jett actually being with Keylee. Were they together now that I wasn't in the picture? I told him I would be back. Would he really resort to taking her out again? The thought broke me in half.

How could he want Keylee? She looked like a damn hyena with her hair teased to the heavens and her stupid fucking smile showing off her fangs. I wanted to flick her in the forehead and then search that rat's nest on her head for a little woodland family that might have taken up residence. I wouldn't be shocked if two squirrels and a rabbit popped up, smoking cigarettes and discussing the threesome they just had. If anyone had woodland debauchery up in their hair, it would be Keylee.

Fucking fuzzy ass fruit.

The last thing I wanted to do was make nice with all of Rex's friends, so when he asked me to go to the bathroom, to excuse myself from his conversation, I was more than happy to take him up on his demand. Frankly, I was too worn out to think about what he and Leo might be talking about.

This morning, when I was training the girls for tonight, I noticed Rex had his phone in the club, and that's when it dawned on me. I would have to somehow grab his phone from him at some point and record my evidence using his own device. The only thing was, how did I go about doing that? How did I go about grabbing his phone from him?

There was another demonstration tomorrow night that I would be able to attend, as well as Rex. I made a mental note to talk to Blane at some point in the morning to see what I could do, because I was done. After seeing Jett, I wanted this all to be over. I wanted to crawl my way back into his arms and just hope and pray he kept his faith in our relationship and waited for me.

Not really needing to go to the bathroom, I meandered slowly to the back, where I could see a long line forming already. I blew out a frustrated breath as I eyed all the women in backless dresses and pearls. I would never get used to the way these people thought, the way they functioned. They had money excreting out of their pores and a good percentage of them didn't put it to good use. The only person I knew of who actually was doing something good in this city was Jett.

Opening my clutch, I went to grab my lipstick when a strong arm wrapped around me and pulled me into a dark room that was opposite the bathrooms. The door clicked shut and my pulse picked up.

"What's going on?" I asked, while looking around, trying to feel for a door. My hand came in contact with a warm body and I screeched. "I will knife hand you!" I warned, as I put my hands up and started swinging them around in the dark, making contact with nothing.

"When you're finished, I would like to speak to you," came the unmistakable voice of Jett Colby.

My gut clenched at the sound of his voice and the fact that we were in the same room, alone.

"Jett," I offered, as I tried to find him. His hands stilled my shoulders and turned me around.

Light from the moon poured through the window, casting a small glow on Jett's face when I finally saw him. My body seized on me from the hard stare on his face. His jaw ticked as he studied me. His face was freshly shaven, begging for my hands to touch him, caress him, and just get lost in the feel of him.

He was utter perfection and it hurt too damn bad to be standing in front of him with my hands tied behind my back, not being able to tell him how I felt or show him how much I want him, how much I need him.

My body ached to have his arms wrapped around me and his head buried against mine, his eyes telling me how he truly felt.

Right now, he was wearing a mask, a professional mask I've only seen a couple of times, a mask that was most definitely not reserved for me, and it hurt knowing that he could turn that face on when seeing me for the first time since I'd left the club.

Nervous, I just stared up at him, waiting for him to say something, because I knew anything that came out of my mouth was not going to be intelligent from the way he turned my brain into mush.

His eyes ran the length of my body, taking in the rather revealing dress I had on.

"You look...breathtaking," he said softly, as his hands found my hips. My breath caught in my throat as he pulled me in closer. "Why are you here?" he asked, looking me square in the eye.

"Because Rex asked me," I said meekly. His stare was cutting me in half, breaking down every strong wall I ever built up.

He thought about my answer for a second, and then said, "I asked you to stay with me, but I guess that meant nothing to you."

"That's not true," I said quickly, while shaking my head, but he pushed me away and started pacing the short distance of the dark room. "Jett, I'm trying to make things better."

"By sleeping with Rex?" he gritted out, smacking me in the face with his words.

"What?! No! I'm not sleeping with him."

A sarcastic laugh escaped his mouth. "You're telling me the man who used to pay you for sex isn't fucking you right now?"

The tone of his voice, the way his body moved was terrifying. I had never seen him so angry before.

"No, he hasn't even touched me. That's more than I can say for that stupid kiwi you brought with you."

His head snapped up and he glared at me. "You think I'm messing around with her?"

"Well, didn't you kiss her out there?"

On the cheek, but still seeing his lips caress someone else's skin was like a dagger to the heart.

"And I thought you were too engrossed with your new boyfriend to notice," Jett said childishly.

"He's not my boyfriend, you..." the words died on my lips because, technically, Jett wasn't my boyfriend right now.

"Were you going to say...I am? How is that possible? How could I be your boyfriend when clearly you're with another man? Tell me, Goldie, how does that work?"

Okay, he was mad. I should have seen that coming when I took of my collar, but it was all for a good reason. I was trying to make a better life for us. I was trying to protect him, trying to fix things. He had to understand that, right?"

"I'm not with him, Jett."

Grabbing me by the shoulders, he pushed me up against the wall of the room and stood inches from my body.

"Then, what the fuck are you doing with him?" his voice broke as his eyebrows fell and he said, "Are you trying to intentionally hurt me?"

Just like that, my entire heart crumbled to the floor. The man was hurting, he was weak, and I could see it in his eyes. There was no doubt in my mind that by me leaving, by me handing him my collar, I had destroyed him. It was evident by the way he was staring into my eyes.

I lifted my hand and caressed his face softly, reveling in the feel of his smooth skin against my hand. Lightly, I could feel him push his face into my palm, giving me only the slightest bit of hope.

"Jett, I'm not trying to hurt you. I'm trying to help you."

"I don't need your help," he said gruffly. "I just need you."

One of his hands travelled from my shoulder down the side of my dress. He slipped it into the front of my exposed stomach and drew it up to right below my breast. His touch burned my skin, made me weak in the knees, and reminded me of all the reasons why I was beyond in love with the man in front of me.

My breathing became erratic as his eyes never left mine and his fingers lightly grazed the underside of my braless breast.

"This dress is too revealing," he chastised, as his other hand found the slit of my dress and pushed me up against the wall even harder.

His fingers continued to make feather-like touches across my sensitive skin as they travelled up to my erect nipple. Without touching my breast, his fingers pinched my nipple in the most erotic way possible, making me throw my head back and moan.

A throbbing ache took place between my legs, reminding me that it's been way too long since I've been with this man, this all-consuming man who held my heart in the palm of his hand.

"Say it," he whispered in my ear, sending chills up my spine. "Say it, Little One. Make me forget this unyielding suffering that you've put me through. Remove this pain."

The mixture of his touches, of his hand inching closer and closer to the front of my thong, and the desperation in his voice had me muttering those six little words that he was begging to hear.

"I'm here to submit to you," I said breathlessly.

A light growl came out of his mouth, as his hand found the hem of my thong and started to tug it down, while his fingers squeezed my nipple, sending waves of pleasure rolling through my body.

A deep need crawled through me as he pulled my thong down just enough to grant him access. I needed more of him; I needed him to squeeze more than my nipple, I needed his lips, his tongue.

"Spread your legs," he demanded with his deep southern voice, curling my toes right there in my high heels.

Like it was second nature, my body reacted to his demand, granting him more access. His lips trailed the side of my neck, but never made full contact; it was just a whisper against my skin, an empty promise of what he could offer me.

Instinctively, my hands went to his waist, but he pushed them away and kept me pinned to the wall.

"Did I tell you that you could touch me?"

I shook my head no, as I looked at him through my lashes, trying to read him, trying to see exactly what he wanted. At that moment, I knew what he needed; he needed control, which I was more than willing to hand over to him.

"Put your hands above your head and don't move them unless you want me to leave this room right now."

His threat hit me hard, because there was no way in hell I wanted him to leave, so I raised my hands above my head and waited for his next command.

Trailing both his hands to the front of my dress, he moved the panels that were covering my breasts to the side and stared at my naked skin. He bit down on his lip right before diving forward and taking one of my breasts into his mouth. His teeth nipped at my nipple as his hand squeezed relentlessly at my other breast.

Fuck, I was coming undone. Just from his touch, from the way he moved his mouth over me. He captured my soul with one touch; there was no turning back from him.

When I thought I couldn't take the torture anymore, he moved his head away from me and pushed back. Emptiness consumed me at his distance, but then I saw what he was doing and a burning need took over the core of my body.

His hands moved to the waist of his pants and slowly undid them, pulling out his erection. My mouth watered at the sight of him. It had been way too long since I'd been with Jett, since I'd experienced the mystifying feeling only he could bestow upon me.

I watched as he erotically stroked himself while biting down on his bottom lip, eye fucking me almost to orgasm. Instead of begging, like I normally would, I kept my arms in place and waited patiently for what he was going to offer. I pushed back the thought of how long I'd been away from Rex and how, at any moment, someone could walk in on us, because when I was with Jett, I couldn't think about anything else but the man standing in front of me.

Coming closer, he grabbed the slit of my dress and pushed it to the side, so I was exposed to him. With his spare hand, he spread my legs even wider, and then guided himself into me. I was wet, beyond ready for him. He slid in easily and was pleased with exactly how ready I was for him. It wasn't hard to be wet; just from the sight of him in a tuxedo, I could take him easily.

"Fuck," he muttered in my ear, as he started to move in and

out of me. "I've missed you," he said gently, as he started moving his hips. He grabbed my leg and wrapped it around his waist, making his task of pushing his hips into me a little easier.

The pain in his voice slashed my soul. I hated bringing such a powerful man to his knees, knowing I had such an effect on him. Jett was my rock, the one person who saved me, so to see him weak and full of anguish had my heart breaking.

"I've missed you, too," I whispered back, lightly grazing my lips on his cheek.

With a groan, he started thrusting into me frantically, making a light sheen of sweat appear on our skin.

A mixture of emotions ran through me as Jett continuously worked in and out of my core until I couldn't hold back any longer. From the pit of my stomach, a moan escaped me, just as I was taken over the edge. My body convulsed and clamped around him, causing him to find his own release.

He continued to pump into me until we both ran the course of our temporary euphoria.

With regret in his eyes, he pulled away from me and lowered my dress. He zipped himself back up, righted his clothes, and then turned to me. His gentle hands straightened out my dress, so my breasts were no longer hanging out and my dress fell across my body like it was supposed to. Once I was all in place, he stepped away and straightened his tie with a look of displeasure on his face.

He stepped away without a word and headed toward the door, giving off a rather cold exterior.

"Jett…" I trailed off, not really knowing what to say.

"Don't, Goldie."

His back was turned toward me, and in the dimly lit room, I could still see the tension that rested on him…the distress I was putting him through.

"I'll be back," I choked out, trying to not let my emotions get the best of me.

"You never should have left," he said before leaving the room, dragging my heart behind him.

Why couldn't he understand my urge to take matters into my own hands? To find a solution for the problem we were living in? I wanted to be with him; it was evident in the way I reacted to just seeing him across the room. How come he couldn't understand that?

Taking a calming breath, I gathered myself before I walked back out into the main room. Thankfully, the women's bathroom line was still a nightmare, so if Rex questioned me, I had evidence that there was an abundant amount of pee-ers amongst us.

Scanning the room, I immediately saw Jett walk up to the kiwi and place his hand on her lower back. She looked up at him with adoration in her eyes, as if they were sharing a secret look. The urge to plaster my heel through her skull crossed my mind, but I refrained from causing a bloody scene and sought out the man who'd accompanied me tonight.

In the corner of the ballroom, Rex and Leo were still talking, hunched over, but where Rex looked complacent, Leo looked outraged. His body language read stiff and his hand motions were less than happy. Rex was more casual, with his hands in his pockets, as if he owned the world.

Knowing I needed to at least show my face to him, I started walking their way. He caught my approach and straightened up, cutting Leo off by buttoning up his jacket and walking toward me, leaving Leo in his wake.

"Get lost?" he asked, as he looked me up and down, probably trying to see if there was a hair out of place.

"Long line, almost sprinted to the kitchen to pee in the sink," I grinned, making him cringe.

"Where's your class?" he muttered, as he pulled me by the elbow toward the bar.

"Think I left it in my other clutch," I mumbled, as he guided me across the room, introducing me to more geezers and debutantes.

Like a robot, I shook their hands, charmed them, and then went to the next, all the while thinking about the back room and what Jett just did to me.

Tomorrow, I was going to find a way to bust Rex, because spending another minute away from Jett was slowly eating away at me; I needed this to be over; I needed to be in his arms again.

15
"YELLOW"

Goldie

"That's it, girls, just like that," I called out, as they moved in unison to the music coming through the main room's speakers.

Once again, the girls were naked and slowly moving, snapping to each crack and pop of the music. Rex picked the music, which, can I just say is fucking atrocious? Might as well be dancing to *Lambchops Play Along*, that would be more entertaining than the dreadful show tune Rex picked.

Don't get me wrong, I liked a musical, but naked women bouncing their tits to the beat of *Seventy-Six Trombones* was less than sexy, more comical.

Alright, it wasn't *Seventy-Six Trombones*, but it still had a trumpet in it, and trumpets come off more as nerd bomb material rather than, "Hey, check out my pussy from below."

Being pressed up against the wall by Jett last night still replayed over and over in my head. I was a little sore, which only became a constant reminder of what we did. It was stupid, because if Rex wasn't so engrossed with his little spat he was having with

Leo, we could have easily been caught. But, for the life of me, I can't be sorry for what we did, because it just reminded me why I was going through this creepy sex ring hell. I was doing this because, in the long run, I wanted to be the one Jett brought to events; I wanted to be the one he woke up to in the morning and the one he wrapped his arms around at night.

The music cut out and I looked over at the controls behind the bar. Blane and Rex stood together, looking sexy as hell. Even though Rex was a tyrant with some creepy fetishes and hoarding tendencies, he was still handsome and sinister. He was that man you couldn't take your eyes off of because you wanted to know what he was thinking behind those dark brows. Then there was Blane, blond and beautifully handsome...Blane with enough muscles to make up for all the other members in the club.

"Uh, are we done?" I asked, cutting the silence in the room.

"I need to speak with Mercy," Rex said.

Speak with her...ha! Unless speaking meant putting his dick in her mouth, then they weren't speaking.

Without saying a word, Mercy nodded and headed toward the back rooms. There was something completely wrong with what was going on in her head. I liked all the other girls, but for some reason, I didn't quite like Mercy. I couldn't trust her. She was the epitome of a fem-bot.

"Shall I excuse the other girls?" I asked Rex, as he walked toward me with a devilish grin on his face. I didn't like that grin; I didn't trust that grin.

"I think it's time you start practicing with them, Goldie. We need to even out the dancers, and it might be time for you to get up on stage."

"Excuse me? I thought we had a deal, that I was going to manage for a while." Sweat started to form at the back of my neck.

"Not really a deal, Kitten, more of an understanding, but now that I'm going to win Lot 17, I need more girls, and you are the one the members want."

Was he really going to win Lot 17? Was it because of that Zane guy? I leaned over, my stomach already knotting from the thought of being on stage, and I spoke softly into Rex's ear. "You're willing to share me with the members?"

"You're not sharing yourself with me, so what difference does it make? Either way, I get to see you naked, and that's my goal here. Either comply with my demands, or good luck trying to find a job in this town. Don't forget, Kitten, I know everyone in this city. I can destroy you."

He placed a gentle kiss on my nose and turned away from me, as if his small bit of affection would make up for the threat he just made to me.

"I can't do it tonight," I shouted after him.

"Why is that?" he asked, looking me up and down.

Think…think, Goldie.

"Cramps," I stated with a sad face. "Got the old blood flow going on right now. Hardly think being naked at this time in my life would be appealing to the members."

A look of absolute disgust crossed Rex's face before he turned around and called over his shoulder, "Next weekend, you will be up on that stage."

Thank fuck.

"Sure," I called after him.

I turned to look at both Eva and Bizzy, who gave me the "I'm sorry you're uterus is bleeding look," and then took off toward the back room, leaving me finally alone with Blane.

By no means was I on my period, but it was the best excuse I could come up with to get out of going on stage with the girls tonight…naked. If there was one sure-fire way to make sure Jett never touched me again, it would be going up naked in front of a bunch of people I didn't know. No, that wasn't going to happen.

Casually, I walked over to the bar and asked Blane for a bottle of water. He obliged, never speaking to me. I hated that he couldn't really talk to me. Enough was enough, I needed to take care of everything tonight; it would be the last chance I had until the next weekend, and to hell if I would be going up on stage.

"Can we talk?"

Blane looked around and then nodded his head toward the back. Fucking paranoid man.

He went to the back first, and a few minute later, I trailed after him. Eva and Bizzy were in the girl's room, eating some food, and not even talking to each other. What a sad, sad life. If anything, I wanted to help these girls out; they needed it.

Once I reached the office in the back of the club, I shut myself in the small space with Blane, who was sitting at the desk waiting for me.

"What can I help you with?" he asked with a smirk.

"Seriously? Come on, we need to take some action here. There is no way I will be going up on stage next weekend."

"I don't know, might be fun?" he looked me up and down while licking his lips.

I pushed his head and said, "Don't even think about it. It will never happen. I'm off limits."

"All the good ones usually are. Do you have a plan?"

"I do," I nodded. "But I thought you had one as well."

"That I do, but I wanted to hear yours first."

"Typical," I said, while folding my arms across my chest. Trying not to get irritated, I started divulging the details of my plan. "So, Rex never leaves his phone in a lock box. He has it on him at all times, and I was thinking, somehow, we can get his phone and use that to record some things around here, text it to…oh, shit," I muttered.

"What?" Blane asked, looking a little intrigued.

"Rex took my phone away from me. I have no way of texting myself the pictures without him obviously seeing it."

"That's not a big deal; we'll just send it to my phone."

"Wait, how do I know I can I trust you?"

Seriously, Blane sat up in his chair and placed his forearms on his knees while looking up at me. His back muscles flexed in the tank top he was wearing, making me quite aware of how damn sexy he really was.

"Goldie, he practically treats me as a slave here. He has ruined my life. He has taken everything away from me, everything that's ever mattered, and now I have nothing but this club where we are all manipulated by that power hungry bastard. It's time Rex finally gets what he deserves. I've been waiting for someone like you to come around. I need your help just as much as you need mine."

Well, that was convincing. From the look in his eyes, the look of desperation, I could tell he wouldn't cross me. I could trust him because, from the very beginning, since I'd met him, he looked like he'd been putting on an act, never really living life. Maybe he really had to be let free of Rex's grasp to get what he needed.

"I guess we can text to your phone. Do you think my plan would work?"

"Possibly," he said, while studying his hands. "I had the same idea, since I see him with his phone all the time. He and Leo both carry their phones around in the club."

"Leo actually comes here?"

"He does," Blane nodded. "He actually is supposed to come tonight."

"Really? Hmm…do you think it would be easier to steal his phone, rather than Rex's? I mean, I have this idea, but I really don't have any clue how to actually get the phone without asking for it."

"How are you at pick-pocketing?"

"Uh, terrible. Never really mastered that fine art."

"Well, you might want to practice before tonight. It's your only option."

"You're acting like this is some *Ocean's Eleven* shit. I like to believe I could be as badass as Matt Damon with a fake nose, but honestly, I have no clue how to go about grabbing a phone from someone's pocket."

"Do you know how to give someone a lap dance?"

"That's insulting that you even had to ask that. Of course I know how to give a lap dance, I know how to make a man cum just from the thrust of my hip against his crotch, but the two don't compare. There is no way you can say giving a lap dance is just like pick-pocketing."

"I wasn't going to say that," Blane stated, a little annoyed. "God, you talk too much sometimes."

"Eh, it's a fault of mine. At least I don't go around slicing people's necks or something like that or punching random people in the head. Although, the shock factor would be hilarious, because what person walking down the street would expect a fist to the old noggin? Not many, unless you're a criminal; if you're a criminal, you can pretty much expect a punch on a daily basis. Talking too much can almost be entertaining, so to call it a fault really isn't that bad. You know?"

"You done?"

Blushing, I nodded and allowed him to continue.

"Like I was going to say, you can give Rex a lap dance at some point tonight and grab his phone then. He won't know what's happening, because he'll be too distracted with you on top of him."

I thought about it for a second and realized it was a good plan; there was only one problem.

"That's a great idea and all, but do you really think Rex is going to allow my crotch anywhere near him after I practically told him my uterus was ripping itself apart?"

Blane cringed and shook his head. "Fuck, that is so nasty."

"Hey! I'm not really on my period. I just said that to get out of being on stage tonight."

"Can you not say period?"

"Such double standards! Guys can talk about snot rockets and jizzing all up in their pants, but I can't talk about my monthly? Something I can't help?"

"It's not proper," he smiled.

"Oh, fuck off," I laughed. "But, seriously, I won't be able to give him a lap dance. He wouldn't want that, and I don't feel comfortable giving Leo a lap dance. I think the world would blow up if I ever let the man touch me."

"Fair enough. I would offer to give them a lap dance, but pretty sure that would go over just as well as your attempt."

"You never know, you could probably work it just enough to entice them," I wiggled my eyebrows.

"Yeah, I'm depressed here, but not that depressed; I still have my self-respect." We both laughed while Blane rubbed his forehead with his fingers. "Did you really have to say you have your period?"

"Sorry, it was the only thing that came to my mind."

"That's really inconvenient. What if we get Eva involved?"

"You think we can trust her? Get real. These girls are so brainwashed it's ridiculous."

"No, what if we get her to give Rex a lap dance, and maybe you help her out? Wear something low cut tonight, and when she's giving Rex a lap dance, maybe you go up behind him and you know, be all touchy and shit. Guys love girl on girl action."

I was about to turn his idea down, but then I thought about it for a second. It would be pretty easy to grab his phone if he was busy with someone else.

"It would have to be Mercy. I'm pretty sure Rex wants nothing to do with Eva. If we have Mercy do it, Rex for sure wouldn't pay attention."

"You're right," Blane snapped his finger as he got excited. "While she is giving him a lap dance, you should play around with him a little, and then take his phone. Once you grab it, hand it off to me, because I will have some free time before my demonstration. You can handle the bar, right?"

"Pretty sure my middle name is liquor. Believe me, booze is

my friend. I know how to handle a bar."

"Right on, this should be easy then," Blane said, with his heavy Australian accent making him that much more attractive. "Why are you looking at me like that?"

Shaking my head and straightening, I said, "Nothing."

Blane poked my side and said, "You were staring at me. You find me attractive."

"Yeah, that's if I enjoyed humping chicken cutlets," I scoffed, avoiding all eye contact with his bulging muscles.

"Chicken cutlets? Wow, you hurt me," he held his heart.

"You're fine. I should get back out there. By the way Rex looks at Mercy, pretty sure he would blow early from whatever she was doing. So, we're on for tonight?"

"We're on, babe."

"Don't call me that," I pointed at him.

A wicked grin spread across his face as he stood. "Got it, sweet cheeks." He slapped my ass and walked out of the small room.

Fucking men.

Nerves ran through my body as I thought about finally taking control tonight. I would end everything tonight and then flee Rex's house to go back to Jett. It would all be over tonight. Tomorrow night, I would be held tightly in Jett's arms, that or being fucked sideways in the Bourbon Room, either way was appealing.

16
"BEG FOR IT"

Jett

"A Mr. Black to see you," Jeremy said, as he stepped inside my office.

"Please show him in," I replied, as I got up to grab two glasses of bourbon for myself and Zane.

Last night, Zane let me know that everything had gone according to our plan, and set up a time to discuss the details with me today. I couldn't be more eager about gathering the information from Zane, not just because I would be able to finally lock up the feud between myself, Rex, and my dad, but because it meant I would be able to take my Little One back. At least, I hoped she would want to come back.

I was still very sour about the whole situation, and I hated that she showed up with Rex, actually despised the whole notion of her being on his arm. After I got a light taste of her last night, it only made me crave her more. It was a slice of heaven that wasn't guaranteed, which made me realize, even though she was with me in that moment, it didn't mean she really wanted to be with me.

Goldie leaving me wouldn't be the first time a woman had left me for Rex. The thought made me sick to my stomach. I wanted to convince myself she wanted to be with me and she wanted nothing to do with, Rex but there was always that nagging thought in the back of my mind that brought me back to the day Natasha left. It happened once; it sure as hell could happen again.

The door to my office opened and Zane Black walked in, wearing a black suit with a white button-up shirt that was undone at the top. The man exuded confidence, but wasn't too cocky about it, something I respected about him.

"Z, it's nice to see you," I greeted, while handing him a glass of my favorite bourbon.

"Jett, always a pleasure," he tilted the glass toward me and took a sip.

"Please, sit down."

We both sat down in the seating area of my office, offering a more relaxed environment.

"I sent you an email with all the data and evidence I was able to collect," Zane started off. "Have you received it?"

"I have, but haven't had a chance to look at it quite yet. I thought I would allow you to tell me everything. I plan on sending it off to my detective friend and giving him a call once we finish our meeting."

"I'm sure your friend will be excited. You were right about the phone, Rex collected it right before I walked through the doors. The man knows he's conducting illegal business and is doing everything in his power to make sure he's not caught."

"Did the watch work out alright?" I asked.

"Perfectly. I was able to record everything Rex said and take some pictures. Some of the things on there are a bit graphic because, I'll be honest, what Rex has going on in there is rather indecent. I won't go too far into it, but the main reason he is able to keep staff on board is because he's blackmailing them all. The employees look depressed, lifeless actually."

Thoughts of Goldie ran through my mind, and I wondered if she was one of the ones Zane saw. She and Rex were late to the event last night, so it did cross my mind that Zane might have seen Goldie, but I refused to ask; I didn't want to drag Zane into that aspect of my life.

"That's sad," I responded, feeling sorry for the girls who were stuck under Rex's grasp.

"I wasn't able to get any proof of the quote unquote contracts Rex had his employees sign, but I'm sure your detective will be able to find them. Even though those girls are selling their bodies to the men in that club, they clearly don't want to be there, you could see it in their eyes."

Was Goldie one of the girls he was talking about? The curiosity was starting to burn a hole in my soul. I couldn't stand to think of Goldie exposing herself to such men, letting them touch her.

"Are you alright?" Zane asked, as he tried to gather my attention.

Clearing my head, I nodded. "Long night last night. Do you believe you got enough material to take them down?"

"I do," Zane responded. "I recorded Rex talking about the club; no doubt will they be able to put him away for this."

The thought of Rex and my father in jail brought a smile to my face. That was exactly where they belonged, and thanks to my connections in the city, I would be damned if they got away with anything less than jail time.

"Well, I can't tell you how appreciative I am to you for you going in there for me and gathering evidence."

"Hey, it was kind of fun," he laughed. "Plus, I would have sold my soul for the Expressway. I can't tell you what this will do for my business."

"I'm glad I could help, which reminds me." I stood up and walked over to my desk, where I had put together an envelope for Zane. I handed it over to him and said, "Inside is the deed to the Expressway, as well as blueprints, layout, and zoning restrictions. Plus, I added some of the contacts I know around the city for you to help get around some of the restrictions, as well as construction companies who would be more than willing to work for you. They all know we are friends, so they should be a pleasure to work with."

"Wow, thank you," Zane said, while looking down at the envelope. "Lot 17 really means a lot to you, doesn't it?"

More than he would ever know.

"It's an opportunity for me to give something back to the community, which needs it. This city has been through hell and back, and if I can help it out in any way, help the children of this city have a better life, then I will do it."

"That's very honorable of you. You're not the man I thought you were. I'm glad we were able to work together."

"Me too," I agreed.

"I hope, in the future, you'll come up to my speedway and indulge a little."

"I would enjoy that," I said, as Zane got up from his chair and headed toward the door. I grabbed his cup from him and put it on the buffet that held my bourbon.

"Who knows? Maybe you'll start your own racing team for my Speedway; just remember, no one beats Black Top Racing," Zane said with a wink.

"Wouldn't dream of even trying."

We shook hands and I guided Zane out the front door of the Lafayette Club. Once again, we thanked each other and made future promises to visit each other. Zane would be spending some time in New Orleans because of the Expressway, so I reminded him to call me when he was in town; I would be more than delighted to show him around the city that made me the man I was today.

The minute Zane was gone, I sent a text message to my detective and let him know I would be sending over the write-up Zane put together about Masquerade, as well as all the evidence he was able to gather.

I was in my office, sending out the information when Kace knocked on my door. I looked up to see he was looking somewhat distraught.

"What's wrong?" I asked, while looking away at my computer, making sure I had everything in place.

"Lyla is driving me fucking insane," Kace responded, while slouching on my chair. "That girl has more of a mouth than Goldie, and she's impossible to shut down."

"You chose her," I said, while finishing up, ignoring the pang of hurt that ran through my veins at the mention of Goldie's name.

"I thought I was doing us a favor, trying to find Goldie. She had some great ideas, but fuck, now she's just annoying the crap out of me."

"It was never your concern to find Goldie."

"What's crawled up your ass?" Kace asked, while slouching in his chair. "I thought you saw her last night."

"I did; she was with Rex."

"That doesn't mean anything."

"How do you know?" I asked, getting angrier by the second.

"Because, she told me..." Kace trailed off, knowing he'd divulged some information he wasn't supposed to.

"What are you talking about?" I asked, anger lacing my voice.

Clearing his throat, Kace shifted in his seat before looking me in the eyes. "I went to go see her one night; I wanted to make sure she was okay."

"That is not your place," I yelled, while slapping my desk. "I told you to stay the fuck out of it."

"Someone had to do something!" Kace yelled back.

"I had it under control. I have it under fucking control!"

"You might now, but you didn't then. I needed to make sure she was okay. Fuck, Jett, she set out to save your pathetic ass. Who knew what she was getting herself into? But that doesn't matter; what matters is that she told me she wanted nothing to do with Rex. She only wants you, Jett. She was devastated to know you were hurting."

"Why would you tell her that?" I asked, feeling rage pouring out of my body. "You had no right to tell her any of that."

"Why is it so hard for you to show someone your feelings?"

"Pot calling the kettle black there, Kace."

"Don't, don't fucking compare me to you. I've lived my life. I fucked it up. I have no need to show feelings. I'm an emotionless man walking through the phases of life until my day comes. We both know that, but you're different. You have your life in front of you, but you refuse to let anyone in your fucking world."

"I was raised not to show feelings," I shot back. "Showing feelings is showing weakness. The moment I showed any kind of emotion, everything was taken away from me, Natasha was taken from me..."

"You didn't even love her," Kace cut in.

"That's beside the point. I don't let anyone in. I didn't until Goldie came along, and do you know what fucking happened? She ripped me apart. The moment I let her in, the moment I dropped the walls erected around my heart, she broke me. She fucking broke me," I trailed off.

"Not on purpose," Kace defended.

"I don't want to hear it," I held up my hand.

"She wants nothing to do with him," Kace pushed on, just as

my phone signaled an incoming text.

Expecting a message from my detective friend, I looked down at my phone to see a text from Rex. I pulled it open to see a picture of a naked woman with the same honey colored hair that had run through my fingertips on more than one occasion, mounted on him. My chest restricted, my breathing became shortened, and my legs started to go numb. I read the text that came along with the message.

Rex Titan: Just like I remembered. Goldie has by far the sweetest pussy I've ever had the chance to fuck. Thank you for fucking up, because not only do I have the girl, but I will also have Lot 17. The best man always wins.

Swallowing hard, I turned the phone to Kace and held it up so he could see it.

"You can't tell me she wants nothing to do with Rex when this is proof that she went back to him. Tell me that isn't her."

Kace looked at the picture as he started to chew on his bottom lip. He was silent. He knew I was right; there was no mistaking that was Goldie in the picture.

"That's what I thought," I said while closing out on the text message, just as my phone rang.

Detective Brown.

Taking a deep breath and trying to will my thundering heart to slow down, I answered.

"Jett Colby."

"Mr. Colby, I received your email. I was able to briefly go over it, but we have enough material to go in tonight. I know you have some restrictions about some of the employees; do those still stand?"

He was asking if I still wanted to give Goldie immunity. At the moment, I didn't care what happened to her, not after the blatant betrayal I was just privy to.

"No, do what you need to do. Will you call me after you get everything settled tonight?"

"Will do, Mr. Colby. Thank you for bringing this to our attention. We will be sure to honor you for keeping this city clean."

Not wanting to keep up with the pleasantries, I thanked him and got off the phone.

"What was that about?" Kace asked.

"Taking care of things. Lot 17 will be mine tomorrow morning. Rex and Leo will be in jail, and their club will be shut down."

"What about Lo?"

Staring at my computer, trying to act like I wasn't affected by his question, I just shrugged my shoulders.

"Don't know. Most likely she will be taken to jail as well for working at the club."

"You can't let that happen," Kace said, outraged.

"I can," I responded quietly, while turning away from him in my chair, dismissing Kace from my room.

"She loves you, Jett."

"If she loved me, then she would never have taken the control out of my hands. She left me helpless and turned to Rex, something I will never forgive her for."

17
"I DON'T MIND"

Goldie

I was quivering from my fucking hair follicles to my lady folds to my damn toenails. I liked to believe I was some strong confident woman with the ability to go all secret agent on someone's ass, but when it came down to it, I was more nervous than a teenage boy sitting next to a porn star.

Both Rex and Leo were in attendance tonight, shaking hands with members and enjoying the perks of the club. Rex continuously kept his eye on Mercy, which made me believe that maybe, just maybe, we would be able to pull off the phone grab. The only problem was, we had to distract Leo, so he didn't see me grab the phone. The other problem was, I had no place really to stuff it, since I was wearing the outfit of a German milkmaid. Not my choice, by any means; the outfit came from the oh-so-cliché mind of Rex Titan. The man needed to expand a little on his fantasies, because they were as stale as the pantaloons hanging on his wall.

The girls' show was over and Blane was getting ready to do

his demonstration, but there was a period of time we had between the demonstration and now, a small time frame where we could possibly grab Rex's phone.

Two of the members spoke quietly to Rex, and I could see him eyeing me with an evil thought in his mind. He was going to make me do something; I just knew it. From the sinister look he was giving me, I knew I was going to be called on.

Sweat trickled down my back as I thought about what was going to happen. What was the worst that could happen? I'd have to give a man a handy; that wasn't a big deal.

"You ready for this?" Blane asked from behind me.

Startled, I didn't turn around as I answered, "You can't talk to me right now."

"Don't worry about it, Rex knows I have to communicate with you about the girls occasionally."

"What's happening right now? Are we going to have time?"

"We have to do it now, because after the demonstration, the members will disperse, and Rex usually takes off after that. It's now or never, sweet cheeks."

"Fuck," I mumbled, as I felt my hands start to get sweaty.

Taking a deep breath, I grabbed Mercy and walked casually over to Rex, who was still talking to two of the members. I wasn't sure if I was allowed to talk to Rex while he was with the members, but I didn't care, I had to take charge and get this done.

"Hello, fellas," I said with a bright tone.

Rex sneered at me, pretty sure I saw his lip quiver. While Rex was giving me the evil eye, the other two members looked Mercy up and down with appreciation in their eyes. Even in my ridiculous outfit, I was still getting eye fucked; I couldn't imagine what it felt like to be Mercy, completely naked in front of all these people.

"Goldie, must I remind you not to interrupt the members' conversations?"

Batting my eyelashes, I pulled Mercy forward and said, "Mercy and I have a surprise for you."

This morning, I approached Mercy about surprising Rex with a lap dance. Of course, she was more than happy to participate. I showed her everything she needed to know in order to make a man forget his name during a lap dance. It wasn't hard, especially if the girl was naked. A little bend here and a little touch there with a perfect hip swivel and the man would be putty in your hands.

"A surprise?" he asked, while eyeing Mercy up and down. I nodded my head, hoping Mercy would pull him away from his conversation. "Just as well, these two fine gentlemen were just about to go back with Bizzy and Eva. Blane," Rex called Blane over.

Confidence exuded from Blane as he strolled over to Rex's call, whipping a towel over his shoulder and placing his hands on his hips.

"How can I help you?" Blane asked, not portraying the domineering man I had come to know in the short amount of time I'd known him. He was different around Rex, and it was probably because Rex had Blane by the balls.

"Please set up Eva and Bizzy in the back; these two gentlemen would like to have some fun."

The way Rex spoke made my vagina want to crawl inside itself. How was I ever attracted to this man, this creepy, manipulating man? It made me shiver just from the thought of being with him. I must have been pretty damn desperate for money, that and I guess I never really knew who Rex was until I moved in with him…well, temporarily took up residence in his house.

"Not a problem," Blane answered, as he took off toward the room, calling Bizzy and Eva with him.

There was always intermission when it came to the events of the night. Rex allowed for members to take some of the girls to the playrooms, that way other members could take them back after the demonstration. It grossed me out, sickened me, to know these girls were being used like this, and I would be damned if Rex got away with it for much longer. This club was coming to an end tonight.

"Now, what's this surprise?" Rex asked, while rubbing his hands together and sizing up Mercy and me.

Strapping on my lady balls, I smiled brightly and said, "Come, sit down for us."

Holding in my revulsion, I grabbed Rex by the hand and guided him to a chair that would allow me access to his pockets from behind, it was the first step I had to complete in order to make this happen. Luckily, Rex let us lead him.

Blane came from the back just in time, and I nodded at him to start the music. With a wink, he went behind the bar and played the one song I knew would be perfect for a lap dance, the same song I played the first time I showed Kace I could give a lap dance, "Nasty, Naughty Boy."

Casually, I walked behind Mercy while trumpets blared through the speakers, setting the mood. Rex's eyes turned dark as I wrapped my arms around Mercy and brought her closer to him. Like we practiced, Mercy allowed me to move her with the music.

Sinking in his chair, Rex spread his legs and got in position for a lap dance. The man wasn't stupid; he knew exactly what was happening.

I moved Mercy into the triangle zone of Rex's legs, the perfect position to start conducting a lap dance, and like we practiced, Mercy leaned forward and placed her hands on Rex's legs. Bending over her back, I moved my hands from her shoulders down her arms until I pressed against her forearms. From there, I came back up to move her hair to the side, exposing her neck.

Rex bit down on his bottom lip as he watched me feel up the apple of his fucking creep-ass eye. Poor Mercy.

Moving my hands back down her back, I backed away and slapped her ass, making the crack of my hand against her skin echo through the room. That was her cue. She turned on her moves and started moving against Rex's body. She turned so her back was toward him, and with a bend at the waist, spread her legs and gave both me and Rex a view of everything she had to offer.

Why men thought the women's genitalia was as coveted as the Holy Grail was beyond me. It was a bunch of folds of skin, gah; it wasn't the most amazing thing I've ever seen. Mind you, Mercy had a very nice…vagina, but still, not my cup of tea.

Slowly, I worked my way to Rex's back, while I gradually ran my hand along his body, so he knew I was still with him, still interested. Bending down, I kneeled on the floor and wrapped my arms around his waist, so I could continue to touch him, intrigue him.

Mercy snapped back up and then worked her hips down onto his crotch, while holding onto his legs. A small groan came out of Rex when she made contact with him. Hell, she was doing a good enough job I wanted to groan as well.

Sliding my hands to the front of his shirt, I started to unbutton it, exposing his skin. My hands gradually slipped in and out of his shirt, playing with his nipples and the goosebumps that spread across his body. I had to give it to the man, he did have a nice body. I wish I could say he's like a flabby old man with sand dollar nipples, but damn, he had it going on under his shirt. It was annoying.

Peeking a look at Rex, I could see that he was totally gone, he was enraptured with Mercy, so I started testing the waters. I ran my hands lower, so they rested on his hip bones. I could feel the strain in his pants from his erection, and I held back the giggle that wanted to escape me.

It was time. I glanced over at Blane, who nodded his head at me, while thankfully distracting Leo, who had his back turned toward me. This was it, this was my moment. Wincing, I moved my hand down to his pockets and was about to pull out his phone when the front and back doors crashed in and a barrage of men holding guns came barreling into the club, making me fall back on my ass, tucked in like a turtle and screaming my ever living brain off.

"Freeze. Put your hands in the air," men shouted all around, while moving further into the club.

Someone grabbed me from behind and made me stretch out my rigid body so they could push it against the floor and strap some cuffs around my wrists.

What the fuck was happening?

Words like prostitution, investigation, and solicitation filtered through the screams filing in and out of the main house. One by one, from the corner of my eye, I saw Mercy be pinned to the ground, as well as Blane, Rex, Bizzy and Eva, even Leo. Members were brought down as well, and one by one, we were escorted out of the club and into rows upon rows of cop cars that lined the street.

Tears fell from my eyes as I tried to figure out what was going to happen to me. Blue and red lights flashed, causing a scene outside. Jail time was in my near future, because even though I wasn't doing anything, I was still guilty by association.

For the first time I could remember, I actually feared for my future. I've been through hell and back, fighting for a couple of dollars to stay afloat, but this was beyond my control. I was caught red-handed and there was nothing I could do.

I was fucked.

***

Getting my mugshot taken was a less than flattering moment for me, especially since I was in a German milkmaid outfit. My hair was plastered to my face, thanks to the tears, sweat, and smashing of my face against the floor at the club, thank you, police officers. My makeup was dripping off my face, so to say I would take world's most hideous mugshot was an absolute guarantee. I looked like a poorly liquefied mega-beast. Not my finest hour.

The community cell I was placed in held a combination of New Orleans' finest. Drunk Diane was sitting in the corner, trying to take her pants off, but luckily was too drunk to work the buttons of her jeans. Hobo Helga was sniffing her armpits while sitting with her legs spread wide enough to welcome a marching band. Sticky Fingers Stephanie was scratching her crotch and picking her teeth at the same time, portraying the whole multi-tasking hand thing, which was quite impressive and rather entertaining, because damn was she digging deep.

Mercy, Eva, and Bizzy were decorated in some oversized jumpsuits to cover up their nudity, and they were huddled in the corner together looking absolutely terrified. I didn't blame them; I felt the same way.

Honestly, I've never been so frightened in my life. I didn't know what to expect, what would happen to me. Was this going to be on my permanent record? Uh, yeah, duh Goldie. You had a mugshot taken.

Fuck.

A door outside of the cell opened and a few police officers came through, looking into the cell. I prayed they were here for me, but then again, I hadn't even made a phone call yet. If anything, they would be here for Sticky Fingers Stephanie, since she already had her one phone call, plus she was just in the cell for shoplifting. I was in here for possible prostitution. Damn, I was so fucked.

The balding police officer walked over to the cell and nodded at me. "Milkmaid, your time is up."

Opening the cell door, he escorted me out and held onto me as he weaved me through some hallways.

"Um, is everything going to be okay?" I asked, not really knowing what was going on.

"You posted bail," the man said, as he went behind a desk and started filing some paperwork.

"Posted bail? By who?"

Who knew I was even here? There was no way it was Rex, because the man himself was locked up. I was pretty sure he was in more trouble than I was, and then it hit me. Rex was in jail, and so was Leo. They were busted, the one thing I wanted.

An overwhelming weight was lifted off my shoulders as I thought about the possibilities of what this meant. I could go back to Jett; I could finally be with the man. Rex and Leo's names were tarnished. Even if they were able to post bail, they still had a black mark on their names.

"Miss, sign here," the police officer said, growing annoyed.

"Sorry, I was daydreaming. I do that often. Usually it's about something stupid like what would happen if you shook a bottle of soda up with a paint shaker and then poked it with a needle. I think it would explode in my face, which is why I haven't tried it yet, because I'm too terrified. What do you think?"

Working his jaw, he pointed at the paper and said, "Sign."

"Oh, yeah, sorry." As I signed the paper, I asked, "Um, who posted bail for me?"

The officer pulled the sheet from under my hand and ripped off the bottom half. "That man over there," he pointed, as he handed me my paperwork.

I glanced over and my heart stopped as I saw Jett putting something in his coat pocket. He glanced up in my direction, and for the briefest of moments, the world stopped, and everything around me faded as I made eye contact with the one and only man that owned my heart.

Like I was a complete stranger, he shifted his eyes away and walked out the door, not taking a moment to wait for me.

"Am I excused?" I asked, wanting to run after him.

"Yes," the officer said, annoyed with my questions.

Not giving the officer a chance to lock me up for something asinine I might say, I took off toward the front to catch Jett. I thought he might possibly be waiting for me outside with an idling town car, but when I exited the police department, the street was clear of any cars except for a faint gleam of red taillights pulling away.

Why didn't he wait for me?

18
"WHEN I WAS YOUR MAN"

Jett

"With the recent findings against Rex and Leo, and Zane Black dropping out of the race, you are automatically awarded Lot 17," George, my lawyer, said excitedly through the phone. "I couldn't be happier for you."

"Thank you, George," I stated solemnly.

I should be excited, I should be celebrating a well-earned win, but there was not one bit of excitement running through my body. Instead, rage boiled in the pit of my stomach, waiting to erupt.

The picture Rex sent me was constantly on replay in my head.

She told me to my face there was nothing going on with her and Rex...that I was the one who held her heart, but she lied. She fucking lied.

"Are you there?" George asked, a little concerned.

"I am. I'm sorry George. I'm just a little tired. Do you mind if I call you tomorrow to finalize the details?"

"That's perfectly fine. Get some sleep. I know how stressful this whole campaign for Lot 17 has been, but rest easy, you're the owner now. You can finally make the park you wanted. You're a good man, Jett."

Swallowing hard, I nodded, even though he couldn't see my acknowledgement, and then hung up the phone.

Lot 17 has been an entity that has inspired me, disappointed me, hurt me, dragged me through the mud, and given me hope. I've been waiting for this day, the day where I found out I was able to secure the property for the kids, but when it came down to it, without Goldie by my side, I just felt empty.

A part of me wanted to leave her to fend for herself after Masquerade was busted, but I couldn't do that. I saw the frightened look on her face when she was escorted out of the club and into the cop cars. I couldn't be the one responsible for keeping that look on her face, that was why I posted her bail, but that was it. I couldn't let her talk to me after that.

I was burned from the inside out; there was no soul left in me. I was a heartless man, the definition of bitter and foolish. To think a woman would be able to look past my faults, my demanding exterior, and see me for the man I want to be was an irrational thought.

The bitter taste of my bourbon did nothing to soothe the ache that took up place in my chest, nor did it help me forget. How could I forget? How could I forget the sassy mouthed, honey-haired girl who captured my heart?

It was impossible.

A small knock came at my door, and without turning around, I beckoned whoever was on the other side to come in. My thoughts were lost in the darkness of the streets as little footsteps padded across my floor and the click of my door shutting echoed through the room.

I didn't have to turn around to see who it was. I should have known she would have come to me after she left the police department.

"Jett…" she practically whispered.

Involuntarily, my eyes shut from the sweetness of her voice. I missed her so God damn much, I didn't have the strength to face her. It would be too painful.

"Jett, please turn around."

With shaky legs and an unsteady heart, I turned my chair and came face to face with my Little One.

Her face was covered in smeared make up, her costume—which was hideous—was crumpled and dirty, and there was a small red patch on her face, probably where she was pressed against the ground. Even though her hair was in disarray and her bravado was lacking, she was still the most beautiful woman I had ever laid eyes on.

"What are you doing here?" I asked, trying to steady my voice.

"I-I thought you would want to see me," she said with a shaky voice, her hands twisting in front of her.

"And why would you think that?"

I could tell with every angry word coming out of my mouth that I was hurting her, but I had to protect my fragile heart.

"Because I told you I would be back."

"You're back because you got caught, not by choice."

"That's not true, Jett. I was going to be back here tomorrow, actually. Right before the police showed up, I was going to steal Rex's phone and gather evidence. I had it all planned out."

"Did you?"

"I did," she said, puffing her chest out.

"And what were you going to do with the 'evidence'," I said while using air quotes.

"I was going to give it to you, so you could show someone, and finally win Lot 17. I was trying to help, Jett."

"I didn't need your help, Goldie. I had everything under control."

I could see the moment her attitude switched from scared to pissed. It was almost comical.

"You had everything under control? So, hiding me away, keeping me in the dark and fraternizing with a kiwi is having it under control? Well, shit, I would hate to see what it's like when you're completely out of your mind. It would be rather entertaining." She crossed her arms and looked down at me.

"I knew what I was doing," I said strictly.

Blowing out a frustrated breath, she asked, "Does it really matter? It's all over now, can't we just move on? I told you I would be back, and here I am."

"Do you really think it's that easy?" I asked, while standing. "Do you really think you can walk back in here as if nothing happened? You stole the one and only thing I asked for you to give me. You stole my control. You took that away from me. You didn't trust the fact that I could take care of you."

"I did too!" Goldie shouted. "I just was sick of hiding under a rock, living my life in a shadow. I wanted to live my life with you, Jett. I wanted to help protect you; I wanted to help."

"I didn't need your help," I gritted out.

Throwing her hands up in the air, she said, "God, you're infuriating. You can't control the world, Jett. Sometimes you have to put your trust in others."

"When I put trust in others, they end up hurting me. You can't trust anyone in today's society, not even the people you think would never hurt you."

Goldie sucked in her breath at my statement. "Are you saying you don't trust me?"

Losing my temper, I punched my desk and shouted, "You left me! You grabbed my heart from my chest and left me. You left me to go to the one person who could make or break me."

"To save you!" Goldie shouted back. "I did it for us."

"You wanted to save me, Goldie? You wanted to protect me? Then you should have fucking stayed; you should have protected my heart, which I'd handed to you. You took advantage of it, though, and gave me back my collar."

Tears welled up in Goldie's eyes as she ran her hands through her hair in frustration. "I did that to help you, to help us, Jett. I want to live my life with you. How come you can't understand that?"

"Then you should have stayed," I stated, while turning my back on her and gripping onto the edges of the window.

"What happened to having faith?" she whispered, throwing my words back at me. "What happened to having faith in the power we have, Jett? Did you just forget that?"

Gritting my teeth, I swung around, pulled out my phone from my pocket and opened up the picture Rex had sent me. I tossed the phone on my desk for her viewing, and said, "My faith went out the window the minute I realized you lied to my face. Not interested in him, Goldie? Then fucking explain that picture."

I watched as she pulled the phone toward her eyes with shaky hands for better viewing. Her eyes widened as she studied the picture. She shook her head and then put the phone on my desk.

"Do you really think that's me?"

"Are you going to deny it is? Don't bullshit me, Goldie."

Nodding her head and pressing her lips together, she started to back away from me, making her way toward the door.

"Are you going to deny it?" I repeated, needing to hear her answer.

"I don't need to answer that question. You, out of everyone, should know better, Jett."

"So, you're going to deny the fact that is you in the picture…that Rex is fucking you from behind?"

Anger billowed up in her face as her hands clenched at her sides. She charged toward my desk and opened my pone back up, shoving the picture in my face.

"Look at it," she yelled. "Look at the picture. Tell me what you see."

"Don't belittle me," I said, looking away.

"Belittle you? Seriously? You're the one who thinks that I have zero loyalty where you're concerned when all I've been is loyal to you ever since I walked into this house. You've been the only man I've thought of, that I've wanted to be with, even before I officially met you. You owned me the minute you ordered your drink at Kitten's Castle, so how dare you fucking say I have no loyalty to you? You're the only person I've ever wanted to be a part of my life."

She took a breath and flashed me the picture again. "This, Jett, is Mercy, one of the girls at Masquerade."

The stubborn me came out and said, "And how can I believe you?"

"Well, I would like to say you trust me, that you kept your faith in me while I was gone, but, apparently, that's not enough. Look closely, Jett, is there a heart-shaped birth mark above this girl's tailbone?"

Flashes of Goldie's unique birthmark ran through my head as I studied the picture. All the color from my face drained as realization dawned on me.

"Yeah, that's what I thought," she said, while she tossed the phone on my desk. "You know what really hurts, Jett? Is that you didn't even give me a chance to prove to you how much I care for you, how much I love you. Yeah, love, that's right, I used the scary L word. Oh no, commitment and opening up are coming at you," she said, while making scary fingers at me. "I sat by and waited for you to open up, to realize that, in fact, I'm the best thing that's ever happened to you. I waited while you tried to figure out this Lot 17 bullshit, and I waited as you took the kiwi out to events, events I should have been attending. I even stood by, trusted you, when there were compromising pictures in the tabloids of you two. I stood by your side and had faith in what you were doing for us, what you were trying to give us, but the minute I try to do the same, reciprocate the affection, you turn away from me, you drop me like a bad fucking habit and leave me to fend for myself."

Taking a deep breath, she shook her head and pulled away. "I've dealt with enough bullshit in my life that I think it's about time I figured out what's best for me without an over-domineering man telling me what I can and cannot do. I gave you a chance, Jett; I gave you everything I had from my body, to my soul, and you lost it. You handled me with a hand full of razor blades and have cut me open. Well, you know what? I don't need this club, I don't need the Bourbon Room, and I don't need you, Jett. I'm an amazing woman with a heart of gold and the determination to make something of myself. If I have to take the long route to make that happen, then I will. Don't give yourself so much credit; you can't save everyone."

With that, she turned on her heel and walked out of my office and out of my life without a backward glance.

19
"BRAND NEW ME"

Goldie

Arrogant, self-centered, asshole!

I busted through my old bedroom door to see my art supplies packed up, my clothes in bags, and my makeup sitting in boxes. The man didn't even give me a chance.

I hated him; I fucking hated him.

My heart sunk to the floor the moment I found out that he thought I would cheat on him…that he would think I turned to someone else when he was all I ever needed.

All I wanted was to be the one who took care of him, who made him happy, who made him come alive and shed the walls he'd put up years ago.

No matter how hard you try, how much passion and love you give someone else, they might never change. I thought I'd made it quite clear to Jett that I was the only one for him, that I wanted nothing more than to be the woman by his side, but, apparently, he couldn't get that through his thick-headed skull.

Unfortunately, anything I had taken with me to Rex's house

was a lost cause now, since I wouldn't be going back there, so I had to pack up some clothes, grab my personal items I left behind, and get the hell out of this house, because the longer I stayed, the unhealthier I could feel myself get.

My body wanted to retreat back upstairs and beg to be a part of his life, for him to love me the way I love him, but I refused to lower myself to such a demeaning state. For once in my life, I needed to figure out what I wanted, not what someone else wanted or what I needed to do to stay afloat.

I had money now, thanks to my short stint as a Jett Girl; I needed to make use of it.

It was depressing, seeing my room so empty, as if my time at the Lafayette Club meant nothing.

Slowly, I went around and gathered some clothes, make-up, and shoes. Opening my night stand drawer, I took my credit card that was connected to the account Jett set up for me. I never thought I would touch it, because when I was at the Club, I didn't need it. Everything was taken care of for me, but now I needed it, and I knew the first thing that I was going to do with that card.

I packed up a few of my art supplies, mostly the ones I came to the club with, and then turned to look at the room that held so many memories for me.

There were multiple times I'd stayed at the Lafayette Club when I'd threatened to leave, where I was on the verge of packing up and taking off, but I was always stopped. Now, I knew there was no stopping me. This was the last time for me in the club.

You can't make someone love you, no matter how hard you try.

With a deep breath, I took one last look at the yellow room that sheltered me, my sanctuary for a short period of time, and turned to walk out my door when I slammed into Lyla and Kace.

"Where do you think you're going?" Lyla said, with her arms crossed over her chest.

"Please don't, Lyla, just let me go."

"Yeah, that's not going to happen. What the hell is going on? All we know is there was some big bust down at Rex's place."

Taking a deep breath, I said, "There was, we were all thrown in jail. Jett bailed me out and left me there. I came back here to talk to him, but he wanted nothing to do with me, because Rex sent him a picture of what he thought was me in a compromising position. Jett believed Rex, and that's that. I'm out."

"That picture wasn't you?" Kace asked.

I flashed an angry glare at Kace. "What did I tell you the other day, Kace? Do you really think I would do that to Jett?"

"Then, tell me it wasn't you."

"It wasn't me," I shouted. "Fuck, why doesn't anyone believe me around here?" Frustration overtook me and tears started to form in my eyes once again. I hated crying, but when I became so overwhelmed with frustration, I couldn't help it.

"I believe you," Lyla comforted with a hug. I looked over at Kace, who had a distressed look on his face, like he wanted to believe me, but it was hard for him to do so.

Pulling away, I walked over to Kace and pushed his chest. "What is wrong with you? Why are you having a hard time believing me? I can see it all over your face."

"It looked like you, Goldie."

"How would you know? You've never seen me bent over like that." Kace winced at my nasty tone. "But I guess you would take Jett's side. We're not friends, right, Kace?" He was about to speak when I stopped him. "Save it. Not that I need to explain, but that was a picture of Mercy, one of the girls who worked at Masquerade. She might look very similar to me, but she was missing one thing. My birthmark on her lower back. Check the picture again, Kace."

I shook my head and pushed past Kace.

"Goldie, don't leave," Lyla called out.

I turned and shrugged my shoulders as I looked at her. "There's nothing left here for me, Lyla. I need to find out who I am, and I'm not going to do that living here, pretending like the man upstairs actually cares about me."

"Where are you going to stay?"

"I'll figure something out."

"Stay with me," Lyla said, moving forward. "I'm done here. I was only here to help because you were gone. I don't need this."

I glanced up at Kace and noticed how his features turned from confused to troubled at Lyla's words. It was clear he cared for her, maybe more than he cared for me.

"No, you do need this, Lyla. You can't stay at Kitten's Castle forever; you're better than that. Stay here, earn an education, and start a new life. You deserve it."

"But, Goldie…"

"Lyla, I love you, I really do, but you have to let me go. I'll be fine. I've been through hell and back; this is just a minor speed bump in the shitty life I've had."

The lies that were pouring out of my mouth were convincing enough for Lyla, but did nothing to affect my mood. I wanted to believe that leaving this house was a good move…that I would be happy, but I knew I wouldn't. Jett owned me; he owned every piece of me, and getting over him would be the hardest thing I ever did, harder than saying goodbye to my parents, and harder than selling my body to make it in the world. Jett Colby was someone you just didn't get over; Jett Colby was a staple in my life, an unyielding presence that will forever be a part of my heart.

With a sad smile, I turned away and headed down the stairs, secretly praying Jett would come after me. That he would come flying down the stairs and stop me from leaving, beg for my forgiveness, but he never came. He never showed up; he never begged.

***

"He will be right out, ma'am. You can have a seat if you would like."

"Thank you," I replied, as I took a seat on one of the worn out blue chairs.

My mind was still reeling from the emotional trauma I was just put through. I was cut in half by Jett not trusting me, but the icing on top of the cake was Kace not believing me. We've always had a love hate relationship, but we've always been honest with each other, so the fact that he automatically thought I would turn my back so quickly against Jett hurt.

A buzz rang out in the sterile room I was sitting in and a door opened. Wearing a borrowed shirt and the same pants he'd been wearing earlier was Blane, but instead of the normal mischievous look on his face, he was more somber, concerned.

"Hey," I said, as I stood up.

Blane stopped in his tracks when he saw me, shocked at my being the one in the waiting room.

"Goldie, what are you doing here?"

Twisting my hands together, I answered honestly. "I couldn't leave you behind. I feel like we were in this together, and we have to finish it together."

"Wow, I don't know what to say," he replied, while pulling on the back of his neck. "Did you post my bail?"

"I did." It was the first purchase I made with my Jett Girl money, and I was damn proud of the decision. Everyone deserves a second chance, and it was Blane's turn to make a new life for himself, a life without constraints.

Smiling at me, he walked toward me and wrapped me in his arms. "Thank you," he whispered near my ear, sending goosebumps down my skin.

"You're welcome," I replied, while hugging him.

I didn't know Blane that well, but what I did know, I liked. He was a good guy who'd made some bad decisions. Not everyone is perfect.

Blane wrapped his hand around my shoulder and we walked out of the Police Department together. We were greeted by the muggy night, which only New Orleans could offer. The night was just beginning for many, but for me, I was ready to call it, to bury my head in a pillow and end this horrible day.

"How did you get out?" Blane asked, as we started walking toward the French Quarter.

"Jett, he posted bail."

"So, why aren't you with him right now then?"

Cringing, I said, "That's not going to happen."

"Why not?" Blane pressed.

"Classic Rex, the scumbag, sent Jett a picture of him and Mercy together. The picture could have easily been me, since we look so similar. Clearly, Jett thought I was with Rex, and wanted nothing to do with me. We said some pretty bad things to each other, and I left, for good. He didn't come after me."

"Seriously?"

"Yes," I nodded. "I'm done with the Lafayette Club, I'm done with being a Jett Girl, and I'm done with Jett Colby. I feel like he's caused me nothing but heartache."

That wasn't true; the man had caused me a lot more than heartache. He taught me how to live again, how to enjoy life and live it to its fullest. He taught me that people are allowed to have second chances and can actually climb out of the pit of despair they might have fallen into. Jett changed everything about my life; he showed me what it was like to hand my heart over to someone. He was everything to me.

"Seems like you still care about him," Blane pointed out, as we walked down Canal Street.

"Of course I do," I sighed. "It's hard not to when you love someone so deeply. It's hard to just clean them out of your life. It's going to take some time."

"I can believe that. Was he the one who busted Rex?"

"I'm pretty sure. He didn't come out and say it, but it's kind of obvious. He knew everything that happened." I thought about our fight and sighed again. "I also kind of messed up."

"How so?"

"Jett is a man who needs to have control over every aspect of his life, and by me leaving, I took that away from him."

"I'm going to stop you right there," Blane interrupted me. "You left to help protect him, to find a solution. By no means should he be mad at that."

"You don't get it," I argued. "You're a dom; you need control…"

"In the bedroom."

"Not in real life?"

"Well, I guess in some ways," he admitted.

"Jett needs it in all ways. By me taking charge, in his head it looks like I didn't trust him to protect me, to take care of things."

"Is that how you felt?"

"No," I said softly. "I just…ugh, I just wanted everything to be normal. I'm so beyond impatient. It seemed like things were never going to end, and I wasn't sure how much more of the hiding I could take. I thought that if I went out there, tried to find a solution, I might be able to make things better. Instead, everything just blew up in my face."

"Seems like we should be walking in the opposite direction, toward the Garden District."

I shook my head no. "No, as much as my heart is begging for me to go back to him, my brain is winning out. I need to figure out what I want outside of Jett Colby, what I want to do with my life, because stripping down for men and offering them lap dances is not going to pay the bills forever."

"I can respect that. So, where to now?"

We stopped in front of our destination and Blane gave me a

quizzical look. With two knocks on the door, I waited for it to be opened.

I could hear someone running down the stairs to open the door. Locks clicked open and light spilled through the entrance. Standing in only a pair of sweats, looking fine, as usual, was Diego.

"Goldie, what are you doing here?" he asked, as he rubbed the top of his head and held onto the door frame.

"We need jobs and a place to stay. Can you help us out?"

Diego sized up Blane and smiled.

"I think we can arrange something."

20
"SAY YOU LOVE ME"

Jett

"Are you nervous?" Kace asked me.

"No, have I ever been nervous?"

"When you went to ask out Christina in high school you were. I don't think I've ever seen you sweat so much."

I gave him a pointed look. "I was fifteen and she was a senior with a rack that had every guy in school sweating. Pretty sure I have an excuse for that."

"Still, you were nervous," Kace said with a smirk.

I shrugged and looked out the window. For some reason, New Orleans looked less exciting than normal. I used to enjoy the sights and sounds only true natives of the town could appreciate, but right now, everything seemed so bland. I tried to ignore the reason, why I'd been walking around the club for the past week like a ghost, as if my soul was sucked right out of me, but I knew the reason.

I threw away the best thing that ever happened to me.

It wasn't hard to see. I destroyed the trust we'd built, I let my stubbornness get in the way, and I was blinded by pride. I deserved the loss of Goldie.

"Are you ever going to talk about what happened?" Kace pressed.

The incessant best friend of mine wouldn't drop the subject of what happened at the club and why Goldie left. I knew he knew exactly why Goldie left, because I heard him talking to her near her bedroom with Lyla, but classic Kace wouldn't let it drop there.

"It's over; why bring up the past?" I asked, while adjusting the cuffs of my shirt.

"Because you're not the same person. When I'm in one of my self-induced exiles, you make me talk about it."

"That's because I'm afraid you're going to do something stupid, like commit suicide," I smirked at him.

"I wouldn't make it that easy on you. Come on, man, just fucking tell me. I hate all this whiney bullshit you've been putting the whole house through."

"Whiney? Last time I checked, I don't whine."

"Well, you sure as hell aren't a shining beacon caressing us with angel kisses and cuddling clouds."

I eyed Kace up and down. "Lose your balls somewhere on this ride?"

"Sometimes, I think I did," Kace said, while looking out the window.

"Lyla giving you a run for your money?" I asked, grateful for the subject change.

Kace rubbed his forehead in frustration. "She's infuriating. She doesn't ever listen. It's like directions go in one ear and out the other, and the worst part about it is she's influencing the other Jett Girls. When did we lose control?"

I shook my head and laughed. I knew the answer to that, the minute Goldie walked in the house. She shifted the atmosphere of the entire club. The girls always held the cards, but she turned into the fucking dealer.

"I think you know the answer to that."

Kace wiped his mouth with his hand. "I told you Goldie was a bad choice," he smirked.

"You were right when you said she wasn't Jett Girl material; she is so much more than that. She's a complex twist of sunshine and rain, a bright spot on a dull day, a compact ball of fucking sass and defiance."

"But, you can't help but love her," Kace pressed.

Looking out the window, I nodded my head. He was right, I couldn't help but love her and every little defiant and caring bone in her body. I was so fucking in over my head when it came to Goldie that I didn't know how to handle the feelings running through me.

I wanted to protect her, dominate her, care for her, and love her, but I had no clue how to do those things, because for the first time in my life, instead of me being the dominant, Goldie was. She owned every last inch of me, and right about now, I would do anything she said to be with her. Fucking anything.

"Tell me you have a plan."

"Plan for what?"

We pulled up to our destination and I fixed my jacket, making sure everything was in place. The driver walked around to our side of the car to open the door.

"Don't play dumb with me," Kace said. "Do you have a plan to win Goldie back?"

The door to the car opened, and I was greeted with an onslaught of press. Before stepping out of the car, I turned to Kace and said, "I always have a plan."

Adjusting my tie, I stepped out of the car with Kace following me close behind as I weaved my way through the press, who found it necessary to shove microphones in my face every chance they got.

When George called me this morning about a press conference for Lot 17, I was more than accommodating because I wanted everyone to know about my plans for the space. What I wasn't looking forward to were the questions involving my father and Rex Titan.

After the police invaded Masquerade, they were granted access to the inner workings of their business, their books, and everything involved with their bank accounts. Some city elites were brought down, and their reputations were tarnished, but what I wasn't expecting was for Rex and my dad to have a lot more hidden in their closets than I thought.

When I sent Zane into Masquerade, I knew we were going to expose the prostitution ring Rex and my dad were running, but I never expected for them to be exposed for embezzlement and a grand Ponzi scheme that didn't only affect some of the people of New Orleans, but also citizens around the country.

The findings were complete news to me, but when I thought about it, it all made sense. My dad wasn't good at managing his money, which is why he was so desperate to obtain Lot 17; it was going to set up a lucrative business for him, using the people's money and the business model of the Lafayette Club, but with a perverted and highly illegal twist.

Investigations were still underway, but for right now, my dad and Rex were facing charges for prostitution, embezzlement, and fraudulent investments. Pretty much, they were sitting pretty on some prison time. I was looking forward to the day they would pay their much-deserved dues.

George met me in the back of the room where the press conference was being held. We shook hands, and I could tell by the small smirk on his face that he was a very happy man.

"George, you're looking well," I greeted him.

"Mr. Colby, good to see you on such a joyous occasion." He glanced over and saw Kace and stuck out his hand. "Mr. Haywood, a pleasure."

"Hi, George. Good to see you. I can't believe you're still hanging around with this guy," Kace said, while gripping my shoulder.

"I could say the same about you," he smirked.

"He pays me. Have to milk the cow as much as I can."

"Milk the cow?" I asked, while raising my eyebrow.

Kace just shrugged, making George chuckle to himself.

"It's good to see a friendship likes yours stay intact. I've seen so many friendships dissolve throughout the years."

"I'm too invested by now to let go," Kace responded, being more playful than usual.

"Don't let him fool you," I cut in. "The man is obsessed with me."

George threw his head back and laughed. "Never a moment with Jett Colby when he isn't full of himself."

"Why, George, was that a dig at my personality?" I acted offended.

He patted my cheek and said, "Never, my boy, only affection."

"Mr. Colby, are you ready?" someone asked, who was helping run the press conference.

Taking a deep breath, I nodded my head and walked toward the lights of the stage.

The room was full of press with cameras, microphones, voice recorders, and columnists with poised pens, just waiting to take notes and ask questions. They looked like hungry vultures, and I was about to feed them the meal of the century.

George informed me before the conference that I was supposed to address the press with my own statement, and then take questions afterwards. It would be pretty simple, and thankfully I was seasoned when it came to handling the press, so if they started to become too invasive, I would be cutting the press conference short. There was only so much I divulged, and right now, I knew my personal life was up for attack, since my father was looking at such serious charges.

The room fell silent as I approached the podium. Lights shone down on me, blocking out most of the faces in the crowd, making it easier to recite the speech I'd spent the morning memorizing.

"Good afternoon. Thank you all for taking time out of your day to be here with me. As you all know, Lot 17 is a prime location in this great city of New Orleans. I've been very zealous at making it known that this property has been of great interest to me. Last week, I was awarded the property through a bidding process and can now tell you how ecstatic I am about acquiring the property. I am known in this city for my real estate investments and business prowess, but I'm afraid I have been quiet when it comes to my philanthropic work. I've done this because I don't believe in gloating about my charity work. I am in a position where I can spread my wealth, and I believe doing so in silence is a proper way to conduct business, but there are times when you need to talk about such charity work to bring the community together, to make the citizens of New Orleans a cohesive force. That being said, I'm here to announce my plans for Lot 17."

Taking a second to let my words sink in, I paused and then continued.

"Lot 17 will belong to the community, to the children of New Orleans, to those in need of second chances. I plan on making a park with ball fields, soccer fields, walking paths, and a community center, where we will offer free classes ranging from exercise to art for members of the center. Membership will be free to the citizens of New Orleans; all we ask is that you keep the parks clean, you encourage each other, and stay positive. We want to encourage kids and adults to explore different avenues of recreation, whether it be cooking, painting, or even joining a team. It's time to give back to the community, the same community who raised me from a baby to the man I am today. I want every family in this city, no matter their social standing or race, to have a chance to grow and experience life in a way they might not have without the community center. I am announcing the plans for Lot 17 because I want to engage the community, ask for volunteers, and help spread the word about the new opportunities we will be offering to the city of New Orleans. Thank you for listening to me today; are there any questions?"

The room erupted as press raised their hands and shouted out their questions. The moderator of the conference called on individuals to ask questions.

The first question came from a brown haired man with glasses. "How will this community center be funded?"

"Funding won't be an issue...that is for me to worry about, and me alone."

"Does that mean you will be funding it yourself?"

Annoyed with his question, I answered curtly. "Yes, next question."

"Mr. Colby, when do you foresee the community center opening?"

"By the end of the year, hopefully by fall. I've been in communication with multiple contractors in the city, making sure they know what kind of priority Lot 17 will be. They are well aware of my time line. I have full confidence we will be seeing a community center soon."

The moderator called on an elderly gentleman in the front, who had been chewing on his pen for the whole conference.

"Mr. Colby, can you release a statement on the investigation your father is going through?"

That was quick, I thought to myself, as I geared up for the question.

"My father and I have been estranged for years now. He's conducted business in a way I didn't want to emulate, so when I was eighteen, I separated myself from him. I believe in the judicial system and know that if the findings in the way my father has conducted business are correct, then I expect for him to be punished appropriately."

"Did you know about his embezzling and Ponzi scheme?"

"Like I said, my father and I have been estranged since I turned eighteen. I was unaware of his financial status and the inner workings of his business. Next question."

"Mr. Colby, you are known to have a strangled relationship with a Mr. Rex Titan. Are you happy to see the recent findings of the way he conducted business?"

"I find it improper to talk negatively about relationships I have with other individuals in a public setting."

A blonde raised her hand and asked, "Is it true you and Miss Keylee Zinc are engaged?" The local gossip magazine. I refrained from rolling my eyes.

"Miss Zinc is a wonderful woman, but we are just friends. Any rumors about Miss Zinc being connected with me romantically are just that, rumors. Our relationship is a strictly platonic one."

"Are you in a relationship with someone else?" she asked, pressing her luck.

"I don't believe that is the media's business. I am a private man and would like to stay that way. If there aren't any other questions about Lot 17, then I believe I will end this press conference."

Before I ended, I answered a few more questions about Lot 17, and then thanked the press one more time before taking off. Kace stood on the side of the stage, waiting for me, with his hands in his suit pockets and a smirk on his face.

"Community center?" he asked with a questioning brow. "I thought you were just going to make a park."

"Plans changed," I said, while I thanked the assistant who handed me a bottle of water. Both Kace and I walked toward the waiting town car, said our goodbyes to George, and took off.

"When did your plans change?" he asked, once we were settled in the car.

"The moment I lost Goldie. I knew I had to make some changes in the way I conducted business. The Lafayette Club isn't the same without her, and I need to give the girls other opportunities."

"What do you mean?" Kace asked, concerned.

"I'm closing the club."

"What about the girls?"

"They will work at the center, teaching the children and families, while they still pursue their education. I don't want to expose them any longer. With this new business venture, I can have the members of the Lafayette Club become donors to the center. We will still allow meetings to be conducted in the Toulouse Room, but the girls won't be performing anymore. Those days are over."

"I see," Kace said, while looking out the window. His silence said it all; he was worried about his place in the club.

"Don't worry, if you accept, I would love for you to manage the center and offer exercise classes to the community, including boxing."

Kace's head whipped around and his jaw was slack as he stared at me for a second.

"Are you serious?"

"Very much so. Your talent and services are better used in that capacity. You have so much to offer young teenage boys who might be lost. I have the utmost confidence in the fact that you can make an impact on these boys."

"Wow," Kace responded, while rubbing his chin. "I didn't see that coming. I don't know what to say."

"Say you'll take the job."

"How the hell can I say no to that?" he smiled. Silence fell between us as Kace looked at me seriously. "I have to say, Jett, I couldn't be more appreciative of your friendship. You've been there with me through everything and never once judged me. I would be lost without you."

"I feel the same," I admitted. Kace nodded and smirked. I jabbed his shoulder and said, "I can't believe you were going to cry back there."

"I wasn't going to cry," Kace replied, offended.

"Oh, please, I saw the tears in your eyes."

"Fuck you," he laughed. "God, you're a dick."

Laughing, I nodded, as I looked out the window. This was my city, the place I was born and raised, the place where I grew into a man, the place I met the love of my life, and now that

I'd settled my business affairs, it was time I settled my personal ones, because to hell if I was going to let go of the best thing that ever happened to me..

21
"UPTOWN FUNK"

Goldie

"No, you're getting it all wrong. You have to bend first, stick your ass out, and then snap up," I instructed both Diego and Blane, who were standing in front of me with giddy looks on their faces.

"I don't get it," Diego said. "Can you show us one more time?"

"It's not like you're making a penis out of a can of worm meat and dental floss," I said, while getting in position.

"Worm meat? Is that even something?" Blane asked, his voice thick with his Australian accent.

"Possibly," I giggled. "Would you eat it?"

"What would I get if I ate it?" Blane asked, eyeing me up and down.

"What do you want?" I said, losing my balance; damn alcohol was going to my head.

"I think you know what I want," Blane replied, while licking his lips.

Oh, fuck, did I know. The man had been relentless ever since he found out Jett and I were no longer together. He made his feelings for me quite clear and wasn't shy about them. He said when he knew I was still attached to someone, he respected my space, but apparently to him, I was fair game now.

Diego had been more than accommodating when it came to helping us both out. I went back to assisting Diego at his club, like I had before I left to try to save my relationship with Jett, what little help that was. The rooms were almost fully painted and my work was really coming together nicely with the overall theme. Diego was pleased, and that was all that mattered to me.

I've kept to myself most of the time, because frankly, I didn't want the boys to see me cry over a guy who I wasn't sure ever really truly cared about me. It was embarrassing. But Diego only let my personal exile last a couple of days; he didn't feel that wallowing in self-pity was a productive way to conduct my days, so that's why I currently found myself almost twisted off my ass, teaching Blane and Diego how to pole dance.

"Back off, Blane," Diego said, while pushing him away. "If Goldie is going to bone anyone here, it's going to be me. We have history," Diego winked at me.

"There is no way she would fuck you," Blane laughed. "Not with that prissy dancing you do around stage."

"Prissy?" Diego asked while standing tall.

Prissy was the last word I would use to describe Diego. For Cirque du Diable, Diego was the ringmaster, the man who sat center stage, directing all the acts that were conducted. He was the grand MC with a body that would make your lady folds weep, eyes that would have you orgasming on the spot, and a kind of control that would have you dropping to your knees, asking him what he wanted.

Blane gestured toward Diego and said, "Yeah, you're prissy."

"Watch it, bro, your livelihood is being held on by a thread right now, and I can fucking snip it so fast," Diego said with a grin.

Nodding, Blane said, "Aw, I see. So you're going to hold the fact that you gave me a job, a fucking awesome job, by the way, and a place to stay over my head?"

"Pretty much," Diego laughed.

"As long as I know up front," Blane laughed as well. "Still, doesn't mean you get to fuck Goldie. She's up for grabs. That's how I see it."

"There is a no fraternizing with other employees policy here," Diego stated, while crossing his arms.

"Soo, wouldn't that mean you're shit out of luck as well?"

"I'm exempt," Diego smiled.

"No fucking way. If you're banging the employees, then so can I. It's only fair. Don't you want a fair work environment for everyone? Make your employees happy?"

"Not really. I'm a slave driver. I don't want anyone happy unless my dick is inside of them," Diego winked at me.

"Hmm…does that mean I need to bend over?" Blane asked, as if he was contemplating a hard math problem.

"Nah, opening your mouth is perfectly fine."

"Why am I listening to this?" I asked, as I started to walk away, but Blane stopped me with a muscular arm to my waist. He pulled me into his chest and leaned down to my ear.

"You can't tell me you're not affected by me." I could hear the mirth in his voice, and all I wanted to do was smack that stupid grin off of his face.

Moving in with Diego was a smart move on my part because I could continue to paint and earn money while I tried to figure out what my next step in life was going to be. I also felt safe in his club, like no one could harm me. The only problem was, I was living with two of the most flirtatious men I've ever met. Kace and Jett were the complete opposite; they didn't show many emotions at all…they didn't show their feelings. They had mastered the art of emotional detachment, making it impossible to understand what they might be possibly thinking in their gorgeously brilliant minds, but not Diego and Blane. They would lick me as I walked by if I let them.

But, even though Jett and Kace didn't voice their emotions, I could see it in their eyes, especially Jett. He would lighten up when he saw me walk into a room, his eyes would become sinister when I would tease him, and he would soften when I needed him to.

I guess that didn't matter now, though, because even though I thought he might have loved me, what it came down to was, he didn't trust me. Never once had I given him the impression that there was any other man but him, but he couldn't see that; it was as if he had blinders on and he only saw what he wanted to see.

I can't live my life like that. I refused to live my life like that, but now that I made that decision, I was hurting. I couldn't lie about it; I was fucking hurting.

"Hey, where did you go?" Blane asked.

"Sorry, just thinking." I pulled away and grabbed another drink from Diego. Too many heavy thoughts during a fun time with friends.

"Thinking about Jett?" Diego asked, while pulling me into his chest.

"No," I lied.

"Yeah, okay, Goldie. You're the worst liar ever."

"We're not talking about this," I pulled away. "We're learning how to pole dance." I set my drink down and clapped my hands. "Now, line up, I want to see you guys move."

"I need music if I'm going to do this," Blane said with a cringe.

"And another shot," Diego added.

"Ugh, you guys are annoying. Fine, let me get…"

"Ahhhhhh!!!!!" screams came from down the hallway, scaring the ever living piss out of me.

I flung my body up against the wall in sheer panic as the voices filtered in. Getting ready for a complete attack, I put my hands in knife hand mode and got in my karate attack position.

One by one, Pepper, Babs, Francy, and Tootse filed into the room, holding up bottles of booze and screaming at the top of their lungs.

With my hand to my heart, making sure it didn't beat right out of my chest, I asked, "What the hell are you four doing here?"

"Drinking with our girl," Babs said, while eyeing Blane up and down.

Francy tossed a bottle of vodka to Diego and told him to find a place for it.

Pepper grabbed ahold of the cap of the whiskey bottle in her hand and downed some, right before handing it over to me, while Tootse ran up to me with her hands wide open and in attack mode.

In a matter of seconds, I had Tootse's hands squeezing my breasts, Pepper shoving liquor down my throat, Babs whispering in my ear about Blane, and Francy smacking my ass.

"Hold up," I said, stopping the onslaught of Jett Girls. "How the hell did you know I was here?"

With her hand on her hip, Babs gave me a pointed look and

said, "Come on, Lo, we're not that stupid. You were either with your bartender friend Carlos, or Diego. We called Carlos and got the old negative from him, so we thought we would come over here."

"You ladies are welcome over here anytime," Diego replied, while perusing all the girls, sin lacing his eyes.

"Blane," Blane introduced himself to Babs, who would not take her eyes off of him.

"Oh, my God, he has an accent," Tootse squealed, as Babs took Blane's hand.

"Babs, nice to meet you. Are those muscles real or are they the product of those finicky steroids?"

"Babs!" I chastised.

"What? It's a legitimate question. If guys can ask about our breasts, we should be able to ask about their muscles. Listen, I was screwed one time by a guy who took steroids. Let's just say his smallest muscle was hiding in his pants. God, it was like staring at a little piece of macaroni between two ham bones." She shivered as she remembered the small dick man.

Blane chuckled next to her and said, "They're all real, sweetheart. No supplements for me."

"Mmm, I like that."

"What about your tits?" he asked, eyeing Babs' cleavage. "Are those real?"

"Like you even had to ask. They're real, hot stuff. Want to see them?"

"Babs, keep them stuffed away for at least a half hour," Francy scolded. "Remember what we're here for."

"Yeah, but I didn't know we would be meeting this hunk of meat over here."

"Why are you here?" I asked, feeling nervous all of a sudden. Did something happen to Jett?

"We wanted to spend some time with our girl. Just because you're no longer a Jett Girl doesn't mean you're still not one of us. It's time to take some shots; it's been too long," Pepper called out, as she pulled some shot glasses out of her purse.

Classic Pepper.

"So, does this mean we have to leave?" Diego asked. "And, you know I have shot glasses, right?"

"You don't have pink ones," Pepper said, while handing them

out.

"You have me on that."

Once the shot glasses were handed out, Pepper looked at a sad looking Diego and Blane and rolled her eyes.

"God, go get yourself some shot glasses. We usually don't allow men into our little circle, but we'll make an exception, since Babs can't seem to stop drooling and thrusting her hips at beef cake."

"But, you have to take your shirts off," Babs demanded.

"Easy enough," Blane entertained, as he stripped off his shirt, showing off his perfectly built body.

A collective sigh echoed through the room as we took in his well-defined chest, literally bulging biceps, and toned forearms. I never knew forearms could be so attractive. Jett was cut, like fucking seriously cut…to the point that I didn't understand why he was a mortal, but Blane was more muscular in a body builder type of way. Even though Blane was insanely hot, I would take Jett's body over Blane's any day.

No! No, I would not take Jett. Fuck, what was wrong with me? I was supposed to be forgetting him.

"Uh, hello, I'm about to take my shirt off too," Diego complained, as he gripped the hem of his shirt in his hands, waiting for everyone's attention to turn to him.

"Oh, sorry, Diego, please proceed," I giggled.

"That's right," he nodded, as he slowly started taking his shirt off.

His rich mocha skin was slowly exposed as he moved his shirt purposely off his body in slow, seductive movements. Diego's body was just like Kace's, perfectly defined in every crevice, with strong shoulders and well-defined arms. His abs modeled Jett's, with a deep V near his waist making me want to inch closer to him.

"Damn," Pepper breathed out. "We need to hang out here more often. Who knew Lo was hiding all the hotties?"

"I even think I felt a little twerk from my lady folds," Francy said, while pressing her hand against her crotch.

"Oh, my God, honey! My nipples got hard from watching," Tootse confessed, as she hung on Francy's arm.

"I guess that solidifies it; Diego is the winner," Pepper awarded.

"Wait, what?"" Blane cut in. "When the fuck did this become

a competition? If I would have known, I would have gone all out. I demand a redo."

"Too late, the ladies have spoken," Diego said, while smacking Blane in the chest and then taking off to get some more shot glasses.

"This is bullshit," Blane huffed, as he crossed his arms over his chest and sat in a chair.

"Aw, poor baby. You can give me a private show later," Babs winked as she sat on his lap, just inviting herself. Blane seemed to cheer up from Babs' attention. There was no doubt in my mind those two would be banging soon, and fuck if they weren't an attractive pairing with their blonde hair and beautiful skin. Those would be some good looking babies…that was for damn sure.

Once Diego returned, we all held out our shot glasses and watched as Francy poured us some intoxicating liquid. With a collective clink, we cheered, and downed our first shot. The smooth liquid burned down my throat, awakening me for the first time in a while. It was good to have my girls with me; it was energizing.

"Where's Lyla?" I asked, as Francy started to pour more shots.

"She and Kace got in some argument," Pepper brushed off.

"They are so fucking," Babs said. "It's obvious. The tension between those two is ridiculous."

"You really think they are?" I asked, feeling giddy. If I could pick anyone for Kace, it would be Lyla; she would give him a good run for his money, and I would pay good money to sit in the front row of that show.

"No doubt about it," Francy chimed in. "They are either fighting or nowhere to be seen, which can only mean one thing, they're fucking."

"And that hooker hasn't told me," I said, a little surprised. "Next time I see her, I'll be harassing her. No one bones and doesn't tell me. I need to know where all dicks and pussies that are close to me go."

"You keeping score?" Diego asked. "If that's the case, then should I start listing off all the pussy I've seen this week?"

A laugh escaped my throat. "Please, Diego, the only pussy you've seen this week is one on a computer screen."

"What, does that not count?" he smirked.

Infuriating man.

"Alright, what's the game?" Blane asked, while clapping his hands together.

"Truth or dare," Tootse said with excitement.

"Aw, babe, you're cute," Francy replied, with a kiss to Tootse's nose. "So innocent."

"Is that not a good suggestion?" she asked, confused.

"It's perfect," I cut in. "Alright, Diego, truth or dare?"

The devilish grin he had on his face scared me too much, I was going to make sure I only gave him options, because by the way he was looking at me, I could see things getting frisky…fast.

"Dare," he winked at me.

Gulping, I nodded and tried to think of something to dare him.

"Make out with Lo," Babs said.

"What, are we twelve?" I asked. "He's not making out with me."

"I'll take it," he said, while walking toward me, his eyes set on my lips.

Putting my hands out, I stopped him and said, "I asked him truth or dare, so I get to tell him what to do."

"That is how the game is played," Blane defended me, but I was pretty sure he had ulterior motives. Even though Babs was sitting on his lap, he still looked at me like he wanted to eat me up.

"Fine," Diego backed up, but not far enough. His cologne and bare body were fogging my senses, and I could feel my body warming up to the idea of making out with him. He had the most luscious lips ever; he could probably do some real damage to my horny status with those lips.

"You going to pick something there, darling?" Diego asked while laughing.

"Yes," I defended. "Umm, how about you give Blane a lap dance?"

The twisted look on Diego's face had me laughing out loud from my very gut. It felt good to laugh, to just let loose and have fun. It felt like there was a weight on my shoulders for a while, and now that it was lifted, it felt freeing to just relax, to enjoy the company around me.

"Come on, Goldie, spare me."

"Hold up," Babs said, while holding her hand out. "Your name is Goldie?"

It never dawned on me that the girls didn't actually know my real name. They always knew me as Lo, and that was it. Then again, I had no clue what their real names were either.

"Yeah," I laughed. "Is that going to be a problem?"

The girls looked at each other and then shrugged their shoulders.

"You'll always be Lo to us," Pepper said.

"Well, what are your names?" I asked, curious to hear their real names.

"Ahh, that's something you will never find out," Babs smiled. "Now, back to this man on man lap dance."

Diego groaned and looked at me with those beautiful light eyes of his. "Come on, babe, pick something else." Pepper raised an eyebrow at me at Diego's term of endearment. I ignored her silent question. "At least make me give one of the girls a lap dance. I'm too fucking nervous I might turn Blane on."

"Fuck you, man," Blane said, while sitting up a little taller with Babs still on his lap. "I dare you to try to get me up."

Babs shifted and looked Blane up and down. "Did you just ask him to give you a fucking throbbing gristle? I don't think I'm cool with sharing," she smiled.

"What you're worried about is sharing?" Pepper asked. "I think I would be more worried about something else."

"If they want to be gay, let them be gay," Francy waved, as she pulled Tootse in closer to her.

"Yeah, do you have something wrong with the gay?" Tootse asked, while she kissed Francy's arm.

Pepper gave her an admonishing look. "Don't pull that gay shit on me. You know I like the gays, especially you lesbians. Everyone needs a token gay in their group; I'm a lucky girl to have two."

"We are a hot commodity," Francy added.

"It's hard to keep up with the demand. And then there's the whole recertification process we have to go through to maintain our gay license. You should see the holes they make us jump through."

"Is that with two fingers or three?" Babs asked with a smirk.

"Oh, you heteros, what are fingers when you can use fists?" Francy asked, while raising her fist to the sky.

"Oh, fuck," I cringed, just thinking about a fist going up my vagina."

"You've never been fisted?" Babs asked, as if it was the craziest thing she'd ever heard.

"No!" I practically shouted. "Why the fuck would I have ever been fisted? I'd rather not spend every minute of my life doing keegles to get back down to a normal and appropriate diameter for my pussy ring."

"Where's the challenge in that?" Babs asked, while Blane studied her intently, probably trying to gauge if she was serious.

"It's called being kind to your snatch. Am I right?" I asked Tootse and Francy. "Out of everyone, you two should know proper pussy etiquette."

"While studying at the University of LesboLand, we learned in Pussy Principles 101 that a well-treated snatch is a fine ass catch. Keep that garden trimmed, that clit wet, and your hole tight, the classic rules to an orgasmic night," Francy said without blinking an eye.

The room fell silent for a second before we all threw our heads back and laughed.

This was exactly what I needed, my girls, my shots, and the new men in my life. Maybe I wasn't so lost after all; maybe I was going to be just fine without Jett Colby by my side…maybe.

22
"GLITTER & GOLD"

Rex

Fuck.

That's all I could think as I made my way through Kitten's Castle to a black out booth.

Fucking hell.

In a matter of seconds, my life had been flipped upside down; I was taken in for questioning, I spent the night in jail, and now I'm on trial for prostitution, embezzlement, and a fucking Ponzi scheme.

Was I innocent?

Fuck no, I wasn't innocent. I was the furthest thing from innocent. I was so God damn guilty that I was grasping at anything to make this hellish nightmare go away. I would do just about anything to avoid the wrath that was coming my way.

That was why I found myself hunched over in a booth at Kitten's Castle, awaiting my caller. I received a letter this morning, inviting me to talk tonight. I didn't know who it was from or what they were going to say, but what I did know was they wanted to talk about my future, in private.

I was a desperate man, so meeting in such a filthy strip club wasn't an issue to me. I would do just about anything right now.

The club hadn't changed since the last time I paid the rat hole of an establishment a visit, except for the workers...the girls were different. They were far more classless than the previous girls. They didn't seem to care about their appearance, nor how they spoke or presented themselves. The standards at Kitten's Castle had dropped immensely.

Music pounded against the walls as the stage acts grabbed the attention of every drooling man in the vicinity. The girl on stage was a pretty red head, not something I would necessarily touch, but she was nice to look at. She was completely nude except for a miniscule thong barely covering her assets, and her breasts were beyond fake, but enticing enough to make a man yearn.

"See something you like?" a familiar voice asked from the side of the booth. I couldn't quite see who it was, given the darkness of the booth, but the moment he stepped forward, right in front of the table, I knew right away who it was, I would know that silhouette anywhere.

Jett Colby.

Fire raged within me as I realized he was the one who was coming to meet me. My hopes for salvation immediately fell; Jett Colby wouldn't be offering me an out, not after our history.

"What do you want?" I asked, as I sat back in the booth.

Stepping forward, Jett placed his hand on the table and leaned toward me. I could see his face from the flicker of the small candle on the table.

"Let's have a little conversation, shall we? But, before we get started, we need to wait on one more person."

I could guess who it was going to be; there was no doubt in my mind. It was going to be Goldie. I should have known all along. Leo was going to have my head.

"Well, where is she?" I asked, looking around. "Spreading her legs for someone else?"

The least I could do was strike him where it hurt.

"Who?" he asked, not flinching from my words.

"Don't treat me like an idiot. You know I'm talking about Goldie; where is she? I don't have all night to wait."

"You do, actually," Jett corrected me. "Because, last I heard, you were pretty damn desperate to figure any way out of the hole you put yourself in, and for your information, Goldie and I haven't talked since she left. Like I told you before, we're not together. I don't know how many times I have to tell you that until you get it through that dense, disturbingly ugly head of yours."

My jaw twitched as I refrained from raising my fist to the man. The last thing I needed was assault and battery on my record as well, and knowing the prick standing in front of me, he would press charges.

"What the hell are you doing here?" came Leo's voice from the side.

"Ah, just in time, please take a seat...Father." The lightness in Jett's voice had my knuckles itching to be plowed through his face. He was just too damn happy.

Begrudgingly, Leo sat down next to me in the booth, while Jett took a seat across from the both of us. He perched his folded hands on the table, just as a waitress came over and asked if we wanted anything. With a flick of his wrist, Jett answered no for all of us, and then turned his gaze on us.

In the darkness of the booth, I could still see the glint in his eyes. The arrogant bastard couldn't be happier...it was written all over his face. He had everything he wanted, he had me and Leo squirming in our seats, and he had Lot 17. Plus, he had the whole damn city wanting to lick his damn nut sac with the plans he'd laid out for Lot 17. Watching his press conference was worse than spending a night in jail until I was able to post bail. He looked so pompous, up on stage with that stupid smirk on his face...

"I'm so glad you two could join me tonight," Jett stated with cool composure. "Especially given your new circumstances."

"What the hell do you want?" Leo asked, raising his voice. The man was angry. I actually hadn't seen him since the club was raided by the police.

"We'll get to that," Jett smiled. "What I really want to talk about is your embezzlement and financial problems. Father, I thought you were better than that."

Leo leaned back in his seat and crossed his arms over his chest. "You're just finding too much humor in this situation, aren't you?"

"Where is the humor when it comes to you screwing over thousands of people with a Ponzi scheme? A Ponzi scheme! What about your little prostitution ring, did you really think you weren't going to be caught? You're despicable."

"Like you're one to talk, with the Lafayette Club; you don't think that's despicable?" I stated. "You did the same thing as us with those girls, you just cover it up better."

"That's where you're wrong. The Lafayette Club doesn't even come close to what you two were conducting behind closed doors. I offered the girls an opportunity to better themselves, all you did was blackmail those girls and make them work for you. Do you really think that's a way to conduct business?"

"Is that what this is?" Leo asked, "A little economics lesson?" Leo snorted and then leaned forward. "The only reason you're in the position you're in right now is because of me. I suggest you don't forget that."

"Once again, you're wrong. I'm in the position I'm in today because I worked my ass off and utilized the heart my mother gave me, rather than the empty soul you tried to instill upon me. There's conducting business, and there's stealing from others, taking advantage of human beings…and that's where you two faltered. The power got to you, and now, you're going to reap what you deserve."

"You think you're so perfect, don't you?" Leo asked, growing angrier by the second.

"No, I don't, actually. I'm far from it, thanks to you and the manipulative childhood I had to endure."

"Ahh, is that what you're calling it? Manipulative? I taught you everything you know; I gave you a set of steel balls, boy. I suggest you remember that."

Even though I was in a world of trouble and looking at possibly a lifetime in prison, I was rather enjoying the little "Daddy hates me" conversation that was going on. I knew for a fact Leo despised his own son; he'd told me many times. That was why Leo took me under his wing. Maybe it wasn't the smartest decision on my part, now that I think about it.

"The only thing I learned from you is how not to treat people, how not to conduct yourself in a professional atmosphere, and how to push someone as far away from you as possible," Jett trailed off as he looked down at his hands.

It was easy to see his last comment struck a nerve with him, and I knew exactly why.

A laugh escaped me as I pointed out, "Seems look like you

took daddy dearest's advice when it came to Goldie."

A sharp look from Jett tried to split me in half, but I was unfazed by his glares by now.

"Goldie isn't a topic we discuss, ever."

Both Leo and I laughed together. I turned to Leo and said, "At least we were able to take away the one thing he wanted, even though he denied it constantly."

"There is nothing between Goldie and me," Jett cut in. "Like I said…"

Leo held up his hand and cut him off. "Save us the bullshit. We know how much that girl means to you; it's undeniable, so stop making a fool of yourself and trying to contradict your feelings for the woman. I'm just glad she came to her senses and left you."

Jett's jaw ticked as he tried to think of what to say next. I could see his mind working, trying to find a way to justify what happened between him and Goldie, but it was useless. The man knew exactly how he pushed her away, which was punishment enough.

Clearing his throat, Jett sat up and said, "Goldie is not the reason why I came here. I came here to tell you that your assets will be repossessed and will find a safe home."

"What are you talking about?" I asked, while I could feel the fury start to boil up in Leo.

"I'm going to tell it to you two straight. I've already talked to the bank, and once you are convicted, which you will be, there is no denying that, I've made it my mission to own everything you two have ever purchased together, at a very decent rate, thanks to my many connections. So, your little empire that you thought you built, that will be mine."

"You son of a bitch," Leo roared, as he reached across the table. Jett scooted out of his chair just in time to avoid his father's attack.

In rage, I watched as the man who'd been my nemesis ever since I could remember, adjusted his tie and looked down on us.

"Good luck, boys, have fun in prison."

With that, Jett Colby walked out of my life, probably for the last time.

I buried my head in my hands and tried to comprehend what was happening, as my stomach twisted in knots. Never in my life did I think I would ever hit rock bottom, but here I fucking was, without a life saver to be tossed out to me. I was totally and utterly fucked.

"This is your fault," Leo spat at me.

"How is this my fault?" I asked, while looking up at him through my hands. "I do believe the Ponzi scheme was your idea, the embezzlement was your grand plan, and the club was the pinnacle of your scheme to get back at your son, your own son!" I roared. "I should have stayed as far away from you as possible."

"Too late for 'should ofs,' son," Leo said with a menacing tone.

I got up from the booth and adjusted my suit jacket. I looked Leo square in the eyes and said, "Don't ever call me 'son,' you sadistic bastard."

With one last glance, I retreated from Leo and went back to my place. It was time to face my Creator. There was only one way out of this life, and hell if I was going to rot in prison for the next hundred years.

I was a lost man; it was about time I found where I was supposed to be…in fucking hell.

23
"JEALOUS"

Jett

A lone trumpet played in the far distance as I sipped my café au lait and observed the many tourists lining up to get a taste of Café du Monde's beignets. It's been a long time since I've been down to the quarter for my Saturday ritual. Things have been hectic, to say the least, and I wasn't about to visit the Quarter while I was still with Goldie if she couldn't come with me.

Goldie.

My heart still ached from the thought of her. It took me a couple of phone calls, but I was able to track her down. I should have known she would have gone to stay with Diego; they'd had a close connection ever since she went to go help him out with painting his club. I just prayed she wasn't working there with him as well. She had plenty of money from being a Jett Girl to keep her afloat. I wondered if she'd used any of it. I was tempted to look at the bank account I set up for her, but knew that was an invasion of privacy, and the last thing I wanted was to piss her off more.

She was mad. Really mad. I didn't blame her. She was right about everything she said. I didn't trust her, I didn't believe in her, and I had zero faith. I didn't blame her for leaving; I deserved it. I was a master at pushing people away, and I'd done a damn fine job of kicking her out of my life.

But I was over and done with that now. I knew what I wanted. I wanted a life with Goldie; I wanted everything. I wanted her to be mine, to share a home with her, not just as a Jett Girl, but as my girlfriend...as my wife one day. I wanted her to carry my child one day. I wanted nothing more than to grow old with her in my arms.

The only problem was, she wanted nothing to do with me, but that would be changing.

A Vietnamese woman who worked at the café took my money and smiled gently at me, as if to wish me a good day. Her smile carried me out onto the streets, as I observed the bustling sidewalks of Jackson Square.

My life was coming full circle, as I walked the same route I took when I first dropped my business card off to Goldie. It was a risky move, getting as close to her as I did, but there was no stopping me then, like there was no stopping me now. I was on a mission, and hell if I wouldn't follow through with it.

I placed my sunglasses over my eyes, rolled up the sleeves to the button-up light blue shirt I was wearing, and made sure it was tucked into my jeans. Even though it was a casual day for me, I still made sure to present myself well in public; it was the one thing I learned from my father that I would never forget. Image is everything, especially when it comes to someone in my position.

Leisurely, I walked around Jackson square, taking in all the palm readers, side show acts, musicians, and artists. One of the many beauties of New Orleans was you could be as weird and outlandish as you wanted, and no one was going to judge you for it, because they all chalked it up to the atmosphere the city had to offer. Some people may say New York City is full of crazy eclectic people, but that just tells me they've never been to New Orleans, because where else would you find a man painted in gold, a shopping cart turned musical instrument, and break dancing on cardboard? Only New Orleans.

Crowds gathered around someone who was balancing a bowling ball on their nose, a challenging feat for sure, when I spotted a wave of perfectly golden hair flying in the wind.

My Little One.

Even though it's only been a few short weeks since I've seen her, it still felt like it's been months. I missed everything about her. The way she smiled at me through her eyelashes and the little stolen moments where she glanced in my direction to convey how much she really wanted me. I missed her sweet touches, the way my name sounded rolling off her tongue, and the sassy mouth she never seemed to know how to turn off. Fuck, I needed her in my life, desperately.

Taking a deep breath, I stepped forward and started making my way toward her. Like I thought, she was once again selling her beautiful art in Jackson Square. I took in the chalk-covered canvases that hung on the wrought iron fence that surrounded the square. They were impeccable, like always, but seemed almost darker, not as whimsical as I was used to her art being. I wondered if I did that to her, if the edge that was in her art now was because of me.

There was only one way to find out.

Her back was to me, so she didn't see me approaching, giving me more of an opportunity to take her in. Her hair flowed out from under a sun hat and her shoulders were exposed from a red and white tank top she was wearing. Her legs sprouted out from a pair of short denim shorts and a white pair of Keds graced her perfect little feet.

My hand grazed my jaw as I took in everything about her. How could I have been such a damn fool to give up something so good?

Not wanting to wait any longer, I made the rest of my way toward her, just as a bulky man with blond hair sidled up next to her in a spare lawn chair and handed her a drink, while kissing her on the cheek at the same time.

I froze in my tracks at the display of affection from another man. Sweat started to creep down my back as rage boiled inside of me. Did she really find someone else that easily? Was I that forgettable?

I tried to convince myself I wasn't, but then again, I hurt her, I was the one who drove her away. If she found someone else, maybe she was really trying to move on from the hell I put her through.

Looking back at our relationship, I'm now realizing there weren't many moments where we weren't struggling against something trying to hold us back. There was always something between us; it had never been an easy relationship for us. If it wasn't my insane stupidity of stubbornness, it was my dad.

Instead of going up to her, I stood back and observed her interaction with the new man. She laughed easily with him as they pointed at something in the far distance, probably where the man just came from. Goldie took a sip of the drink she held in her hand, and then handed it over to the stranger. With disgust, I watched him wrap his lips around the same straw Goldie used and take a drink.

The urge to punch my hand through a wall overcame me as I continued to twitch with anger at what was unfolding right in front of me. She was with someone else. It was obvious from the affectionate looks they were giving each other, the shared drink they were sipping from, and the easygoing camaraderie they shared.

Turning around, I ran my hand through my hair and tried to figure out what I should do. I couldn't possibly go up to Goldie now and talk to her about my plans, about what I wanted for our future, not in front of Mr. No Neck.

Fuck.

Looking over my shoulder, I eyed them once more, seeing how easily they talked, how the air between them seemed so relaxed, without worry. I hated it, I hated him.

What the hell was I supposed to do? I wasn't expecting another man to be in the picture, to rip my heart out in one smooth movement in front of the tourist mecca of New Orleans.

A sharp pain radiated through my chest as I tried to catch my breath. It couldn't end like this, could it? Was life really this unfair? I didn't believe in happily ever afters, since I've never once seen one in my life, but I did believe in luck, and Goldie landing in my hands, in my club, in my life, that was pure luck, making me the luckiest bastard in the world.

That was until I blew it all with my stubborn pride.

That was the bane of my existence, my pride. It ate me up and turned me into a man I hated, a man who didn't take chances because he was too damn scared to venture out of the protective shell he made for himself.

I didn't want to be that man anymore. I didn't want to sit around, trying to protect my heart so I never got hurt again. No, I wanted to make a change in my life. I wanted to be fucking happy, for once in my life. I wanted to know what it felt like to have a woman, the woman of my dreams, wake up next to me every morning. I needed this girl; she was the key to my happiness, and hell if I was going to let my pride get in the way once more.

Taking a deep breath, I turned back around and faced Goldie and the mystery man. Making sure my shirt wasn't askew, I ran my hands down it and adjusted my belt, making sure it was facing forward. Feeling put together, I walked up to Goldie with my mind set on one thing and one thing only, getting her back.

"Hello, Goldie," I spoke with sincerity. Slowly, I took off my sunglasses and looked down at the shocked look on that gorgeous face of hers.

Her legs that were once propped up on the fence flew to the ground as she sat up and adjusted the hat on the top of her head.

Clearing her throat and scanning me up and down, she said, "Um, Jett. Hi."

Her voice was sweet, but confused; it was so damn adorable, I just wanted to grab her by the waist and take her against the damn fence.

"Your artwork is extraordinary, as usual," I complimented.

"Thank you," she said, while looking down at her exposed thighs. Thighs I wanted to spread as wide as they would fucking go so I could bury myself deep inside of her, the only place I've ever felt completely at peace.

This was going to be harder than I thought.

"Who's your friend?" I asked, while nodding at the man who started sizing me up the moment I walked up to Goldie.

Once I addressed him, he took off his sunglasses, and that was when I recognized him.

Blane Wilson.

Blane went to school with Kace and me at one point. He was a good man, but had gotten in some deep shit.

Why the hell was he hanging out with Goldie?

"Blane?" I asked.

"Jett Colby," he stood up and put out his hand. "Damn, you look good, man. Never thought I would see you grow into those lanky tennis arms of yours."

"I see you're still using the steroids," I joked. Blane was always more developed than anyone we knew. The man was a walking piece of muscle.

Blane nodded his head and smiled, while sizing me up once again. "What can we do you for?"

We? Were they really a we? I glanced over at Goldie, who had her head down, avoiding all eye contact with me. My heart sank at the thought of Goldie moving on. How did I address her now, with Blane at her side, clearly in protection mode? I could hold my own when it came to a fight, easily, thanks to Kace's training, but I couldn't make up for the thirty pounds of muscle Blane had over me.

Trying not to look fazed, I squatted down next to Goldie and lifted her chin slightly, so she had to look me in the eyes. I ignored the glare that was coming from Blane and spoke softly.

"Goldie, can I please talk to you, in private?"

"What you say to her can be said in front of me, Jett," Blane warned, all friendliness escaping his voice.

Taking a deep breath, I straightened, and looked Blane in the eyes.

"Blane, I think you're a good man who's made some poor decisions. I can see you're trying to make a better life for yourself, so I would avoid another bad decision…like standing in my way of Goldie, and move on."

"Funny that you think you can just come back here and act like you didn't break her heart," Blane said, as he drew closer to me.

"I'm afraid what transpired between Goldie and me is none of your business," I answered back, while I stepped forward, ready for what Blane had in store for me.

Moving in closer, Blane responded, "It is my business when…"

"Stop!" Goldie said, while jumping between us and placing her small hands on both of our chests to separate us. It was almost comical to see her try to put herself between Blane and me. She turned to Blane and said, "I can handle this, Blane. Please, watch my paintings for me."

"You sure?" Blane asked, as he picked up Goldie's hand and brought it to his mouth.

Right then and there, I wanted to bury my fist in his mouth. I wanted to crack every perfect white tooth of his. I wanted to make the man bleed, and I wasn't a violent person, but do not touch my girl…ever!

"Positive, thank you."

I watched in horror as Goldie stood on her toes and placed a kiss on Blane's cheek. I felt like I was going to lose everything that had built up over the past few weeks. All the pent up angst, the need for her, the urge to take her the way I wanted…it was all about to come crashing down with that little display of affection.

I felt cold, numb, like I was nothing but an empty void.

Slowly, I watched as Goldie stepped away from him and then turned toward me. With a nod of her head toward the stairs that led into the greens of the square, I followed her with a dejected demeanor, a fucking broken heart, as I realized this was going to be my last attempt to try to win her back.

Leaning up against a stone wall, she looked up at me and said, "What do you want, Jett?"

"Are you with him?" I asked, needing to know, needing to end the misery I was going through.

"Excuse me? I don't think that's any of your business," she said defiantly.

"It is my business," I closed in on her, needing to be closer. "Tell me, are you with him?"

"And, if I was?" she lifted her chin.

If she was? What the fuck would I do? Probably lose my damn mind and go ape shit crazy on the man's ass, but she didn't need to know that.

"That's something I will deal with if it's true. So, are you with him?"

She bit on her bottom lip as she looked to the side and nodded her head yes.

Every bone in my body melted from the confirmation. I felt like my heart burst in my chest, and not in a good way. She was with someone else.

"I see," I said, as I cleared my throat and took a step back. "The least you could have done was to have the dignity to look me in the eye when you say you're with him."

Her head dropped, and all I could see was the sun hat that was blocking my view of her gorgeous face.

"Goldie, look at me."

She shook her head no and turned her back toward me. Needing her to tell me to my face she was with Blane, I gently turned her back around and lifted her chin. Tears fell from her eyes as she looked up at me. I thought I knew pain…that was until I saw Goldie cry.

The need to wrap her up in my arms and make everything better overtook my body as I tried to pull her into my chest, but her hands stopped me.

"Don't," she said between tear-soaked breaths.

"Goldie…" I said softly. "Please, talk to me. Why are you crying? Is he hurting you?"

"No!" her head snapped up. "You're hurting me, Jett. You're the one making me cry, not him."

The memories I have of Goldie are happy ones, sexy ones, heartfelt ones. The Goldie standing in front of me was not a Goldie I knew. She was angry, upset, and mad. I've seen her mad at me before, but not like this, as if she'd lost the spark in her eyes.

I was at a loss. I had no clue how to handle this, how to talk to her without sounding like a tool, but I could feel her slipping away with each passing second. I had to do something. I had to throw myself out there.

"I'm sorry," I said, while trying to take her hand, but she denied me that as well.

"Is that all?" she asked, as she wiped a tear from under her eye right before she crossed her arms over her chest.

"No, I want to talk to you."

"Talk then," she said, while gesturing to me.

I ran my hand through my hair and put myself out there.

"I came here to ask you out."

Her arms uncrossed as she stared at me with the most adorable perplexed face.

"What did you say?"

My heart beat rapidly in my chest as I said, "I wanted to ask you out on a date. Just you and me."

I could see a bit of her eyes start to light up again at my question, which gave me hope…hope that was threatened to be ripped right out from under me with one little word from her.

"Why would you want to ask me out?"

She wasn't going to make this fucking easy at all. I wasn't one to show my feelings, to make them known, especially in a public place, so I was struggling to find the right words, but knew if I didn't, I wouldn't ever see her again, simple as that.

"Goldie, I've been a bastard. I've treated you with disrespect and acted like a fool full of jealousy. I didn't give you a chance to prove your ability to take care of us, and I'm forever regretful about that. I know I can't change the past, but I can start a new future. I want another chance, I want to be able to treat you like you're supposed to be treated. I want a life with you, but I know I have to prove it to you first."

"That's right you have to prove it to me," she snapped at me, while pushing my chest with her finger. A small smile threatened to cross my face, but I held my features together so I didn't piss her off any more. "It's so infuriating how you can just walk in to my life again and disrupt everything. It's not fair. I should be able to have you come up to me and not start sweating or have to clench my thighs together because my damn pussy can smell your dick from a mile away. I mean, damn it, Jett, you have no right showing up here. I'm doing fine without you," she ranted, and then said softly, "I'm doing fine."

Stepping closer, I asked, "Are you sure you're doing fine?"

Her blue eyes glistened up at me as tears threatened to fall over once again. She nodded slowly, but closed her eyes shut, not being able to lie to me. I knew she was lying; it was written all over her face.

"Don't lie to me, Goldie."

"What do you care? You have everything you ever wanted. Now that Lot 17 is your property and your dad is headed for the slammer, what else do you need? What else do you really want? It's not like you're ready to open up that cold heart of yours."

Ouch, but I deserved that.

"That's exactly what I want, Goldie. I want to start from the beginning with you. I want to learn who you are, date you, and spoil you. I want to do this right; I want to do us right."

"There is no us, Jett," she tried to push away, but I didn't let her go far.

"Then, why are you so upset?" I asked, hoping I would strike a nerve. By the look in her eyes, I did.

"Why am I so upset? Hmm, let me see…"

Oh shit, sarcasm at its best was coming my way.

"You insert yourself into my life, like literally don't give me an option other than to follow your rules and do what you ask, because, heaven forbid if your voice isn't sexy as hell. Then you take me up to your stupid Bourbon Room, where you fucking show me what sex is, what it feels like to have a real man bury himself inside of me. You show me a whole new world of sex…and damn it if I don't love and hate you for it. Then I go and get attached to you, because you're this brilliantly sexy man who is oh-so-fucking sensitive and just 'needs time'," she continued, as she used air quotes. "Which is just fucking fantastic, because by then, I'm already attached, I'm already in deep, so thanks for that. And when I finally think we're going somewhere and you're taking me to events, you decide to hide me instead, increasing the craving I have for you. And then, do you know what happened, Jettonathan?" she asked, with her hands on her hips, using the stupid ass name she came up with for me. I'm about to answer when she holds her hand up to stop me. "No, I don't want to hear it; I'll tell you what happened. I went and tried to make everything better, just asking for one simple thing from you. To have faith in me like I had in you, but holy shit was that too hard for you, because the powerful man needs his control," she waved her hands around like a lunatic as she spoke to me. "Heaven forbid the male debutant with the penis of a Greek god doesn't have control for a short period of time. Fuck, Jett, you ruined everything! You ask why I'm upset? Because, since my parents passed, you've taken the one and only thing I've ever cared about. You took away your heart."

What was I supposed to say to that? She was right, everything she said was absolutely right.

Instead of arguing and being the stubborn man I usually was, I nodded my head and said, "I know; I fucked up."

Shock registered across her face as she swallowed my words with her rant.

"Oh, so you agree?" she asked, while she scrunched her nose.

"Completely."

"Well," she looked around and then patted her shorts. "I don't really know what to say now. I wasn't expecting you to agree."

"Do you not want me to agree so you can keep arguing?" I asked with a smile that I knew would hit her hard.

"Oh, no, don't, you can't do that," she said, while shaking her finger at my face.

"Do what?" I smiled again, inching closer to her.

"You know what, that whole charming male dominant thing. I

will not fall for it."

"You sure?" I asked, as I moved inches away from her and rested my hands on her hips.

"Yes, I'm positive," she sucked in a deep breath at my proximity. "Wh-what are you doing?"

"Trying to remove that crinkle between your eyes."

"Blane will see you," she said quickly, trying to deter me.

"Like I give a fuck about Blane; don't bullshit me, you're not seeing him." I took a shot, hoping I was right. I didn't believe she was seeing Blane by the mere fact of how she reacted to me, to our situation.

Looking away, she whispered she was, but I didn't bite; she was lying.

"Look me in the eyes and tell me you're with another man. Look at me Goldie."

Sighing, she turned her head and stared me in the eyes.

"Tell me you're with him," I repeated.

She bit her bottom lip as her eyes searched mine. With a frustrated grunt, she pushed away from me and started pacing the little section of the garden we were in.

"Ugh, you're so infuriating. Of course I'm not seeing him. You happy?"

"Very," I smirked.

"I hate you," she spat back, while she looked at me with fury.

"No, you don't," I smiled back.

Shaking her head at me, she sat down on the half wall and brought her knees up to her chest.

"What do you want from me?"

"You know what I want," I said, as I took a seat next to her. "I want to date you. I want to start fresh with you. Treat you the way you deserve to be treated."

"Because you want sex..." she said, while she buried her head in her knees.

"No," I said softly, as I moved my head down to her ear. "Not because I want sex, because I want you, Goldie; I want your heart, your smart mouth, your defiance, I want everything."

"I hate that I want the same thing," she admitted. "I want to hate you, I want you to leave me alone, but I know that won't fix the numbing ache in my heart. Why does this have to be so hard?"

"The best things in life are hard, Little One," I replied.

Silence fell between us while I gave her time to think about my proposal. I didn't want to pressure her, but damn it if I didn't want to wrap her up in my arms right then and there.

There were moments in my life when I sat back and assessed the decisions I made. Proposing to Natasha was a huge mistake, one that I would regret because the emotional abuse she put me through has set me back in my current relationship…well, the one I used to have with Goldie. Asking Goldie to be a Jett Girl, smartest decision I've ever made, because I found a mirror image of myself in her. I found my counterpart.

Interrupting my thoughts, she finally spoke up. "I won't live with you."

"What?" I asked, as my head snapped to the side. "That's non-negotiable. Do you really think you're going to live with Diego? He's a horny bastard, no way."

Goldie put her feet on the ground and stood up right in front of me so I had to look up at her. She pushed my shoulder with her two little fingers and said, "Do you know what's non-negotiable? My requirements if this is going to happen," she said, while waving her hand between us.

I ground my teeth as I felt the control starting to slip away, once again. It was always like that with Goldie; I never truly had a firm grasp on it.

"Don't tick your jaw at me; I can see it throbbing with uncertainty." She poked the side of my jaw as she spoke. I couldn't help but smile at how tough she was trying to be. "Ugh, and don't smirk either, that's more irritating."

"Sorry," I chuckled. "What are your requirements?"

She thought about it for a second, and then said, "I get to stay with Diego. No sex…"

"No sex," I gulped, trying not to look desperate.

"That's right, Mr. Demonic Devil in the bedroom, no sex."

"Demonic Devil?" I asked with a quirked eyebrow that she quickly rubbed out with her two fingers.

"Don't give me that eyebrow; you know exactly what I'm talking about."

Swallowing hard, I said, "Fine, no sex."

The smile that spread across her face was almost annoying, as if she didn't look so damn adorable already. I hated succumbing to her, but damn, if she gave me that heart melting smile every time, then I would be giving up more often.

"You have to talk about your feelings, you have to open up to me, and you have to trust me. I'm not saying I forgive you or that this is going to work, but I'm willing to give it a try if you don't act so closed off to me. I can't be shut out of your life anymore; I refuse to be. If you want to be with me, then I am requiring that every last part of you to be with me, not just half."

I knew that was coming, and I was willing to be what she wanted. I was willing to open up my wounds again for her because I knew with her by my side, I would heal once again.

"You want all of me, Little One? Then you'll get it, but in good time. I promise you, you will get all of me."

"Good," she said, almost exasperated. "Um, I don't have a phone, so call Diego to set up a date. Until then, take care."

And with that, she walked away, leaving quite the fucking wake.

24
"ARROWS"

Goldie

"That tickles," Tootse squealed as she shifted to the side, making my paintbrush fly to her arm.

"Can you hold still, please? This will take forever if you don't hold still."

"I don't understand why I had to be purple; I think pink would have better suited me," Tootse complained, as she continued to wiggle.

"No one is going to know it's you, and pink isn't a color of Mardi Gras. Just hold still."

"Why did we agree to do this?" Tootse asked, as she looked over at Francy and Lyla, once again making my brush fly to the side.

Pressing my fingers against my forehead, I took a deep and calming breath, and then looked at Francy. "Can you please control your woman? For fuck's sake! I'm trying to be an artist here."

"If painting tits is being an artist, then damn, I want to be an artist," Francy shot back, as she walked over to Tootse and wrapped her arms around her waist and spoke into her ear. "Now, sweetie, can you just hold still for a little while longer while Lo finishes up painting those delectable breasts of yours?"

Tootse instantly relaxed into Francy's embrace and nodded her head.

"You would think I was clamping her nipples off," I mumbled, as I filled more paint on my brush and attacked her breasts.

As I painted, Francy spoke into Tootse's ear, trying to distract her from what I was doing. But, as she spoke, she rubbed her hands up and down Tootse's stomach, making her nipples pucker to fucking bullets. A light moan escaped Tootse as I ran over her nipple, trying to coat it in paint.

"Oh, come on," I said, as I pulled away. "I don't want to be a part of your little sexual experiment right now. Just hold the fuck still, and Francy, step away, I don't need Tootse orgasming."

"You act like you've never been in a sexual experience with us before, Lo," Francy said with a raised eyebrow.

"We don't talk about that," I warned.

"Wait, what?" Lyla asked, as she laughed and walked over to sidle up for story time. "What's this I hear about a possible lesbian encounter? Oh, please, tell."

"You're supposed to be standing in line, go on," I tried to shoo her away.

"Damn, relax," Lyla smiled, as she stood back in place. "Why is this so important anyway?"

I finished up Tootse's breasts and grabbed my canvas as I spoke, "Because, there is an art contest that I want to enter. Whoever wins gets a spotlight in the art gallery on Royal. It would be a dream come true."

"So, you're squishing breasts against a canvas to win?" Francy asked, confused.

"Yes," I said, matter-of-factly. "It's all about interpretation. Now, put your back against the wall, Tootse, and for God's sake, do not move."

Like the good little girl she was, Tootse backed up against the wall and put her hands on her head like we practiced together before I painted her breasts. We had to do a couple of practice rounds, so she knew what she was getting into.

"Are you ready?" I asked.

"Ready," she nodded.

I held the canvas stiffly in my hands and angled it to the side as I pressed it against Tootse's breasts, giving her my own personal form of a canvas mammogram. Pulling away quickly, I looked down at the canvas and was pleased when I could visibly see the outline of her nipples.

"Oh, this is awesome," I praised myself, as I went in for another press, but at a different angle.

As I continued to reapply paint and press Tootse's breasts against my canvas, the girls grilled me about my love life, something I was very much expecting when they came over. I was just surprised it took them so long to ask about it.

"So what's going on with Jett?" Lyla asked, just as I finished up with Tootse.

I took the blow dryer that was plugged in and started drying the canvas, so I could move on to the next pair of breasts without smearing the colors together.

"What about him?" I replied, acting nonchalant. I was still a little uneasy about the whole dating thing. I mean, I wanted to date him, fuck did I want to date him, but it just seemed too easy, like I was giving in too easily. The man put me through a lot, and I felt like I was going against all of womankind by just saying yes.

I could hear the women's rights activists shaming me now, by chanting over and over…doormat, doooormat!

Even though these women were in my head, they could fuck off, because until they had been fully inserted with the tree trunk resting pleasantly between Jett Colby's thighs, they could back the hell off. Plus, the moment he talks to you intimately in that deep southern voice of his, fuck me in the damn meat valley, I can't stay away.

And it's not all physical, hell no, there is an emotional connection I have with him, one that has grown stronger over time. At first, it wasn't that strong, but over time, since he's been opening up slowly, I've come to know the man I've always been curious about since I met him at Kitten's Castle.

I wanted to flip him off, to send him on his way, to show him that he couldn't always control my heart, but I would have been lying if I'd said that. The man had a hold on me, the kind of hold that would last a lifetime, so instead of fighting it, I was going to let it happen. I was going to fall all over again, but this time, it would be on my terms. If he wanted me in his life, in his bed, and in his arms, then he was going to have to fucking work for it.

"Don't act like nothing is going on. Blane told us he stopped by the other day at the square."

Rolling my eyes, I pulled Francy over to my painting area and started spreading green paint all over her breasts. "Blane is such a gossip. I would swear the man spends his nights bouncing on his bed in a pink nightie with his hair clipped in bows while talking on his red lip phone."

"Does he have one of those?" Francy asked, while she raised her arms for me. She was much more professional at getting her breasts painted than Tootse, not that there was really a professional aspect of it, she just wasn't squirming around like a child.

"I wouldn't be surprised if he does," I answered.

"Babs really likes him," Lyla added.

"Who, Jett?" I asked, as my stomach dropped for a second.

"No, Blane," Francy answered. "Come on, Babs and Jett are like brother and sister."

"Who fucked," I said. "Don't use that comparison with them; it's just wrong."

"Understandable, but seriously, to all of us Jett is a friend, and that's it. Once you walked in the club, we knew he was done for."

"So Babs and Blane then?" I asked, while changing the subject off of me and Jett. I wasn't ready to answer those questions just yet. I would use Babs as a distraction for as long as I could.

Eyeing me carefully, Lyla let me change the subject, but I could tell it would only be momentarily. "Yes, you should see the woman, always asking about him, texting him, and drooling over a picture she took with him the other night…"

"She is so masturbating to that picture," Francy pointed out. "I heard some moaning coming from her bedroom last night."

"You did not," I laughed, trying to envision Babs being one to masturbate to a picture on a phone. Well, actually, she most likely would.

"I did, a genuine moan…like her fingers were hitting the right spot."

"Could have been a vibrator," Tootse said, coming back in the room with a top on now and her boobs cleaned up. "She has about four of them. Oh, my God, she was showing me one the other day; it plugs into the wall."

"Shut up, it does not," I giggled.

"No joke," Tootse sat on the floor and leaned back on her hands. "The thing looked like something from the fifties, but when she turned it on, I was pretty sure it jostled my cervix from just standing next to it. What did she call it?" Tootse thought, as she looked up to the ceiling, trying to rack her brain for the name.

Casually, Lyla answered while looking at her nails, "The Earth Quake."

We all turned toward her and gave her a questioning glare. She shrugged her shoulders and said, "It's the granddaddy of vibrators. No need for batteries or the possibility of running out of juice in mid-orgasm. No, it plugs into the wall, has a gel handle for comfort, and rocks your pussy like no man would ever be able to handle. It's called the Earth Quake because the thing rattles your loins like a five on the Richter scale. Want to learn how to squirt? Grab an Earth Quake and sit back, the damn thing does it all for you." Lyla shivered and then fanned her face. "I need to get another one, because just thinking of it has gotten me hornier than a dog in heat."

"You? Horny? That's hard to imagine," I said sarcastically.

"You wouldn't be so horny if you just gave in to Kace," Francy chastised.

With a giant smile on my face, I turned toward Lyla, paint brush mid-stroke, and said, "Kace came on to you?"

"Hell no," Lyla cringed. "That man is appalling."

There was a collective guffaw that rang through the room, as every other woman except Lyla scoffed at her assessment of Kace.

Kace.

Fuck me. If I wasn't with Jett, there was no doubt in my mind I would be spreading my legs, welcoming Kace with flapping wings down below. The man was impossible not to stare at with his rough exterior, devilish eyes, and his brooding attitude. With one glare, he could have you falling to your knees and begging to be taken right then and there. Believe me, I was close the moment I saw him in the shower…naked.

Oh, and his penis, there is only one other penis that beats

Kace's, and its Jett's, but Kace was a close second. To stroke it just once would be all the pleasure someone would need for a month.

When it came to men's genitalia, there were two categories men could fall under: the tree trunks and the twigs, Kace and Jett fell under the tree trunk category...easily.

Lyla was either in complete denial about Kace, or she was starting to float down the tuna river to meet up with Francy and Tootse, which would be kind of hot because Lyla would be one fine ass lesbian. Any pair of tits would be lucky to have her dangling off their arm.

Setting my paint brush down, I turned toward Lyla and folded my arms over my chest. "I call bullshit. There is not one woman on this earth who would look at Kace and say he is appalling."

Tootse and Francy nodded, as Francy said, "Hell, I dig the pussy like every other horny bastard out there, but I still get a little water works down below when I see Kace with his shirt off."

"It's true," Tootse agreed. "Sometimes we role play with Kace..."

"Babe," Francy said in a warning tone. "What happens between a lady and a lady should stay between a lady and a lady."

"Oh, no, please continue," I gestured. "I would love to hear how that sentence ended."

"Of course you would," Francy teased. "You can't get enough of our sex life."

"Not falling for it," I replied, as I started to paint Francy's breasts again. "So, Lyla, tell us why you're in denial."

"I'm not in denial; I can just see past his exterior. Don't get me wrong, the first time I saw him, I wanted to pull off my shirt and let the man motor boat me into the next fucking month, but there is too much under that sexy façade. Things run deep in him."

I paused my paintbrush and looked over at Lyla. "Of course things run deep with him; he has a horrid past, Lyla. Do you really think the man would be all sunshine and glitter? He broods for a reason. You can't be that sexy and not brood about it; I think it's a rule in the romance community or something."

"Well, I can't get involved. I have my own damn problems, taking on someone else's wouldn't be healthy, and I recognize that."

"He needs love," I said softly, as I thought of the Kace I'd grown to love. Yes, he was a bastard most of the time, and he could easily make you want to pull your hair out, but he was kind and sweet and protective. When you were in his inner circle, you were set for life.

"I know he does," Lyla agreed. "But I don't think I'm the girl to give it to him. Plus, I'm not really into the whole relationship thing, and I doubt he is either. And then, there's the whole Pepper thing…"

"Wait, they're still fucking?" I asked, as I finished up painting Francy and grabbed my canvas. "I thought that was a onetime thing."

"I don't think so," Francy added.

"Yeah, Pepper is down there a lot," Tootse said. "Pepper doesn't really talk about it, but apparently, it's just meaningless sex."

"Doesn't seem meaningless to me," Lyla pointed out. "And, honestly, I like Pepper a lot; I don't want to step on any toes. She can have Kace. I'm moving on anyway. I've moved up to the prime time spot at Kitten's Castle."

"Lyla, you can't work there anymore," I responded, while pressing the canvas against Francy. "You're better than that. Don't you want to do something else with your life?"

Lyla just shrugged her shoulders, as if it wasn't a big deal that she didn't have a backup plan. I could tell she was shutting me out; it was typical. She never got too deep or really talked about the future. She was independent, always did her own thing, and never worried about what was to come.

"Not all of us are as lucky as you, girl. We can't just land in the hands of a billionaire," the tone she used was light, but the way she avoided eye contact with me made me think she was being snider than she was coming off as.

"I'm trying not to take offense at that comment," I replied, as I finished up with Francy. "But it seems like it was kind of a dig at me."

"Not a dig, just saying you're lucky, that's all. You know I love you, girl. I'm happy for you."

I eyed her for a second and only saw sincerity in her face. Maybe she didn't mean her comment in a menacing way, but there was a bit of jealousy coming off of her, which I could imagine, since she's had a rough go at life just like me. She deserved her happily ever after just as much as me or any of the other Jett Girls.

"Well, don't get all excited for me just yet. Things are…weird with Jett and me right now. I'm not really sure where we stand or what's going to happen. After everything we've been through, I've got to hand it to him, he had balls to ask me out on a date."

Lyla whipped her shirt and bra off and stood in front of me, ready for paint. "I'm not surprised. The man is infatuated with you. You should have seen him when you were gone. I felt like he was going to start punching holes through any wall that was near him. He would do anything for you."

I knew he would; it was written all over his face every time he saw me. I just wished that he would give me all of him, not just half of his soul. I didn't want half. If I was going all in, then I wanted all of him, despite what shortcomings he might think he had.

It was funny, some women thought the dominant man was an easy one to be with because they knew what they wanted and took it, but they were actually the most difficult to live with because they were prideful, and that pride got in the way a lot, especially when you were trying to share a life with them, that's at least what I wanted. I wanted to share a life with the man.

"Hands up," I directed Lyla, as I brushed off her comment. I wasn't really in the mood to talk about Jett, especially since I didn't know what was going to happen.

"Oh, that reminds me," Tootse shouted, as she started digging around in her purse. She pulled out a phone and brought it to me while I pressed the canvas against Lyla. "This is from Jett."

I eyed the phone and shook my head. The man was impossible.

"I don't want that."

"Just take it," Lyla commanded, while the canvas was pressed flush against her. "Give him a little break and take the damn phone; he is obviously trying."

"When did you become Team Jett?" I asked, as I finished up and then eyed my canvas.

It was interpretative art, for sure. The gallery wanted Mardi Gras, well what was more Mardi Gras than purple, green, and yellow breasts? I was going to do some shading and fillers, but the beginning of my art piece was making me quite happy.

Lyla washed herself off as she talked to me. "I've always been Team Jett, from the very beginning when you got that little black card from him. Remember, I was the one pushing you to call him."

Taking a deep breath, she continued. "He's a good man, Goldie. He may have his faults, but he has the best of intentions when it comes to you. You have to know that."

I just nodded my head because even though I was mad at him, I knew the way he looked at me, the things he did to protect me, but was it enough?

"Are we all done here?" Francy asked, as she got up from the ground and brushed off her bottom. "I have a steak calling my name at the club; Chef's been grilling."

"Steak, such a lesbian thing," Lyla shook her head.

"How is that lesbian?" Francy asked.

"It is when you wear a flannel and eat it without a fork and knife," Lyla countered.

"One fucking night when I was drunk and you're going to hold that against me."

"Honey, when you're drunk, your inner butch comes out. It's okay with me," Tootse kissed Francy's cheek. "It just means you're a terror in the bedroom. You should see how far she can get…"

"Babe, let's not finish that sentence. Remember, things between a lady and a lady?"

"Oh, right," Tootse winked. "Are we done? My girl needs to bite into her lady meat."

"Why does that make me think of something else?" I asked, while cringing.

"Because I was referring to my puss…"

"Tootse, Jesus! Come on," Francy said, while dragging her away and waving to both Lyla and me as she retreated.

Lyla finished cleaning herself up, while I straightened up my paints and washed out my brushes in the bathroom next to my room. I was getting used to the small quarters and enjoyed my two roommates, even though they could be extremely overbearing, just like a certain southern gentleman that consumed my thoughts on a daily basis.

Just as I finished up cleaning, the phone Tootse handed me started buzzing on the table. Both Lyla and I looked at it as Jett's name appeared on the screen.

"Are you going to answer that?" Lyla asked.

"I don't know," I admitted.

Lyla shook her head at me and put her shirt back on. "Don't ruin the best thing that happened to you because of pride."

"Pride? Is that what you think this is? It isn't pride, Lyla, it's not wanting to get stepped on. Jett has a very strong personality…"

"And yours is stronger. Do you really think he is the dominant one in the relationship? Maybe in the bedroom, babe, but in life, you are. You're the one that holds the cards."

The minute the words left her lips, I wanted to ask her if Jett told her to talk to me, because those were his exact words…that was what he'd told me many times before. I was the keeper, the one who called the shots, and at one point, I thought I really did, until he didn't trust me to take care of our business.

"Don't, don't do this, Goldie. Give him a chance."

"I want to, Lyla. But my life can't revolve around him. I want to do something for me. I want to find out who I am, what I'm supposed to do in this world."

With a soft smile, Lyla came over to me and pulled me into a hug while she whispered into my ear. "Sometimes, life has a funny way of helping you figure things out. You might not see it now, but I think Jett Colby was brought into your world so you could finally find yourself once and for all. I love you, girl. I think you know what to do."

She kissed me on the cheek and took off down the stairs before I could yell back at her to give Kace a chance, because maybe he was her Jett Colby. That would have to be a conversation for another day, because hell if I was going to let Lyla get away with not letting Kace into her life. They would be perfect for each other, easily. They would just have to get past their demons first.

Shutting my door for some privacy, I grabbed the phone Tootse had given me, laid down on my bed, and touched the voicemail button to hear what Jett had to say.

"Hello, Goldie. It's Jett. I was calling to inquire about our date. When you have some spare time, I would love to hear back from you. Have a nice day."

I laughed out loud at the professional voicemail he'd left me. I could tell he was trying to control the way he spoke to me, being more cautious than anything, and add his southern politeness on top of that and the voicemail was ridiculous. Just so fucking Jett Colby.

With a quick swipe, I called him back.

The phone rang twice before he picked up.

"Goldie," his voice rang through the phone. It was soft,

almost relieved…it cut straight to my heart.

"Hi, Jett," I held back the giggle that wanted to come out.

"How are you?" he asked, once again, being cordial, not the same Jett I knew.

"Umm, a little concerned."

"Concerned? Why?" he asked.

"Well, you see, I knew this guy, this really hot guy, he kind of umm, took me by surprise by how fast and hard I fell for him, but he's missing now…"

Clearing his throat, Jett said, "Do I want to hear this?"

"I don't know, do you know where the real Jett Colby is?"

"What?" Jett asked, confused, but clearly satisfied that I'd said his name.

"Calling to inquire about our date?" I imitated his deep southern voice, but did a piss poor job at it. "When have you ever talked to me like that?"

A sigh came from the phone, and I could envision the man settling in his desk chair and undoing his tie, then taking a sip from his tumbler full of dark liquid. Just thinking about him in such a position had me wishing I wasn't at Diego's house.

"I'm sorry. I just don't know how to act around you right now. I feel like I don't know how to talk to you anymore."

"Is that because you don't trust me?" I asked, feeling sad.

"No!" he said quickly. "No, Goldie. I just…" he paused as I heard him shift in his chair. "I feel like there's been too much distance between us. I feel like I've lost you."

The pain in his voice was almost too much to handle. I swallowed hard as I controlled the emotions that were threatening to boil over.

I was so up and down with this man. I wanted him, more than anything did I want him, but would he give me what I really needed? It seemed like he wanted to, like he was ready to do whatever it took, but I wasn't sure if I was ready to see. I couldn't be hurt by him again; I just couldn't.

Reassuring him, I responded, "You didn't lose me, Jett, we just need to patch up the crack that has separated us."

"Are you willing to do that?" he asked, hope in his voice.

"I think I am," I admitted. "But we have to both work at it; it can't be a one way street. I can't do everything, Jett."

"I want to put in the work, Goldie. I…I miss you. It's not the same here without you."

"Why, no one busting your balls? I need to talk to those girls, remind them what their real responsibility is."

Laughing, Jett said, "Yes, I do miss the daily ball busting. You really know how to put a man in his place."

"I take great pride in juggling nut sacs."

"I'm sure you do. So, how are you juggling the nut sacs over where you're staying?" I could sense he was curious about my relationship with Diego and Blane, but he wasn't jealous, because deep down, the damn man knew I belonged to him. I could deny it all I wanted, but the man knew.

Fucking cocky bastard.

"Well, trying to get two nut sacs in my mouth at the same time has been challenging, but with a few more jaw stretching exercises, I'm pretty sure I'll be able to accomplish it. Diego said if I get good enough, I could bring it to the main stage as an act. What did he call it?" I paused for effect. "Oh, yeah, testies be gone with your bad self."

Silence rang through the other end of the phone, as I held in the snicker that wanted to escape.

Clearing his throat, Jett said, "Goldie, I hope you're joking."

Letting out a laugh, a good one, one that I hadn't felt in a long time, I settled into my bed and pressed the phone closer to my ear, trying to be as close to him as possible while I spoke.

"Come on, you know me better than that, Jett. I can easily get three pairs of balls in my mouth at the same time."

"Goldie..." he warned, making me laugh some more.

"Fine, I haven't had any balls in my mouth. Does that make you happy?"

"Very. So, how are things with the boys? Are they treating you well?"

"Yes, they've been the perfect gentlemen. I mean, Diego is a continuous flirt, but he's been like that since I first got here, so that's nothing new. I don't think he would ever act on anything. He wouldn't be able to handle me. And, Blane, well, he's like a big brother to me. I could never get with that."

"Good to know."

"What about you? Have you porked anyone lately?"

"How I've missed how eloquent you are," Jett teased. "And, no, I haven't been able to take my mind off of this Little One I know."

"Is that right? So, have you slapped the salami lately to this Little One you speak of? Maybe stroked the log in the shower? Fondled the old fiddle? Playing a little five on one? A little hand to gland combat?"

"Are you asking if I've masturbated to your gorgeous face?"

Feeling a little caught off-guard by his bluntness, I cleared my throat and replied, "Umm, yeah."

"What do you think?" he asked, his voice going an octave deeper. I knew that fucking voice, that was his Bourbon Room voice, that was the voice he used right before he took me up against the wall and took what we both wanted.

Oh, fuck, I was so damn horny; just from his simple question, I could feel myself going wet. It was going to be one hell of a long night at this rate.

"I'm going to say yes."

Seductively, he answered, "Every fucking morning, Little One."

Did pussies actually clap? Because, I swear to God, in that moment, my pussy gave Jett a standing ovation for his answer.

"Wow, um, this conversation got dirty pretty quick," I tried to laugh it off, even though I was pretty sure I was involuntarily licking the phone.

Self-respect Goldie, self-respect.

"I'm pretty sure you're the one who went there," Jett pointed out.

"You're probably right about that, but I will neither confirm nor deny if it was really me."

"Stubborn woman," Jett chuckled.

"Glad you figured that out, now, tell me, what are you wearing?" I couldn't help myself. I knew we had to work on deeper subjects about our lives, but right now, skimming the surface was fun; it was opening up the conversational gates to help us dig a little deeper. It was easier to crack the surface first, rather than trying to dig to the bottom right away.

Mirth laced his voice as he talked, "Black button-down shirt, black pants, and I was wearing a black tie, but that is now on my desk."

Just as I suspected, the man was tie-less. Imaging what Jett Colby was wearing was making my underpants dance excitingly. I loved it when he wore black, because it made his strong features stand out more, plus those eyes of his, fuck me, those eyes could bring me to a bent over position, just begging to be taken care of.

"Are your sleeves rolled up?"

"They are, do you like it when they're rolled up?"

"I do, you have some pretty sexy forearms."

"Forearms? Really?"

"Yeah, they're hot."

"Hmm..." I could hear him wrestling on the other line.

"What are you doing?" I asked.

"Making a note to always flex my forearms when I'm near you. The more I can do to help my case, the better."

"Ugh, you're going to be annoying about your forearms now, aren't you?"

"Most likely," he laughed. "But, then again, you haven't dropped the whole Jettonathan thing, so I could accuse you of being annoying."

"And why would I do that? It's your God given name."

"It really isn't," he laughed.

"It could be. I mean, Jettonathan, it has such a hoity ring to it, perfect for you."

"Hoity, huh?"

"Don't even deny it. You know you love wearing your white sweater sets at the country club, while talking about the latest stock market margins and holding a tumbler in your hand with your pinky out for everyone to see."

"Now, Goldie, what happens to girls who lie?"

"Tell me I'm lying; you know it's true."

"You're lying; I don't hold my pinky out. Never have."

"I've seen you do it."

"Liar," he chuckled, as did I.

"I'm not lying! There was a night when we were drinking..."

"I'm going to stop you right there. Any sentence that starts with we were drinking, I'm not going to believe. Have you seen you drunk?"

"Yes, and I am a delight, just an absolute delight," I responded with my chin held high and confidence in my voice.

"Yes, a total delight. Need I remind you...Cow Vagina?" he asked, referring to a night I "supposedly" started calling him a cow vagina face. I have yet to see the evidence.

"Funny thing is, Jett, you keep bringing that up, but I have yet to see the video on this. How can I believe what you're saying to me? I can't let you drag the great Goldie name through the mud with such lies."

"Come over here right now, Little One. I'll show you."

Fuck was I tempted. I was so damn tempted I actually felt myself lean toward my shoes, but I knew it was a bad idea. By the way he'd been sending shivers down my spine since I got on the phone with him, I knew I was bound to end up in the Bourbon Room with my legs spread and Jett Colby circling me, waiting to see what he was going to do to me.

"Maybe another time," I answered lamely, not really knowing what else to say.

Easily, in a matter of three little words, I busted the bubble Jett and I were living in, and we were brought back down to the painful reality that we weren't really where we wanted to be when it came to our relationship.

The awkwardness resurfaced and the inability to have a conversation with each other took over, rather than the easy flow we'd been enjoying.

Good job, Goldie.

Once again, clearing his throat, Jett said, "Can we talk about the date I would like to take you on?"

"Yes, I would like that," I responded, all too politely. Who was the one with their pinky out now?

"Well, first of all, are you free on Saturday? I'm not sure of your work schedule."

"My work schedule consists of me telling Diego when I want to work, so you don't have to worry about that. Before I commit, because I don't want to be that easy, tell me what you have planned."

"Fair enough," he chuckled.

Can I please just state for the record, I had never seen Jett Colby so…easygoing before? Maybe the man was tense about Lot 17 for so long that I never really got to see the fun side of him, because all this laughter coming from the other end of the phone was warming up my damn heart.

"So, Saturday is the Gumbo festival in the Quarter, and I was wondering if you wanted to go with me…as a judge."

I wanted to clear my ears out to make sure I'd heard him

correctly.

"I'm sorry, did you just say as a judge? Like, I get to eat Gumbo all day and criticize their recipes?"

"Yes, that's exactly what I'm saying."

I was about to scream from the rooftops yes, since I absolutely loved Gumbo, but then the scene unfolded in front of me, and I realized this would be a massive public appearance.

"Are you aware that if I go with you to this thing, we will be seen together in public; it's not like we would just go there and walk around. No, cameras will be taking in the entire event."

"I'm very aware."

"And you're okay with that? Of being seen publicly with me?"

Without hesitation, he answered, "I would want nothing more than to be seen with you by my side. I meant what I said, Goldie. I want to date you, I want a relationship with you, a future. I'm in this for the long run. There is nothing that can get in my way…only you."

Because I held the cards, he didn't have to say it, I received his silent statement.

"Then, sign me up, Jett. I would love to accompany you to the festival."

25
"BRIGHT"

Jett

Why the fuck was I so nervous? It's not like I haven't taken Goldie out on a date before. I took her out before we were even an item, and I was way more confident than I am right now. I've spent entirely too much time standing in front of my mirror, checking my clothes out to make sure they were perfect.

Fuck.

My clothes didn't matter; I tried to tell myself that it didn't matter, but I still ended up changing my shirt five times. I wanted to look casual, to come off as more approachable, more relaxed, but I didn't have casual clothes, so I had to settle for a pair of navy shorts, a white collared shirt with the sleeves rolled up to my elbows, and I matched my brown loafers with my belt. I was able to get a haircut in this week, by some miraculous scheduling, so my hair was freshly shaven on the sides and styled to the side on top.

"You look like you're going sailing," Kace's voice came from my bedroom door. He was the only one who had seen my bedroom, and that's because he didn't give a shit about my rules. Kace had no boundaries. "Should I fetch you your captain's hat?"

"Fuck you, man," I shook my head. "Is it that bad?"

"Is it bad that you're asking me for fashion advice? Seriously, dude, grow a pair."

I ran my hands over my face and gave up on the clothes; it didn't matter, it was trivial compared to the real work I had to do in order to win Goldie back. The other night, on the phone, hell, I felt alive again. To hear her tease me, press my buttons, I missed that. Call me some sort of masochist, but Goldie's defiance and her candid ability to push my buttons was something I now craved. It wasn't the fact that she was a challenge, because she was most definitely a challenge, it was how real she treated me. She didn't take my crap; she didn't care who I was or what social standing I had. No, she treated me like every other person she knew, and that's what I craved.

"Before I leave, I would like to talk to the girls," I stated, while sticking my wallet in my back pocket and grabbing my phone.

"And, there he is, the emotionless Jett Colby. It was nice to see your vulnerable side for a second."

I gave Kace a pointed look. Like he had room to talk. He was a brick wall, and when it came to emotions, he was impossible to talk to.

"This coming from the man who doesn't know how to smile."

"All that matters is that my dick knows how to smile."

"Is it still smiling with Pepper?" I asked, knowing full well that I'd seen them together again.

Pursing his lips, Kace looked me up and down while slowly nodding his head. "It's not very becoming of you to sit outside of my room and listen. You're better than that, Jett."

"Seems like you could do better yourself," I teased Kace. "It's called an orgasm, try giving her one."

"Ahh, your dick is feeling sour, so you have to take it out on me. Fair enough," Kace teased back as he patted my crotch.

Jumping away from him, I punched his arm, and said, "I don't know why you hide your love for me. Just admit it, you want in my pants."

"Nah, I'd be afraid it would take me too long to find that needle dick of yours."

"Take your valium today? Because, fuck, I haven't seen you this lively in a while," I replied, walking out of my room and toward the stairs. "Is Lyla out of the picture now?"

"She was never in the picture," Kace lied.

"Who are you trying to convince? Me or yourself?"

"Both," he replied, while following me down the stairs. "It wasn't meant to be. We're too different."

"Plus, she wants nothing to do with you, can't blame the girl. You can't really make up for all three inches of you, no matter how amazing the motion of the ocean is."

"Well, aren't you a fucking comedian tonight? You trying to sharpen that jagged sense of humor so you can try to win Goldie back? Not sure how that will go."

I turned and eyed Kace with a smirk. "Low blow man, low blow."

"Hey, and I thought you liked a low blow," Kace responded, while wiggling his eyebrows.

"Lame, dude, straight up lame."

He laughed behind me as we walked down the stairs and headed toward the Toulouse Room, where all the Lafayette Club presentations took place. It would be sad to no longer hear the girls practicing under Kace's watchful eye, but it was time to move on. I was changing, and so was the club. The girls needed to move on, and if that meant giving them a little push, then I would.

I walked into the Toulouse Room, where all the girls were wearing their Jett Girl clothes with their masks strewn across the floor, mingling with their heels. They were laughing and most likely gossiping about my date with Goldie, because I'd been receiving little jabs from them since I asked Goldie out.

Getting the girls involved in my relationship was the last thing I wanted to do, but when I needed their help to deliver a phone to Goldie, I really didn't have a choice. So, their ribbing was something I had to swallow. The worst part was, they knew how much it bothered me, but they still did it on purpose.

"Well, if it isn't Scott Disik," Pepper said, making me stop in my tracks.

"What the fuck do mean by that?" I asked, concern in my voice.

"You know..." Pepper said, motioning to my clothing.

"Oh, fuck," I said, as I turned around to head back up to my room to change, making all the girls laugh, even Kace, the asshole, who stopped me.

"Don't worry, you pull off loafers way better than him," Kace winked at me.

"I think you look smashing," Tootse, the oh-so-innocent one said, while coming up behind me. "If I was into cock, I would do you."

"And that means a lot coming from her," Francy called out from behind us.

"Why are you so nervous?" Tootse asked, as she wrapped her arm around mine and pulled me into the room. "It's not like you haven't had sex with her."

"It's more than that, Tootse."

"Yeah, he's trying to actually expose himself to her," Pepper added for me. "For our little Jett, that's hard. The little rich boy has to show his scars."

I eyed Pepper and said, "With the amount of Kace's dick you've taken in, I would have assumed the edge in your voice would have eased by now."

Pepper's mouth flew open as Kace pushed me from behind.

"Oh, please, like everyone didn't know," Babs chimed in.

I took a glance over at Lyla, who seemed to be removing herself from the conversation and playing with a button on her shirt. It was easy to see, as an outsider, that she was uncomfortable with the conversation, and there was only one reason why, she had feelings for Kace. I could tell from the moment I saw them together. They had an electricity between them that was only found between two people who were truly meant for each other; it was the same spark that singed when Goldie was in my arms.

"Maybe not everyone…" Pepper trailed off.

Changing the subject, I started to discuss what I'd gathered them all in the Toulouse Room for. "Ladies, I want to thank you for meeting me before I head out on my date."

"Are you trying to get dating advice from us?" Francy asked.

"No. I want to talk to you about the future of the club."

At the mention of the club and the serious tone in my voice, they all sat a little straighter and dropped the sarcasm that usually laced their features.

"What's going on with the club?" Babs asked, concerned. She was practically a founder, so I could understand her concern.

"After the end of the month, I will be shutting it down."

"What?" They all shouted at once, except for Lyla, who could care less about the news. She said she was temporary, but after being here for a while, I thought that maybe she would change her mind. I guess not.

"How can you do this to us?" Pepper asked. "Where the hell are we supposed to go, Jett?"

"Are you going to kick us out?" Tootse asked with tears in her eyes. Francy gently wrapped her arms around Tootse and pulled her into a hug.

"Jett, are you serious?" Babs asked, looking almost mad.

These were the exact reactions I was expecting from the girls, and I'm glad I got them, because if they could care less about the club, then I would have felt like what I was doing for the past couple of years meant absolutely nothing.

"Ladies, you know I only have your best interest in mind, right?"

"I thought so," Pepper said, while folding her arms across her chest. "But then you go and take away our jobs, so I'm a bit confused."

"Pepper, I would never do anything that would hurt you; you know that. I'm only here to help you, so that's why, when the community center at Lot 17 opens, I want you all to be a part of it."

Confused looks faced me, as the girls tried to understand what I was telling them.

"I'm open about most things, but a strip club at a community center may be a little too eccentric," Francy stated.

"I agree, that's why you will be utilizing the education you've been earning the past few years to help out the community. I will pay you, and if you would still like to stay at the club, you are more than welcome to stay here for as long as you want. I want you ladies to use more than your bodies. I want you to use your brains, your hearts, and your souls. You are some of the most amazing women I've had the privilege of getting to know, and it would be my honor to have you working at the community center. We will have classes ranging from dance to cooking, to exercise. There's a spot for all of you, and I'm open to whatever you would like to teach. Tootse, you could easily give sewing lessons. Francy, you could help with the day care, because I know how much you love children. Pepper, easily, you can run dance classes. There's a spot for each of you."

"What about Kace?" Babs asked, while nodding at him.

I turned to look at Kace and then smiled. "What else would he do? He's already agreed to manage the center for me, as well as give boxing lessons."

"Seriously?" Babs asked, excited for Kace. "Jett, that is so great."

"So, I'm guessing you approve then?"

Babs looked around at the girls and I could see all of them smiling, confirming what I thought…they loved the idea.

"Does this mean we can wear normal clothes?" Babs asked.

Laughing, I nodded my head. "Yes, please wear normal clothes."

"Well, just that would make it worth it," Francy said, as she plucked at her shirt. "If I never have to see another dress shirt again, I would be a happy woman."

"But, you look so hot in them, and you know how I love ripping the buttons off," Tootse whined.

"Ah, I see. So your kinky sex is why I had to keep buying button up shirts for you two," I asked, while shaking my head.

"What can I say? I know how to please my lady," Francy shrugged her shoulders.

"Hey!" Tootse said. "I thought we were supposed to keep things between a lady and a lady."

Francy patted Tootse's bright blonde hair and said, "Babe, I didn't say anything revealing."

"Oh, okay. So as long as I don't talk about how you like me to use my left hand on you…"

"Babe!"

"Are you ambidextrous?" Babs asked Tootse.

"When I'm knuckles deep, yes."

"Jesus," Kace muttered from behind me.

I checked my watch and noticed it was time for me to leave, and not just because I didn't want to be late for my date with Goldie. I really didn't want to hear about Tootse going knuckles deep.

I said my goodbyes and listened to the girls try to tease me one last time about my outfit before I left. I ignored them and popped into my Aston Martin, the car I used when I took Goldie out on her first date with me. I felt like being a little nostalgic, plus I knew how much she liked the car. Maybe, just maybe, I would let her drive it. That would be a very big maybe. Knowing her, she would be the worst driver ever.

Pulling up to Diego's apartment made me even more nervous than ever, and not because of my date with Goldie, but because of the last time I talked to him. I was an abhorrent bastard, blaming him for my problems. Diego didn't deserve that kind of treatment, and I owed him more than an apology. I just wasn't sure whether he would accept it or not.

I parked my car in the back alleyway and headed up to the back entrance. The door was unlocked, so I let myself in. I called out, but no one came to the back, so I headed up the stairs to Goldie's room, hoping she was ready to go.

As I approached her door, I could hear her talking, so I paused to make sure I didn't walk in on a private moment. When I only heard her voice, I grew slightly confused, so I pushed forward to see what she was doing.

Her door was cracked just enough that I could see her standing in front of her mirror...talking to herself.

"Oh, this old thing? I just pulled it from the closet, but thank you, it really does accentuate my breasts, doesn't it?" she leaned forward and showed off her cleavage. "Eat your heart out, Jett Colby," she said in a deep voice, while shimmying at herself in the mirror. "What's that? You want to take me in the port-a-potty? Why, Jett Colby, I thought you had more class than that, but if it's a dream you've always had, then who am I to stop you from achieving your dreams? Just make sure you wash your hands afterwards. Who knows what happens in those things?"

She brushed her hair out of her face and then curtseyed with the bright green dress she was wearing, which was tight around her breasts and waist and then fell loosely at her hips. It was a gorgeous sundress for a gorgeous woman.

In a hoity voice, she held her hand out and said, "Why, I do believe we've met, Mrs. Havershire. Yes, I'm the woman who fucked Jett's brains out at the event a while ago, yes, that's right, you smelled my puss..."

"Mrs. Havershire?" I asked, before she could finish her sentence.

"Fucking hairy balls," she shouted, as she backed up into the mirror at being startled. I quickly caught her before she fell over. "Why, why would you do that?" she asked, while she pulled herself away and tried to right her dress.

"Because I couldn't help myself," I answered with a grin. "What were you practicing?"

"Who knows who we will meet today? I wanted to make sure I was prepared."

"By talking about when I banged you up against a wall at an event?"

"Yes," she replied with her chin held high.

"Okay, I'll make sure to introduce you to everyone as Goldie, the girl's pussy you smelled..."

"Stop it," she laughed, while covering her face, making her absolutely adorable. "Do not introduce me like that," she warned.

"Or what?" I asked.

"Or I will make sure I embarrass you in the most horrid way possible."

"You think you can embarrass me?"

With a big grin, she nodded and said, "Oh, I know I can embarrass you."

"Why are you so confident?" I asked, while nudging her chin with my finger.

"Because, you're Jett Colby, Mr. Social Standing. You have a façade you have to live up to. One mention of the wrong thing in front of the right person, and I'll have your face turning bright red before you can unzip your pants and introduce everyone to the Douglas Fir you keep locked up in there."

"Douglas Fir? Really? Not a Redwood?"

Rolling her eyes, she grabbed her purse and asked, "Are you ready?"

"Not quite. I bet you I can embarrass you more than you can embarrass me."

She placed her hands on her hips and looked up at me with disbelief on her face. "You can't be serious. You and I both know I could make Charlie Sheen blush with the things that come out of my mouth, let alone a little debutant like yourself."

"Alright, game on," I challenged her.

She paused for a second, while eyeing me carefully, and then said, "Fine, what are the stakes?"

"If I win, I get to come back here with you tonight."

"No sex!" she said, while pointing her cute little finger at me.

"No sex, just..." I bit my lip for a second and said, "I just want to hold you."

Her face relaxed as my words sank in.

"Ah, hell, that's not fucking fair. You can't say things like that."

"And why not?" I asked.

"Because it makes me have all the feels, and I don't want to feel for you right now. I still want to be mad at you."

"Okay," I laughed. "When are you going to stop being mad at me?"

"I'll let you know," she smirked. "Okay, if you win, we come back here, but if I win…I get to drive your car."

I knew that was coming. I'd called it the moment I stepped inside the Aston. Even though my car was my baby, nothing was more important to me than Goldie. The bet was by far worth it, especially if I had a shot at staying with Goldie for the night.

"Deal," I agreed, while I held out my hand to shake on it.

She shook my hand with a giant smile on her face.

"Oh, you are so going down, Mr. Colby."

"Keep dreaming, Little One. I don't lose."

"We'll see about that," she said, as she brushed past me, leaving a trail of her intoxicating perfume behind her. Fuck, I needed to start thinking of embarrassing things to do to her, because hell if I was going to lose. Nope, I would be ending my night in her small room with the average-sized bed and with my Little One in my arms. There was no other choice for me.

26
"SHUT UP AND DANCE"

Goldie

The drive from Diego's apartment to Armstrong Park, where the festival was held, was a short five minute drive, but it felt like half an hour as I was trapped in the small confines of Jett's Aston Martin, watching the muscles in his forearms flex as he shifted gears. Life was so unfair. When did a guy's forearms become the sexiest part of their bodies? Well, one of the sexiest parts of their bodies, next to the cock, abs, and dick divots.

"Did you just say dick divots?" Jett asked, as he parallel parked into a spot on St. Phillip Street.

Did I really say dick divots out loud? Was I talking out loud that entire time?

"Um, what are you talking about?" I asked, trying to pass it off.

He cut the engine and turned toward me, swinging his arm to the back of my seat, making him that much closer. "You were mumbling to yourself and the only thing I caught was at the end, you said dick divots."

"Huh, imagine that," I smiled, as I tried to get out of the car, but of course the infuriating man stopped me.

"Goldie, please explain to me what dick divots are."

"You're annoying, you know that? Can't you ever let something go?"

"No," he smiled brightly.

Huffing, I crossed my arms over my chest and said, "Dick divots are those little things that point to your dick, turning every honest woman into an idiot as they direct their gaze down a path past your waistline and straight to your...redwood. You know...the v-cut," I said, while pointing to his side.

"Not sure what you're referring to. Can you show me? Need me to lift my shirt?"

"No!" I practically yelped, not wanting to see one bit of Jett's body. It was bad enough the man wore his sleeves rolled up and the top few buttons of his shirt undone, showing off his perfectly bare and tight chest.

Fuck, he was a walking god. All bronze-like with his designer clothes that were simple but looked so damn good on him, like he was a walking Ralph Lauren catalogue.

"Come on, Little One," he winked, as he got out of the car and came to my side to open the door for me, always the gentleman.

Helping me out of the car, he grabbed my hand and shut the door, just as a man walked up to us for Jett to toss him the keys, once again the guardian of the car, just like our first ever date. Some things never changed.

The entire walk into the festival, Jett held onto my hand tightly, making my heart beat rapidly in my chest. It was just a little hand holding, but it was who the hand was attached to that had my tongue hanging out of my mouth like a cat in heat.

"Have you ever been to the festival before?" Jett asked, as he led us through the crowd with ease.

"No, surprisingly I've never been."

"That is surprising, given your infatuation with the classic dish." I gave him a sideways look which made him laugh. "Chef told me how much Gumbo you used to eat at the club; I made sure he cooked it once a week."

"So, you're the reason I had to work my ass off in the gym every week?"

"You didn't have to work anything off," he smiled while

squeezing my hand.

Charming, just too fucking charming. I could feel myself slowly slip into the Jett Colby world he was sucking me into. Not good, it was only the first ten minutes of our date and I was already losing it. Time to start thinking about my game plan on how to win the bet we made so I could get my hands on his perfect little car. All I had to do was act inappropriate in front of the right people, and I was good as golden.

Music from the brass band filled the air, as festival-goers walked about with their hands full of gumbo bowls. The smell of the spicy and favorable dish hit me hard as we walked deeper into the festivities. My stomach growled at me, practically begging me to feed it. I patted my stomach and secretly told it to be patient; good things were coming its way shortly.

"Over here," Jett directed, as he led me to a tented off area where people milled around giant cooking vessels.

The cook-off.

Best date ever! Shoving my face full of food and having no shame while doing so was one of the best date ideas I could ever conjure up. The man knew me all too well.

"Jett Colby," a deep voice spoke out as we passed through a tent opening.

The mayor walked up to us while holding out his hand to Jett. The mayor of New Orleans, what a perfect subject for Mission Embarrass Jett. It was almost too easy.

"Mayor Rupert, what a pleasure to see you. Are you judging the contest today as well?"

"That I am," the mayor said, as he patted his stomach. "And, may I ask who this lovely lady is who seems to be attached to you?"

"How rude of me," Jett said in an apologetic voice. "Mayor Rupert, this is Goldie, my girlfriend."

Girlfriend? How easily the man forgot about our relationship status, but I would let it slide because the damn title sounded so good to me. Bested again by the conceited man.

"Goldie, I'm very delighted to meet you," Mayor Rupert said, while taking my hand in his.

"It's a pleasure," I responded, as I looked up at Jett, gearing up for my embarrassing moment.

"Will you be judging the contest as well?" the mayor asked

me.

"I will be. Gumbo is my all-time favorite dish, so I can't wait to sit back, shove my face full, and belch out the winner, am I right?" I asked, as I nudged the mayor in the stomach, showing less class than expected from me.

The mayor chuckled and Jett just smiled, not affected one bit. Hmm, this was going to be harder than I thought.

"I'm right there with you," the mayor said. "Gumbo is a New Orleans staple. I'm always fascinated to see how different chefs try to reinvent the classic dish."

"Me too. I eat gumbo like a son of a bitch eating out a lady for the first time. Although, seafood gumbo isn't my favorite, I prefer chicken sausage. Any sausage really, isn't that right, Jett?"

The mayor pulled on his ear a bit to make sure he was hearing me correctly, as Jett stood there with a stoic smile and his eyes beaming with pride, as if I was the most majestic woman he had ever met.

Mother fucker.

Clearing his throat and pulling on his collar, the mayor totally fake laughed at me and said, "What an interesting description."

"Given the fact that you have a gorgeous blonde that sleeps next to you, I would guarantee you prefer seafood gumbo over the old saw-seege," I said, while wiggling my eyebrows, embarrassing the mayor more than anything.

A small trickle of sweat from the awkward moment I put myself in started to gather at the base of my back, and I ignored the fact that my plan was backfiring tremendously, and I was the one who was about to be embarrassed in a few seconds.

Jett, on the other hand, was just smiling widely, proud as could be. Bastard!

"Um, yes, I do appreciate seafood," the mayor said uncomfortably, his face bright red. Oh, Jesus, this was not going the way I wanted. "It's a shame this is a vegan gumbo cook off."

"A what?" I practically shouted as I looked up at Jett. "A vegan cook off?"

Jett snapped his finger and said, "Oh, did I not tell you? Yes, it's a vegan cook off, but don't worry, sweetheart, I packed an extra pair of clothes for you in the trunk." Sweetheart? What was he up to? He looked up at the mayor and put his arm around my shoulder as he said, "You see, my girlfriend has a bit of an…irritable bowel, so if she eats too many soy products her bowel flares up and she has a bit of a sharting problem. You know, a shit and fart come out together, but it's okay, I've got back-up underwear in the car at all the times. It's like her own personal diaper bag. Isn't that right, Goldie?" Jett asked, as he tugged on my shoulder and smiled down at me.

My mouth hung open as I tried to figure out what the hell to say. To say I was mortified was an understatement. Point Jett.

The mayor nervously laughed and then turned in the other direction without a word, leaving Jett and me alone.

"Oh, my God!" I shouted as I pushed Jett away. "I can't believe you said that."

Laughing a little too much for my liking, Jett held on to his stomach and tried to speak through the tears forming in his eyes. I've never seen him so loose before in my life, and even though it was at my expense, I still loved it. It was moments like this, when he dropped his control and had some fun, that I craved. Don't get me wrong, I demanded the dominant man who could make me scream his name in seconds, but I also craved this real man, this man with feelings and emotions.

"You should have seen the look on your face," Jett said while pointing at me. "Oh, that was fucking priceless."

"If I would have known bodily fluids were in play, I would have opened up with Jett just blew up the port-a-potty and gave himself a ten out of ten on the shit scale."

"Too slow, gorgeous," he continued to laugh.

"Laugh it up, pretty boy. Have fun holding onto a stiff body tonight."

"I will enjoy every second of it," Jett said, while grabbing my hand and bringing it to his lips.

"Ugh, that wasn't fair," I complained.

"How so?"

"Because I lost," I whined, making him laugh again.

"Well, if you're a good girl today, maybe I will let you drive the Aston, but I make no promises."

"And what qualifies me as a good girl?" I asked with a suspicious tone. The man knew exactly what he was doing.

Shrugging his shoulders, he led us over to a table where we would be testing the different bowls of gumbo, and said, "I don't know. Maybe a kiss here and there; if your hand so happens to land on my crotch, then I wouldn't be opposed to something like that either."

"You're incorrigible, you know that? I'm not about to grab your crotch in public."

"Then the port-a-potty? It seemed like you were having some kind of fantasy about it back at Diego's place."

"Eck, don't be disgusting, that was not a fantasy and no, I won't be kissing you. Nice try though. Remember, I'm still mad at you."

"That's right," he smirked, as he pulled out my seat for me and helped me into my chair. "How much longer are you going to be mad at me again?"

"As long as I want," I replied like a child, while crossing my arms over my chest, making my cleavage stand out.

Jett's lingering gaze on my chest caused a slow throb to grow at the juncture of my damn thighs. Slowly, I watched as he licked his lips and ran his eyes up my chest until he was staring into my eyes. His heated gaze ate me alive and I wasn't sure if I would make it through the contest without jumping his bones in front of everyone at the festival. If the mayor thought he was uncomfortable with all of the sharting talk, then he was in for a rude awakening, because me riding Jett like a mechanical bull in front of the gathering crowd, tits flopping about, was going to absolutely mortify him.

"Mr. Colby?" A voice from the side pulled us out of our heated ogling.

With a lazy smile on his face, Jett retreated from our stand down and greeted the man trying to get our attention.

My mind didn't follow anything they were saying, as visions of Jett in the Bourbon Room overtook every last thought in my mind. Me, bent over in the bathroom, staring at myself in the mirror as he ate me out from underneath, me strapped to the beam, hanging upside down, me on the velvet table, being plunged by Jett until I couldn't take it anymore.

Oh my fuck was I randy and more than willing to be taken by the Demonic Devil himself, as I'd so properly named him.

I couldn't though; I couldn't fall into the same old pattern. I had to stay strong. I would stay strong.

At least, that's what I tried convincing myself.

"Thank you," Jett said, as he sat down next to me. "Did you

hear any of that?"

"No," I said sheepishly.

"I didn't think so, I could practically feel your tongue licking the zipper of my pants."

"Nuh-uh," I defended myself...so eloquently.

"Little One, you act as if I can't feel your gaze on me, as if I can't read what's going on in that pretty little mind of yours."

"Oh, really? Well, please enlighten me, what was I thinking?"

"How you want to be with me, how you want me to take you, but you're holding out, you're being strong because you're not ready to fall back into the world we were living in."

Damn it! Exasperating man!

"You are so wrong," I shook my head and laughed at him, as I tried to pull off that what he just told me wasn't spot on. "I was actually thinking about how those shorts were very unflattering on you."

He looked down at his shorts and then back up at me. "Lying is not the least bit flattering on you," he called me out while he pinched my chin. "But, you're still adorable. Now, are you ready for this?"

Trying not to get irritated with how confident he was, I nodded and looked around as people started to enter the tent for the judging. The other judges took their seats as well, lining the long table on stage. The mayor sat as far away from us as possible; I didn't blame the man, he most likely didn't want to fall victim to my "irritable bowel."

Fucking Jett Colby.

"How does this work? And is it really vegan gumbo?"

"It is. The festival wanted to try something new and embrace the new food lifestyle."

"But what is gumbo without sausage? I don't understand how that can even be something."

"Have an open mind; you never know, you might like it."

"Yeah, okay. You're so buying me real gumbo after this," I said, while poking his rock hard chest. Stupid Kace and his workouts that made Jett all strong and man like. It's like they were working together to take down every woman in New Orleans.

"Anything you want, Little One. Now, there will be five bowls that we will try, and all you have to do is write down your favorites in order. The scores will be tallied at the end, and then they will crown the winner. Simple."

"Except for the fact that we're eating vegan gumbo."

"Would you have still come if I told you it was vegan gumbo?" he asked.

"No," I lied.

Shaking his head, he replied, "Lying will get you in trouble, Little One."

"Yeah? What are you going to do about it? It's not like you can take away my orgasms," I spoke softly, lighting up the heat in Jett's eyes. Damn it, that look easily started to tear down the walls I put up around my vagina so she wouldn't get confused.

Jett was about to answer when the MC for the contest lit up the speakers and started warming up the crowd. The moment between us was lost, as we both turned in our seats to face the crowd. Onlookers gazed at me as I looked down at them from my perch up on the stage. It was interesting to me that so many people cared about a vegan cook off. Maybe there was more to the cuisine than I realized.

As I scanned the crowd for a familiar face, a warm hand gently found its way to my thigh. Not going too high, Jett gently rubbed my skin with the pad of his thumb, turning me into a pile of mush in my seat.

"What are you doing?" I asked from the side of my mouth.

"Touching my girlfriend," Jett answered without skipping a beat.

"You keep saying girlfriend, but I don't remember giving you back that title."

"Deny it all you want, Little One, but you're mine and you know it, so a little title shouldn't bother you one bit."

"Your hand on my thigh is bothering me."

"No, it's not," Jett whispered in my ear, sending chills down my entire body.

I turned to him and smiled brightly as I moved my hand to his crotch and grabbed ahold of his package. Two could play at this game.

Luckily, there was a cloth hanging over the table, so no one could see what we were doing underneath it.

Ready to see the taken aback expression on his face, I looked up and was greeted with a shit-eating grin.

"A little to the left," he winked at me.

"Gah, you're annoying," I replied, while removing my hand and turning away from him.

Out of the corner of my eye, I could see his chest rise and fall from the silent chuckling he was doing. Never did I think Jett would have the joking personality of Diego, or the ability to infuriate me like Kace. It was like all the men in my life came together and morphed into one mega man to drive me bat shit crazy and make me horny as hell.

For the rest of the contest, I ignored the piercing hand of Jett Colby, burning through my skin as I tried all different types of vegan gumbo.

Honestly, it wasn't that bad. They had all the classic flavoring of the dish, it was just the textures that were different, which I tried to ignore, because if I thought about it too much, I started to gag. There was one bowl that said it had faux chicken in it that was a brown square in a pile of rice and gravy. That was the hardest bowl for me to swallow because what kind of "chicken" is a perfect little square? Fuck was it nasty, but like a good girl, I swallowed it down and held back the shiver that wanted to overtake my body from the "chicken" burp that followed. Needless to say, "chicken" gumbo didn't win.

Once the winner was crowned, a very excited lady wearing a peasant skirt and a tank top with no bra—it was obvious—Jett helped me out of my seat, shook hands with the judges, and then led me out to the festival. Job one, get some real gumbo to help me forget the brown chunk I had to take down.

"Did you have fun?" he asked, as he guided me flawlessly through the crowd.

"I did, but can we just discuss that chicken bowl?"

"I'd rather not. I think I'll have some indigestion problems from that bowl for a while."

"Thank you!" I said relieved, glad I wasn't the only one who had a problem with it. "I don't care what you say, you can't pass tofu off as chicken. There is something just so wrong about that. If you're going vegan, then own up to it."

"Yeah, bad move on that person's part. Although, it looked like the mayor rather enjoyed that bowl."

"The mayor liked every bowl."

"True," Jett laughed. "So, what's your pleasure? You have your pick of any gumbo dish out there. What can I get you?"

"Chicken and sausage, I need the classic stuff right now," I requested.

"Right this way," Jett said, as he took me to a small station off to the side where a large black woman stood over a pot of gumbo, stirring it with a giant spoon. Her form reminded me of someone I knew, but I couldn't quite place her until she turned around.

Miss Mary, the she-devil herself stood in front of me with her wooden spoon in one hand and a towel in the other. Flashbacks of her ruler smacking my arm rest during "reform school" flashed through my mind and I winced as she moved toward us. The lady still scared the ever living fuck out of me.

"Why, if it isn't it Miss Lo and Mr. Colby. How lovely to see you both." The smile on her face seemed absolutely genuine, but I didn't trust it for a minute. I knew what she was capable of, so I kept my distance.

"Miss Mary, so glad we were able to find you in this crowd of people. My girl here is looking for the perfect bowl of gumbo, think you can help us out with that?"

"Always a charmer," she winked at Jett as she grabbed two bowls and dished us both a heaping scoop of gumbo. Steam rose off of the bowls as she handed them over to us with spoons.

Jett reached into his back pocket to pay for our food, but Miss Mary held up her hand and shook him off.

"Your money is no good here, son. Just enjoy."

It wasn't like Jett couldn't afford the gumbo, the man was dripping in cash, but he knew when to step down. Miss Mary wasn't one to mess with.

Jett held the bowl up to Miss Mary and gave her that devilish grin of his. "Thank you, Miss Mary. I appreciate it."

"Anytime," she winked again and then went back to stirring her pot, leaving us both alone.

The interaction with Miss Mary almost made her seem human, not like a ruler-wielding, crazy eyed, manner police.

As we walked to a bench in the back of the park, I asked, "Do you and Miss Mary have a close relationship?"

"You could say that," Jett said, as he stared down at his bowl of gumbo.

"Want to tell me about it?"

This was a test; if he was serious about making something happen between us, of having a relationship, then it was time for him to open up. It was time to bring some substance to this uncontrollable force that was bringing us together.

Clearing his throat, Jett leaned back on the bench and said, "Miss Mary was my nanny growing up. She took care of me when my dad was taking care of his businesses; she's the one who raised me and she was the one who made sure I still saw my mom, despite my father's demands."

Right then and there, I felt like my mind was blown. I didn't know much about Jett's mom, except for the fact that she died from AIDS, but I never would have thought Miss Mary raised him. They didn't seem that close; maybe they kept a more distant relationship.

"By your silence, I'm assuming that's not what you were expecting to hear."

"It wasn't," I admitted. "I just thought she worked with you occasionally. I never thought she could have been your nanny. What was she like back then? Was she mean? Did she threaten you with a ruler too?"

Chuckling, Jett shook his head as he spooned some of the gumbo in his mouth. Once he swallowed, he said, "She was strict, really strict, but she was kind and caring as well. She made sure I did everything that was demanded by my dad, and then made sure I had fun by letting me hang out with Kace and do things my father wouldn't normally let me do, like visit my mom."

"Why wouldn't he let you visit her?" I asked, as I put a spoonful of gumbo in my mouth. "Holy shit, this is good," I stated with a full mouth.

"I told you it was good."

"You would never guess by the way she's so aggressive with that damn ruler; you would think she practices her intimidation skills day in and day out, but that broad can cook."

"That she can."

"So, are you going to tell me about your visits to your mom?"

Jett looked up from his bowl and shook his head no. "Let me save that story for a more intimate setting. Is that okay with you?"

Sincerity rang through his voice. It was hard not to agree with him when he spoke straight from his heart.

"Of course," I agreed, not wanting to make the man open himself up in a public place. "So, tell me, did you get a lot of this kind of cooking growing up?"

"I did. Miss Mary was all about Southern cooking, but only when my dad was away on business trips. When he was home, we had to eat salads and basic meals that were approved by my dad. I looked forward to him going on business trips, not just because of the good food that came my way, but because I couldn't stand the man, and when he was gone, it was like I could breathe in my own home."

"Was he really that hard on you?" I asked, as I finished up my bowl.

"He was," Jett nodded. "I had everything I ever wanted when it came to my dad, except for a childhood. I would spend hours in his office, listening to how he conducted deals. He would show me the ins and outs of his business, educating me constantly into becoming a tycoon. Unfortunately for him, I didn't turn into the cutthroat man he wanted me to be. Instead, I went in the opposite direction, making him madder than I ever could have expected."

"That must have been hard," I said, as I placed my hand on Jett's.

"Not really, it was the best decision I ever made, freeing myself from his pressing grasp. It took me a little bit of time to get settled, to land on my feet, but once I did, I took off and never looked back."

"Is that why you're so...jaded at times?" I asked, wanting to know why he was always so closed off.

"It's a combination of things, but my dad is a big factor." Taking my bowl, Jett stood up and said, "It's getting late, shall we get back to your place? I would like to talk to Diego before we call it a night."

"You're not going to lecture him, are you?" I asked, while I followed behind Jett just as he tossed our empty bowls in a nearby garbage can.

"No, on the contrary, I owe the man an apology."

"An apology?" I asked, as I stopped in my tracks. "For what?"

"Nothing that is of your concern," Jett replied, while he grabbed my hand and tried to walk me toward his car.

"Oh, no you don't," I stopped. "You can't keep things from me now, Jett. If you want this to happen between us, then you better start opening up."

I could tell he was counting to ten in his head. This was new for him, divulging every last thing. He was a man who kept to himself and took care of business. He didn't need to spread his problems around or cause drama. It just wasn't the kind of man he was, and I appreciated that about him, but I was tired of being kept in the dark about things, so it was time for him to open the flood gates.

Finally, he lowered his head to mine and said softly, "The night you left me," he took a deep breath and continued, "I was hurting; I was a torn man, and instead of keeping to myself, I took it out on Diego and blamed him for your departure. It's about time I apologize for my wrongdoing."

"Oh."

I will admit I didn't handle that night with the most finesse. I could have spoken to Jett differently. I could have explained to him what I had in mind, but honestly, I knew he wouldn't let me go if I actually told him what I was doing, and at that point, I had to go, I had to do something to change the way we were living our lives, even if in the end, it did nothing but mess up the one good thing in my life.

"Nothing you need to worry about, Little One," Jett said, as he grabbed my hand and walked me toward the car.

"But the reason you were mad was because of me, so I do kind of have to worry about it."

"No, you don't. I shouldn't have reacted the way I did. Now, let it go, okay?" he said sweetly.

The sweet tone in his voice was compensating for the dominant demand he was handing out, and damn it if it didn't turn me on. Would he always be able to do that to me? Control my emotions with his words?

Most likely, he knew me too well.

We walked hand and hand across the park, toward his car, where the man with the keys stood in front of the Aston Martin, protecting it. The whole scene was absolutely absurd, but Jett protected his cars like he protected his girls, guess I couldn't blame him for that.

The keys were tossed to Jett, who caught them in the air and then held them out to me. I looked down at his palm in shock and then back up at him. He was smiling brightly at me, as if he was offering me the world.

Oh, fuck my heart, he was slowly killing me, one smile at a time.

"You're serious?" I asked.

"Of course, I would let you do anything, Goldie."

"My, my, my, you would do just about anything to get in my pants."

Wrapping his arms around my waist, he pulled me in tight and said, "No, actually, I would do just about anything to get into that beautiful heart of yours."

Like second nature, I ran my hand up his chest and gripped the lapels of his shirt. I brought him closer and spoke softly.

"You're in there already, Jett. You just need to take up a permanent residence now."

"That's my goal."

Lightly, he kissed my forehead and helped me into the driver's seat. The smooth leather welcomed me as I checked out the polished steering wheel. I really couldn't believe Jett was going to let me drive his precious car, but hell if I was going to miss out on this opportunity.

Jett got into the passenger side and started giving me instructions, but once I started the car and felt the rumble of the engine underneath me, I blocked out what Jett was saying and took off, letting the wind whip through my hair and the man next to me grip onto the handles for dear life.

27
"I BET MY LIFE"

Jett

I sat in my car, staring out the windshield, trying to recollect the last ten minutes that just flew by me as Goldie whipped around New Orleans, cutting in and out of one way streets and traffic from the festival. Pretty sure I lost a few years on my life from her "driving."

"Oh, my God, that was so much fun," Goldie cooed, as she put the car in park and turned to face me. "I know why you love driving this car so much. You barely have to press down on the gas pedal. Did you see me zip through those streets? It was like we were in some kind of super speed time machine thing. You know what I mean? It seemed like you enjoyed yourself, you weren't even saying anything, just taking in the sights. Hey, are you okay? You look a little strange," she asked, as she pressed her hand against my cheek. "You're all clammy; are you going to be sick?"

I shook my head no and gulped as I looked over at her. "No offense, but you're an awful driver."

Insult crossed her face as she took in my words. "I am not! I'm a damn fine driver. If I was a bad driver, I would have hit somebody."

"We almost took out a street performer, they jumped out of the way before they could be taken out by your absurd driving."

"Jett Colby!" she practically shouted. "I'm not a bad driver."

Nodding my head, I got out of the car, but not before I pulled the keys out of the ignition and pocketed them. I didn't have to turn around to hear her stomping behind me and slamming the driver's side door shut. I lit the fire and I was about to be burned.

"I'm not a bad driver," she repeated herself. "I have just as good of driving skills as fucking Jeff Gordon, maybe even better. Hey, I'm talking to you," she stomped behind me.

Her little finger poked my back as I opened the back door to Diego's apartment for her. She didn't proceed inside. Instead, she continued to poke me.

"Say it, say I'm a good driver."

"Goldie, you're a terrible driver."

"How can you say that?" she said in complete outrage.

"You drove on the sidewalk!"

She opened her mouth to retort, but then stopped herself while she thought of what to say. She crossed her arms over her chest and held her chin high as she said, "It was a low sidewalk, and was hard to see. Anyone could have made the same mistake."

"Okay," I shook my head and grabbed her hand, pulling her into Diego's place and leading her up to her room.

I could hear the slight beat of music playing in the main hall, letting me know Diego must be practicing one of his acts, something I very much wanted to watch at some point, not just because it interested me, but because he worked really hard at his club, and I'm sure he'd like to show off his hard work.

Goldie kicked and argued all the way up to her room, and once we were confined in the small area, she turned on her heels in a fit of rage.

"You can't just manhandle me because you're bigger than me."

"Are you done?" I asked, waiting for her to explode even more.

"Am I done? Are you kidding me right now? No, I am not done. I want you to tell me why you think I'm a bad driver."

"I told you why. You drove on a sidewalk, you almost hit a person, and you, by far, surpassed every speed limit in the French Quarter."

"So?" she asked, looking adorably frustrated.

"So, you're a bad driver, but that's okay, because you still looked fucking hot driving my car."

Bam, just like that the crease that was forming in her forehead vanished and her eyes lit up from my compliment. It wasn't a lie; she looked hot as hell in her little green dress with her hair blowing in the breeze as she cornered my car around the narrow streets of New Orleans. It was a shame I was too terrified out of my mind to enjoy it.

"Well, I guess I can accept that," she smiled.

"Good, now go get ready for bed. I'm going to go talk to Diego."

"Alright, but don't be long."

I raised an eyebrow at her and asked, "Do you have something special planned? Maybe you're wearing something a little revealing tonight?"

"You wish," she laughed at me. "I'm going to bed in a turtleneck and corduroys."

"Have I told you how much a woman in corduroys at night turns me on? Might want to reconsider."

"I'll take my chances," she laughed. "Now, hurry up."

"Remember, Little One, with great patience, comes great reward."

"Fuck your patience," she stated with a chasing smile as she walked toward the bathroom.

"Maneater," I mumbled to myself, as I pulled away from the gorgeous honey-haired woman who'd stolen my heart.

Needing to make things right with Diego, I left Goldie to herself, hoping she really wouldn't be sporting a turtleneck when I got back, and found my way around Diego's club. The man had impeccable design taste, and given the outside appearance of the club, you would never know it was so posh and sophisticated inside. I was quite proud of Diego for coming so far.

As the music grew heavier and vibrated against the narrow hallway I was walking down, light started to peek through, casting a red glow in the club, making it look almost sinister. The lights were set to coincide with the music, so with every pulse of the deep beat, a darker red light would flash, making it almost seem like the walls were bleeding. I was instantly fascinated.

The moment I turned the corner, I was presented with a view of Blane and Diego, bare-chested and wearing tight leather pants with top hats and ropes in their hands as they hovered around a girl who was comfortably hanging from the ceiling.

The scene in front of me was wildly erotic and something I didn't want Goldie seeing, because I didn't want her getting any ideas from being near these overly sexual men. Easily, they could steal her away from me, no doubt in my mind they had the potential to swipe my girl, a worry I faced every day.

I watched as Diego's body moved smoothly with the music, while the red lights beat off his mocha skin. The man was fluid with his movements, gliding around the floor while twisting and turning with each switch of the music. I could see how successful the club could be, given the ringmaster in charge.

Diego spun on his heel and turned in my direction, where he stopped immediately once he saw me standing in the hallway watching him. As if I was an unwanted guest in his club, an intruder, Diego grabbed a remote from his back pocket, turned off the music, and turned on the lights.

"Dude," Blane complained while covering his eyes. "You have to worn a guy before you blast the lights. My fucking pupils need a second to adjust."

Without looking at Blane, Diego said, "Take down Marissa and help her lotion her wrists. Practice is over for tonight."

Blane looked my way and quickly understood the instant tension that filled the room from my presence. Quietly, Blane undid Marissa and escorted her out of the room, leaving me alone with Diego. Not once did Diego's eyes falter from mine while we waited for Blane to leave, a tactic I taught him when I first took him under my wing. Never back down; never show weakness.

"Why are you here, Jett? Care to blame me for some more of your problems?"

The urge to run my hands through my hair was overpowering, but I held back from showing the nervous tick that I resorted to when I was in a stressful situation. Instead, I held my composure and walked closer to Diego, so we weren't speaking loudly across the room to each other.

"Would you mind taking a moment to talk to me?"

"I have all the time in the world, talk," Diego gestured.

Fucker wasn't going to make it easy, and I didn't expect him to. I would be disappointed in him if he let me off easily, because that would mean everything I taught him about being a strong confident man was a waste of time.

"May we sit?" I asked, as I gestured to one of the tables that sat around the center stage.

"I would rather stand," Diego responded stubbornly.

Not trying to exhale in frustration, since this wasn't going to be easy, I took a deep breath and said, "Diego, I want to apologize for what I said to you about Goldie. I was out of line and in pain. I decided to take my problems out on you when, in fact, you were just being a good friend to Goldie, something I should have been appreciative of."

Diego tried to hide the shocked look on his face at my apology, but I caught it before he could put on his mask.

Instead of letting him speak, I continued, "I want to thank you for taking Goldie in and being a pillar in her life when I was too much of an idiot to be one. I want to thank you for being respectful enough to not try anything with her, even when Goldie and I haven't been on the best of terms, and I want to thank you for taking care of her when I couldn't. I'm very grateful for the friendship you've given me, even in times when I didn't deserve it."

Silence fell through the room as Diego soaked in everything I said. I wasn't nervous that he would tell me to fuck off, because from his body language, I could tell he wasn't mad anymore. I was just anxious to get this conversation over with so I could get back to Goldie.

It felt like minutes ticked by before Diego finally opened his mouth.

"Didn't ever expect to see Jett Colby thanking me for something in my lifetime, given the amount of generosity you've bestowed upon me, but I'm not going to lie, I kind of enjoyed it," Diego responded, as a smirk crossed his face.

Dickhead.

"I see, so you just wanted to see me grovel."

"Pretty much," Diego laughed, while he came toward me and held out his hand, which I shook in relief. "If you want me to pull my pants down so you can kiss my black ass, I would be okay with that too."

"Don't push your luck," I warned.

"Fair enough," Diego chuckled, but then grew serious for a second. "I won't lie, I flirted with the girl often, don't think I was a gentleman while you were apart. You found a good one, a rarity in this city, and if your dumb ass was stupid enough to fuck it up, then I wasn't going to let the opportunity pass me by."

My lips twitched with his confession, and I tried to take a deep breath before I reached over and choked him.

A loud laugh escaped Diego as he gripped his stomach with one hand and pointed at me with the other.

"Oh, damn, the look on your face is worth the ass beating I'm most likely about to get."

"You think it's funny, flirting with my girl?"

"Yeah, I do, and I wasn't the only one. Blane found a liking for her as well. And, you know what? Fair game, man. You fuck up and it's fair game."

"Well, lay the fuck off now," I warned, making Diego laugh some more.

"No need to warn us, dude. Goldie wanted nothing to do with us. For some foolish reason, she seems to have some kind of feelings for you. No worries about her loyalty, but fuck is it satisfying goading you. I don't think it will ever get old."

Needing to lighten up a bit, I let the knot that was forming in my chest loosen just a little as I realized that even the men who threatened me in my thoughts were turned down by Goldie. There was something to be said for trust, and I owed Goldie all of my trust, something I wasn't able to give her before, something I've been working on trying to hand over now.

"Glad I can amuse you," I replied, while relaxing the tension in my shoulders.

Slapping me on the shoulder, Diego said, "Always a pleasure with you, Jett Colby. I'm assuming the little hellion is waiting for you in her room?"

"Yes, but not in the way you're thinking. We're taking things slow."

Diego shot me a pointed look that said he didn't believe me one bit, but I didn't have to convince him.

"Okay," Diego replied skeptically.

Not wanting to get into a debate about where I stood with Goldie, I smiled at Diego and asked, "Are we good, man?"

"We're good," Diego replied easily.

"Thanks," I said sincerely before shaking his hand one last time and heading back down the hallway. "Glad I could make up with my honorary Jett Girl."

Diego flipped me off and called out, "Don't fuck it up this time, Colby."

Little did he know, I had no intention of ever letting Goldie out of my life. She would soon be a permanent fixture in my life if I had any say in it.

I quickly walked back down the long hallway and up the short staircase to Goldie's room. With excitement building up in the pit of my stomach, I lightly tapped on Goldie's door to let her know I was coming in, and then opened the door.

The soft glow from the light on her nightstand greeted me as I walked in her room and saw her sitting cross-legged on the bed, wearing a pair of shorts and a tank top that clung to her every curve. Her hair was tied up in a high bun on the top of her head and her face was free of all make up. She looked absolutely beautiful.

"Don't look at me like that," she said, pointing her finger at me.

I shut the door and walked toward her, reminding myself to keep my hands from getting too frisky with her.

"Like what?"

"You know, like you're thinking about all the different ways you can bend me over and fuck me till morning."

"Actually, I was thinking how beautiful you are, but now I'm thinking about what you said," I said casually, as I started to untuck my shirt from my pants and unbutton it.

"Hey now," she said, while backing up on her bed. "What do you think you're doing?"

"You don't expect me to sleep in my street clothes, do you?"

"You don't expect to sleep naked, do you?" she countered.

"No, just in my boxer briefs," I said casually, as I undid the last button of my shirt and let it fly open as I started to undo my belt. As if she hadn't seen a man's physique in years, she ate me up with her eyes in a matter of seconds, making this night that much harder on me.

"Can't you borrow pajamas from Diego or Blane?" she asked while she gulped.

"I'm a grown man, Goldie. I'm not about to ask Blane and Diego if I could borrow pajamas, something they probably don't possess anyway. You lost the bet, now you have to deal with the consequences, and honestly, I think you're getting the better end of the deal."

"Is that right?" she asked, while crossing her arms over her chest. "And how is that?"

I took off my pants and shirt and folded them as I spoke to her. "You'll see. May I use your bathroom?"

Confused, she nodded her head as I went to the bathroom to quickly brush my teeth with my finger, of course…anything is better than nothing, and then use the toilet. Once I was ready for bed, I turned off the bathroom light and walked toward her. She was leaning against her wall while sitting on her bed waiting for me. I was one lucky son of a bitch who she'd stuck through everything with. I still had a way to go, but she was still here, and that was all that mattered.

I rounded her bed and casually slipped under the sheets. Holding them up for her to crawl in, I said, "Why don't you join me, Little One?"

"I don't trust that you're not going to get all handsy with me."

"You have my word; I just want to hold you, nothing more."

"When have you ever wanted to just hold me?" she asked, as she crawled up the bed and under the covers with me. She rested her head next to mine on her pillow and curled up into a ball while staring me in the eyes.

Sincerely, I moved a stray wisp of hair out of her face and let my fingers caress her soft cheek as I said, "Since the minute you walked into my life; I've just been too damn afraid to admit it."

Carefully, I placed my hand on her hip and pulled her in a little closer, forcing her to unfold her legs and stretch them out so she couldn't use them as a barrier between us. The quick intake of air from her made me realize she wasn't quite expecting my intimate touch, but she wasn't protesting either.

"Is this okay?" I asked, making sure she was comfortable.

"I guess so," she responded, while trying to study me. "Do you really mean the things you say? Or are you just trying to win me back so you can go all dominant on me again?"

"Why do you say that with a negative tone?"

"I don't know," she shrugged. "Because you like controlling

my life."

Disappointment ran through me, as I saw for the first time how she truly saw me as a person. She didn't see me as a protector or someone who truly cared about her soul. No, she saw me as a controlling man, who wanted nothing more than to tell her what do in her life.

"I see," I nodded, while I refrained from getting out of the bed and putting my clothes back on. If I wanted Goldie in my life, then I was going to have to fight for her, in every aspect of our lives.

"Am I wrong?"

"Yes, Little One. I'm afraid you are. I don't want to control your life; I want to protect you, to take care of you, to erase any worry that might come across that beautiful face of yours."

"I don't want to talk about that right now."

"Why? Do you not believe me?" I asked, while slightly running my thumb up and down on the side of her hip.

"I do, that's the problem. I'm still mad at you, remember?" she scrunched her nose all cute like, making the need to kiss her that much stronger.

Clearing my throat, I nodded and asked, "Then, what do you want to talk about, Little One?"

She pondered my question before answering. "Tell me about Kace as a kid. Was he a trouble maker?"

I didn't think I could be caught more off guard. Out of all the questions she could ask me, I didn't think she would ask about Kace. I didn't like it one bit, her wanting to know more about Kace. She was supposed to want to learn about me, not the man who was stiff competition for Goldie's heart.

"Didn't think you were going to ask about Kace," I responded, trying not to sound sour.

"Why not? The man is so mysterious, so hot. If he was a main character in a book, I would want to know all about him. He's always brooding and umm, hello, he's an ex-boxer; if that doesn't scream panty pudding, then I don't know what does. I want to know everything about the man, what makes him tick. So, tell me, what was he like as a kid?"

Goldie's eyes lit up as she spoke of Kace, making me that much more jealous.

Trying not to blow up, I shifted on the bed, trying to get

comfortable. This was not the way I'd envisioned my night.

"Well…"

I was about to tell her Kace was an ass most of his life, until she threw her head back and laughed, making the most amazingly beautiful sound slip from her lips. I watched as the column of her neck moved up and down with her laughter, enticing me to run my tongue along it, to take what I've wanted since the first moment I met her.

She was so fucking mine.

"Why are you laughing?" I asked, enjoying her laugh too much.

She looked at me with tears in her eyes, tears of laughter, and said, "Oh, my God, you should have seen the look on your face." With a scrunched up face and a deep southern voice, she said, "I'm Jett Colby and I'm mad because the girl I like wants to talk about another man." She threw her head back and laughed some more, hopefully more at her terrible impression of me than at my expense. A man could only hope.

"Oh, you're too easy," she said, waving her hand in front of her face. "If I knew life was going to be this much fun dating a dominant man, I would have dated one a while ago. You can fuck around with them so easily."

Damn was she right. One thing that didn't go my way, and I was ready to have a coronary over it.

Pulling her in closer, I rested my forehead on hers and lined our bodies up properly while I stared into her eyes.

"Does that mean we're dating?" I asked, while moving my hand to her back and lightly stroking her bare skin. I felt her breathing grow heavier with every stroke, making me an extremely satisfied man.

"Umm, maybe," she said, while licking her lips and looking at mine.

Temptress, but hell if I was going to make the first move.

"Do you know why it's so much fun dating someone like you?"

"Why?" she asked, pulling her eyes away from my lips for a brief moment in time.

"Because, with one touch, you're putty in my hands. I don't have to do much, just a light graze or a soft whisper in your ear," I said, while leaning forward, brushing my lips against her ear lobe.

"You really think it's that easy?" she said, while her chest rose and fell at a rapid pace.

Stroking her cheek with my thumb, I answered, "Little One, I know it's that easy."

Just as I leaned forward, letting her know I would love to take her lips, I pulled away, causing her to groan out loud from my abandoned position.

"You're a tease," she complained, as she pushed my chest, trying to put distance between us, but I didn't allow for it. No, I just pulled her in closer.

"If I'm a tease, then that means you wanted what I was offering. If that's the case, Little One, all you have to do is ask."

"Nice try, Jett. You're not going to get into my pants that easily."

I just nodded as I allowed my thumb to graze her bare skin, causing all kinds of emotions to run through her expressive eyes. Her body was heated and pouring into mine, making my job of not making the first move that much harder, but I was a man of my word. Even though she slowly moved closer to me, inch by little inch, I kept my mental distance and decided to focus on getting to know Goldie, on letting her get to know me.

Continuing to touch her in every way possible, I asked her, "So what do you want to know about me? I'm an open book, ask away."

"Anything?" Her eyes lit up and I could see the inner cogs of her mind working, trying to come up with some of the juiciest and invasive questions to ask me.

"Easy now, I can see your mind is up to no good. Take it easy on me, Goldie, I'm new at this sharing thing."

"Alright," she smiled softly at me while pressing her hand to my cheek, a gesture that fucking melted me right into her damn palm. "Tell me about your mom."

Fuck, she wasn't going to take it easy at all. It was time to man up.

"My mom was a beautiful woman, who was dealt a bad hand in life. She fell in love with my father, unfortunately, and was manipulated by him until my father got what he wanted, a son to pass his enterprise onto. After I was born, my dad decided he didn't need my mom anymore, divorced her, and proved her to be unstable, so my dad gained custody of me. I was torn away from her right after birth and raised by Miss Mary."

"Oh, my God," Goldie said in but a whisper. "I can't imagine having my baby taken away from me like that. Your poor mother. Did she at least get a good settlement?"

"No," I shook my head. "She was left with nothing and had to fend for herself; she wound up trying to make a living on Bourbon Street, but wasn't too successful. She wound up with AIDS and died right after I was able to escape my father's wrath. She spent her last days with me in the Lafayette Club, enjoying the sunshine and my company."

A small tear rolled down Goldie's cheek as she looked at me with sincerity.

"That is so sad."

I wiped the tear from her cheek and agreed with her. "It is; that's why I created the Lafayette Club, to seek justice for women like my mother, to give them a second chance. I like to think I brought some honor to her."

"You have," Goldie agreed. "So, Miss Mary would help you see your mom when your dad was gone? Were you able to give her money?"

"No, my dad kept a tight hold on the money I earned, said I would appreciate it when I was older. So, instead, I would take my mom food and anything she could possibly pawn without my dad noticing. It helped a little, but she still lived in a freezing cold apartment and went hungry most nights." I took a second to breathe as a tight ball formed in my throat. I couldn't think about my mom this much; the thought of her suffering while I was provided for still gutted me to this day.

"Why would your dad do something like that?"

"Because he's heartless. He doesn't care about anyone but himself and the power of controlling what's important to him. I told you he was a bad man, Goldie, do you understand now?"

"I do," she said softly.

"He taught me how to be ruthless, how to take advantage of those weaker than me, and he taught me how to turn my heart into a cold abyss of darkness. Emotions are not my thing. I'm not very good at expressing myself or accepting compliments. I have a hard time relating to people and can be just as ruthless sometimes when it's something I want."

My thumb ran up her side to her face, where I slowly stroked her bottom lip. "I want to give you everything you want, Goldie. I want to please you, to protect you, but I know there are aspects about me that are rougher around the edges than others. You deserve more than me, your heart deserves to be paired with one that is full and bright, one that matches yours, not a cold black heart like mine."

"But, it's not black, Jett," she replied, while her small hand pressed against my chest, right above my heart. "You think it's black, but it's the furthest thing from it. You might have a hard time expressing yourself, but you do a damn fine job expressing who you are through your actions. You've proven to be a rescuer...an angel to me and the girls and even Diego. You save people, Jett. As much as you want to deny it, you are full of love, you're a hero..."

"No," I shook my head. "I'm not a hero, I'm just..." my words fell short at Goldie's lips on mine.

Her hands encased my face as her body slowly moved on top of mine and her lips gently nipped at mine.

There was only so much a man could take before he snapped, and having Goldie's small body on top of mine was my snapping point.

Instinctively, my hands found her hips where her shirt had risen from her movements, giving me a great expanse of skin to press my hands against. She was so soft...delicate but hard at the same time. She didn't take crap from anyone, especially me. She was a stark contradiction of soft and hard, something I loved about her.

She wiggled on top of me just enough so our bodies were directly in line with each other and her hands never left my face as she deepened our kiss. Every instinct in my body wanted to push her off of me and into the mattress, to take over the intimate moment, but I held back, I allowed her to control the situation, something that was entirely new to me, but worth it if it meant I had my Little One in my arms.

Sadly, she pulled away and stared down at me, her eyes searching mine for some kind of indication of what just happened, what she was doing on top of me. The moment she realized what she was doing, she quickly tried to retreat, but I stopped her, I couldn't help it, I wanted to have her warmth spread across me for a few moments longer.

"Please, don't go," I asked. "You don't have to kiss me, but please just let me feel your skin on mine for a moment longer."

With understanding, she nodded and rested her head on my chest, while her fingers lightly stroked the spot above my heart. My hand found her hair and played with the silky strands while we held each other, our breathing falling in step with each other.

"Thank you," I whispered, grateful for the moment she was granting me.

Not saying a word, she continued to stroke the spot above my heart, letting me know she was there for me and, hopefully, she wasn't leaving.

28
"MY HEART IS OPEN"

Goldie

Yup, I was seconds away from fucking the man I was laying on top of. My legs quivered as I tried to keep them from straddling him and taking what I wanted.

Did he really think he could get away with telling me that story about his mom and not get fucked? I mean, damn, my heart ripped right out of my chest for his mom, for the little boy who deserved his mom, who deserved the love he would have gotten from her.

I needed to touch him, to show him how much he's loved, how much of an amazing man he was, a man he didn't believe he was himself. The only way I knew how to do that was to kiss every inch of him, to show him with my body that he was loved, that he was cherished, but I'd told myself I wasn't going to have sex with him.

I couldn't.

What kind of woman would that make me look like? A hussy…that was for damn sure, but fuck, he way too damn sexy.

The moment he stripped down to his briefs, I knew I was in trouble. I was pretty sure that since we've been apart, he's become more ripped and more defined. I've never been able to truly resist him, and now with this whole sensitive side of him showing…I was so fucking gone.

His need to feel my skin touch his was something he's needed from the very beginning, and I know it's because he feels the closest when our bodies are touching so intimately, but right now, all it was doing was turning me on even more.

I was a sexual being and not being able to ride the fucking bologna pony to pleasure town was torture; it actually made it hard for me to breathe.

Did I say hard to breathe, no, I meant it made it hard to keep my finger out of my vagina.

Fuck, I was so horny, and being on top of Jett, with his hand stroking my hair and him just breathing me in had my pussy wetter than a fucking typhoon blowing up a flesh valley. My hip occasionally would rub against his, and I could feel his hardness, his beautiful cock against my thigh. What I wouldn't give to see that cock right now, to feel it in my hands, to torture him with my fingers, with my tongue.

It would be so easy, I would just start lightly grazing him, letting him know that, yeah, I was interested. Maybe tease him a little by wrapping my fingers all the way around his cock, but then pulling away to keep him on his toes. But, fuck, I couldn't pull away for too long because I wouldn't be able to stay away. So, I would return, but this time, I would apply more pressure, running my fingers along the veins that would be now showing from how turned on he was. I would…

"Goldie," he whispered in a strained voice. "What are you doing?"

"Laying here, what are you doing?" I asked, confused as to why all of a sudden his body was stiff.

"I'm wondering why your fingers are wrapped around my cock."

Testing my left hand, I felt it under my body out of the danger zone, but when I went to locate my right hand, I found it under Jett's briefs, squeezing his cock.

"Jesus," I muttered, as I pulled my hand away and reprimanded my rogue appendage for misbehaving. "Umm, just making sure you still had a dick. It's been some time, you know, just wanted to make sure things didn't fall off," I mumbled, as I scooted off of him and back to my side of the bed.

Skin on skin contact was a bad idea. No, it was the worst idea in the world because right now, every last inch of me was tingling, my hands were itching to go back into the dark cave of Jett's briefs, to test his cock one more time, to see if it was just as hard as I thought it was.

Instead of turning toward him, I flipped on my back and stared at the ceiling, waiting for him to say something. He shifted on the bed and drew closer; he knew exactly what he was doing, he was enticing me, trying to get me to crack.

It was working.

He smelled so good, like he took a two hour bath in pheromones and forgot to dry off. The urge to hump his leg, to drool all over his chest, to stuff his cock in every orifice I had, including my belly button was overpowering. Something was going to happen; the pull was too strong. I needed something from him, a little touch, a little taste. My pussy was begging for it.

"Can you not be so close to me?" I snapped, while I pulled on the blankets and wrapped them up around my chin to try to block the delicious smell of the man and keep a protective blanket layer between us. I practically swaddled myself to keep from having any more villainous hand expeditions.

Fucking phalanges, can't trust them, can't live without them.

"I'm sorry, do you want me to leave?" Jett asked, all sweet and concerned.

I wanted to flip him off, to punch him in the crotch, and kick him square on the shin.

No, I didn't want him to leave. That would be saying, "No, ma'am, I don't want the corn dog that's made out of gold," or something to that effect. What I wanted was for him to have never fucked things up between us because if he was able to control his temper, his psychotic-ness, then we wouldn't be in this mess. I wouldn't be sexually frustrated, and I wouldn't be wavering between wanting to poke him with a fire stick and letting him poke me with his stick.

What a predicament.

Without saying another word, Jett started to get out of the

bed, making me want to scream at the absurdity of the situation.

"Ugh, don't fucking go," I said in an annoyed tone.

"That's convincing," Jett responded with a half-smile.

"Stop it, just stop it," I demanded, while poking him in the chest. "God, I'm so annoyed with you right now. You're acting all sweet when I need to be mad at you. I want to be mad at you."

"But, you're not…"

"I am! It's just that, my horniness is taking over. I can't think clearly when your rock hard body is pressed against mine. Do you really think that's fair, Jett?"

"Fair? Are you serious right now? You're wearing a thin tank top with no bra and you were just laying on top of me. I could feel every movement of your nipple against my chest, and then you go and grab my dick like you're digging around for gold. Do you think that's fair?"

"Oh, poor rich billionaire, a girl was fondling your dick," I said in a smarmy voice. "Grow a real problem."

"You're quite sassy tonight."

"No, Jett. I'm horny," I sat up and pulled the sheets down. I pointed at my crotch and said, "There is a dried up lady cactus down there; she hasn't been cleaned out and rehydrated in weeks. She's desperate."

"What do you want me to do about it?" he said, a smirk playing on his lips.

Refraining from smacking him on the head, I held my hands down and said, "Oh, you're just enjoying this all too much, aren't you?"

"Just a little," he admitted, but held up his hands before I could go bat shit crazy on his ass. "I only admit to that because, ever since I met you, you've been a maneater, teasing me, disobeying me, making my life that much more difficult in the bedroom, so it's a fresh breath of air to see you struggle."

"Oh, is that right? You like to see me struggle? Fine!"

Without a word, I stuck my hand down my shorts and found my clit, not even giving him a warning. I started playing around with the little beast that's been tormenting me the past couple of weeks.

A low growl escaped Jett as he watched me finger myself. Ha, take that, you fucker!

He watched me with determination, and when I thought

I'd cracked him, when I thought he was going to lose that stone veneer, he pulled his boxer briefs down, freed his erection, and started stroking himself while he watched me.

Tou-fucking-che.

Instantly, my eyes flew to his cock, where his hand squeezed tightly around his shaft and pulled on it, tugged the fuck out of it, and then rounded the head of his cock with precision.

My mouth filled with saliva as I watched what he was doing with fascination. Every stroke of his hand hardened his length, and a small glisten of moisture formed at the tip of his beautiful cock.

Oh, hell.

Like a razor to a stray pube, I felt myself move toward him. Fuck, I was gross. Note to self, don't use that analogy again.

His eyes were trained on me as I moved closer; he knew exactly what he was doing; he knew he was enticing me, and damn if it wasn't working. I only had so much willpower, and the minute Jett took off almost all of his clothes, my last shred of willpower was used. It was only in time that I found myself moving closer and closer to him.

"You're not playing fair," I said.

"Hey, I'm only participating in what you started. You can't play with fire, Little One."

"How am I playing with fire?" I asked, while I ran my hand up his leg, making his breathing pick up.

"You know damn well what you're doing."

"And, like you don't know what you're doing? You think I can sit next to you and just watch you touch yourself and not be intrigued? I might be mad at you, but I still want you."

With a smirk, Jett nodded at me and said, "Prove it."

It was his bait; he was trying to get what he wanted, but hell if I wasn't a stupid flopping fish because I grabbed right ahold of his bait and let him reel me in.

Not even thinking about it, I pushed his chest down so he was lying flat on the bed and pulled his briefs all the way down to his ankles, exposing that fantastic cock that had tortured me many times in the Bourbon Room.

Straddling Jett's Legs, I grabbed a hold of his hands and pinned them to his sides and started to lower my head.

"Goldie, don't," Jett said, abruptly, shocking me a bit.

"What? Why?" I asked self-consciously.

"You don't have to do that. I wasn't playing fair."

"Do you not want me to suck your cock?" I asked with a raised eyebrow.

"No," he shook his head. "I want nothing more than for your perfect lips to be wrapped around me, but I don't want you to do anything you told yourself you wouldn't."

I pulled away for a second and studied him. "You know, I like this new sensitive Jett, where you talk to me and express your feelings, but right now, with your erection playing tiddlywinks with your belly button, I kind of want the dominant man."

"You can't have both," Jett answered honestly, shaking me out of the cock-induced stupor I was in.

"What do you mean I can't have both?"

"I can't be both for you, Goldie. If I'm dominant, then I'm going to be cold and unresponsive..."

"No," I shook my head and interrupted him. "Not acceptable. That is not true at all. There have been plenty of times when you've been sweet and endearing in the bedroom, don't give me that bullshit."

"It's not a switch I can turn on and off."

"Jett, I'm not asking for you to cry when we come at the same time; I'm asking you to share with me when we're sharing and I'm asking you to be the fucking man I want when I need him. It's not an either-or type of situation." I pulled away and shook my head. "Maybe this was a bad idea."

"What do you want from me?" Jett asked, as he pulled up his briefs. "I'm trying to be the man you want me to be."

"I want you to be you," I said honestly. "I want you to be exactly who you are, but not afraid to tell me things, to open up to me."

"That's not who I am," Jett said sharply, as he ran his hands through his hair. "I'm afraid, Goldie. I'm so fucking afraid."

"Why?" I asked, feeling exhausted.

"Because I'm fucking in love with you," Jett said with his back turned toward me.

Everything in the room turned dark and all I saw was the silhouette of Jett Colby, looking away and looking almost pained.

His back moved up and down with his breath as I tried to comprehend the monumental moment that had just transpired between us. I wanted to jump on the bed and smack my tits together in joy, but knew that wasn't quite appropriate. So, instead, I carefully crawled toward him and wrapped my arms around his stomach.

Exhaling, Jett wrapped his arms around mine and allowed me to pull him closer. Lightly, I pressed my lips against his while my hands cradled his face, letting him know I wasn't going anywhere.

I felt the light pressure of his fingers grip my hips in almost a needy manner, like he needed me to prove to him that everything was going to be okay. Well, I had no fucking problem with that.

Placing one last kiss on his lips, I pulled away and ran my hands down the front of my body until they reached the hem of my tank top. Like the seductress I was, I deliberately took my time gripping my tank top and moving it off my body until I exposed my breasts and dropped the tank top to the side. Jett's eyes were fixed on mine until he couldn't take it anymore, then he took his time perusing my half-naked body.

My nipples were hard…just from his stare, they were ready to pop right the fuck off. My nipples had always been a fan of Jett, and tonight was no exception.

Needing to be naked for him, I took off my shorts and tossed those to the side as well. Jett cleared his throat as I moved closer to him and wrapped one hand around the back of his neck and straddled his lap, allowing my knees to hold my weight as I used Jett as my personal stripper pole.

With my signature movement, I started to rotate my hips just right so I was stroking his hardened length perfectly. I looked down at Jett, whose eyes were fixed on my exposed lower half, watching my every movement. He was biting his lip, as if trying to hold in obscenities that wanted to escape.

His hands glided up my thighs, making me moan out loud; it was a movement I couldn't act like didn't affect me because once his hands finished moving up my thighs, they hovered right above my heated core. My pussy was throbbing, fucking throbbing, begging for the man, needing there to be no material between us.

When I thought his hands were going to work their way down south, they actually travelled north, up my sides, lightly gliding over my ribs and just under my breasts, where his fingers played with the soft and sensitive skin.

Fuck me.

He made small movements, movements that didn't seem like much, but between the combination of my pussy rubbing against his dick and his small touches, I was about to scream in frustration. I wanted it all; I didn't want to be teased.

Needing more, I ran my other hand down his stomach and to the waistband of his briefs. I pulled away for a second, so I could release him from his confines, but before I could grab ahold of what I really wanted, Jett flipped me on the bed and straddled my body so he could hover above me.

"How wet are you?" he asked, in that dominant voice I craved.

"Very," I said in a breathless heroine-type voice that you only hear in fifties movies.

Scanning my body, he took a deep breath and asked, "Do you want this?"

"More than anything."

"The whole package? Everything that's fucked up about me. You want this?"

"Yes," I nodded my head and placed my hand on his cheek. "I want this."

With a curt nod, Jett grabbed my hands and pinned them above my head. "Do not fucking move those, do you hear me?"

I was pretty sure my "burning loins" heard him and submitted.

I watched as the man pulled off his briefs and tossed them on the floor. Oh, hell yes, this is what I needed; this is what we needed. Fuck talking right now, we needed to talk with our bodies.

Jett's mouth found mine in a frenzy of heated passion. He kissed with force, with meaning, with the idea that this was it, we were it for each other. His lips were to the point of bruising mine; he was so rough, so possessive, but I wanted it, I wanted him to brand me, to make me his. I needed the reassurance.

Yes, we still had things we needed to talk about. Jett still had issues he needed to work through, but I was positive we could work through them together.

So much for my no sex policy. That lasted a good couple of hours. I have so much willpower it's overwhelming…not.

His hands ran up my arms and then back down, sending

chills up my spine. His fingers grazed the sides of my breasts, making a world of wet flow between my legs. With one small touch, he had me wiggling in place, searching for him to take me.

His hands continued a journey down my sides to my hips, where they rested and pulled them up. He moved forward ever so slightly so the tip of his cock just barely grazed my pussy. I wanted to fucking scream, to grab his dick and shove it inside of me, but that would mean moving my arms, and hell if I was going to do that. So, instead, I let him torture me.

Releasing my lips, he pulled up and looked down at me with the sexiest smile I had ever seen, like he was showing me how beyond happy he was that I was his. I watched in fascination as he grabbed his cock and started moving it up and down my slickness, gathering it all at the tip of his cock. He tortured my clit with small movements, little thrusts until I screamed.

"God! Please," I begged, on the verge of happy tears. I just wanted him, I wanted to feel him inside of me; there was nothing I wanted more.

"Patience, Little One."

Fuck his patience, he could take his patience and shove it up his dick hole as a cork to see how it felt not being able to orgasm when you wanted.

Continuing the torture, I watched the veins in Jett's neck pop as he tried to hold onto the little control he had left. I could see the moment he cracked, when I moved my hips just at the right time when his cock was close to my hole, allowing him in just enough. With a growl sprouting from his chest, he dropped down over me and thrust his cock inside.

"Fuck!" I screamed, trying to keep my arms above my head, but wanting to wrap them around him.

He filled me perfectly, to the point where I didn't think he could go any deeper, but with a tilt of my hips, he did. He found that one spot that could make me shake my leg and start spewing obscenities. With each stroke, he hit the spot and made the orgasm that was slowly building up come forward like a tidal wave.

"Oh, God, I'm going to come," I told him, not being able to hold on too long.

"Me too," he grunted, surprising me. The man always lasted longer than this.

His lips found mine once again and our tongues met in the

middle. I was lost in him and before I knew it, my body was shaking uncontrollably as we both came at the same time, chests bumping against each other and lungs gasping for any kind of air to help the beating of our hearts.

There's something to say about delayed gratification and all the wait and pent up anger…it was worth it, because right now, I had Jett wrapping his arms around me and holding me close to his chest just after giving me one of the most explosive orgasms of my life.

Once our hearts grew steadier, Jett pulled us both under the covers and made sure I was pressed tightly against his chest. My fingers danced across his skin as his hand ran through my hair, playing with the individual strands. The sweet gesture had my eyes shutting instantly, calming everything in my body that had been disrupted. This was all I never needed.

I rubbed my cheek against his chest and said, "You didn't ask me if I was here to submit to you."

He kissed the top of my head and said, "I know."

"Why not?"

"Because, you're mine now, Goldie, forever. That means I don't ever have to ask you again."

"Oh," I replied, as butterflies did somersaults in my stomach.

I was his, forever.

29
"JUST GIVE ME A REASON"

Goldie

Oh, sweet Jesus, I was sore. I didn't think Jett was that hard on me but now that I lay in bed with the sun shining on my face, I could feel every sore inch of my body from the multiple ways Jett took me last night. The man was relentless once I gave him the green light. He took me in bed, up against the wall, on the floor, in the shower…I don't think there was one piece of my room that Jett hadn't pushed me up against and fucked me blindsided.

"Mmmmm," I moaned, as I flopped to the side, looking for a warm body to snuggle into, but coming up short when I was met with cold blankets.

My eyes opened just as my pupils told me to F-off from the bright sun. I felt around, but there was no hot and sexy man next to me. It wasn't a dream; I knew that.

Slightly panicked, I forced my eyes open and looked around the room. My lamp was still on the ground, my clothes were on the floor, lotion was smeared on the nightstand, and one of my heels was hanging off the curtain rod…oh, yeah. I smiled to myself as I thought about my heel. I am just so classy.

The one thing that I did notice that gave me hope was Jett's clothes that were still folded up to the side. He was still here.

Giddy, I wrapped my robe around my body, not bothering with any other clothes, and opened the door to my room. The smell of coffee greeted me, pulling me to the kitchen. The door was closed, but I could hear voices on the other side, so I made sure my robe was extra tight and then swung the door open.

Standing together were Jett, Diego, and Blane, all shirtless, wearing various types of pants, except for Jett, who was in his briefs still, holding cups of coffee and grinning at me like they were posing for a calendar.

All they needed was Kace and the whole room would spontaneously combust from too much sexy. Seeing all of them side by side was too much for one horny pussy to handle. Yes, Jett took care of me last night, but my lady bit was insatiable, since she'd been out of commission for a while.

"Are you just going to stand there and stare or are you going to come give me a good morning kiss?" Jett asked with a smirk over his coffee cup.

"Actually, I was going to give Diego a good morning kiss," I answered defiantly, as I walked toward Diego, who straightened up from leaning on the counter and held out his arms.

I was moments from falling into his open arms when Jett pulled on me and led me into his territory. His chest was heated as it pressed against me and his arm wrapped around my body, claiming me as his.

Whispering in my ear, Jett leaned over and said, "Don't even test me, Little One."

Chills ran down my spine and scattered across my skin from his warm breath pressed against my ear. His heated skin seared through my thin robe as he pulled me in closer, gripping onto my hip so I was unable to move away from him, not that I really wanted to.

Looking up at Jett, I gave him my most innocent smile, which made him shake his head in laughter. Even though I felt like he owned me in every way, I really did own him. I had the ability to bring this powerful man to his knees. He would do anything for me, and sharing wasn't even an option.

He loved me.

Holy shit, he loved me. This all-encompassing, powerful man loved me. He could have any woman he wanted, but he chose me, he chose to open his heart up and let me in. He fucking loved me!

Clearing his throat, Diego said, "So, I'm assuming this means Jett is no longer a fuck-up?"

I looked up at Jett, who was taking a sip of coffee from his mug. I watched as his throat gracefully swallowed the hot liquid, warming me in all the right ways.

"Unfortunately, he's still a fuck-up, but I'm a sucker for fuck-ups," I said, while smiling at a surprised Jett.

"A fuck-up, huh? I wouldn't say I fucked up last night, or this morning," Jett wiggled his eyebrows.

"Dude, we all know what you did last night," Blane said, while taking a seat in one of the kitchen chairs.

"What? You heard us?" I asked, feeling slightly embarrassed.

"Kind of hard not to," Diego responded. "Especially when Jett is trying to hammer you through the wall. I mean, fuck dude, do you have a jackhammer in your pants?"

"I don't know, ask Goldie."

All three men looked down at me, making me feel incredibly exposed.

"What, you're all clammed up now? That's hard to believe," Jett teased.

"She's all talk," Diego added. "Girl can't handle being picked on."

"You would think, with how sassy she can be, she would be able to defend herself in front of three strapping men," Blane said, while taking a sip of his coffee.

"She's shy," Jett cooed in my ear.

"She has no game," Diego poked.

"She can't even handle…"

"Jett has a needle dick," I shouted, trying to think of something offensive to say. Puffing out my chest, I nodded and said, "Yup, he has a needle dick, can't even find it in his pants. It's like a little piece of macaroni floating around in a world of big meat balls. Yeah, you heard that right, he has big balls and a small dick. It's like, where's your dick, man?" I said, while holding my hands out and adding a nervous laugh. "Like, uh, hello, are you even a man or am I staring at a giant moose knuckle?"

Diego, Blane, and Jett all fell silent as they just wondered what the hell was going through my head.

Sheepishly, I said, "Yup, big balls, small dick," just to confirm my point.

Silently, Diego walked toward both Jett and me and looked Jett up and down before squatting in front of him. He moved his head closer to Jett's crotch and Jett swatted him away.

"What the hell do you think you're doing?" Jett asked, offended.

"Looking for the giant moose knuckle, this I have to see."

"Get the fuck out of here," Jett laughed, while grabbing ahold of my arm. "Looks like someone needs to learn a lesson."

"Oh, no, not another game of find the needle in the haystack," I rolled my eyes, making both Blane and Diego throw their heads back and laugh.

"Damn, Jett, do you need to talk to us?" Blane asked. "We can maybe hook you up with an enlarger or something."

"Well, now the hammering makes sense," Diego said in between laughter. "The man is just trying to get his damn dick to penetrate the poor girl."

A very un-lady like snort came out of me, just as Jett grabbed the waistline of his briefs.

"You really want to joke?" Jett asked me, as his hands started to pull his briefs down.

"No!" I shouted as I grabbed ahold of his hands and stopped him. A giggle escaped me as I said, "Please, don't embarrass yourself. Not in front of these guys, it will be too humiliating for you. I can't let you do that."

Looking me dead in the eyes, Jett said in a firm voice so only I could hear him, "You are in so much fucking trouble, Little One."

Gulping, I looked at how serious he was, and damn if I didn't instantly turn wet. His kind of trouble was my kind of pleasure.

"Uh oh, looks like someone is going to get a spanking," Diego teased. "How did it go last night?" Diego turned to Blane for help, who stood up and rubbed his head.

Blane bent over and started smacking his ass while saying, "I think something like 'oh, yeah Jett, oh, yeah, big boy, give it to me harder." Then he squealed liked a little girl.

Diego clapped his hands together and fist bumped Blane. "Nailed it, man."

Jett ticked and shook his head no at the same time. "You

couldn't be further from the truth."

"Thank you," I said, while scooting closer to Jett, offended by Blane's horrible impression of me.

Jett patted my shoulder and said, "She doesn't squeal; she does more of a snort-type thing, like a pig drowning in water." To my horror, I watched as Jett bent over and started snorting like a pig, while adding a bit of a gargle in his throat, causing both Blane and Diego to practically fall over from laughter.

I watched as all three men tried to impersonate the pig gargle orgasm sound in the kitchen, making each other laugh hysterically. With my hands on my hips, I stomped my bare foot on the ground like a child.

"You're all just hideous men," I called out before making my way back to my room, completely unable to take a joke.

I slammed my door shut, sat on my bed, and folded my arms over my chest, just waiting for the pig snorter himself to walk in. I could have counted down the seconds until he opened the door.

It was right on cue when he opened my door and shut it without taking his eyes off of me. He stood there, silently, just taking me all in, owning the fucking room with one breath, with one tick of his jaw.

"Why are you looking at me like that?" I asked, feeling myself wilt under his stare.

"Like what?" he asked, as he approached me with the kind of swagger that would make your clit pop right off.

"You know," I shifted on the bed, as I readied for his pounce; it was inevitable, especially with the way he was approaching me. "Like you want to eat me."

"Is that a problem?" he asked, as he stood right in front of me, making me shrink in place.

"Yes," I squeaked out. "Wouldn't want to pig snort again."

Smiling, Jett said, "Well that won't be a problem, given the fact that I have such a small dick that you need a pair of tweezers to pick it up."

"Yeah, about that..."

"Yeah, about that," Jett copied me as he leaned forward and pushed me back on the bed. His muscles flexed as he held himself right above me. "Funny that you're so quickly able to lie about my misfortunes."

"Someone has to pop that ego of yours," I gulped, as his hand found the knot of my robe and started to undo it.

"Ego?" he asked with a raised eyebrow. "Is that what you think it is, an ego?"

"What else could it be?" I asked, just as my robe was parted, exposing my breasts to the cold morning air, puckering my nipples in such a fantastic way.

"Confidence," Jett responded. His finger trailed the outline of my nipple as he said, "Confidence in a man can often be mistaken for an ego, but do you know what the difference is, Little One?"

As he pinched my nipple, my chest lifted off the bed and I shook my head no.

His fingers continued to do torturous loops around my nipples as he spoke, "The difference between having confidence and an ego is that a man with an ego can be very self-involved, but a man with confidence doesn't need to puff his chest to prove his self-worth; he is bold, he is sure, and he knows how to fucking please a woman."

His last words ricocheted through my mind, as his mouth fell down onto my breast, while his other hand quickly made work of my free nipple. The feel of the rough five o'clock shadow that grazed his jaw and his tongue lapping around my taught nipple was a new feeling of euphoria I felt like I hadn't experienced yet.

Unlike every other time in the bedroom, my hands were free of his constraints, so I took advantage of it by running my hands down his strong and solidly muscular back to the waistband of his briefs. With a quick intake of air as he bit down on my nipple, my fingers grasped his briefs and pulled them down, so I could grab a handful of his tight ass.

Like a fucking lunatic, I felt my hands go crazy with pleasure as I gripped his ass as firmly. I wasn't much of an ass person, but I had to admit, I was going to grow quite fond of the two hammy hams between my fingers.

"Hammy hams?" Jett asked, as his mouth lifted off my nipple and he looked up at me with a fucking adorable smirk.

"What?" I asked, delirious from what he was doing to me.

"You were mumbling hammy hams."

Thank God I was a complete embarrassment to myself, because what else would help keep me grounded? Jesus.

"Yeah, um, you have nice hammy hams. It's the first time I've really been able to explore your ass, so I kind of went a little crazy with it."

"Clearly," he chuckled. "Just don't go digging around in there."

"God, no!" I practically shouted.

"What? Is my ass that nasty to you?" he asked, feigning insult.

"What? No, your ass is nice," I backtracked. "I just...I mean, I don't do the finger in the hole thing. I mean, that's your job...wait! No, I mean, finger in the hole, yes, but not in the stink, just in the pink. You know, the vagina..." I let out a long breath, as Jett just let me ramble on, so I said, "You know, this ass talk is far above you, where are your manners?"

"Someone told me I needed to loosen up a bit, so I'm trying that new approach. I've found it to be quite rewarding," he smirked.

"Why? Because you get to hear me ramble on like a moron who doesn't know how to stop?"

"Exactly."

"Hmm, well, I'm glad you're getting pleasure out of this."

"I am," he smiled once again and then perused my body. "Now, Little One, it seems like you need to be punished for your lying in the kitchen. Since you were not so kind to the size of my cock, I thought I would really show you how misinformed you were."

"How would you do that?" I asked, watching him pull himself away from me and pull his briefs off. He toed them to the side, giving me a great view of his very impressive erection.

So, when I was in the kitchen, discussing Jett's little macaroni, what I really meant was the man was sporting a cannoli fit for the Jolly Green Giant...if the Jolly Green Giant was gay and could open his mouth wide enough to fit a grapefruit in it.

It was a tree trunk, a cannon sitting between his legs, the arm of a grown man...and it looked like that arm was about to fist me.

Fuck, the thoughts in my head were so wrong, but damn if I wanted to be right.

In my mind, I wanted to put my hands out and wiggle my fingers while saying, "Gimme, gimme, gimme," but knew that not only would give me a pass straight to restraint-ville, but it would also move the mood from sexy as hell to brand new virgin confused as to what sets the mood.

"Get your eye full?" Jett asked, cutting into my thoughts.

"Can you actually turn to the side a little?" I asked while directing him with my finger.

He shook his head no and approached me. "Up on your knees," he commanded.

And just like that, with that domineering voice of his, which had a southern charm to it, I was stripped of my robe and getting on my hands and knees, preparing myself for whatever he had planned.

He came up behind me and placed his hand on my lower back. His fingers spread wide, he pressed down just hard enough that I knew he meant business as he ran his hand up my spine. His body came up close behind me, and I could feel his erection against the back of my thigh, enticing me to beg.

He hovered over my back as his hand found my neck. His fingers ran through the small wisps of my hair and dug into my scalp, massaging my nerves, and sending impossible chills all over my skin.

The hardness of his body pressed against me as his mouth grew close to my ear.

"Little One, I have a little bone to pick with you. You see, I'm afraid you gave the wrong impression of my cock back there in the kitchen. Now, do you know what happens to you if you lie?"

"You spank me like a bad girl?" I asked, giddy at the thought.

"No, that would be too much pleasure for you. If you're to be punished, then I want you to be punished. So, do you know what that means?"

"Dinner in my room?" I asked, trying to be charming.

"One more smart mouthed comment from you and I'll make sure you don't see pleasure for a week."

Well, that fucking clammed me right up.

"Better," Jett said, pleased with my silence. "As a punishment, I will touch you, I will bury myself deep inside of you, to the point where you don't think you can take anymore, and just when you think you can't take it anymore, when you feel every part of your body turn numb, I will pull away, tie you up, and leave like that so you can't orgasm."

"What?" I practically cried, as I turned to look at him.

"Eyes straight ahead; don't make me ask you again."

Obeying him, I looked straight ahead and cautiously asked, "Would you really do that to me?"

"Do you think you deserve it after that conversation in the kitchen?"

"You made fun of me too…"

Snap.

With a quick flick of his wrist, his hand connected with my ass, sending a shock of surprise and then pleasure through my body. Oh, fuck, yes.

"Remember who is in charge here, Little One."

"Yes, Jett," I answered.

"Now, do you think you deserve that punishment?"

Knowing that I didn't want that punishment, I wanted to say no, but if I agreed with him, he might take it easy on me, so instead of acting out and showing my defiance, I swallowed my pride and nodded my head.

"Let me hear you say it," Jett said forcefully.

"Yes, I deserve that punishment," I replied breathlessly at the way his hand started to move over my back again.

He traced my spine carefully and then ran his fingers down to my ass, to the backs of my thighs and then travelled on to my innermost sensitive skin, to a spot that was sore from last night, but more than happy to accommodate Jett's current needs. I grew even wetter as his fingers teased my core, played with my responsive skin, my skin that made me shake and quake under his touch.

My breathing grew heavier as I tried to control my hips from thrusting into his fingers. Self-respect, Goldie, self-respect.

"Does my punishment turn you on, Little One? You're very wet."

"You turn me on," I responded, wanting him to push his fingers inside of me, anything to lessen the pressure that was building up.

"Good answer," I felt him smile behind me. He leaned forward again, so his mouth was close to my ear, as his hand still continued to tease me, while the other hand ran up my stomach to my hanging breasts. He took turns tweaking each nipple, causing me to moan out loud.

"You're so responsive, Little One. For that, I will forgo my punishment and teach you a lesson a different way."

Thank fuck!

"What do you have planned now?"

"Since you seem to forget how large my cock really is, I'm going to take it upon myself to remind you."

"How do you plan on...oh fuck!" I screamed, as Jett plunged himself inside of me.

Just as Jett was gentle and loving last night, he now turned right back into his dominant self, and I loved every little moment of it. Don't get me wrong; I liked it when I was allowed to touch him, to explore him, but right now, with him gripping onto my hips and deep inside of me, I was more than happy to see this side of him.

His fingers held tightly onto my skin as he filled me with every glorious inch of him. Yup, definitely not a little macaroni.

I waited patiently for him to start thrusting into me, to show me how deep he could go, but he just held still, growing inside of me, but never moving. I thought of helping him out, reminding him of the typical movement one conducts in such a position, but knew that could only cause trouble, so instead, I opened my mouth.

"Jett," I begged, letting him know that I was ready for whatever he had planned.

"Were you asked to speak, Little One?"

"No, but, I just...fuck, I need you, Jett."

"Very well, you just have to do one thing."

"What's that?" I would do just about anything right now to get the man to move his hips.

"You need to shout at the top of your lungs how big my cock is, so Diego and Blane can hear you." I could hear the mirth in his voice and it took all my strength not to turn around and slap his cock like it was a wet piece of bread.

"You can't be serious?"

"Oh, I'm very much serious right now, Little One. I don't joke around when it comes to my cock. Now, you have two options, you can either scream at the top of your lungs that my cock is trying to swallow you whole, or I can go back to option number one, the original punishment."

The cocky mother fucker.

"You really want me to say your cock is trying to swallow me?"

"Yes, I find that will prove the point of my size. Your choice."

Like I had a choice right now. The man was ten inches deep

inside of me, ready to make my fucking day, of course I was going to shout.

Rolling my eyes, I cleared my throat and said, "Jett's cock is swallowing me whole."

Jett tsked at me and started to pull out, causing me to clear my throat and shout one more time, "Jett's cock is swallowing me whole!"

Jett pondered for a second and then said, "You can do better than that."

Gah! If it wasn't for what was going to come, I would have punched the man behind me.

One more time, I sucked in air, and then shouted as loud as I could, "Jett's cock is swallowing me whole!!"

"We heard you the first time," Diego said, while shouting past my door, heating my entire body with embarrassment.

"Oh, my God," I mumbled, as Jett chuckled behind me. "I hate you."

"No, you don't," Jett said, as he leaned over me, inserting himself all the way in. "You don't hate me at all. Admit it," he demanded with a tweak to my nipple.

"I don't hate you."

"Good."

With that, Jett forcefully moved his hips forward and held on tight to my body as he continued the movement. His mouth nibbled on the back of my neck, while his hips did all the work. I steadied our position by digging my hands into the bed, trying to keep as still as possible with each stroke.

He slipped in and out of me with ease, putting more and more pressure on my neck with each passing moment, to the point where I didn't think the goosebumps on my skin could grow any larger.

One of his hands slipped from my hips to my breasts and started kneading them with precision, slightly stroking my nipples, teasing the undersides, and then gripping them whole. He was a fucking mastermind, and I was there for him to play with.

Just when I didn't think he could go any deeper, he pressed his hand to my neck, making me lower myself to my forearms, and that was when he thrust deeper, reaching a place I didn't even know existed.

"Oh, God," I practically cried, pleasing him.

He pulled away from me, gripped my hips, and started making long slow strokes with his dick. The movement was luxurious; it was too good to be true; it was almost too much to take. My mind went blank and all I could feel was the friction he was causing. His hand ran to the front of my clit and he pressed on the little nub with his finger and then made long strokes against it, the same stroke he was making with his cock.

That was all it took. My head buried in my hands and I cried out as my body ricocheted with pleasure, convulsing in all different ways, turning numb to the point that I felt like I was floating on a cloud.

My mouth was held wide open, as I screamed and pressed into the now-rapid movements Jett was making. He stiffened above me and groaned as I felt him orgasm; just the thought of pleasing such a man shocked me with another round of pleasure, sending me into fit of pure euphoria.

Slowly, Jett shortened his movements until he collapsed on top of me and pulled himself out. Without even taking a second chance to think about it, he flipped me around so I was now resting my head on his shoulder and he was holding me tightly against his body. My hand found his taut stomach, where I started to lightly stroke it with my fingers.

"That was so fucking good," I said, while kissing the side of his neck. "Thank you for my punishment."

"Don't ever forget how big my dick is," he chuckled.

"How could I, after you tickled my brain with it?"

"Let's not exaggerate," he laughed, as he pulled me in closer and kissed the top of my head. His chin rested there as his breathing evened out.

This is what it felt like to be loved by Jett Colby. He fucked you like he owned your body, and then he held you as if you were the most precious thing in his life. I could get used to this.

"Jett?"

"Hmm?" he asked into my hair.

"You know, last night, when you said…"

"I love you," he finished for me.

"Yes, did you mean it?"

"I mean everything I say to you, Goldie, don't second guess that. I love you. I never thought I would find this feeling, this excitement, when it came to falling in love, but it's here; it's so fucking prevalent in my body that I sometimes don't know what to do with it."

Swallowing hard, I nodded and said, "Well, um, I just wanted to tell you that I love you, too. I know I didn't say it last night, but I wanted you to know."

Pulling me on top of his body, Jett placed both of his hands on my cheeks to look me in the eyes and said, "Thank you, Little One. I'm so sorry for everything I put you through, and I am beyond grateful for your understanding and for your love. I can't tell you how much it means to me."

I was about to answer when Jett's phone that was on the nightstand of my bed started ringing. I looked over for him and saw that it was Kace calling.

"It's Kace."

Jett took a deep breath and reluctantly reached over to grab his phone, while still holding onto me; clearly, he didn't want me going anywhere.

"This better be good," Jett said, answering the phone.

Jett was silent as his jaw grew tighter and tighter. I could hear Kace's voice, but I couldn't make out what he was saying. Whatever he was telling Jett, it was not something Jett really wanted to hear, because when he hung up, he tossed his phone to the side and ran his hands over his eyes.

I swear to God, if whatever Kace told Jett was going to once again prolong the moment that I could stay wrapped around Jett, someone was going to be castrated, and since Kace was the man who delivered the information, it wasn't looking good for him right now.

"Is everything okay?" I asked, just as Jett slipped out from under me, leaving me cold. I pulled the blanket on my bed up around my chest, so I didn't feel as exposed when Jett spoke to me.

"No," Jett gruffed out, as he started to dress himself.

"Are you going to tell me what's going on?"

"No, this doesn't concern you," Jett said, falling back into his old non-expressive ways.

Grabbing my robe, I threw it over my body, tied the knot, and stood in front of him while he buttoned up his shirt.

"Jett Colby, you better tell me what's going on, or I will push you out the door and send you on your way; I don't care how much your dick swallows me. I will not stand by while you once again keep everything from me, do you hear me? This is not a fucking joke."

Realizing the pattern he was slipping back into, he raked his hand through his hair and then grabbed my hands. He kissed my knuckles and said, "You're right, I'm sorry. I'm just so used to taking care of everything. I'm sorry."

Well, pinch my nipple right off, the man knew how to realize when he was wrong. I wanted to hang my jaw in surprise, but knew it wasn't the time; I would gloat by myself later over my small victory.

"Thank you. So, what did Kace tell you?"

Jett took a deep breath and said, "Rex Titan was found dead in his home; he hung himself, what seems to be a few days ago."

Just like that, everything around me blurred as Jett's words rang through my head.

Rex Titan was dead.

30
"RUN RUN RUN"

Jett

The car ride to the Lafayette Club fell silent between Goldie and myself. After the phone call from Kace, the jovial mood we'd been experiencing turned sour quickly, and not because of the fact that Rex committed suicide, which was shocking news to find out, but because of Goldie's reaction.

She cried!

Goldie fucking cried! She was still crying. As the driver took us back to the Lafayette Club, she cried next to me, little sobs escaping her. I wanted to reach over and pull her into my embrace, to tell her it was going to be okay, but the rage that was boiling deep inside of me kept me at a far distance from her.

I tried to control my temper, to realize that she did have a history with Rex and the information came out of nowhere, but the devastation in her eyes was hard to swallow. I couldn't help but wonder if she would react the same way if something was to ever happen to me. How would she react? I would hope to God she would be more hurt than she was now. Then again, she looked pretty wrecked at the moment.

The car pulled up in the back driveway that connected to the garage and I quickly let myself out of the car, not waiting for my driver to open the door. The crunch of the gravel behind me let me know Goldie was following close behind. I was surprised she was able to pull herself out of the car, since she was so torn apart about what happened.

Shaking my head in disgust, I walked to the back entrance of the club, threw the door open, and then quickly walked up the back steps to the third floor. I avoided all the common areas because I was in no mood to talk to anyone.

Funny how fast the mood could change between two people with one phone call.

"Jett," Goldie called after me, but I ignored her and found my way to my office, where I quickly poured myself two fingers of bourbon. The warm liquid coated my throat, easing some of the tension that was building up inside of me.

"Jett," Goldie said again, as she walked through my office and slammed my door shut. "What the hell? Why are you running away from me?" she sniffled.

"I wasn't running," I corrected her, as I took a seat in my office chair and turned it to look out the window.

I turned my chair away from her so she would get the hint that I didn't want to talk to her, but I had a feeling that wasn't going to matter. She was a stubborn girl, and if she wanted to talk to me, I could only imagine she would result to climbing over my chair, if need be, to get me to open my mouth.

Yes, I was resorting to my old ways of shutting her out; I knew exactly what I was doing, but right now, it was because if I told her how I felt, I knew I wouldn't be able to hold back.

The top of my chair was gripped by a small hand and I was forcefully turned away from my window; I was greeted by a very red-eyed and very mad Goldie, who had her arms crossed over her chest and was looking down at me, ready to unleash.

"You have two fucking seconds to tell me why you are acting like a dick right now or I am taking off. You can't keep resorting to shutting me out. I am not fucking kidding, Jett. I will not stand for this."

Running my hands over my face to give me a second to think, I took a deep breath and said, "I would love to have this little heart-to-heart with you, but I'm afraid you're not going to like what I have to say."

"What? Do you think you can only tell me things I like to hear? That's not reality, Jett; probably fifty percent of the crap that comes out of your mouth is something I won't like…"

"Fifty percent?" I asked with a questioning look. "That number seems absurdly high."

"Don't, don't distract me from what's going on here. Tell me why the hell you're acting cold towards me."

"You really want to know?" I asked, as I got out of my chair and started pacing my office.

"Yeah, I really want to know," Goldie said in a mocking voice, trying to impersonate me. The woman knew how to press my buttons, and she was doing a damn fine job of it right now.

"Fine, I can't stand the fact that you're crying over Rex's death. The thought of you being sad over him makes me physically nauseous. Seeing you weep over a man who did nothing but try to separate me from you is like a fucking knife to my stomach. Right now, I don't even want you near me."

"You can't be serious," Goldie responded, shocked.

"I don't fuck around, Goldie," I said, getting in her face. "You should know that by now."

She stood her ground as I hovered over her, trying to startle her out of my office before I said something more damaging.

"You want me to leave?"

"Yes, I want you to leave," I said without blinking an eye.

She crossed her arms over her chest again and said, "Well, too fucking bad; I'm not going anywhere."

Frustrated, I blew out a long breath and went over to my bourbon to fill up my glass.

"Resorting to your bourbon again…you're becoming a real lush, aren't you? Can't face reality, you have to hide behind a glass of amber liquid. I guess it's your upbringing, push everything behind a fake wall so you don't have to deal with it, then drink yourself into oblivion. Maybe you're more like your father…"

I slammed the glass of bourbon into the wall as I turned toward her and said, "Don't you ever fucking compare me to that monster, do you hear me?"

My rash actions startled her, as she kept her mouth shut and nodded her head. I could see that she started to visibly shake from the anger pouring off of me.

"Leave, you need to leave," I commanded, pleading in my mind for her to listen to me, for once.

With a quick nod, she started for the door, but when her hand reached the knob, she stopped in her tracks and glanced in my direction. A lone tear streaked down her face as her eyes connected with mine. Right then and there, my fucking heart was ripped out of my chest and thrown on the floor. No matter how much I was mad at her for feeling for Rex, I still couldn't take the hurt look in her eyes.

Pressing my hand to my forehead and trying to massage the aggravation that was trying to consume me, I said, "I can't stand the fact that you have feelings for him."

"I don't have feelings for him," she said, as more tears fell down her face.

"If you don't have feelings, then why the hell are you crying? Why does it seem like you lost the love of your fucking life?"

A crease formed between her eyes as she processed what I was saying. She let go of the doorknob she was holding onto and walked toward me, never taking her eyes off of mine.

"You really think this is the way I would react if I lost the love of my life? You're sadly mistaken because, first of all, Rex was nothing to me…"

"Then why are you fucking crying?" I shouted, entirely frustrated with the situation.

"Because it was a shock to me," she shouted back. "I would have cried if you told me your milk man died. For fuck's sake Jett, I have a heart. I don't walk around all dark and moody like you and Kace; things affect me. I can't help it. I cry during that stupid Budweiser commercial with the dog; it's who I am. Why does it bother you so much?"

"Because…because…"

"Because why?!" Goldie spat at me.

"Because he stole Natasha from me, which turned me black, but when I found out he took you," I shook my head and said, "When I thought he took you, my soul died. I thought I was hurting when Natasha left me, but I didn't know what pain was until you left me, Goldie. I had no fucking clue what misery was until the day you took off. You can't imagine the flashbacks I went through, the gut-wrenching agony I had to deal with by you taking off, trying to save the day."

"I was trying to make things better for us."

"By you 'making things better'," I quoted her, "You made them exceedingly worse."

"Because I asked you to trust me? Because I wanted you to try to have faith in me?"

"Because you abandoned me," I choked out.

Feeling vulnerable, I turned around so Goldie didn't see the open wound in my chest that was starting to pour out. I didn't do fucking feelings, this was why, because I wasn't able to control them.

The room fell silent as I waited for her to say something, but instead of her coming back at me with a smart remark, I heard her feet pad across the floor until she stood directly behind me. Her arms wrapped around my waist and her head pressed against my back as she hugged me tightly.

"I'm sorry, Jett. I didn't even think about how my leaving might affect you; I didn't know it would hurt you so much."

"Goldie, you were there. You saw the pleading look on my face when you said you were going to leave; you heard me beg for you to stay. How can you say it wouldn't have affected me?"

She turned me around so I was forced to face her. Her hand went up to my face, where she caressed my jaw and said, "How was I supposed to know how you really felt, Jett? You never told me; you barely showed me. For all I knew, you moved on without me here, hired a new Jett Girl, which you did."

"Because I thought you'd moved on. You were with Rex, Goldie. Rex, the one person who made it his mission to destroy me every chance he got. He was one of the main reasons, besides my dad, why we couldn't be together."

"And how did I find that out? Oh yeah, from Diego, not from you, the person who was supposed to be my boyfriend."

Completely frustrated, Goldie let go of me and pulled away. I could see the tension radiating off of her. Did I really want to dig deep into our issues? Not really, but they were out now. They had to be resolved once and for all.

"How come you can't just trust me?" Goldie asked, aggravated.

"Because I don't trust anyone except for Kace. Everyone in my life has either left me or treated me more as an accessory than a human. Trust doesn't come easy to me."

"Have I done anything for you not to trust me?"

Valid point, she hadn't. She'd actually been extremely loyal, but because I'm a fucked-up bastard, I can't readily admit to her being welcomed into my inner circle.

"No," I admitted.

"So then, why are you treating me like everyone else? Why are you clumping me in with all the other people who've hurt you? It's not fair, Jett, for you to pre-judge me like that."

I didn't know what to say; I didn't think she would understand.

"Jett, talk to me," she practically begged. "Tell me why."

Wanting this to be over, I finally said, "Because you're the one person who could annihilate me, Goldie. I've never in my life felt so strongly about a person before, and it terrifies me because with one sentence, with one wave of your wrist, you could take everything away from me. You literally hold all the power. You're the definition of gold. You think you're just a small girl who came from Bourbon Street, but you are so wrong. You're so much more than that. You hold the colors in the palm of your hand."

"Colors?" Goldie asked, confused.

I walked over to her and opened up her palm. With my finger, I traced a J, F and P on her palm.

"Purple is for justice, something you were able to accomplish while staying at the Lafayette Club. Green is for faith, even though it might not seem like it, I have more faith in you than anyone. And finally, gold, for power. The colors of the city are yours, Goldie, the colors I live by, and fuck if you didn't just come into my life and take them all away."

"I just wanted to be a part of your life, Jett. I still do; I love you."

Needing her close, I pulled her into my chest and kissed the top of her head.

"I love you, Goldie. Fuck, do I love you. Three words I never thought would come out of my mouth, but the moment I saw you drawing my mother's gravestone, I knew I was in trouble. I knew, at that moment, my mom was trying to bring us together, it just took me a little longer to accept the help she was sending me."

"Why is this so hard?" she asked innocently.

"Because I'm fucked up and have trust issues. I have Daddy

issues. I have little rich boy issues..."

"Little rich boy issues for sure," she giggled into my chest.

"I'm sorry, Goldie. I want to be better. I just need you to understand that when you thought you were doing something for us, you were really destroying me. I don't do well with being left behind. I was left behind my whole life. It's hard for me to see something I care about so much leave me. I can't fucking take it."

"I understand," she said softly, while rubbing my back, erasing all the stress out of my body. "Can I ask you to do something for me?"

"Anything," I said, almost in desperation.

She looked up at me and patted my heart with her hand. "This right here, this heart belongs to me, and I need you to open it up, to let me fully in and to be vulnerable, to be scared, to drop the alpha mask when you're with me and just be. I will not judge you and I will not leave you; I'm here and I'm not leaving. Do you understand that? I'm not leaving, Jett, it's time you accept that and help us move on with our relationship."

She was right, I needed to stop pushing her away and finally let her all the way in, throw my balls to the wall and dive in headfirst to the unknown. Fuck was I scared, but with Goldie by my side, I knew it was going to be alright. It had to be alright, my mom brought us together for a reason. My mom knew Goldie was the one for me; it was about time I started living my life and stopped living in fear.

"I can do that," I whispered, as I carefully brought my lips down to hers.

She sighed in my embrace and let my lips take control of hers. With my tongue, I pried her mouth open and tasted her beautiful self. She was intoxicating, debilitating, and so fucking mind altering that at times, I forgot who I was.

Needing to prove to her that I was fully in this relationship, I pulled away, eliciting a cry from her, but then grasped her hand.

"I need to show you something."

"Okay..." she drawled out. "But before you do that, can we address one thing?"

"Sure."

"Rex, what are you going to do about him?"

"What do you mean?"

"I mean, are you going to do anything about what happened?"

"There isn't much I can do, or would want to do. Do I feel bad that the man drove his life into the ground by following my father and wound up killing himself? Yes, I don't think any person, no matter how horrible they are, should die under such circumstances. But you have to remember, Goldie, underneath his fake façade, he was a bad person. He was blackmailing every single person in his club, making them work for him. He committed shady acts throughout his entire life, and when it came back to bite him in the ass, he couldn't handle it. I'm sorry for the way he left this world, but I'm not sorry for what he had coming to him."

"I see," she said, while nodding her head, making me nervous. "I guess you're right, he deserved what was coming to him…his jail sentence that is, not his death. I guess it just seems so sad to me that a person's life could be that bad to them that the only option they think they have left is committing suicide."

"It is sad," I agreed. "But it's not our problem. I can't have you dwell on this. I'm not a very strong man when it comes to jealousies, Goldie. I need to know that you're not truly upset over his loss."

"I'm not. I'm just sad for the circumstances, that's all. He was by no means the love of my life, and he never even had a shot at it. You, on the other hand, I don't know what I would do if something ever happened to you. I honestly don't know how I would go on."

"I feel the same about you. Can you see why I was so upset now?"

"I can….drama queen," she teased, causing me to roll my eyes. "Don't deny it; you're a little drama queen."

"Tease me some more, see where it gets you."

"Hopefully strapped to the beam, hanging upside down with your cock dangling out of my mouth."

"I really see that my class has rubbed off on you."

"You can try all you want, Mr. Colby, but I will forever be the girl you plucked off of Bourbon Street."

"And I wouldn't want it any other way. Now, come on, I want to show you something."

"Is it your dick?" she asked, as she followed behind me out of my office.

"No, but keep talking like that and it might be."

"Oooh, another threat that only entices me, keep them

coming Jettonathan."

"Seriously?" I asked, while turning to face her. She just shrugged her shoulders and laughed. Shaking my head at her, I brought her over to the only room she hadn't been in since she moved into the Lafayette Club, my bedroom.

"Oh, my God, are you going to show me your room?"

"Yes, I think it's time I stop hiding and let you take over my entire life."

"I like the sound of that," she responded, while rubbing her hands together. "Now, before you open the door, do you need to warn me of anything? Am I going to find little superhero toys everywhere? Maybe some Barney memorabilia, Care Bears?"

"Do calm down, Little One, you're starting to foam at the mouth."

Wiping her mouth with the back of her hand, she said, "I'm just so excited. I feel like this is the last puzzle piece I've been waiting for; now, open the door!"

Trying not to smirk at the glee that she was portraying, I opened the doors to my bedroom and let her in. She silently walked into the large room and immediately took in her surroundings.

My bed was situated in the middle of the room up against the wall, making it the focal point. A giant rug took up half of the wood-covered floor; I always hated stepping onto cold floors in the morning, so a rug was a must. My walls were sparse, as well as the rest of the room; it almost felt cold and sterile, but now with Goldie in the room, I could start to feel what I've been missing my whole life…love. Everywhere she walked, she rained love upon me. She was all I needed, all I ever needed.

"So, what do you think?" I asked, nervous for her approval.

After examining everything, she turned toward me and said, "Yeah, this room kind of sucks."

Umm, not what I was expecting her to say.

"What?" I asked, entirely confused.

"Your room, it's…boring. Where are the pictures, the textures, the rich fabrics? I feel like I just walked into an operating room. Is this where you really sleep at night? No wonder why you're so fucking moody all the time; it's like you purposely incarcerated yourself." With a cute expression on her face, she asked, "You don't expect me to sleep in here, do you?"

"Well, I was thinking…"

"No, definitely not," she said, while holding up her hand. "I refuse to sleep in an old ice bucket. I mean honestly, Jett, I thought you were better than this. I mean, the Bourbon Room is warmer than this place. What is that? A cow's tongue?" She pointed to a sculpture on my dresser.

"No, it's art."

"Looks like a cow's tongue to me," she said, while walking over and examining it. "Yup, it's a cows tongue, you can see all the taste buds. Looks like this cow liked sour things."

"Oh, that's right, I forgot you are quite knowledgeable on different cow parts, like vaginas and whatnot," I teased, reminding her once again of her drunk shenanigans.

"Still need proof of that," she shouted, as she took in the "Cow's tongue" some more. "Gah, this thing is nasty. Why on earth would you have it in your room?"

"I have an appreciation for art."

"Well, your appreciation reads like a bloody vagina. You need some new taste, and because I'm so kind and loving, I will offer my services."

"Is that right?" I asked, as I moved toward her. "What kind of services would that be?"

"You know, curtains, wall paint, blow jobs, throw pillows."

"Blow jobs? Is that extra?"

"When I'm trying to find a needle in a haystack, yes. Extra fifty for you, big boy," she said, patting my chest.

"What did I tell you about girls who lie?" I warned.

"They get utterly fucked by their hot billionaire boyfriend?" she wiggled her eyebrows.

"You're impossible," I huffed, as I walked away, hearing her trail behind me as I walked straight into the Bourbon Room; it was time to get down to business.

31
"THE DAYS"

Goldie

"Where do you think you're going?" I asked Jett, who was butt ass naked and walking toward his room. That ass, damn. If I hadn't just been thoroughly fucked in the Bourbon Room, I would be chomping away until I grabbed a piece of it.

"What? You want more?" Jett asked, as he turned toward me, giving me a full frontal.

Sigh.

Yeah, I sighed, don't judge me.

"I always want more," I replied, while slipping my hand into his, which he took as an invitation to ravage me once again.

Pushing me up against the wall of the hallway, he locked me in with his arms on either side of my head and lowered his mouth so it was only inches from mine.

"Can you handle more?" he asked, now starting to slowly nip away at my neck.

No, I couldn't handle more; I was already so incredibly sore, but my damn pussy kept awakening every time Jett came near me.

His lips worked their way up my neck and to my jaw, where he peppered kisses along my skin until he hit my lips. Not even giving me a chance to recover, he pulled my bottom lip with his teeth and then bit it, making me squeal.

A low and sexy laugh came from his chest as he started to sooth my lip with his tongue.

Oh, fuck me.

My legs involuntarily widened, as his hand found its way to my hip, just under the silkiness of my robe.

Was this really happening again?

His other hand glided up to the knot of my robe, and the two sides fell open, exposing my skin to Jett's heated body.

Yup, this was happening.

"You taste so fucking good," Jett said, as he ran his tongue along my neck. I wasn't really into the whole licking thing, but damn if I didn't want to make a prosthetic of his tongue and run it up and down my body all day long.

His mouth descended down my neck to my chest, where my nipples were so incredibly hard, just begging for him to touch them. His hands, which were on my hips, glided up my body until they were gripping my breasts with a kind of force I hadn't ever experienced from him. The way he squeezed me, making me stand on my tippy toes from the pressure, had me begging for more, needing more.

With skillful fingers, he pinched my nipples, hard, and then worked his mouth down my stomach until he nestled right between my legs. He spread my legs wider, until I thought I was going to fall, and then he pressed his hands against my hips to hold me up better and ran his tongue up my slit.

A moan escaped me as his wet tongue slid up and down my most sensitive area.

Yes, this was exactly what I needed. Even though I loved Jett's dick, fucking craved that meat sword, I occasionally wanted to be loved like this, tenderly.

I relaxed into the wall as I let Jett's tongue do all the work, allowing myself to feel every swipe, every breath, and every hum he laid on me.

Faster than I expected, I felt my orgasm coming on; my legs started to feel like noodles and my core began to burn from the onslaught of pleasure I was experiencing.

I gripped Jett's head and prepared myself. With one deep swipe, I was riding Jett's tongue, exploding from the inside out, screaming for the entire club to hear, until there wasn't any more orgasm left inside of me.

My eyes were closed, trying to figure out how Jett was able to literally turn me inside out, when I felt him pick me up and walk toward his room. He moved the door open with his foot and walked me toward his bed.

Carefully, he placed me on the very comfortable mattress, which made me temporarily forget where I was, until I opened my eyes.

Jett was in his closet, pulling on a pair of briefs, when I sat up and looked at him.

He was hard, really fucking hard, and I knew it was because he was turned on from getting me off. How could you not love a man for that?

"Come here," I said, waving my finger at him.

"Why?" he asked, at the same time as he leaned against the door frame of his closet and crossed his arms over his impressively cut chest.

"Because I want to soothe that rather massive ache you have in your briefs; now, get over here."

"Not necessary," he replied, walking toward me. He grabbed ahold of my robe and ran it carefully over my shoulders. Was he trying to turn me on again? Because he was doing a damn fine job of it.

Wanting to take charge, I ran my hand up his thigh until I reached the juncture of his legs and grabbed ahold of his balls.

He inhaled a sharp breath and looked down at me, telling me through his eyes that I was in so much trouble, but at the moment, I really didn't care, because I was seeing how much I was turning him on, and that was all that mattered to me.

"What do you think you're doing, Little One?" he asked in that dominant southern voice that rumbled through my body every time he spoke.

"Taking care of your little problem here."

"You know damn well it's not little. How many times do I have to remind you of that?"

Shrugging, I said, "Maybe one more?"

Without letting him respond back, I grabbed the top of his

waistband and pulled down his briefs, allowing his cock to spring free. My mouth watered at the sight. I felt like it had been so long since I'd had the distinct pleasure of taking him in my mouth.

Licking my lips, I grabbed his cock with my hands, and guided it to my mouth. Jett took a deep breath and then relaxed in his stance, preparing for what I was about to do to him.

There were many things I enjoyed about the "new" Jett, and one of them was the fact that he relinquished control a little more, allowing me to do what I wanted, when I wanted…with some exceptions. There were times where, if I muttered a word he let me know about it, but right now, he was more relaxed, more open, and I was going to take advantage of it.

I wrapped my lips around his length and reveled in the feel of him. So hard…for me.

His fingers dug into my scalp and entwined with my hair, helping my motions by pulling and tugging ever so slightly. The feel of him still trying to direct me should have made me mad, but it only turned me on more.

One of my hands sat at the base of his penis, while the other started to massage his balls. A low moan escaped his throat as I continued to work his heated length.

In and out, it was almost like a dance I was conducting, pulling him and tugging while carefully running my tongue along the underside of his cock. It was so easy, so carefree to want to please this man, to want to make him burst in ecstasy.

"Fuck…" he drawled out, now starting to thrust his hips in my mouth.

He was at an impossible length, almost too much for me. I held back my need to gag at how far I'd started to take him, and instead, relished the feel of him riding my mouth.

His hand gripped tighter in my hair, needing me to give him an orgasm, so with a light tug on his balls and a sharp suck of my mouth, he threw his head back and reared into my mouth, all the while calling out my name.

I felt him come, use me as a mechanism of pleasure, until he was completely sated.

Slowly, he pulled out of my mouth, still breathing heavily with a look of absolute pleasure crossing his gorgeous face.

Satisfied, I sat back on his bed and smiled up at him, taking in the reaction I was able to garner from him.

Without a word, Jett leaned over and placed his hand on my shoulders, pushing me down on the mattress. He stared into my eyes, searching them for something I didn't know. His eyes glistened in the dark room, making me fall in love with the man all over again.

"You make me so incredibly happy," he said softly, before claiming my lips with his.

When he pulled away, I asked, "Because I give good head?"

"No, because when I look in your eyes, I see true adoration for me. No one has ever looked at me the way you do, Goldie. I've never experienced what love was like, I never knew what it felt like to be unconditionally loved by anyone until you came along. You love me and being loved by you, and only you, is, by far, the best feeling I've ever experienced. Your love is something I will never give up again, no matter what the circumstances are. I refuse to lose this feeling."

Tears threatened to spill over my eyes as I took in his words.

Never did I think the mysterious man who'd dropped off the black and purple card was going to end up being the one I held closest to my heart. I was looking for a way to survive, an olive branch, and what I found was a heart that matched mine, a soul to forever make me warm.

"I love you, Jett. I will never stop loving you."

While looking down at me, he caressed my face with his thumbs and said, "Shall we call it a night? Or do I need to ravish you one more time?"

Laughing, I replied, "I think if you ravish me one more time, there will be nothing left to ravish."

"Have I been taking it too hard on you?" he asked with concern.

"No," I smiled and caressed his speckled jaw. "But I might be a little sore after what happened in the Bourbon Room."

"Don't mouth off and you won't be sore," he quipped.

"Now, where's the fun in that?"

"Maneater," he teased.

"Tyrant," I teased back.

With a growl, he scooped me up and brought me to the head of the bed, where he tried to put me under the covers, but I clung to him instead like a spider monkey, not letting him drop me down.

"It's going to be hard to sleep like this," he joked.

"Yeah, about that, I'm not sleeping here."

"Excuse me?" he asked, slightly offended. "Are you saying you would rather sleep away from me?"

"No, drama queen," I joked. "But I'm not sleeping in this jail cell of a room you have. I mean, honestly, Jett, no wonder you're always in a bad mood…look at this place. There's no color, no brightness; it's just a cold room with some meaningless objects in it. I mean, fuck, you have a cow tongue in here. I'm kind of embarrassed for you."

"Embarrassed?" he asked, more intrigued now.

"Yes, embarrassed. You hold yourself to such high standards, and then you go and have a room like this? Eck, gross. Thank God you never brought women here; they would have run for their damn lives." Lowering my voice I looked around and added, "It looks like a fucking psychopath's room."

Jett threw his head back and laughed at my assessment.

"It does not look like a psychopath's room."

"The hell it doesn't," I stated boldly. "No personal items, everything has its proper place. Uh, yeah, you're a fucking psychopath."

"Yeah, and you just sucked this psychopath's dick, so what does that say about you?"

Thinking about it for a second, I said, "Never said I was perfect, plus, I felt pity for you."

"Bullshit," he chuckled, and pulled away from the bed. "So, if you don't want to sleep here, then where do you plan on sleeping? Don't say Diego's place, because I don't think I can sleep in that bed one more night. I can't believe you've been sleeping on such piss."

"You're such a snob."

"A snob whose cock you can't get enough of."

Rolling my eyes, I pointed to his door, and said, "Take me to my old room. I refuse to stay in this place one more second."

"Pretty sure I'm the one in charge here. If I say we're staying in this room, then we're staying," he said in that beautiful voice of his.

"Oh, yeah, well…" well what? What did I have on him? "Well…I have a pussy!" I shouted.

Laughing, Jett picked me up and started walking us toward the back stairs to take us to my room. "That you do, Little One, and you have the most beautiful pussy I've ever had the pleasure of fucking."

"So romantic," I cooed.

We were almost to my room when there was a slam of a door and stomping feet coming in our direction. I looked up from Jett's face and saw Kace storming toward us. He stopped in his tracks when he saw half-naked Jett and me in a robe in the same hallway as him.

"Get out of my way," he stated gruffly.

Jett obliged for some reason, probably because he wanted to get me back in bed, but I wasn't about to let Kace storm off; I was too damn nosy.

"Wait," I called, as I struggled to get out of Jett's grasp. "What's going on?"

I was now rotating my body, so Jett was forced to hold me by my stomach rather than my back. I took the moment to prop my chin in my hands and kick my legs up.

"Trouble in paradise?" I teased, knowing full well Lyla was giving the man a run for his money.

"Drop it," Kace said sharply.

"Oh come on, Kace. Sharing is caring."

Kace turned around, looked up at Jett, and said, "Take care of your woman and get her off my back."

"Hey!" I shouted, completely offended, as Kace walked away and Jett walked toward my bedroom. "I don't need taking care of; I can handle my own! Come back here; I dare ya!"

"Easy, killer," Jett said, as he closed the door to my bedroom and walked me over to the bed that held so many memories for me. "Let him do his thing."

"He's handling Lyla all wrong."

"That's his business, not yours." I was about to fire back a response when he stopped me with his fingers to his lips. When he was satisfied with me not opening my mouth, he went to work on my robe again, and said, "Tonight is about you and me, no one else. Do not bring him into this bedroom with us. Got it?"

His tone was serious, but loving. How could I not listen to him?

"You're not into threesomes? You two would be hot together," I joked, garnering a look from him. "Guess not," I gulped.

Once my robe was removed, he slipped us both under the covers of the bed, and we allowed the comfort of the mattress to swallow us whole. Maybe Jett was right; the mattress Diego gave me was piss, but it was nothing compared to the mattress over at Rex's place.

The thought of Rex made me sad, but I didn't dwell on it because, not only did Jett not want us talking about other people, but he would flip shit if he knew I was thinking about Rex. Not a smart move on my part.

"What are you thinking about?" Jett asked, as if he could read my mind.

Racking my brain for something, I shouted the first thing that came to mind, "Leprechauns!"

Leprechauns? Seriously?

"That's slightly random," Jett stated, while chuckling.

"Yeah, you could say that, but my train of thought would tell you otherwise."

"Oh, yeah? What was your train of thought?"

Shit…

"I don't want to bore you with such trivial things."

"Enlighten me," he said, while pulling me in close to his body, making sure our skins touched.

Fuck…

"Well, I was just thinking about mattresses and how sometimes they're hard and sometimes they're soft, and then I thought about how manufacturers made the mattresses so soft. I mean, were they quilted by bears, like that toilet paper? Maybe there was a different animal in charge of mattresses. You know, bears have toilet paper covered, geese monopolize the pillow district, and then maybe kangaroos are in charge of mattresses. But then a kangaroo being in charge of a mattress made no sense at all, I mean, how fucking silly is that?"

Jett looked at me confused and said, "Silly."

"I know, right?" I stated, getting more into my story. "Like, uh, hello Mr. Kangaroo, if you were in charge of anything, it would be pockets, am I right?" I asked, while nudging Jett's side. "So then that left me wondering who is really in charge of the mattresses. Well, mattresses are soft and cloud-like and then, bam, I thought unicorn."

"Naturally," Jett laughed.

"But what does a unicorn have?"

"Too much glitter?" Jett asked.

"No! Well, I mean, yes, they fart glitter, but no, they have horns," I said, while forming one with my hand and connecting it to my forehead. "Horns can poke right through mattresses, so that wouldn't be safe, so they would have to hire someone to make the mattresses, since hooves and horns can't quite sew pockets of floating ecstasy. And who are unicorns friends with?"

"The Easter Bunny?" Jett teased.

"No!" I said. "They are friends with Leprechauns!"

"I see," Jett nodded, taking in my ramble. "I don't think I will ever ask you about another train of thought again. I don't think my brain can wrap around it."

"Takes a special kind of mind," I stated, while patting his face.

"Apparently." He took a deep breath and then said, "Goldie, I need to talk to you about something."

Yeah, I didn't like the tone of his voice. Whenever he became serious Jett, not dominant Jett, but serious Jett, he was always about to tell me some bad information. Right now, I could only imagine what it would be, most likely how he wants to be with me, but can't, the same old routine that we've been going through since I showed up at the Lafayette Club.

"Why do I feel like I'm not going to like what you're about to tell me?"

"Because you probably won't…"

"No," I said while sitting up. "I refuse to listen to you turn me down once again. What is it this time? Not man enough to handle me? You have another business deal in the works, and I'm not good enough to go to your parties with you? Are you starting another club and need to spend time with those 'Jett girls?' God, I'm such a fucking idiot. Why do I keep coming back to you? Thinking things are going to change? Well, fuck this shit," I said, while scrambling to get out of bed.

"Goldie, stop," Jett stated in a commanding voice. "This has nothing to do with our relationship. But it's comforting to see what kind of faith you have in us."

"Do you blame me?" I asked, feeling like an ass. I got back under the covers, but kept my distance, something Jett let me know was not acceptable by pulling me in closer to him.

"I don't," he answered honestly, "and I get that it's going to take time to earn your trust back, but please give me a chance to talk to you before you go running off. Promise me that?" he asked, while rubbing my cheek with his thumb, a loving gesture that calmed my heart.

"Promise."

"Good," he kissed my forehead softly and pulled away. Looking me in the eyes he said, "I need to tell you that I've shut down the Toulouse Room."

"What do you mean?" I asked, confused as to what he was trying to tell me.

"The Lafayette Club will no longer be offering presentations."

"Why?" I asked, lifting off the bed. "What about the girls? What about me?"

I needed to pace, I needed to think about the ramifications of what Jett was telling me. I wanted to do my own thing, but knowing I still had the Lafayette Club was a good back up plan to have until I solved my future plans.

Once again, Jett grabbed ahold of me and lowered me back down to the bed.

"It's time to offer something new to the girls. I've decided to close the doors of the Toulouse Room and open up new ones," Jett stated soothingly.

"Where?" I asked, trying to let his warm hands that were rubbing my back relax me.

"Lot 17. I will be offering up a community center where the girls will now work, as well as Kace. We will be offering free classes to the community and the girls will help teach them. They will be able to apply the education they've been earning during their years with me to help those in need, those who also need a second chance. I've also made connections with local businesses, which will be providing educational classes as well, to help those get back on their feet. Kace will be offering classes in self-defense, boxing, and general exercise. There will be housing in the back for those who might need a place to sleep at night, and a soup kitchen as well."

Oh, fuck...my heart was a puddle in my chest for the man right in front of me.

"After Katrina hit, this whole city was rolled over. A lot of people, including yourself, lost everything they ever had, and they lost hope. I want to help bring back that hope, to help those who might have lost everything land back on their feet. My mission is to make Lot 17 into a place of refuge, a place of rebuilding, and a place of challenge, but I can't do it without you, Goldie. I need your help. I need your bright, shining personality to help encourage people to turn their lives around, to find a new hope to strive for."

Shaking my head, I asked, "How can I help them?"

"Art therapy," Jett said, smiling sweetly at me.

No, this was not how it was supposed to happen. I'm supposed to figure out my own life, not let Jett figure it out for me.

"No," I shook my head. "You can't just come swooping in here with your amazing ideas and figure everything out. I need to figure out my own life; I can't rely on you anymore."

Perplexed, Jett studied me for a second and then said, "Little One, it's my job to protect you, to provide for you, to make you happy. I wouldn't be doing my job as your dominant, as your boyfriend, if I wasn't doing those things. Let me love you and care for you; it's what I strive for...what I need to do. It's a part of me."

Damn it...damn it!!

"Think about it," Jett kissed my forehead. "I'll understand if you say no, but please, just consider it."

How could I not when he asked me so sweetly? When he looked at me with those deep blue eyes, begging me to let him take care of me?

"Thank you," I whispered, curling into the man who controlled my heart. "Thank you for wanting to take care of me. I haven't felt this safe in a very long time."

"I would do anything for you, Little One. I hope you know that."

"I do, without a doubt in my mind, Jett."

We sat in silence and just held each other. Jett ran his hands through my hair, as I brushed my fingers along his chest, memorizing every sculpted line.

Life was changing quickly. What I once thought was normal, what I relied on, was now turning into something completely different. The Lafayette Club was shutting down...it was still hard to believe.

"How did the girls take the news?" I asked, worried about their futures.

"They took it well and have been working together to try to figure out what classes they want to offer. Babs will be in and out, now that she is about to start her own make-up line, but she is still very much dedicated to the effort. Francy and Tootse would like to head up a day care, so parents can drop their kids off to gain a better education. Pepper will be offering dance classes to keep our youth active and cultured. They all have a place at the center."

"What about Lyla?" I asked, worried about my best friend.

Jett quirked his lips and shook his head. "She's not so quick to jump on board. I have a meeting with her and Kace tomorrow to go over some things. I don't know why she is so stubborn when it comes to changing her life."

"You can't fix everyone," I told Jett. "Some people just don't want to change."

"But her life could be so much better."

"Maybe she's happy with the way things are going in her life. Believe me, I've tried; you can't force her to do anything. She's more stubborn than me."

"That's hard to believe," Jett said with laughter in his voice.

"Watch it," I warned, as my fingers hovered over his nipple.

"Don't you fucking dare."

"I'm not afraid," I said with a smile.

"You should be."

With that, Jett was on top of me, straddling my body and taking off his briefs.

Insatiable man.

32
"STEAL MY GIRL"

Goldie

"When will you be back?" Jett asked, as he stood in the doorway of my bedroom, freshly showered and wearing a pair of black pants and a white button-up shirt that was unbuttoned on the top. His sleeves were rolled up, showing off his forearms…tease. He was handsome, couldn't argue that.

"Why do you care?" I teased, as I finished tying my shoe.

"I don't like you going out on the streets by yourself."

I walked up to him and grabbed ahold of his hands. "Do you fail to realize I'm a grown woman and can handle myself? Oh, and there is no more threat. Time to let go, Jett."

"I still don't like it," he complained, acting slightly like a child, a side of Jett Colby I hadn't seen.

"Well, deal with it," I smiled and patted his cheek.

His hand caught my wrist and pulled me flush against his chest, making my pulse pick up a notch.

"Careful, Little One. I still have no problem punishing you for misbehavior."

"Something to look forward to later," I stated, while giving him a kiss...one that he turned into something deeper as his hands ran up my back to my neck and straight into my hair.

I sighed into him as his hands messed up the ponytail I just fixed my hair in. He turned us so I was pressed against the doorframe, and he used his body to hold me in place as his hands explored me.

The feel of his hard body pressed against mine had me thinking I'd had the wrong idea in going out for a jog.

Just as his hand started to run up the back of my shirt, I realized what he was doing, and I pressed my palms on his chest, pushing him away slightly.

"Don't even think about distracting me; you have a meeting to get to, and I have a grave to visit."

"You're going to the cemetery?" Jett asked, his swollen-kissed lips staring down at me.

Shaking the naughty thoughts out of my head, I nodded. "Yes, I need to talk some things out."

"Things, as in me?"

"Maybe," I responded, while fixing my hair back in the ponytail.

"Trying to decide if I'm worth it?"

"Oh, I know you're worth it," I said, kissing his lips one last time before I took off. "I just need to think some things through. Don't worry, I promise I'll be back."

"Okay," he said a little skeptically.

"I love you, Jett."

His unease vanished at my words, and a sexy grin popped up in replacement.

"I love you, Little One."

One last kiss...I snuck one in before pulling myself away and making a note to take advantage of that sexy grin later tonight.

"Be careful," he called over his shoulder.

"Always am," I responded, while I put my phone in the holster that was strapped to my upper arm.

I walked down the front staircase of the Lafayette Club for the first time without my Jett Girl gear on. I almost felt naked, sans mask and heels, but a little invigorated, like I was starting a new chapter in my life.

I ran out the front door of the club and out the gates that I once thought were intimidating. To think, when I first came to the club, I was naïve, desperate, and in the need of a helping hand. I never thought I would end up finding the man I would spend the rest of my life with, nor did I think I would form some of the most important relationships of my life.

The Jett Girls and Kace were my family now; they meant the world to me, and I would do anything for them.

I lightly started to jog through the tree-covered streets of the Garden District, my absolute favorite part of New Orleans. The houses were gorgeous, painted in pastel colors with shutters gracing every window, evoking an old southern charm. The sidewalks were rough, uprooted by trees and cracking all over, but they added character to the historic part of town. The humid heat of Louisiana hit me hard in my first couple minutes of running, but I soon found my stride, while listening to Britney Spears pump through my ear buds. The woman was a goddess, and she knew how to motivate.

I turned the corner to make my way toward the cemetery when I ran into a still body. My earbuds fell out of my ears as I tried to recover from smacking into someone.

When I looked up, I saw Mercy standing in front of me, looking like she was just walked over by a Mardi Gras parade. Her eyes were sunken in, her hair was strange and un-brushed, and her clothes were disheveled.

"Mercy, oh my God, is that you?"

Slowly, her eyes worked their way up to mine, and the minute we made eye contact, a deep chill ran up my spine and goosebumps spread over my body. I was not getting a friendly vibe from her.

"Goldie," she said without emotion in her voice.

Backing up a bit, I asked, "Um, how are you?"

She didn't respond; she just stared at me as her hands twitched behind her back. I wanted to ask her what she was hiding behind her, but was too afraid to ask. Visions of the demonic woman stabbing me repeatedly ran through my mind as a light sheen of sweat started to pour over my skin.

I was about to ask her what she was up to, when she sidestepped me and said, "Excuse me."

She started walking away, and when I saw that she was holding a shirt behind her, I had to know what was going on.

"Mercy, wait, are you okay?"

Turning around, she brought the shirt up to her face and rubbed the fabric against her cheek...all the while maintaining eye contact with me.

"I see that you have your man back," she said, not looking like the same woman I once knew.

Gulping, I nodded my head.

"How nice for you."

"Um, it is nice," I responded, not really knowing what to say.

"I lost mine," she said, narrowing her eyes at me.

Was she talking about Rex? She must have been, but were they really that close? I examined the shirt she was holding against her face and saw that it had small splatters of blood on it, making my head want to spin around in a "holy fuck" kind of moment.

"I'm, uh, I'm sorry to hear that."

"Me too," she responded, as she tilted her head to the side. "It would be a shame to see it happen to you."

"See what happen to me?" I asked, as my heartrate picked up.

She just shrugged, and said, "Lose your love," then she turned back around and walked away, leaving me completely helpless in my thoughts.

Quickly, I ran to the cemetery and pulled my phone out of my holster. I dialed Jett as fast as my fingers allowed and waited impatiently as the phone rang.

On the third ring, he picked up.

"Little One, are you okay?"

"No," I practically cried in the phone.

"Where are you? I'll come get you."

"No, don't come get me. I just, I just had to make sure you're okay."

"Tell me what is going on right now," he demanded into the phone.

I recalled my interaction with Mercy and told him about her connection with Rex.

"She looked deranged, Jett, like she was high or something."

"I'm coming to get you."

"No!" I practically shouted. "Don't come get me, I just...I just wanted to make sure you're okay."

"Why wouldn't I be okay? You're the one who's out in the open. I knew this wasn't a good idea," he mumbled.

"Because she said it would be a shame if something happened to you. I didn't know if someone was trying to kill you."

"Don't be silly," Jett said into the phone. "I'm not the one to worry about. Goldie, listen to me, I want you to be safe. Can I please send my security detail to watch over you? It would put my mind at ease."

"What about my mind?" I asked in a panic. "There wasn't something right about her, Jett."

"Which is why I would prefer for you to be protected. I can take care of myself. Please, Little One, please let them at least watch over you for a little while until I can get my men to check out this Mercy woman. Please do this for me."

The strain in his voice had me caving.

"Fine, I'm at the cemetery."

"I know; they'll be there shortly. They'll give you privacy, I promise."

"Thank you," I said sincerely, grateful he understood my need to talk to my parents.

"I love you; please be careful," he said softly into the phone.

"You do the same," I added seriously.

"Say it," he responded.

"I love you," I added.

With a sigh, he clicked the phone off, leaving me to spend some time with my parents. Feeling a little bit better, I walked over to their gravestone and sat in front of it. It's been so long since I've come to visit them that guilt washed over me when I saw the dead flowers that sat in front of their grave.

Holding back the tears that threatened to spill over, I placed my hand on the cold stone and said, "I'm sorry I've been such a lousy daughter and not come to visit you more often. Things have been a little crazy lately. You guys remember Jett, right? I talked about him a couple of times. Well, I kind of fell in love with him."

Sighing, I shook my head. "Who am I kidding? I didn't kind of fall in love with him; I full on threw my heart off the edge and tumbled down the side of Love Lane. I'm so far gone when it comes to that man. I feel like I've developed the kind of love you two would have wanted for me. It's taken a while, and we've had our ups and downs, but I feel like we're in a good place now. I just know he was meant for me."

A rustling came from behind me, causing me to whip my head

around only to see one of Jett's security people had made himself present. Once I spotted him, he pointed to where he was going to be. That was quick, but the man wouldn't be working for Jett if he wasn't quick.

I nodded and waved, trying to calm my racing heart.

"Jesus, I'm losing my mind," I said to my parents. "Being with Jett isn't easy, that's for damn sure. It seems like the more money you have, the more people want to destroy you. You were right when you said money isn't everything in life. I'm finding that out rather quickly."

Changing the subject, I traced the outline of their names and said, "I would give anything to have you two back in my life right now. I'm kind of stuck as to what to do with my life. I don't want to dance anymore. I know I have so much more potential with my art, but I don't know where to take it. I really want to figure this out on my own, to provide for myself, but Jett has this idea in his head that he needs to take care of me, to provide for me and protect me. Hence, the burly men hovering over our conversation. He kind of offered me a job that...God, it would be so amazing. An art therapy job to work with those looking for a second chance in life. It would be perfect for me, but the only thing wrong with it is it's just one more handout I would be taking from him. I don't want to be helpless anymore. I want to be able to provide for myself."

Shaking my head and looking down at the dirt, I thought about what I was saying. This was my second chance, why was I so opposed to taking it? Because, once again, Jett came to the rescue?

Yes, that's exactly why, because Jett was involved. I really wanted to do something that didn't involve him, to prove that I could be self-sufficient.

"Ugh, what do I do? Why is he the one who had to offer the opportunity? Why aren't you guys here with me?" I asked, as a tear rolled down my face, just as a breeze picked up, wrapping a tight wisp of air around me. Dirt swirled in circles as the wind picked it up and scattered it around the gravestone.

Sun broke out between the tree's leaves and shined down on me. Warmth spread through my body from the heat, and right then and there, I knew my parents were trying to comfort me, to let me know everything was going to be just fine.

The wind tossed around some more until a twig flew off the

tree above me and struck me in the head. I grabbed the twig and looked down at it. It was in the shape of a "Y," and in my own twisted and convoluted head, I surmised that the twig was from my parents, telling me "Yes" to take the job and not worry about where the offer was coming from, but to appreciate it.

At that moment, I knew no matter what happened to Jett and me, what transpired in the future, I would forever be a Jett Girl.

Damn, twigs were wordy.

I sat there for a while, just experiencing being as close to my parents as I could, something I used to do often when working at Kitten's Castle.

I clutched the twig to my chest and smiled at the gravestone, just as a whirlwind of fire engines whipped past the cemetery, echoing through the canopy of trees.

My heart stopped in my chest at the blaring and dread filled my gut. Instantly, I shot off the ground and turned to the security guy standing a few feet away.

"I need to get to Jett, now!"

33
"FIRE AND RAIN"

A few moments earlier...

Jett

"Say it," I said through the phone, as my heartrate started to slow down.

"I love you," Goldie's sweet voice rang through the phone.

Those three little words would never become old to me, not when they were directed at me from the most beautiful and sassy woman I had ever met.

Thankful that she allowed me to send security to be with her, I held my finger up at Kace and Lyla, who were waiting for our meeting to start, and called Jeremy.

"How can I assist you, Mr. Colby," Jeremy asked into the phone.

"Send security to the Lafayette Cemetery to watch over Goldie."

Without another word, I hung up the phone and placed it on

my desk. I looked up at both Kace and Lyla, who were doing everything in their power not to look at each other. The tension was rather uncomfortable, but since Kace was the new manager of the community center, I needed him in the room.

"Is everything okay?" Lyla asked, looking slightly concerned.

"Yes," I answered curtly, not wanting to get her involved in what was happening with Goldie. The only person who needed to worry was me.

"Then, why does she need security?" Kace asked gruffly.

Turning slightly to the brooding man, I said, "It's none of your concern. It's being taken care of. Now, let's discuss why you're here, shall we?"

Kace's jaw worked back and forth, as he refrained from challenging me. I knew he wanted to know what was going on with Goldie, but I wasn't about to bring it up in front of Lyla; it wasn't her concern.

"What's this all about?" Lyla asked, as she crossed her legs and popped a piece of gum in her mouth. Her lips smacked together, as if she was in some kind of fifties movie, ready to strike a deal.

"Lyla, I wanted to talk to you about your future here."

"There is no future," she interrupted. "I spoke with Marv; I will be heading back to Kitten's Castle starting in a week. "

"Lyla, I'm going to be honest with you."

"I wouldn't expect anything less."

Her confidence was slightly annoying to me. From the way she carried herself, I knew this conversation wasn't going to make much of a difference.

"You have no future at Kitten's Castle. You need to think about what your next step is going to be. You need to take advantage of the education I'm offering and make something of yourself."

"I don't need it," she said, while crossing her arms.

"The fuck you don't," Kace mumbled to the side.

"Excuse me?"

The tension that was bubbling between Kace and Lyla just boiled over as Lyla turned in her chair and stared Kace down. His body language read, don't fuck with me, but Lyla could care less. The woman was fearless, just like my Little One.

"Don't be fucking stupid, Lyla."

"Oh, the big man has an opinion," Lyla said, while mocking Kace's stance. "Frankly, Kace, why the hell would I take advice from you? If anyone needs to get their life together, it's you. You walk around here, stomping around like some stupid petulant giant, making every room you walk in quickly ice over from the black that is shooting from your heart. You think I need help, turn that fucking finger around, because if anyone needs help, it's you."

"You know nothing about me."

"You're right," Lyla agreed. "And that's because you're so shut off that you don't let anyone in. All you care about is working out and having sex with Pepper."

Kace's hand ran over his face at Lyla's statement. So, Kace and Pepper were still fucking? Interesting.

"Seems like you're jealous," Kace said, once he'd most likely counted to ten, since he looked like he was about to explode.

"There is no way in hell I would be jealous over you. Yeah, you're a good fuck, I'll give you that, but that's all you are. You're a hollow shell of a man, Kace. There is nothing to you other than muscles. There is no substance; why would I be jealous...?"

"Enough!" I said, while slamming my hand on my desk. I stood up and looked down at Lyla. I pointed to the door and said, "You may leave. Pack your things and leave. I refuse to have you talk about my friend in such a negative way. You may be Goldie's friend, but Kace is mine, and I will not tolerate you bashing him. You have no clue what he's been through..."

"Jett," Kace warned, barely looking at me. "I don't need you fighting my fights."

"That's fine," Lyla said, as she stood up and started unbuttoning her dress shirt. She took it off and tossed it at Kace, along with her heels. "Here's my uniform, I don't need this place. Good luck with everything."

"Lyla, don't do this," Kace said, while looking down at the ground, not able to even make eye contact with her.

She stood there, in a bra and thong, and grabbed Kace by the face so he had to look at her. The heat that came from his eyes when he looked her up and down was unmistakable; Kace wanted her. Anyone could see it.

"Don't tell me what to do. You're not my protector; you're nothing to me. You made that quite clear."

"You're the one who made it clear," Kace shot back.

To say I was confused was an understatement. I knew Kace was having problems with Lyla, but not such emotional problems…issues that clearly were cutting deep between them.

"I made it clear? The minute you shut me out was the minute you told me you want nothing to do with me. I offered to be there for you, Kace. I offered to talk, but you don't want to. How am I supposed to stick around after that?"

"It's not that easy," Kace gritted out.

"How convenient for you," Lyla responded, while placing her hands on her hips.

Kace shot out of his chair, dropping Lyla's shirt and shoes, and said, "You think this is convenient? Living with this guilt, with this black cloud hovering over my fucking head every God damn day? It's not."

"What guilt? You see, I have no clue what you're talking about. How am I supposed to have any kind of relationship with you if you won't talk to me? I should have known this was going to be a bad idea. I told myself time and time again this was a bad idea, but Goldie needed my help." Lyla shook her head and stepped away from Kace before looking at me. "Jett, I'm sorry for insulting your friend. Thank you for taking care of my girl, for making her feel special, and I appreciate the opportunity you've given me."

She started to walk away when I called after her, "Lyla, wait. Please, don't leave. I apologize for my outburst. I still want to talk about open opportunities for you. I would like to help, if you will let me."

Lyla turned around and gripped the molding of the door frame. "Jett, I appreciate your offer, but like I said, I can handle myself. I've been handling my own life ever since I can remember. I will be fine. Take care of Goldie for me; she deserves your kind heart."

She started to walk away, and I watched Kace battle with himself as to what he should do. His mouth opened for a second, but nothing came out. Instead of chasing after her, he sat back down in his chair and rested his elbows on his thighs as his hands pulled on his hair.

I watched, as the man I've known since I was young, the one person who knows my demons and has stuck by my side, wrestled with his own demons, his own thoughts and concerns.

After giving him a little bit of time, I asked, "Do you want to talk about it?"

"Does it look like I want to talk about it?" Kace answered back.

"Do you ever want to talk about it?"

"Is this one of those conversation where we only ask each other questions?"

"I don't know, is it?"

Shaking his head, a small smirk peeked through his lips, but was briefly wiped away when he sat back in his chair.

"She wants to talk, she wants to know what happened to me, and I don't want to tell her."

"Why not?" I asked, wondering if the man in front of me would ever move forward and forget about his past, if he would ever forgive himself for what he did.

"Why not? Jett, I don't want anyone knowing what happened. If I told her, she would judge me, she would treat me differently, and she wouldn't look at me the way she looks at me now."

"You don't know that. It seems like you both have rough pasts. It might be good for both of you."

Shaking his head at me, Kace laughed. "You fail to realize something, Jett, I will never get the chance to be happy again; I don't deserve it."

"Kace, what happened was so long ago…"

"Yes, but do you think that little girl will ever forget losing her dad?" Kace shot back, now leaning forward and threatening to get in my face. "I took away a father…"

"It wasn't your fault," I said sharply. "He provoked you, he got in your face, and he started the fight; you warned him…"

"I should have backed away, Jett. I knew better; I should have backed away."

Once again, we were at a standstill.

I hated seeing my best friend like this, distraught, hurting, and angry. I remember when he was on top of his game, when he was winning match after match, when he was one of the best boxers in the country. He was happy, he was satisfied with himself, and he had a spark of life inside of him.

Now, all I saw was a black soul, floating around, just living a day to day life…never looking toward the future.

"You can't punish yourself for the rest of your life, Kace."

"You don't get to decide my punishment," Kace said, as he

looked down at his hands.

The fight he was having within himself was hard to watch. To see a man who was so vivacious, so full of energy, slowly deteriorate to an empty shell killed me. I knew Kace's potential, I knew who he could be, but that man was gone now.

Getting up from his chair, Kace tapped the desk and said, "Is everything okay with Goldie?"

"Everything is fine; no need to worry." I looked at my watch and realized what time it was. "I have some things I have to take care of, if you don't mind," I gestured to the door.

"Not a problem," Kace replied, as he helped himself out.

"Hey," I called after him. Kace stopped, but didn't turn around to face me. "I want you to live again, Kace."

"I don't deserve this life," Kace replied.

He left me alone in my office to attend to my business. I had a lot of things to take care of and a lot of plans to finalize. Unlike Kace, I was moving forward with my life. I was done living a life with no emotion. If I wanted Goldie, I had to break down the wall I put up around my heart and let her in, and I couldn't be more ready to do so.

My phone started ringing, and I looked down to see it was my security detail.

"Jett Colby," I answered.

"Mr. Colby, we've located Goldie and have informed her we are here now."

"Thank you, did you see any suspicious behavior on your way over there? She was talking about a girl she ran into on the streets."

"We weren't able to locate any suspicious behavior, sir. We will watch our six, though."

"Keep her safe; that's my life you're watching."

"Yes, sir."

Satisfied, I hung up the phone and tended to my business. I had a lot to get done.

34
"DEMONS"

Goldie

"Why isn't he answering his phone?" I cried, as I got in the back of the security agent's car. "Didn't you just talk to him? He always has his phone on him. Get in the damn car," I screamed at the security guy, who was shutting my door. "I can close my own damn door; start driving."

Yes, I may be acting like a bitch, I might be over-exaggerating, since the sirens could be for anyone, but I just had a feeling, a really bad feeling.

"Drive!" I shouted, while pointing forward like I was leading a pack of angry ass Braveheart men, whatever they were called.

"Ma'am, you're going to have to buckle up..."

I gripped the driver's ear and twisted it while leaning over his seat. "If you don't start driving this damn car, I'm going to Mike Tyson your ass and eat your ear as a snack. Fucking drive!"

That got his attention and he pressed his foot down on the pedal to get the car moving.

"Good boy," I said, as I patted and stroked his ear.

I watched as the pastel colored houses flew by as my driver disobeyed every city speed limit set. We weren't that far away from the Lafayette Club, but it almost felt like we were going at supersonic speed.

We turned the corner to Jackson Street, where the club was located, and that was when we were hit with a billow of smoke, fire trucks, and blazing flames. My heart sank in my chest as I saw the Lafayette Club burning down at an alarming rate.

"Oh, my God," I cried, while I tried to get out of the car, but the doors were locked. "Open the door!"

"Hold on, ma'am."

"Open the fucking door!" I screamed, while grabbing ahold of his ear and yanking on it. "You son of a bitch, open the door. Open the door! Open the Goddamn door!"

He swatted my hand away and pressed the unlock button. In a flash, I bolted out of the car and tried to make my way through the crowd that was forming. People from around the street milled about, taking in the sight of the infamous Lafayette Club going up in flames, flames that were so large I was actually nervous they would spread and burn up the historic Garden District.

The trees that surrounded the Lafayette Club danced with the flames, threatening to light up. There were three fire trucks, taking up angles all around the building to calm the roaring flames.

Pushing my way forward, I called out Jett's name, to the point where I felt my voice start to go hoarse, but my voice went unheard from the sounds of the sirens, the shouts of the firemen directing each other, and the crowd that had gathered to watch everything unfold.

"Move," I said, as I shoved a lady to the side, not caring who I took out. "Jett," I screamed while looking around.

Nothing. I saw absolutely no one, not even Kace or one of the girls. Were they still in the building?

I pushed my way to the front of the crowd until I was able to make it to where firemen were blocking the crowd from getting closer. I tried to peek over the giant fireman in front of me, but I couldn't see anything, so I took it upon myself to make my own ladder and hopped on top of the man standing in front of me. I knocked off his hat by accident and heard it clang to the ground as he spun around and started yelling at me.

"Lady, what the hell do you think you're doing?" he asked, trying to grab me from behind, but I clung on like he was my lifeline and used him as my lookout post to find a familiar face.

"You're moving too fast, slow circles," I directed him, while I continued to climb up his back.

"Get the hell off of me; I have a job to do," he yelled, still grabbing at me.

I used the top of his head to help me gain a little more height as I planted my hand on his hair and pushed up.

"Just give me a second," I said, while I continued to look around. "Why can't I see anyone?"

"Lady, get off of me!"

I was about to snap at him and tell him to be a better ladder when a strong pair of warm hands grabbed me by the waist and lowered me to the ground. Quickly, I turned around and came face to face with the brooding man himself, Kace Haywood.

"Kace," I cried, as I threw myself in his arms. "Where is everyone?"

"We're all around the corner, past the trucks," he said. "We exited out the back of the club."

"Oh, thank God," I said relieved, letting my heartrate return to normal. "I was at the cemetery and I had this horrible feeling that something bad was going to happen after creepy Mercy talked to me."

"Who's creepy Mercy?" Kace asked, as he moved the crowd to the side and showed me where everyone was huddled.

"Rex's plaything. You should have seen her; she looked like a psychopath. She was hugging a bloody shirt…"

I was interrupted by a loud creak and pop. We both turned to the house to see an explosion go off from the back of the house.

Holy shit.

Then it hit me, the club was burning down; there was no way to salvage it.

My sanctuary, the place where I made everlasting friendships, the place that had become my home, the place where I fell in love, where I expected to spend the rest of my days.

Tears welled up in my eyes as firemen exited the building in a hurry so they weren't trapped when it collapsed.

"Clear the area; clear the area," shouted one of the firemen into a walkie talkie that was strapped to his shoulder. "Is everyone out?"

"Yes, sir," all is clear.

"Wait," Kace said, while looking around, "Where's Jett?" Where's Jett?!

My heart bottomed out as my vision around me turned black and my eyes narrowed up to the third floor window, from where I'd seen Jett look down at me many times. In the midst of all of the smoke and flames, there was a body moving up on the third floor, clearly pacing back and forth.

A shrill cry escaped me as I charged toward the house, but was grabbed by the waist.

"Goldie, stop."

"He's up there!" I screamed and pointed. "He's up there; we have to get him."

Another explosion ricocheted through the thick smoky air, sending sparks around the area.

"Start covering the perimeters," a fireman said, "Save the areas around it; the house is unsalvageable."

I grabbed his walkie talkie and shouted into it, "There is a man in there still; stop everything you're doing and..."

The walkie talkie was ripped away from me and the fireman spoke into it, redirecting them to their original duty.

"What are you doing? There's someone still in there. Go save him."

"I'm sorry, ma'am, it's too dangerous. I'm not going to send my men in there when the house is creaking and ready to fall."

"Are you fucking kidding me? What kind of firemen are you?" I screamed, as I charged towards the house to go get him myself, but was grabbed once again. "Put me down! He's in there; I need to save him. He's in there!"

"Goldie, stop. We can't go in there," Kace's voice spoke softly into my ear. "There is nothing we can do."

"Fuck you, there is nothing we can do." I screamed as loud as I could up to the third floor, hoping Jett could hear me. "Open the window and jump. Jett, jump!"

From the floor of the third level, a hand reached up and hit the window, then slowly slid down the glass, as if it was his last ditch effort to save himself.

"No!" I cried and fought Kace, who was now pulling me away. "Fight, Jett, fight!"

My last words died on my lips as the fire burned and the house collapsed in on itself, causing sparks and smoke to explode from underneath the house.

"Put me down," I sobbed, as I watched the house repeatedly implode in on itself until there were only a few beams standing tall.

My heart sank to the ground while Kace carried me to where the other Jett Girls were standing, huddled together. When I reached them, I scampered off of Kace and looked around for Jett.

"Where is he?" I searched around them, hoping that maybe this was some kind of sick joke.

"Where is who?" Babs asked, growing more concerned at how frantic I was.

I looked in the boxes they had scattered around, then I checked their purses, thinking maybe he took a shrinking pill before he left the club. I was reaching, big time reaching, but I refused to think about him up in that room; I refused to acknowledge that was his hand hitting the glass, reaching for me.

"Where's Jett?" I screamed, continuing to look around.

"Goldie," Kace said softly, while his hand grabbed my shoulder.

"No, don't touch me! Don't fucking touch me," I cried, tears streaming down my face.

"Goldie, come here," Babs said, reaching her arms out for me, but I swatted them away. I didn't want to be held, I didn't want to be consoled, I wanted Jett. I wanted my man back, I wanted the Lafayette Club back, and I wanted my life, the life I knew as mine, to come back.

In one single moment, everything I've ever wanted, that I've ever cared about, was taken away from me.

I heard the girls talking around me and saw the look of total devastation on Kace's face as my vision blurred. Before I ran off, I saw a small tear peek out of Kace's eye, which he quickly wiped away, but that was it for me. I couldn't stay; I had to bolt…I had to forget.

"Goldie, where are you going?" Babs called after me, as I sprinted through the crowd, pushing people to the side, trying to get as far away from the smoke and the creaks and cracks as I could.

As I ran, visions of Jett being suffocated by the black smoke ran through my mind, turning my stomach raw. I paused on a sidewalk, held onto a tree and threw up, multiple times, until I could only dry heave. Convulsions shook my small frame and a cold sweat ran over my skin. Once there was nothing left in me, I looked around to see where I was, and I ran to the last sanctuary I had. In front of me was Jett's mom's gravestone; the original location that brought me to Jett. In a sick way, my life was coming full circle.

My body felt lifeless, tired, exhausted, so I collapsed in front of the gravestone, pressing my body up against the cold marble stone.

Broken pieces of the grave dug into my skin, but I welcomed the pain, anything to dull the torment that was running rampant through my veins, the unyielding agony that wouldn't ease in my slowly dying heart.

I rested my head on my hands and cried in front of the grave, while the black smoke from the house started to pool over the cemetery, making the atmosphere dim and bleak, like my future. To say there was a black cloud over my life was an understatement.

Tourists milled about me, spoke softly to each other about the crazy woman, crying in front of a gravestone at the ever-so-popular Lafayette Cemetery. Children cried when they saw me and two people took pictures of the crazy lady. If I had enough strength in my bones, I would have flipped them all off, but there was nothing left in me.

I wasn't sure how long I laid there; time seemed to escape me as I tried to envision my life without Jett. It was impossible. How was I supposed to give up something that I just recently obtained? How was I supposed to let go of the fact that I fell in love with the most complicated, charming, and sexy man I've ever met? How was I supposed to move on from this?

Thoughts of pulling a Romeo and Juliet ran through my mind as a heard footsteps walk up to me. Expecting it to be a tourist wanting to poke me with a stick, I didn't look up until they stopped right in front of me. My vision blurred from my tears, but I knew those shoes.

In a sheer panic, I wiped my eyes and looked up to see Kace looking down at me. Disappointment washed over my body, as I thought the man who was standing in front of me was going to be Jett. I was sadly defeated.

I rested my head back down on the ground as Kace squatted

in front of me.

His hand ran across my face and tried to wipe away the continuously falling tears that would not stop. Carefully, he sat down next to me and pulled up my upper half so my head was resting on his knee. We sat silently as he stroked my back and I cried.

His warm embrace should have been comforting, it should have made me feel some kind of semblance of "home," but I still felt empty inside.

"Please tell me it's not true," I squeaked out, my voice hoarse from crying. I gripped onto his hand and said, "Tell me it's not true."

Kace cleared his throat, but said nothing. Through blurry eyes, I looked up at him and saw that his eyes were just as red as mine, just as puffy, and his demeanor looked like he literally just lost his best friend.

"What are you not telling me, Kace?" I asked, trying to wait for the blow.

"Goldie…"

"Fucking tell me!" I shouted.

"They found a body…" Kace choked on a sob.

"Wh-what? No, no, this is not happening."

I blocked out the hand on the window; I convinced myself this wasn't true. It just couldn't be true. There was no way that whoever was writing this fucking story of my life could take Jett away. I couldn't believe it. We were supposed to spend our lives together, we were working things out, and we were going to finally live our lives the way we wanted to. We were finally given a chance.

"This can't be happening…" I whispered softly, falling into Kace's arms. "I love him, Kace. I fucking love him; he can't be taken away from me."

"Goldie…" that voice haunted me, that deep southern voice haunted me as I cried into Kace. It wasn't until I was transferred into another set of arms that I looked up to see Jett staring down at me.

At that moment, it felt like my veins busted and white bursts prickled my skin, making me numb and unable to function. His hair was tossed to the side, his clothes were wrinkled, and he was disheveled. His eyes were glistening, and that's when I realized he was real.

"Jett," I choked out a sob and squeezed him until I took his breath away. I looked up at Kace, who had his hands in his pockets and was looking down at us. He looked relieved and satisfied. Quickly, he wiped a stray tear, gave me an almost sad smile, and then turned on his heels, leaving us in his wake.

I wanted to scream at him not to go, to come hold me as well, but it was time to let him go, to eternally thank him for his friendship, his love and his protection, and move on.

After saying a silent goodbye, I pulled away from Jett and gripped his face. With shaky hands, I brought him close and carefully placed a kiss on his lips, reveling in the feel of his warmth, of his body pressed up against mine.

His hands ran up my back and carefully gripped the back of my head as he kissed me forcefully. I felt the need in his touch and the tension release from his body at finding me. His lips parted and mine did as well as his tongue slipped into my mouth, pushing our kiss further. Deep yearning ran through me as I straightened and sat on his lap, wrapping my legs around his back, making sure I was as close I could be to the man.

Needing answers, I pulled away and looked into his deep blue eyes as tears clouded my vision.

"Little One..." he said softly, pulling me into his embrace. I wrapped my arms around him and let his head bury into my hair.

I loved this man, everything about him...from his moody tendencies, to his inability to let go of control, to his kind heart and his rare show of humor. I would bleed for this man, I would kill for this man, I would die for this man. He is my light, my savior, my fucking everything.

"Jett," I whispered, while shaking my head. "Wh-where were you?" I hiccup-sobbed, sounding not in the least attractive, but was too far gone to even care. I knew there were pools of mucus falling out of me, but I just let it happen, because all that mattered was I was holding my man in my arms.

"You scared me," he said, while kissing the top of my head. "I couldn't find you once I found out the club was on fire. All I cared about was finding you," he said relieved. "When security said they lost you..."

"Wait, what?" I asked, pulling away, completely confused. "You thought you lost me? Do you realize that we all thought you were dead? That we saw someone on the third floor and thought it was you?"

"Why would you...?"

"Why didn't you answer your phone?" I interrupted him. "I tried calling you, but you wouldn't answer. You always have your phone."

Jett searched my eyes as he thought about it. "I left it in my office when I left. I was in a hurry earlier. I had some things to do."

"You left it?" I hit his arm and said, "Don't ever fucking do that again. Jesus Christ, Jett. I thought you were fucking dead. We all thought you were fucking dead."

"Shhh," Jett cooed. "I'm here, Little One. I'm sorry. I'm sorry I put you through so much distress."

"I thought you were dead," I whispered, burying my head into his shoulder. "Who was on the third floor?"

"I'm here," he replied softly. "We think it was the girl you ran into. The police found her car not too far away from the club, full of cans of gas, kindling, and a very vivid diary of her plans to take back what she lost."

"I knew something wasn't right. I wish I would have gone back and warned you, none of this would have ever happened."

"There was nothing you could have done, Little One."

I shook my head in disbelief and replied, "I love you. I love you so fucking much. Please don't ever leave me."

"I don't plan on it," he said, while placing a kiss on top of my head.

"The club. What happened?"

Jett sighed and gripped me a little tighter. "It's gone."

"I know," I teared up again. "Our sanctuary, your beautifully built club is gone."

He nodded. I felt him sag a little from defeat. I couldn't imagine what he was feeling. His club, his mansion was his pride and joy. He spoke so highly of the establishment, of what it represented, of what it offered and who it helped. It wasn't just a home, it was a place of new beginnings, a place full of second chances, a place where family by soul came together.

"I'm so sorry," I said, while kissing his cheek.

"We will rebuild," he replied, with that deep dominant voice of his. "We will rebuild and we will thrive, Little One, and do you know why?"

"Why?" I asked, while I placed my head on his shoulder and

allowed him to stroke my hair with his fingers.

"Because we're a triple threat. With justice, faith and power, we will thrive and rebuild. There is no one to stand in our way now. Together, we can do anything, Little One. Together, we have the power to accomplish anything."

"Together?" I asked.

"Together," he said, while nudging me and lifting my head.

He smiled brightly down at me and lifted his hand up to my view. His hand opened up and inside was a ring with a large yellow diamond and small little yellow diamonds surrounding it. I gasped and quickly looked up at him to see if he was serious. His smile was devastating as he grabbed my hand and never strayed from my gaze.

"Never in my right mind did I think I would meet such a sassy, gorgeous, foul-mouthed, and kind-hearted woman like you, Goldie, but the moment I saw you in this very spot, tapping your foot to the music running through your ears and drawing my mother's grave, I knew I had to make you mine. I knew my mom brought us together for a reason. It took me some time to actually accept my fate, to know you were meant for me, to care for my heart, and I'm sorry for all the heartache I put you through, but if you will allow me, if you will so kindly grant me the honor of handing over your heart to me for eternity, then I promise you, I will do everything in my power to guard it. Goldie, will you do me the honor of marrying me?"

My heart beat rapidly in my chest as my eyes wandered from Jett to the ring and then back to Jett. Was he serious?

"Oh, my fuck, kick me in the crotch and call me fucking Sally! Of course I will marry you. I'm going to marry you so fucking hard."

Jett shook his head and laughed, as I wrapped my arms around his neck and kissed the ever living piss out of him.

35
"AMERICA'S SWEETHEART"

Goldie

"Stop fidgeting," Jett whispered in my ear as we walked down a very small red carpet that was full of flashing cameras and shouts from the press covering the rather popular event we were attending.

Turning toward him so the press couldn't read my lips, I said, "I'm pretty sure I'm going to piss myself."

Nervously, I gripped my collar that Jett so thoughtfully replaced, after the one he originally gave me was caught in the fire. This one matched the diamonds in my ring, showing just how thoughtful the man I loved was.

Chuckling softly, he kissed the top of my head and said, "Don't be nervous, Little One. You deserve this."

"Mr. Colby, Mr. Colby," reporters called out, trying to gather his attention. "Is it true you're engaged? Mr. Colby, do you have time to answer a few questions?"

"Throw them a bone," I said, while patting his chest, glancing at my ring. It was something I did very often, not because it was a fucking boulder sitting on top of my finger, nope, it was because it was Jett's mark on me. Once and for all, I was his, forever I would be a Jett Girl.

The day of the fire, I couldn't even think about it, it still made my skin crawl. It's been a few weeks, but it still seemed too fresh, seeing the movement on the third floor, thinking it was Jett, not being able to contact him; it all boiled down to the worst moment in my life, next to losing my parents.

After they were able to put out the fire, investigators went in and were able to confirm that Mercy started the fire. She apparently spent a good amount of time dumping gasoline along the front perimeter of the house, making sure to ignite the damn place. She then helped herself inside, through a window she broke, lit the gas on fire, and then trailed her tank throughout the house until she made it to the third floor; she was practically a human blow torch, igniting everything in sight. I'm still shocked the girls and Kace were able to evacuate as quickly as they did with some of their things. Thankfully, Mercy missed the "servant's quarters" when she was lighting shit up.

Fucking crazy ass bitch.

It's scary to think Jett could have been on the top floor…that he could have been trapped, but thanks to one simple phone call from a jeweler, a jeweler I will forever suck dick for, he snuck out the back and went to get my ring. Not even Kace knew about the proposal.

It's so weird how little things, like a phone call, can save your life, or how a small coincidence of drawing a gravestone over and over again can bring two helpless souls together.

"Come on," Jett said, as he pulled on my hand, knocking me out of my thoughts.

I trailed behind him, holding on to his hand tightly as he curtly nodded to a reporter at the end of the pit. Jett adjusted his tie and cleared his throat, "Mr. Cardone, what a pleasure to see you."

"Mr. Colby," the man said, while shaking Jett's hand. "Thank you for coming over here; may I ask you some questions?"

"Of course," Jett said kindly, as the other reporters crowded around Mr. Cardone, sticking their recorders as close as they could get to have a chance at the little Jett Colby exclusive being conducted.

"Thank you. I promise to be quick. Can you make a statement on the recent engagement rumors?"

"I can," said proudly, as he pulled my hand up to his lips and kissed my knuckles gently. He looked down at me with the sexiest smile I had ever seen and he said with great pride, "Mr. Cardone, please meet my fiancé, Goldie Bishop, the woman who's stolen my heart and the talented artist who will be showcased tonight."

In one quick wave of light, cameras pointed at me and started flashing at an unsurmountable rate, making it hard to keep my eyes open. So, instead of looking toward the pit, I looked up at Jett and smiled.

"Congratulations," Mr. Cardone said. "You are one lucky man."

"That I am," Jett agreed.

"Can you tell me how you two met?"

"Through the true luck of serendipity." Jett kept it simple because, apparently, she was a hooker that I pulled from the pit of Bourbon Street wasn't as romantic as the word serendipity.

"Do you have a wedding date?"

Jett tore his eyes off of me and looked at Mr. Cardone. "Not at the moment; we're just enjoying being engaged right now."

"An honored tradition," Mr. Cardone added. "The news about your mansion being burned down has been a popular subject in the city, any plans to rebuild?"

"Yes, we will be meeting with contractors soon to preserve the look and feel of what the Lafayette Club used to be. The club is just a possession; I'm just grateful no one who matters to me was hurt."

"In the meantime, where are you staying?"

Jett gave him a pointed look and said, "That's not really the media's business, but I will say that we are staying at one of my many properties while we figure out the rebuild of the club and continue to concentrate on the construction of the community center, which is my top priority. Until the center is complete, we will hold off on construction of the house. I have plenty of places to stay, but there isn't a community center where people can gain a second chance."

We were currently staying in a hotel Jett owned on Canal

Street, and the proximity to the French Quarter was dangerous for me because every Saturday, I was drawn to Café du Monde for my weekend intake of beignets. Jett refused to miss our new tradition, but my ass was starting to wish we'd skipped a weekend or two. Jett thought differently; he rather enjoyed the extra little curve to my ass, fuck did he enjoy it.

Even though we didn't have the Bourbon Room to play around in, the man came up with new and exciting ways for me to submit.

Did you know there are suction cups strong enough to hold up a grown human against a floor to ceiling window? Yeah, me fucking either, but holy hell is that an experience.

"Do you have a name for the center yet?" Mr. Cardone asked.

Without skipping a beat, Jett answered "Justice," not explaining the meaning; he didn't have to; the title spoke for itself.

"Very fitting," Mr. Cardone complimented. "Can I get you to make a statement on your father's upcoming trial?"

Jett's jaw tensed at the mention of his father. Leo was up for trial in a few weeks and his outcome was looking like incarceration for an obscene amount of time, meaning, he would be dying behind bars. The man deserved every bit of his punishment, but after some long talks with Jett, he still felt sad about losing a piece of himself.

Jett was by no means sad for his father, no, the man was pure evil, but it was the notion of losing something Jett never had to begin with. No matter what, Jett will always strive to impress his father, to prove to his father that he is an honorable man, a man of society, a well-respected impact on the community, but would never receive the praise he craved. When Jett admitted his feelings to me, I cried for the little boy inside of him, and now I make it my duty to show him how important, valuable, and needed he is. I try to deliver the love he's been craving since he was a little boy.

Gripping tighter on my hand, Jett answered, "All I have to say is my father deserves whatever the truth unveils."

Nodding his head, Mr. Cardone turned toward me and asked, "Miss Bishop, congratulations on your first showcase, shall we be seeing more of your art in the future?"

Caught a little off-guard, I smiled and nodded, trying not to let the words "fuck yeah" slip out of my mouth.

Jett nudged me, indicating I should say something. Clearly, he didn't want to be engaged to a mute.

"Yes," I squeaked. "I hope so, at least, but if not, I'm okay with that because fortunately I've been offered a job at Justice as an art therapy teacher, so I'm quite excited to help those in need."

"That is great to hear," Mr. Cardone said, while writing a quick note. He looked up at Jett and me and said, "Thank you so much and congratulations. I can see how the city is just going to fall in love with you two; it's quite evident you are infatuated with each other."

Jett nodded his head and guided me toward the entrance of the art gallery.

"Infatuated with your dick," I said, as I cuddled up close to Jett and whispered in his ear.

"Trying to get yourself in trouble already, Little One?" he asked with a smirk.

"Is it working?"

"It's always working," he insinuated while looking down.

I placed my hand on his chest and slowly started to move it down to his waist when he caught it and sternly looked me in the eyes.

"Behave yourself," he commanded, turning me on like a mother fucker.

"And if I don't?"

"Haven't you learned not to play with fire?"

"My pussy is wet, come on, bang me in the bathroom. Pretty please! Look, my nipples are hard; rub them, do something. I'm a wanton woman with the need for that tree trunk, you know...the one that sits between your legs, the one that plows me like a fucking mac truck?"

Jett leaned forward and pressed his mouth against my ear as he spoke, "I know perfectly well what my dick can do to you; I don't need reminding. Now, you are going to behave for the next few hours, and if you're a good girl, I will reward you, but if you get out of hand, you won't like your punishment, and I can fucking promise you that."

His southern voice rumbled down to my very core, kicking up the heat level in my body. Yup, I was going to be a very good girl.

"Understood?" he asked, pulling lightly on my ear with his teeth.

"Fuck, yes," I said breathlessly.

"Watch your mouth, Little One."

"Yes...sir," I smiled, making Jett roll his eyes and pull away.

"Now, show me your painting."

When I got the call that my picture was picked for the showcase spotlight, I squealed and ran around Jett's apartment naked, pushing lamps and pictures over just for the hell of it. I remember Jett standing in the middle of the room, mouth open, watching me pelvic thrust the air in joy. After I got off the phone, he spanked me on the ass for my behavior, and then fucked me up against the couch in celebration. Do we know how to celebrate, or what?

Since then, I'd kept my mouth shut about my painting so it would be a complete surprise to Jett. Thinking about my piece and what I did, I was nervous to show him. He was a possessive man; he was not going to like what he saw.

"Over here," I guided him, as we pushed through the crowd to the back of the room, where my picture was hanging. A light shone over it, casting the perfect glow on my picture of Jett Girl tits in marked up purple, green, and gold hues. In the center of the canvas was a paper mâché cast of my own breasts, colored white, with one single Mardi Gras nipple tassel hanging off of a nipple. It was, by far, the most offensive piece of art ever made, but it was the definition of Mardi Gras. Just below the canvas was a plaque that held the name of my artwork.

Jett bent down to take a look at the title and then raised an eyebrow at me. "You named your artwork, 'Where the Fuck is my Titty Tassel?'?"

Giggling to myself, I nodded and asked, "Isn't it fitting?"

He shook his head and examined the canvas for a second before recognition washed over him. His brow creased and his jaw turned hard as he looked down at me.

"You are in so much fucking trouble, Little One."

Gulping, I asked, "Whatever for?"

He pressed his lips to my ear and said, "You know damn well why." His nose nuzzled the side of my face as he continued, "I will be buying this tonight; there is no way in hell anyone else will own a piece of you, even if it's a pair of paper mâché breasts. You're mine, Little One, you're all fucking mine.

To think I thought I knew what happiness was. I was so fucking wrong, because right here, in this moment, resting in Jett's arms, this is what happiness was. This is what it meant to be this overjoyed, this satisfied in life, to have the feeling of complete euphoria.

After everything I've been through, losing my parents, losing our business, losing my education, and selling my body just to make ends meet, I never in my wildest dreams thought a dark and mysterious stranger would stumble upon me and try to save my soul, but he did. Jett Colby saved me, and for that, I will be eternally grateful.

People of fortune see life through rose-colored glasses, but not me. I see through purple, green, and gold-colored glasses. I live life through three simple words: justice, faith, and power. Justice for those striving for second chances, faith in the people involved in my life, and the power of love. With those three words, those three meanings, I can finally sit back and live my life with the infamous Jett Colby by my side.

EPILOGUE

Kace

I could feel my jaw twitching as I watched Lyla walk across the room in a black strapless dress that hugged every fucking curve of her body. She was taunting me. I wasn't a moron; I knew her game. She'd been taunting me since she left the club, since she told me without holding anything back that I wasn't the man for her.

We were celebrating Goldie and the achievement of her first showing in a French Quarter art gallery, but all I could focus on was Lyla and every intentional movement she made. I watched as she flirted with every man in the gallery, touched their arms and laughed at their pathetic attempts at jokes. She was putting on a show, purposely making me jealous, and fuck if it wasn't working.

I knew I wasn't the man for her. I knew what she said was right, that I was an empty shell, that my soul was black and I had nothing but a warm body to offer her. I've known that since the moment my fist connected with Marshall Duncan's head.

All it took was one wrong word, one wrong turn, and one wrong punch, and just like that, my life was over.

People like to celebrate the day they were born, the day they were married, the day they met the love of their life. Not me, I celebrate the day I let someone provoke me, the day I made the worst decision of my life, the day I took the life of another man…the day I fucking died.

BOURBON SERIES SPIN-OFFS TO COME

1. Kace—for all of you Kace fans, he will be getting his own story. Rest assured, I am not through with this brooding and damaged ex-boxer.
2. The Ringmaster—Cirque du Diable is Diego's erotic club where he is the Ringmaster, controlling the circus surrounding him, but can he control the one woman who wants nothing to do with his lifestyle? I can't wait to introduce you to Diego's story…he's so yummy!
3. The Black Top Racing Series—Zane Black, mogul and entrepreneur who owns an underground raceway in New York City's abandoned subways will have his own series. Zane's story is already in the works; I will keep you updated.
4. Life After (being a Jett Girl)—This is a possibility for Francy, Tootse, Babs, and Pepper to tell their stories. We will see…

Thank you for reading Forever a Jett Girl! I hope you enjoyed it. If you did, please help other readers find this book:

> 1. This book is lendable, so send it to a friend who you think might like it so they can discover me too.
> 2. Help other people find this book by writing a review.
> 3. Come like my Facebook page: Author Meghan Quinn - https://www.facebook.com/meghanquinnauthor?ref=bookmarks
> 4. Find me on Goodreads - https://www.goodreads.com/author/show/7360513.Meghan_Quinn
> 5. Don't forget to visit my website: www.authormeghanquinn.com

ABOUT THE AUTHOR

Born in New York and raised in Southern California, Meghan has grown into a sassy, peanut butter eating, blonde haired, swearing, animal hoarding lady. She is known to bust out and dance if "It's Raining Men" starts beating through the air and heaven forbid you get a margarita in her, protect your legs because they may be humped.

Once she started commuting for an hour and twenty minutes every day to work for three years, she began to have conversations play in her head, real life, deep male voices and dainty lady coos kind of conversations. Perturbed and confused, she decided to either see a therapist about the hot and steamy voices running through her head or start writing them down. She decided to go with the cheaper option and started writing… enter her first novel, Caught Looking.

Now you can find the spicy, most definitely on the border of lunacy, kind of crazy lady residing in Colorado with the love of her life and her five, furry four legged children, hiking a trail or hiding behind shelves at grocery stores, wondering what kind of lube the nervous stranger will bring home to his wife. Oh and she loves a good boob squeeze!

Made in the USA
Middletown, DE
06 July 2024

56974709R00179